# LOST
# MOUNTAIN
# PASS

A TRUSTY DAWSON, DEPUTY U.S. MARSHAL WESTERN

# LARRY D. SWEAZY

# LOST MOUNTAIN PASS

## PINNACLE BOOKS
Kensington Publishing Corp.
www.kensingtonbooks.com

PINNACLE BOOKS are published by

Kensington Publishing Corp.
119 West 40th Street
New York, NY 10018

Copyright © 2021 by Larry D. Sweazy

This book is based on the short story "Lost Mountain Pass" by Larry D. Sweazy, copyright © 2011 by Larry D. Sweazy, first published in *The Traditional West* anthology copyright © 2011 by The Western Fictioneers

All Kensington titles, imprints, and distributed lines are available at special quantity discounts for bulk purchases for sales promotion, premiums, fund-raising, educational, or institutional use.

Special book excerpts or customized printings can also be created to fit specific needs. For details, write or phone the office of the Kensington Sales Manager: Attn.: Sales Department. Kensington Publishing Corp., 119 West 40th Street, New York, NY 10018. Phone: 1-800-221-2647.

PINNACLE BOOKS and the Pinnacle logo are Reg. U.S. Pat. & TM Off.

First Printing: October 2021
ISBN-13: 978-0-7860-4677-5
ISBN-10: 0-7860-4677-5

ISBN-13: 978-0-7860-4678-2 (eBook)
ISBN-10: 0-7860-4678-3 (eBook)

10 9 8 7 6 5 4 3 2 1

Printed in the United States of America

*To Matthew Clemons,*
*Trusted friend and gentle soul.*
*The world needs more of the likes of him . . .*

# Chapter 1

*Kosoma, Indian Territory, May 1888*

Three pair of boots burst through the gallows, toes aimed straight to the ground. The simultaneous snap of necks echoed on the wind like someone had stepped on a thick collection of brittle tree branches. In a quick last breath and the final blink of the eye, three Darby brothers swung from the gallows, two of them wet from the waist down, one staring sideways in a state of shock like he never thought he was going to die. Embarrassment and pride belonged to another world. This one was cold and harsh, awash in black-and-white judgment, law and order, and relief from the violence of angry men—if only for a moment.

Nothing moved beyond the lifeless bodies, not even a crow. Two of the shiny black birds stood atop the pitch of a nearby roof staring down at the crowd, hankering for something to steal. A few clouds lingered overhead, white, puffy, pausing to see if the truth of the human drama would finally be revealed. A baby started to cry in the distance. The piercing, uncomfortable sound of discomfort and need was quickly hushed. The townsfolk who had stood witness to the hanging needed a little time to digest the end of one life and the start of another. Madness and rage had been silenced. Peace and prosperity were at hand in Kosoma—if only for a moment. The baby wailed again, then was shushed by a solid, embarrassed hand clamping over the suckling mouth. New life could never be silenced for long, even in the shade of death, deserved or otherwise.

Murmurs started to grow in unison like an amen at the end of a long prayer. The entire town stood still, too nervous to leave, eyes shaded, directed toward the three dead Darby men, making sure the twitching and struggling was finally done and over with before they felt free to move, to breathe, to say a silent thank-you to the judge who had passed the execution order on the deserving gang of three. Regardless of what they saw, the crowd found it hard to believe that the Darby brothers, Cleatus, Horace, and Rascal—evil bullies, overbearing toughs, and unpredictable gunmen—were really dead, no longer a bother, no longer a threat to their daily comforts. The Darbys' terror had reigned for too many years to count. No one in Kosoma ever thought this day would truly come.

"Looks like my job here is done, Trusty," Eastern District of Arkansas Judge Gordon Hadesworth said. The judge held jurisdiction in Indian Territory along with Isaac Parker in the Western District. Hadesworth was a stately-looking gentleman with a well-trimmed goatee, bleached white by age, and wore a fancy dark blue suit that, like all of his suits, had been shipped to him directly from New York City by the tailors of his favor, Brooks Brothers. A lifetime spent poring over law books had left the elderly man stiff, arthritic, and hunched over; straight and upright he would have been as tall as an October cornstalk. A walking cane, carved from oak with a highly polished brass lion's head that served as the handle, helped keep the judge vertical and moving forward. The educated man's icy gray eyes stared forward at the gallows and bore no concern for the dead; their souls and their legacy were no longer his worry. The law had executed its judgment and it had been carried out to the fullest extent. Some scoundrels deserved to die because of the foul deeds they had committed. Judge Hadesworth made it clear to anyone within earshot that he was not in the salvation business.

"I suppose you'll be wantin' a bite of dinner before we start out toward Muskogee?" Deputy U.S. Marshal Sam Dawson—often referred to as "Trusty," by judges and outlaws alike—said.

Trusty didn't much care for the moniker folks called him by, but there wasn't much he could do about it. He couldn't argue against the reputation that he was reliable and trustworthy. Those were born traits, along with good eyesight when it came to pulling a trigger, and had got him out of more jams and scrapes than he cared to admit. Besides, he'd been called worse things than Trusty by men far more powerful than Judge Hadesworth. There were worse things that he'd had to force himself to live with.

Trusty stood stiff next to the judge, a good three inches

taller and straighter in physical form than the jurist. The extra height gave Trusty the advantage of wide sight, allowing him to survey a crowd for any apparent or rising threat. The Darbys had their fair share of supporters in Kosoma. A gang like them had deep roots in the town and in Indian Territory, even though the majority of townsfolk looked to be relieved by their deaths.

The Darbys' demise had been a long time coming. The blood and carnage they'd left behind in their wake was the stuff made of fireside stories, some true, some not, but real enough and valid enough to give Trusty reason to be suspicious of every man who itched the back of his neck or reached inside of his coat for a toothpick. The last straw had come when the three brothers had killed a beloved storekeeper in cold blood on a sunny day, in the middle of the town square—with no regard to the law or the man's right to live peacefully. No one claimed to know what had started the ill-fated confrontation, but even the most silent of citizens spoke up and demanded that something finally be done about the Darbys' lack of respect for life once and for all. Judge Hadesworth's appearance was called for a day later after a reluctant sheriff overpowered the trio and locked them up. The wounds were still raw, but Trusty hoped that the dangle of toes would put an end to the Darby troubles in Kosoma once and for all.

"Between you and me, Trusty, I'd just as soon get out of this stinking town as quick as possible," the judge said, lowering his voice so no one could hear, or take offense, to his comment.

Trusty nodded in agreement. The spring day was cool,

and he wore a long coat over his utilitarian canvas pants and blue cotton shirt, concealing an 1880 Colt Single-Action, outfitted with custom-carved ivory handle grips that had come as a gift from his captain when he'd separated from the U.S. Army. His military days were well behind him, but he still wore the dark blue felt Cavalry Stetson, only without the customary ropes, braids, and accoutrements that came from being active-duty army. Trusty had missed out on the War Between the States, being a child when that war had been waged. A Winchester '73 was loosely strapped to his left side, also hidden by the coat but always close to his touch. He was confident that the two weapons, along with his skills with them, could get him and the judge out of any trouble that might show itself.

"Suits me," he said to Judge Hadesworth. "Let's wait until the crowd starts moving out before we head to the hotel to get your things."

"If I never have to come back to Kosoma again it will be too soon," the judge said. "But something tells me that I will have to return sooner rather than later. It takes weeks to rid myself of the smell."

Kosoma meant "place of stinking water" in the Choctaw language. There was a myriad of bubbling, steaming springs fingering off the Kiamichi River, and they were all thick with putrid sulfur. Not even the smell of opportunity provided by the railroad, one of the first to get a land grant through Indian Territory more than ten years prior, could vanquish the residue of the springs from the senses or threads of the cleanest man's clothes. The St. Louis–San Francisco Railroad, referred to as the

"Frisco," had built a rail line, completed in 1887, running from the north to the south, straight through the Choctaw Nation, connecting Fort Smith with Paris, Texas. Kosoma was perfectly located to capitalize on the rail line, smell or no smell, or the fact that it sat in the middle of Choctaw land. The future had been arriving every day with trainloads of Easterners, opportunity hunters, thieves, and speculators all hedging for a spot at the opening of Indian Territory land a year off, now that the Springer Amendment had passed through Congress. New ideas, the promise of change, and redskin conflict hung in the air alongside the pungent air. Most folks who had lived in Kosoma for any length of time were opposed to any kind of change—with the exception of exterminating toughs like the Darby brothers.

Trusty figured he hadn't been in town long enough to reach the point of immunity to the smell by any of his senses and had no intention of staying any longer than necessary. He was relieved to hear that the judge wanted to leave town immediately. "Not one of the nicer places I've ever been either."

The judge smiled, waiting for Trusty to lead him out of the crowd. "Not from the stories I've heard tell. There's a line of whorehouses and saloons from San Antonio to Abilene that tell of your exploits."

They had stood far enough from the gallows to make a quick escape if the need arose, but there was still a gathering of people milling about around them. More in front than behind. Main Street and arranged safety were just around the corner in an empty bank vault. Trusty didn't like that plan, but he was pretty certain that any threat would come from up close, or the rooftops overlooking the execution square. For now, everything was clear, but that didn't stop him from scanning the crowd like a scout expecting to find an ambush. His army training was never far away.

"You'd think a judge would be immune to embellishments and hearsay," Trusty said.

"We like rumor and gossip as much as any other man. Besides, you've a reputation to uphold. I am only endorsing your résumé and contributing to the myth that you are in the process of building, as well as living vicariously through your exploits. I am a bit jealous." The judge nudged Trusty with his elbow, then offered a smile to prove he was serious.

Trusty's face flushed red. There was no question that he had always liked the company of women and had a taste for good whiskey, but there was more to his past adventures than the judge knew or that Trusty wanted to share. He had only loved one woman in all of his life, and that ill-fated love had left him broken and bothered, in need of a salve that could never heal the wound—if he ever found it. He avoided touching that hurt, or thinking about that lost love, as much as possible. "Ain't nothin' but tales about me anyways, Judge. The past is the past. I've become a reformed man."

"You mean you've found Jesus?"

"Not in any of the places I've been lately. 'Course I ain't been lookin' much for Him neither. I was still an energetic boy after I left the army, before I took up the law as my calling. Besides, a woman tends to complicate a man's life, at least *this* man's life. I've always got some place to go, a judge to protect, a scoundrel to round up; you know, chasin' trouble is what I like to do best.

It's been my experience that a fine woman likes to settle, live in a nice house, tie a man down, and extend roots into hard ground. I like to ride, see the country, have an adventure or two, while I still can. I'm not the marrying kind, Judge, simple as that." Trusty tapped the Deputy U.S. Marshal's badge on his chest with his stubby trigger finger and smiled. "This is all of the commitment I need these days."

"You just keep thinking that, Trusty, and we'll all have plenty to talk about for a long time to come. But I'll offer you some advice if you'll have it."

"I'm always open to listening to a man of your stature and education about the nature of life."

"Well," Judge Hadesworth said, "look at me standing here next to you without Mrs. Hadesworth in sight. She's most likely back in Muskogee on another shopping excursion of one kind or another, keeping the fire lit for my return. It's been that way for nigh on forty-one years. I ride the circuit and she is waiting at home keeping things nice and warm. Distance does a marriage good, Trusty. It always has mine. The return is a sweet and welcoming adventure worth traversing the drudgeries of humanity for. Even at my age, if you're wondering."

"I wasn't. But I'll take your advice under advisement, Judge. Not that I'll heed to it, mind you. My duties on the trail are longer and less predictable than yours, and I do enjoy a dose of variety in my life."

"Me too," the gray-haired man said with a wink and another elbow nudge. "Me too."

Trusty laughed uncomfortably. "Let's get your belongin's from the hotel and dust our way out of here before the sun starts to dive west too fast. I'd like to get to Lost Mountain Pass before night settles in."

"Expecting trouble, Trusty?" the judge asked with a raised eyebrow.

"I'm always expectin' trouble, Judge. 'Specially after a hangin' as well-deserved as this one. I know a spot on the pass that's about as safe as I can get us for tonight," he said, looking past the judge at a flush of movement that had caught his eye.

Two men were pushing through the crowd toward them, one as big as a bull, the other short and bulky as a boxer, reaching inside his duster for something that Trusty could only imagine to be a gun of some kind. "Anybody plottin' trouble for us will be waiting for us on the road south. I aim to head north, take a night in the pass to wait them out, then circle around south Kosoma from the west, and get you home as soon as possible."

Judge Hadesworth nodded with approval. "I like how you think, Trusty." He started to walk toward Main Street, back to the hotel.

The sight of the men heading toward them caused Trusty to plant his feet and extend a hand to impede Judge Hadesworth's forward motion. "Stop," Trusty said in a low, "don't argue with me" command.

The hunched man ceased to move immediately, silencing the click of his cane; even the old man's breath restrained itself, hidden, pulled inside himself. A serious look fell over both men's faces. Trusty had been responsible for the judge's life on more than one occasion—ten, as a matter of count—and the two men were past developing a shorthand and wordless manner in sight of a threat. The judge, always happy and accustomed to being in the lead, submitted to Trusty's instinct and drew back without question.

Trusty reached inside his coat to grip the Colt. The holster was unhinged and a cartridge sat in the chamber, ready to be called into action with a quick pull of the trigger. One yank and the pistol would be let loose into the world to prove its purpose: protect and kill.

The two unknown men continued their hard walk toward the judge and the deputy in step, on a mission, anger hanging on their faces as apparent as an OPEN sign at a barbershop. The crowd parted, pushed aside by the apparent suggestion of confrontation. Murmurs of acceptance and relief from the hanging quickly turned to fearful chirps, gasps, followed by an uneasy silence. All eyes were on the four men.

Trusty edged around the judge so the adjudicator was shielded from the coming threat as completely as possible, then he reformulated his escape plan. This one called for the swift death of the two approaching men. Wounding them would not do. Any threat to a federal judge's life had to be dealt with in the most severe terms. Trusty pictured two shots to the heart, if possible. If those shots weren't clear, then the target would shift to just above the bridge of the nose, square between the eyes—a head shot meant to stop both men in their tracks. Trusty and the judge would flee to safety before both bodies hit the ground. Refuge would then be taken in the bank vault in case there were more than two men—because there were always more than two. Always.

The Colt felt cold and ready as all of the sound drained from Trusty's ears. No distractions. No focus on anything but the approaching threat. His heart beat as steadily as if he were napping. Sweat retreated and no force of blood rushed through his veins. He was as calm and ready as the judge had been when he'd read the Darby brothers' verdict. Killing and protecting came as easily to Trusty as it did to the Colt in his grip. The army had given him license to do deeds untoward and inhuman that came natural to him but shouldn't have. Men that deserved to die did not haunt his dreams.

The boxer and most serious looking of the two men— the one who had reached inside his duster—made eye contact with Trusty, then glanced away and let his hands fall clear, out into the open so it was possible to see that they were empty. That did not give Trusty cause or a reason to relax his stance. Both men were heavily armed with two six-shooters, and probably more by the sound of the iron *clank* accompanying their strides and the determined look in their eyes. Revenge never wore a mask.

The crowd remained frozen in place. No one said anything out loud, or called the men by name, but there was wonder in the air. Wonder if these men had come to settle a score for the hanging of the Darby gang. Such a thing had been as expected as the sun arching across the perfect blue spring sky.

The other man—the bull—eyed Trusty, too, and kept walking forward, not wavering his route one inch. If the bull kept moving, one or two of the men would have to step out of the way. Trusty was firmly planted, and Judge Hadesworth stood as erect as an ancient oak could, refusing to sway in the wind, leaning forward on the cane instead of backward in retreat. Intimidation was something the judge reacted to. Gordon Hadesworth didn't have the capability to show fear. That had been lost a long time ago.

The two men veered at the last second, cutting past Trusty and the judge, pushing a bookish-looking man out of the way like angry rats sweeping past a meek mouse. They said nothing, but kept walking, determined in one way or the other to be done with the hanging.

All Trusty could do was watch the men disappear and hope that this would be the last time he ever saw them. "Come on, Judge," he said. "It's past time we put this dot on the map behind us." He didn't relax his grip on the Colt until the two men had vanished around the corner and the crowd sighed in relief.

Trusty took a last look at the three dead Darby brothers, stiff as planks now, swaying in the wind, starting to attract blowflies. Hangings and their aftermath had always unsettled Trusty, and this one was no exception.

# Chapter 2

There were two hotels in Kosoma with the promise of a third on the horizon. One, the Margate, was little more than a flophouse across the street from the train depot. The other, the Hobart House Hotel, was a three-story building with a fancy redbrick façade that aspired to be grand, but failed in the attempt from a lack of imagination, materials, or enough investors to see the original vision brought to fruition. The building looked hastily thrown together because it had been. The inside was as bland and disappointing as the outside, offering little in atmosphere or comfort. All of the carpets were drab, the walls bare of original paintings, and the sour eggy smell from the outside had taken up residence inside the fabric of everything that graced the inside of the hotel. It was rare that Trusty spent time on a soft feather bed, but he had come to enjoy his stays in hotels around Indian Territory and out of it. But the beds in the Hobart House Hotel were as hard and bumpy as the jagged rocks in the Osage lands and just as barren. One more reason to get out of town. Sleeping on the ground offered more comfort and relief than the Hobart House mattresses. ·

The judge's room was on the first floor. He had opted for a single bed instead of what surely would be a disappointing presidential suite on the third floor at Trusty's urging. Upper rooms offered fewer escape routes. Judge Hadesworth wasn't a fussy man, and Trusty was glad about that. He shared the adjoining room, which allowed him access to the judge at all hours of the night; it turned out that was as much a mistake as staying in the Hobart House in the first place. Gordon Hadesworth was a world-class snorer. Mrs. Hadesworth probably looked forward to the nights the judge was out of town. She was probably catching up on sleep instead of the shopping excursion the judge had imagined.

"I've already packed most everything," the judge said. "Why don't you go on and get the horses ready, and I'll meet you at the livery."

"Not going to happen, Judge. I'll wait."

Hadesworth took a deep breath, puffed up his chest the best he could, and started to protest, but suddenly retreated with a shake of his head. "Do you ever relax?"

"Of course, I relax. We talked about blowin' off steam earlier. I'll get to that when the time is right. But that's not a concern at the moment. We need to get on the trail. I don't like the feeling in this town. The voice in the back of my head says I need to get you out of here as soon as possible. Those two toughs made a big show of themselves for a reason. I don't know what that reason was, or is, but I think if we stick around here long enough, we'll find out."

"Those two men in the crowd really set off your alarms, didn't they? They looked like typical trouble-makers to me."

"They *did* set me off."

"You know them?"

"Nope. Never seen either one of them before, but I know their type. They looked like hired men to me."

"It's a little brazen for assassins to show themselves in broad daylight, don't you think?"

"Maybe. But I'd rather overreact than not react at all. You're not leaving my sight unless you make a demand of it. I'm not going to rest comfortably until I deposit you on your doorstep to Mrs. Hadesworth. Then she can look after your every move, and I'll go about relaxin' the best I can. There's a fine blonde in Muskogee I plan on callin' on when I get there. Does that strategy suit your myth-making?"

"It does, though I'd require a little more detail."

"You'll have to use that imagination of yours while we travel."

"Well, in that case, I do require use of the toilet."

"You can have all of the privacy you need. I'll wait."


The judge stood at the entrance of the livery, well within Trusty's sight, regaling a Mexican groomer with a long, drawn-out story while Trusty cinched the saddle on his horse. He rode a roan gelding that he'd never got around to naming. He called the horse *Horse*, and the easygoing beast didn't seem to mind the name at all. The two of them had traveled a lot of miles together, knew each other pretty well, but Trusty wasn't one to hold a high affection for any animal on a long-term basis. There was a job to do and that was that. Attachments were a danger to the job. The escapade with his object of lost love had taught him that. The past held a stink to it that could outlive the current smell in Kosoma.

He kept one ear cocked toward the front of the livery, and looked toward the judge every second or two, like a wary bird, hoping the judge was doing the same thing. But at the moment, almost like every other moment, Gordon Hadesworth didn't seem ruffled or threatened at all. He acted normal, invincible, unconcerned about any enemies that might be lurking around the corner.

"I was hoping I would find you here."

The voice was a young female. She startled Trusty. He jumped and reached for his sidearm at the same time. The Winchester had already been packed into the scabbard. Trusty hadn't heard anyone come up behind him, which concerned him. Letting your guard down for one second on a hanging day could get you and your charge killed, and he knew it.

"I'm sorry, ma'am, do I know you?" he said, letting his hand fall away from the Colt.

She shook her head. "No, sir, you do not." She looked more like a girl than a woman. Lucky to be twenty years old at best, but probably younger, truth be told. Dressed in a black Bolero coat closed up tight at the neck, and a long skirt, deep black, too, parts of it matte, other parts shiny, sewn in a tight horizontal pattern, along with traveling boots and a fancy black bonnet with dangling chin straps. Her face was hard set and she bore a crow-like nose, eyes the color of granite, and dark brunette hair pulled back and swept up under the bonnet—all of which were stacked up on a skinny, unfulfilled body. There was nothing about the girl that Trusty found attractive at all. She instantly annoyed him, considering her stealthy skills and the darkness she carried with her.

The livery was quiet, not much going on. It was just the two of them inside as far as Trusty knew. A few stalls over, a horse snorted, then took a healthy piss. The judge was fully engaged with the groomer and hadn't noticed the woman talking to Trusty or didn't care.

"I understand that you are on your way to Muskogee?" the girl said.

"Yes, ma'am, that would be correct. How did you come upon that knowledge?"

"There are few secrets in this town, though there should be."

"That didn't answer my question," he said. This bit of information confirmed that his plan to exit Kosoma to the north and make his way through Lost Mountain Pass was necessary.

"I would like to secure passage in your company."

Trusty wiped his hands. "I'm sorry, ma'am, I'm a Deputy U.S. Marshal, not an escort. You'll need to make other arrangements. I don't hire out."

"Are you not Trusty Dawson?"

He flinched at the nickname. "I am. Sure as it's day-light, I am." He thought about telling the woman that his real name was Samuel but let that thought slide away. Something told him not to get too familiar with this one. She looked like she could peck his eyes out.

"Most folks call you Trusty, and that is the only reason why I have sought you out. Your reputation as a drinker and a womanizer is overridden by the fact that your gun skills are rumored to be superb, the best in the Territory from what I understand. You have never lost a charge under your care, and a man to be reckoned with by the worst of the worst. It is a fine reputation you carry, and I need protection, Deputy, or I will surely not make it out of Kosoma alive."

"Your life's in danger? How is that, ma'am?" He stepped away from Horse, his attention fully on the woman now.

She stared at Trusty like he had just asked the stupidest question in the world. "Fine. This was a waste of my time, just as I suspected it would be," she said, spinning in perfect balance on the heels of her polished black boots with the intention of stalking off. "My blood is on your hands, Deputy. Remember I said that."

By the time Trusty caught up with the girl, she had hurried off twenty feet away from him, nearly to the barn's rear double doors that stood wide open. A slight breeze pushed stinky air through the barn, mixing with the smell of animal excrements and sour straw. He really wanted to get the hell out of Kosoma.

"Wait," Trusty said, catching up to the girl. He grabbed her arm and brought her to an unexpected stop. "There's no need to go gettin' all haughty. Just tell me what's going on. If you're in trouble, that's another thing entirely. I'll help you if I can."

With a glare that cut through her tear-filled eyes, she said, "It's too late. I might as well succumb to my fate. You were my last hope. I will approach this journey on my own and take my chances, thank you very much."

Maybe it was the tears in her once rock-hard eyes, the

vulnerability now apparent, but her features had softened. There was a beauty to her that Trusty had failed to
initially notice, had overlooked at first glance. She was
not the kind of woman he'd consider pursuing, but she
wasn't such an ugly little bird either. Wearing a black
coat and skirt didn't help her none. Her skin was white
as paste, and it looked like it would crack if anyone dared
to touch it.

"Let's start over," Trusty said. "What's your name,
ma'am?" he asked in the softest, kindest voice he could
muster.

"Amelia. Amelia Darby." She watched Trusty's reaction closely, surely accustomed to a negative response.
"Cleatus was my brother. Horace and Rascal too. And
just because I'm of the same blood as those three, people
think I'm a killer, a thief, and a liar too. Folks around
town think all us Darbys are meaner than snakes and not
fit to walk on this earth. That I'm just like them. I guess
I can't blame them. The three boys robbed anyone with
a nickel in their pocket, and when they finally took to
killing, they did it like it was fun and games with no consequences. Old Man Robinson, the one they hanged for,
was target practice. They emptied their guns on him long
after he was dead. Why should I be surprised, then, that
everyone, and probably you, think I'm no better than
them? I'll never get a fair chance in this town, and most
likely this Territory. If I had the money to get myself to
California, that's exactly what I'd do."

Trusty let his hand slide away from Amelia's arm.
"I'm sorry, I had no idea who you were."

"How could you; you're not from these parts."

"I'll talk to the sheriff, see about gettin' you some protection. Maybe it'd be best to just let things settle down a bit before you go makin' a rash decision like leavin' town."

"I have had pig's blood thrown on my porch. Service refused me at the mercantile. No one will extend credit to me or hire out my skills as a milliner. I am nearly broke, sir, left with no kin to fall back on or any prospects for the future in this town other than the certainty of my death. Just this morning, someone fired a gunshot through my front window. It was only a matter of luck that I was not walking through the front room, or I would be soon lying in a coffin in Poor Man's Hill alongside my brothers. I fear for my life, Deputy, surely you must understand that."

"There's no family left to help you out?"

"None that can help me. My brothers made sure that all of our ties within a hundred miles were broken beyond repair. I am alone in this world, sir, with no one to help me but you."

Trusty shifted uncomfortably. "How do I know that this isn't some kind of ploy to exact revenge on the judge for renderin' a well-deserved death sentence on your brothers, ma'am? How do I know that you don't have a plot to kill him? I'm sorry to say so, ma'am, but I have to consider such a thing. The judge is my responsibility. I've taken an oath to give my life for his if it comes to that. You sure don't look like no killer to me, but I've seen some real sweet ones, let me tell you, in my line of work."

Amelia Darby stared at Trusty with her deep gray eyes, unflinching. She had wiped away her tears and it was like they had never existed in the first place. "I would expect that you would think such a thing. Three things should be reason enough to believe me, Deputy. One. I have never hurt a fly. Never. You can ask anyone in this town. I, too, have worked at maintaining my character, for all of the good it's done me. Two. I am the last of the Darbys in Kosoma. When I am gone, there will be no legacy for anyone to shoulder, and all of my family's debts will be paid in full. I have made sure of that, which is why I have little money left. The Darbys will be a bad memory, quickly forgotten, and unknown to the greedy hordes that are filling the town and the territory in search of their fortunes. Three. I hated my brothers and what they stood for. They deserved to hang. They were cold-blooded killers and earned their punishments. They deserved what they got in the end. I have no mind for revenge, no need to set the record straight by bringing any harm to Judge Hadesworth. My only desire is to start a new life as far away from Kosoma as possible. It's that simple, Deputy. I long to open a milliner's shop in Muskogee or thereabouts. It is my dream, and I aim to fulfill it while I can still breathe and have the wherewithal to accomplish such a thing. That is my story and there is nothing I can add, other than the guarantee of my word that I mean no one any harm, especially the judge. You can take it or leave it. My fate is in your hands."

Trusty took a deep breath and stared up at the rafters. "I'll have to clear it with the judge, you understand."

"No need," Amelia said, "I already have."

### St. Louis, Missouri, summer 1865

Iron clanked against iron as regular as the tick of a clock. Only the sound was no tick. It was a hard slam fueled by demand, necessity, and an underlying rage that always seemed to exist in the palms of seven-year-old Sam Dawson's father's massive hands. The hard hit of a cross-peen hammer against soft red iron was powered by muscles developed from years of blacksmith work and the determination to bend the ore into something useful, tools or weapons, never decorations. Markum Dawson saw little difference between a boy and a piece of metal that needed transformed into something useful. It didn't matter by what method—heating, holding, hitting, or shaping. Flesh or steel bent the same way as far as Markum was concerned. Once the blacksmith decided on the creation of something, he persisted until whatever it was came into being on his American wrought anvil. Sam wondered sometimes if his father wanted to set his head on the bench, take his hammer to it, and fashion a completely new person out of his skull and the brain inside it.

The shop was the place of his boyhood. The dim sooty cave of a worn slat barn where he had been forced to apprentice as a blacksmith whether he wanted to or not. That had been his plight as an only child. The last thing that Sam wanted to be when he grew up was a blacksmith. He didn't want to be anything like his father. But he had no choice. Sam was trapped in his father's world. He couldn't escape if he wanted to. Not at seven, or seventy, if he could even consider such a thing.

"What are you doin' just standing there, boy? Go fetch a bucket of cold water. We got rods to cool and more work to get to before the sun starts to set. Did you get your ma her breakfast before you left her this morning?"

His father had a booming voice that echoed inside

Sam's head like a bullet looking for a place to exit. Markum Dawson was a towering behemoth of a man, wide in the shoulders, thick arms rippled from his daily work, his belly round from his nightly consumption of beer and food. "Big as an ox" didn't suffice as a description, but that was always what came to Sam's thinking when he pictured his father in his mind or had to face him. Sam had always thought his father looked like a giant beast of burden built of iron muscles and a heart made of steel. There was nothing small about Sam's father. His hands were as big as black skillets, and his eyes were always wide open, making them seem larger than normal. Even now, there was no way to know what color his father's eyes were; blue was the assumption, but everything in the shop was tinged with soot. Markum's face was always smudged black, mixed with sweat; even with a good bath it was hard to get off. He always looked overbaked, nearly burnt to a crisp, as dark as the footman on a fancy coach. Blacksmithing had left Markum Dawson stained in more ways than one.

"Yes, sir," Sam said. He lowered his head. His mother had suffered from consumption from the time Sam could remember. She was Mamie to everyone who knew her, but Meredith to her parents and the church. A bony woman, short in stature but tall in spirit, she was exactly the opposite of her husband: soft, pliable, comforting. She fought her way through every day, in the shadow of the blacksmith shop and the life it provided, doing her best to obey and serve her husband, even though she could barely stand to breathe the smoky fumes left in the big man's wake. As much as Sam was a bag of failure made of flesh and bones according to his father, Sam was a rare jewel in his mother's eyes. He was her one great contribution to the world, even though birthing him had nearly killed her. "She said she wasn't hungry, so I left the bowl of porridge on the table next to her bed," he said.

Markum Dawson stopped hammering and shot the boy an angry look. "Can't you do anything right?" He shook his head, then turned away from Sam. "I told you to make sure she ate something. She's never hungry."

"Sorry," Sam mumbled. He moved toward the door, saw his failure as a way to escape the shop.

"You best get to work and start turning those hanger eyes. I need a dozen of them."

Sam stopped, knew it was useless to go any farther, nodded, and said, "Yes, sir," then grabbed up an iron rod with a pair of oversized pliers out of a crate next to the blazing forge. He was angry, upset at being yelled at one more time, and didn't measure the rod. He jammed the rod into the fire until it glowed red, then hurried it to the anvil and started hammering the bend.

"You've got a long heat," Markum yelled. "You're making more work for yourself and weakening the iron. Sizzle that damn rod and do another one like I've showed you a thousand times over."

Sam kept on hammering, bending the rod until it snapped, ruining it, at least for the hanger it was intended for, and said to himself: *I'll show you. One of these days, I'll show you that I can do everything right. I won't give up until I do. You wait and see.*

### Kosoma, Indian Territory, May 1888

They rode toward the end of town, three horses abreast, Amelia Darby in the middle between Trusty and Judge Hadesworth. A few white people stopped on the boardwalks and glared at the trio. Indians, mostly Choctaws, dressed from the same shops that had denied Amelia credit, kept on walking without notice or care about the three riders. Some of those that took notice turned their backs, shunning Amelia Darby purposefully, leaving no question to what their hateful intention was. The sight of such disregard for the woman fortified Amelia's story and made it seem true. Trusty was relieved more than he was appalled by the shuns even though he didn't say so. He remained quiet, still uneasy about the new alliance and responsibility for the woman. There hadn't been a chance to ask the judge when he had given Amelia Darby permission to ride with them, but that would come at the first chance. The two of them, the old man and young woman, seemed to have an easy, warm rapport and that concerned Trusty. Something he'd have to keep an eye on. He still wasn't completely convinced that the Darby girl wasn't up to something.

Amelia stared straight ahead, her eyes set on the horizon, not allowing one gaze that fell across her face to dent her attitude or touch her heart. At least that was what she showed on the outside from her reaction to the folks on the boardwalk. Trusty knew her insides were another matter from the conversation they'd had inside the livery. The shunning would be another wound, a final nail in her reasoning to flee the town. *Good riddance*, Trusty imagined her saying inside her head. Good riddance. All the while her eyes remained cold as January icicles.

Trusty shifted the Winchester rifle that lay comfortably across his lap, and one hand dangled inches from his Colt, signaling to those who stood in watch that

Amelia was under his protection. Horse had his ears erect, alert, sensing the tension in the air. One ear was white, the other red, or strawberry roan, depending on who was doing the describing. Trusty liked to think Horse's ear was red. Like a sunset falling behind a snow-covered mountain. Strawberry sounded sissified, and there was nothing about Horse that suggested he *was* sissified in any way.

Just as they were about to cross the last street before leaving Kosoma, a wagon passed in front of them, causing all three horses to come to a stop and wait. Trusty surveyed the crowd on both sides of the street, searching for the two men—the bulldog and the boxer—that he had seen earlier, but there was no sign of them or any other outward-looking toughs. Just normal folks in town for the hanging, making a trip out of it, a reason to shop and stock up before heading home.

The wagon was loaded with the Darby brothers' coffins, heading toward a cemetery on the opposite end of town, the place Amelia had called Poor Man's Hill. There was no parade of mourners following along with the wagon. The preacher sat shotgun, next to a glum Teamster, both of them stiff and on tenterhooks as if they expected something to happen at any second. They weren't alone. Trusty had an itch in his trigger finger, a sure sign that trouble was lurking about.

Judge Hadesworth leaned toward Amelia in his comfortable, well-worn saddle. "You sure you don't want to attend the funeral of your brothers, Miss Darby?"

"No, sir. I have no more tears left to shed for those three. Rascal held the greatest amount of promise and I will miss him the most. But in the end, his deeds were influenced by the other two, competing to be noticed and accepted, so they wouldn't treat him as a dunce or a punching bag. It never happened. Rascal died trying to impress Cleatus and Horace. Whatever awaits them on the other side of this life will be no different, I imagine. If there is such a thing."

"You are not a believer, then?" the judge asked.

Amelia turned her attention away from the coffins and stared Judge Hadesworth directly in the eye. "Let's just say I have questions. And you, Judge?"

Trusty stayed out of the conversation, his eyes darting to the rooftops and to the shadows of the alleyway that cut alongside a mercantile and an empty storefront with a FOR RENT sign in the front window. He felt the same tension in the air Horse did. The air smelled faintly of gunpowder and lead, but that could have been his imagination playing tricks on him, all things considered.

"My father was a Methodist minister," the judge continued. "I was raised in the ways of the Lord. But I am not one to proselytize, so you have no need to worry of my pestering you for a conversion or deep conversation based on verses put to memory as a child."

Trusty remained stiff in his saddle, listening to a story he'd heard from the judge about ten times over. One way or the other the Lord always worked His way into a conversation with the judge—whether He was welcome or not.

"Being pestered by you is the least of my worries on this journey, Judge Hadesworth," Amelia said. "I'm just grateful to be in your company and have the protection of Trusty Dawson. I fear I wouldn't have made it out of this town alive." She turned her attention to the wagon and the coffins as it moved on and cleared her throat. Trusty thought her eyes were glazed with a tear or two, but he couldn't be sure. It could have been the dust raised by the wagon and team of bored horses that were pulling it.

A wavering cloud of flies chased after the makeshift hearse, drawn by the smell of death and the opportunity that three rotting human bodies provided. The dead brothers were a jackpot of food and a virgin breeding ground. Flies obviously knew a boomtown when they saw it too.

"Your decision is final then, ma'am?" Trusty asked. "You're sure you want to leave today and not pay your respects to your brothers?"

"Yes, Trusty, my decision is final. The sooner I'm out of this town, the sooner my new life begins." Amelia started to nicker her horse, a skinny chestnut mare that needed a good brushing, but the judge reached over and grabbed her by the arm in a gentle, but forceful way to stop her from moving on.

"I understand your reluctance, Miss Darby," Judge Hadesworth said, "but I would implore you to reconsider your decision. Regret adds to the venom of bitterness at unknown and unwelcome times. Those men are your brothers. Blood kin. No matter their vile actions on this good earth, you need to pay your respects. It is not our burden to open or close St. Peter's Gates, and I would suggest that not making a condemnation might lighten your ride, and the rest of your own journey going forward. Leave your anger and grief in Kosoma where it belongs instead of carrying it with you wherever you go."

Something flickered across Amelia's face that Trusty couldn't read. At first he thought she was angry, enraged by the judge's touch and suggestion, but the harsh look in her eyes melted away into something else. Surrender or admiration, he wasn't sure which it was. A confusing mix, at least to Trusty, if there was one.

"Your years as a litigator have served you well, Judge Hadesworth," Amelia said. "I suppose you are right. I owe it to my brothers and my parents, may they rest in peace, to attend their funeral. Especially Rascal's. We were friends once, along with being brother and sister. He looked out for me when he could, when he still had a pinch of goodness on the surface of his heart." With that she gently urged her skinny horse forward, taking lead of the trio, following after the wagon full of coffins with her face void of any further emotion and her head down, in shame or prayer, it was hard to tell.

Trusty had no choice but to follow after Amelia Darby, even though he was concerned about the delay in leaving town. It still stank, and something told him that the threat he'd felt earlier in the day hadn't been left behind at the hanging. The back of his neck tingled with eyes on it, even though no one seemed to be paying him any mind at all. Everyone's attention was on Amelia Darby.

# Chapter 3

*Paris, Texas, May 1888*

Vance Calhoun dodged a punch, then retaliated with a double-fisted attack that came as fast as a poisonous snake lurching forward, fangs drawn, from a hidden stand of grass. A straight hit to the nose was quickly followed up by a blasting uppercut to the surprised chin of the man who had insulted Calhoun. The crunch of bone reached over the spew of blood, and the fragility and slap of flesh echoed inside the silent saloon in a chorus of shuddering pain. Piano keys had gone silent at the first suggestion of a fight. Conversations ceased; breaths drew in and held. The air inside the dingy saloon smelled of yeast and sweat from ten men and one woman looking for respite against a warming sun and the demand of spring labor. The poor sap on the receiving end of Calhoun's fists, an unknown rider off the most recent stagecoach stop, had no clue who he was dealing with until it had been too late to take back the innocent words that had come out of his mouth: *Well, don't you think you're something.*

Everyone in Paris, Texas, knew that Vance Calhoun

had the temperament of a thin-skinned rattlesnake; he was that snake in the grass, quick to strike, slow to retreat, always protecting his territory whether the threat was perceived or the boundaries were crossed accidentally. Any man with one good eye could have seen that Calhoun had been spoiling for a fight the second he'd pushed through the batwings of Dottie Lynn's Silver Sargent Saloon.

"Let that be a lesson to you. Maybe you'll think of this meetin' the next time you elbow your way into a conversation you don't ken nothin' about," Calhoun said, as the battered man, skinny as a broom handle, dressed in a ten-year-old natty gray pin-striped suit, stumbled against the wall and slid down, eyes closed to the heavens. The stranger's nose had twisted sideways as he was knocked out by the assault, and his face was covered in bright red blood that looked like it might make a permanent stain on his pasty white skin.

No one came to the victim's aid. They knew better, even Dottie Lynn, who stood back in the shadow of the bar, frozen like the statue of a renowned opera singer from Paris, France, who was fully aware of who she was dealing with. Calhoun stood over the injured man waiting for a sign of resistance, another chance to strike, another bone to break—something deep inside of him liked the sound of snapping bones and the presence of pain that followed—with his fists still curled in a snake head pose. When there wasn't any opportunity for more of a fight to be had, Calhoun relaxed his hands, stalked back to the bar, sat down with an open seat on each side of him, and took a swig of beer from his waiting mug, unconcerned about any repercussions from his actions.

*He was something.* And everybody within a hundred miles knew it.

Vance Calhoun was a regular in every saloon in Paris, Texas, and carried with him an entitled seat at the bar and the first order of anything he wanted—drink, woman, fight, or otherwise. If somebody had something he wanted, he took it. He owned a four-thousand-acre spread with as many cattle as there were stars in the sky, or so it seemed, and hoped to be a minority owner in a railroad soon, St. Louis–San Francisco Railroad, the "Frisco" that ran to Fort Smith. His wife Jessica was the daughter of one of the railroad owners, Theodore Marberry, and Calhoun knew if he played his cards right, he could become richer and more powerful than he ever thought he could be. Ranching was one thing, owning a railroad was another.

Calhoun didn't look rich and wealthy most of the time. He worked the land, ran his ranch with an iron fist, and took to wearing suits like a lizard dancing on ice. It didn't happen. He was tall enough that he had to shy forward when he walked inside a door with his boots and hat on, and was well-muscled from the daily work he did because he wanted to, not because he had to. Scottish by descent and attitude, quick to anger, a relentless Texas fighter, the War Between the States had set him off on a tirade that had continued long after he returned home, battered, broken, and angry by the defeat. He wore a battle glaze in his eyes at certain times of the day, torment from the past that refused to die with the setting sun. He didn't speak of the loss and time in battle unless he was drunk enough to wipe away the barriers he had set up for himself. The man on the floor most likely indicated in one way or the other, true or not, that he was a Yankee, and that would have been enough to load Calhoun's fists into the deadly weapons that they were. Or it was an insult spoken unawares like so many in the past had done. Saying Calhoun thought highly of himself could have been taken as a compliment, but this time it wasn't.

Calhoun, originally Colquhoun, but changed on the shores of New York so most Americans could pronounce the name, had come to the country as a boy from Aberdeenshire. He worked hard, went to war, fought for the cause that he believed in, then headed west with ambition, a head for numbers, an unquenchable appetite for success, and a secret load of cash stolen from a Union train in the final days of the war. Success, real or filched, was the only way he knew how to get revenge, other than go on a killing spree, which he restrained himself from doing unless there was reason and the high chance of getting away with it. Calhoun couldn't bear the thought of sacrificing the empire he had worked so hard to build or spending another day—or night—in prison. He'd spent six months at Camp Morton in Indianapolis after being captured at Shiloh. His experience as a prisoner of war remained shuttered in the shadows of his mind, adding to his bouts of melancholy and unquenching thirst for whiskey. When the lights went off, blue-hatted demons kept him awake, which is why there was always a lamp burning next to his bed. He hadn't slept in the dark since he had returned to Texas.

Calhoun set down the mug after emptying it of beer and looked over his shoulder as a pair of men walked into the saloon. Spurs jangled. Boots thudded on the wood plank floor. They walked past the battered stagecoach rider without acknowledging him or showing any concern about the state of his health or life. No one in the saloon did. They knew better.

"Get you another, sir?" the barkeep said with a tremble in his voice. He stood back, out of arm's reach so he couldn't be dragged across the bar and beaten to a pulp. It had happened before.

"No. Looks like the posse has been set upon me to come and drag me home," Calhoun answered, spiraling the perfect gold ring on his wedding finger, his brogue lighter, easier to understand. He dug into his pants pocket, pulled out a couple of silver bits, and tossed them to the barkeep. "Buy that fella there a drink when he comes around and tell him it was compliments of Vance Calhoun."

The barkeep snatched the coins out of the air and cupped them into his sweaty palms. "And if he don't wake up?"

"Well, I suppose you'll have to call after the undertaker, now won't you?" Calhoun stood up and met the two men who had walked into the saloon. One, Haden O'Connor, was his right-hand man and overseer of the day-to-day chores on the ranch. Calhoun trusted Haden as much as he could trust any man—which was very little. The other man, Haden's younger brother, Gladnal— that everybody called Gladdy—Calhoun didn't care for or trust at all, but the O'Connor brothers came as a package deal. They had ever since they had all served in the same regiment, the 9th Texas Infantry, in pretty much the same power structure that still existed, with Gladdy bringing up the rear. Gladdy had his uses, maniacal, cold-blooded, but Calhoun didn't like it that the man thought he owned more power around the ranch than he actually did. Gladdy O'Connor had a high opinion of himself that he hadn't earned and didn't deserve. But having Haden at Vance's side was worth the discomfort of Gladdy's bad attitude and smelly breath. Haden O'Connor was well equipped to follow the same kind of orders he had in the past. Haden wasn't a thinking man—he was good at doing what he was told and more grounded than his brother, but Calhoun knew better than to give the Mick an opening to steal or lie to him. He didn't trust Haden that much. He didn't trust anybody that much—except for one person. The only person of his own blood on the ranch, his older sister, Sally, the true overseer in his absence of the ranch.

"She's askin' about you, boss," Haden said, stopping a foot in front of Calhoun. Haden was a typical skinny, blue-eyed, Black Irish who had come across the water in search of food, as long as it wasn't in the form of potatoes. Age had settled in his belly, round as a bonnet and just as soft, but there was still a young slant to his face even with the gray stubble in his beard. Gladdy was a younger version of his brother, only dirtier and shorter.

"And she thought to send you to fetch me for no cause, then?" A twitch rode up Vance Calhoun's high cheek on a spark of anger that came to rest in his dark gray eyes.

Haden shook his head, clacking his sidearm against the knife sheath he wore on his belt. "No, boss. It was

Sally Hoyle who sent me to ferret you out. There was pain in the new missus' belly and a worried note in old Sally's voice 'less there's a storm of some kind brewin' on the horizon. I figured I'd best get you home as quick as I could."

The Bar-C-Bar Ranch sat in a lush valley bordered by the jagged Red River to the north and a line of perfect barbed wire to the south. Four thousand acres equated to a square six miles long and six miles wide, but the land Calhoun owned was shaped more like a hatchet with a long handle than a square. From one end of the property line to the other it was a good ten-mile ride. Long enough for a man like Vance Calhoun to relax once his horse's hooves touched ground that he owned the deed to. But there was no relaxing on this day, not with an alarm set about the fate of his first-born child at stake.

Calhoun rode a grullo Chickasaw horse, gray as a shadow with a dun mask and bottom-of-the-well black eyes as serious and deep as its rider's. The horse was fast off the hoof and only got faster at Calhoun's relentless urging. Head down and free to push itself, the joy runner knew how to get its owner home on the tip of the wind, spry and fast, every snake hole and trip-worthy rock on the trail committed to memory. The gelding could have made the ride with his eyes closed, which was a good thing because Calhoun was not an expert horseman. He was smart enough not to get in the way of the gelding's desire; the horse loved to be given its head more than anything. Even an idiot would have known that about the beast, horseman or not. If there was ever a time Calhoun needed the grullo's independence and speed, that time was now.

The afternoon sun beamed down on the land that had welcomed the turn of the earth from winter to spring. The vibrant color of fresh green was everywhere the eye fell. Crisp, new, and pulsating with promise, especially for a man who traded in cattle and relied on healthy grasses to grow his wealth. Blooms that would bear fruit as the seasons passed offered a sweet fragrance to the air—nectar to contribute to the drunkenness of the waking world, animals and insects alike. Even though the ground and the sky throbbed with hope and opportunity, all Calhoun could see were the clouds brewing over the hills, white puffs tinged with gray, casting greedy dark fingers over the highest ridge. There was wind and bad weather in those innocent-looking clouds, he was sure of it.

It had only been hours ago when Calhoun had lost sight of the season, and the situation he had found himself in allowed his old ways to dominate his changed present. His young wife, the once-widowed Jessica Marberry Tennyton, high-blooded from St. Louis, was a beauty made of curved porcelain and golden locks that gave her the look of a regal painting no matter the light or time of day. The pregnant Jessica demanded that Calhoun, more than thirteen years her elder, change his ways, once and for all. An argument had ensued. Cross words had been spoken, not for the first time, or the last given the position each of them, man and woman, had taken in their lives with minds of their own. Both were accustomed to mounting a campaign and winning their way—by force or desire, one way or the other. Young Jessica was as spirited and fast as the grullo, proud of making her own rules and hell-bent on answering to no one, not even to Vance Calhoun, much to his chagrin and surprise. He didn't scare her, intimidate her, or hold any power over her, or so she had convinced him with her expert gun-handling skills and unwillingness to back down from him; she dared him to strike her. He didn't, but he wanted to. They were a lot alike, headstrong, independent, reluctant to need anything that they couldn't provide for themselves. That had been the attraction. There had been a lot to like about the woman, the girl really in comparison to the women that Calhoun usually found himself attracted to and in bed with.

Life with Jessica had started with a whirlwind romance, one that had surprised Calhoun, had come unexpected, out of nowhere, on a quick trip to St. Louis intended for business, not love. Her father, Theodore Marberry, was a railroad owner who was interested in negotiating shipment fees, saving the grueling, risky, and often unprofitable cattle drives. Dinner at the man's fine house had proved more fateful than Vance Calhoun could have ever imagined. He'd had no idea that Marberry had a young daughter, widowed and childless, living in the stately home with him. Calhoun was smitten with Jessica at first sighting. She glowed golden like a Roman statue lit from the inside out—and she seemed to like him, too, which had been even more of a surprise.

Vance Calhoun had never been a man to seek out a mate, a partner, or a relationship that required sharing a bed for more than an hour. The company of a woman usually came with the exchange of a coin and the change of bedsheets. He could walk away, confident that no emotional transaction had been made, and carry on with his life; romance was for fools. An heir, or a family, had never been in Calhoun's plans. Not until he laid eyes on Jessica Marberry—whose married last name was Tennyton—and was given the indication that she could be his if he was lucky enough to throw all of his chips into the game of love and pull an inside straight. All he had to do was learn how to live with a woman and be willing to trade her beauty for the individual that came along with it, opinionated and strong as she was—all packaged up in a luscious body that could never be bought for only one night. Having and keeping Jessica Marberry Tennyton was a long-term investment—a deal that Calhoun still wasn't sure was going to pay off. He was as shocked as everybody else that Jessica had said yes to his marriage proposal and had been willing to leave the comforts of St. Louis for his ranch in Paris, Texas. He had been more surprised when Jessica came up pregnant weeks after the wedding.

The grullo sped toward the ranch house with Calhoun leaning forward in the saddle. The house was a modest single-story three-bedroom affair with a wraparound porch that sat on a ridge overlooking a creek. Shaded by a grove of towering oaks, and within walking distance of a well-outfitted horse barn, the house seemed simple and small, especially in comparison to the new three-story Victorian house in St. Louis that Jessica was accustomed to.

A bunkhouse sat opposite the barn, and at any given time, there were between ten and twenty hands working on the ranch, the O'Connor brothers included. A cook and maid, Miguel and Maria, lived in a small cabin a hundred yards up the creek. Both were Mexican, married

long enough to grow white-haired and into a pair who
looked like they belonged together; a set of brown-
skinned salt and pepper shakers from the old country.
Sally Hoyle, Calhoun's only true trusted adviser, was his
sister, a colonel's widow since the war. She had come to
live in the house with him and was in charge of all things
domestic until Jessica had showed up. Then it was an old
cat learning to adjust to a young cat who had an eye on
the future, unconcerned about fitting in, or what the older
sister's role or relationship with her brother was. Sally
had mellowed in her territorial warfare at the first show
of Jessica's bulging belly, but only because she had no
children of her own and knew Vance was in need of an
heir himself. The air between Sally and Jessica had never
warmed, and there had remained a cautious distance
even after the pregnancy was certain. Jessica was queen
of the house, and Sally was a mere servant, no better than
the Mexican, Maria. Calhoun didn't notice the power
struggle or care about it. He had his own place in the
house to find with Jessica in charge.

If there had been any drink or drunkenness left inside
of Calhoun's body from his visit to the Silver Sargent
Saloon, it had drained out on the ride home via sweat
and worry. He hadn't considered anything could go
wrong with the pregnancy. Jessica was young, healthy,
and untroubled throughout the whole ordeal as the child
grew inside of her. Calhoun had, of course, seen healthy
cattle lose calves at birth, or shortly after to the scours—
relentless diarrhea that left the young calves dead in a
matter of hours, and the mother cow bereft by the loss.
There was nothing more melancholy than a grieving cow.
Unless, of course, Calhoun was willing to look in the

mirror when he was taken by one of his own dark moods, which, of course, he was not. He expected the baby to come like they always did, in secret, behind closed doors, with women huddled around the bed, coaxing the child into the world safely without any problems at all.

There was the possibility that Haden O'Connor had read the signs wrong and misunderstood Sally's message and intent. There was still hope for that, even though Calhoun could feel it in his bones that something was wrong. His luck had been on a good streak for too long. Something was bound to go awry, all things considered.

The grullo hustled across the final paddock with Calhoun barely aware that he was mounted atop a horse. His focus was on the house. Even from a distance, he could see Sally pacing the front porch, waiting for him to arrive. She met him on the hard dirt that separated the house and the barn. Haden and Gladdy followed, but kept on going, intent on putting up their horses. Their job was done. Calhoun was home. It was hard to tell by the look on Sally's face whether he had made it on time, or if his worst fear had come true.

Calhoun jumped off the horse and rushed to his sister, a stout woman a head and a half shorter than he was. She wore black hair that was losing the battle of time to strands of gray, pulled up tight with a braid at the back. Sally Hoyle was a severe-looking Scotswoman even when she laughed, which was an event rarer than a blue moon.

"What were you thinkin' leavin' at a time like this?" Sally said, accosting Calhoun with dagger-sharp eyes and a hard look that was just short of provoking a slap to his face. She had done that before, especially when they were children. Calhoun didn't fear his sister, but she had her ways of lording over him, making him uncomfortable so he would toe the line. He respected her, and if there was anyone on this earth who could tell him what to do and how to do it, it was Sally Hoyle.

Calhoun rubbed the sore knuckle of his right hand with his left, pushing away the thought of the stagecoach rider. "I needed to blow off some steam."

"With that woman in the state she's in? With the baby about to come?" Sally's brogue wasn't as thick as Calhoun's. She had tried her best to rid her tongue of Scotland the best she could, but her attempts betrayed her when she was angry. Especially when she was angry.

"What do I know about birthin' babes?" Calhoun said. Haden and Gladdy had disappeared inside the horse barn. It was just Sally and Calhoun standing before the house. A slight breeze had kicked up into a wind, riding over the top of the southwestern hill. He could taste rain on the tip of his tongue and feel a change of temperature in the air. "Am I too late?"

"The baby is born." Sally stiffened, looked away from her brother for a brief moment. "Maria is seeing to it."

"It's okay, then?"

"She is fine. Healthy with a deep set of lungs."

"A girl?" There was disappointment in Calhoun's voice.

"Yes, you'll have to think of a name for her."

"I'll leave that to Jessica."

Silence settled between the two of them like an iron partition had been dropped from the sky. Sally didn't need to say anything. Calhoun could read her face. His feet headed for the door, but his sister grabbed him back. "That might be a problem," she said.

"What do you mean? Is she all right?"

"The birth was too much for her. There was a lot of blood."

"Is she dead?" Vance Calhoun's knees started to quake, and the feeling in his body began to fade. His mouth was as dry as a desert and his hands trembled like an old man's.

"No, she is not dead, but she's not responding. I sent Miguel after the doctor. He should be here shortly."

"Did she call for me? Say anything? Anything at all?"

Sally looked away, unable to bear the sight of her brother on the verge of collapsing. "Are you sure you want to know?"

"Yes," he yelled, "tell me what she said."

"She called for a man named Samuel over and over again," Sally said. "She didn't ask for you one time, brother. Not one time."

# Chapter 4

*Kosoma, Indian Territory, May 1888*

Three graves had been hastily dug and stood open, waiting for the Darby brothers' arrival. The sky above was clear with the sun ticking toward the western horizon quicker than Trusty would have liked. He was more than a little annoyed about the judge's intervention in Amelia Darby's decision to attend the burial of her brothers.

A red-tailed hawk screeched overhead, its white underbody contrasting dramatically with its russet fan tail. The raptor wasn't interested in the burial or the bodies in the coffins. Death and human flesh were better left to vultures; this bird was on the hunt to feed its young, unconcerned about the human drama underneath it. A perfect shadow of the wings floated over the trio, causing Trusty and Judge Hadesworth to look up, the brims of their hats shielding their eyes. Amelia didn't move, didn't flinch. Her focus was on the wagon and its load of coffins. Her face was white as the hawk's belly and just as void of emotion as the bird's piercing yellow eyes. Not one tear had fallen from Amelia's own eyes, and Trusty had found her coldness troubling from the moment she had snuck up on him and asked him for his protection.

Poor Man's Hill was more of a bump than a hill, dotted with neglected wood crosses and lazy cairns of rocks built to placemark the final resting spots for the dead. There were no gravestones. That took money and effort. As far as Trusty knew, the closest limestone carver's shop was located in Missouri. Kosoma was a ten-minute ride behind them, with the cemetery offering a full view of the tightly constructed town. The railroad, void of a train, looked like a perfectly healed scar as it ran north and south without its own end and beginning. Lost Mountain poked up into the distance, an hour's ride away. The pass was hidden, unreachable. They should have been there by now.

The Teamster had brought the wagon full of coffins to a stop at the head of the open graves. Both men, the Teamster and the preacher, sat staring at Trusty and the pair of riders who rode with him with distrust and anger in their beady eyes. Amelia continued to sit stiffly in the rigid saddle on her skinny ride, while Judge Hadesworth waited next to her. He watched over the girl like a concerned parent, or a husband waiting for his wife to fall off a horse, overcome with emotion by the situation. There didn't appear to be anything to worry about as far as Trusty was concerned. It was hard to tell whether Amelia was still breathing or not. She looked like a statue upon the horse, who Trusty felt sorry for. The beast looked wore out, on its last shoe, in need of a pasture to be put out in. He wondered if the beast could make it to Muskogee.

"We don't need no trouble," the Teamster finally said,

followed by a spit of tobacco juice to the dry ground. He was a hatless man with stringy black hair and wore a jaw that jutted out a little too far. The man's face cast a comical shadow to the ground, even though there was nothing to laugh at at the moment. A crow could have easily shit on the man's chin without going to any trouble at all. He wore work clothes that looked like they hadn't been peeled off his skin in weeks, and he looked even more unhappy about being in the cemetery than Trusty did.

Trusty was a little surprised by the depth of the Teamster's glare. "This here's the Darby sister come to pay her respects. We're not here for trouble."

"We know who she is," the driver said. "Everybody in Kosoma knows who Amelia Darby is, don't they, Miss?"

Amelia didn't acknowledge the man. She stared at the coffins with her granite eyes. It was as if she was in the world all alone with no one around her.

The preacher didn't have any trouble letting the Teamster do all of the talking. He was dressed in black, holes patched on his elbows, with a gambler's bowler perched atop his head. A three-day crop of whiskers prickled up on his sun-drenched face, and a cigarillo dangled from his dry, cracked lips. The only way to tell the man was a true representative of the Lord was the faded Bible clutched in his left hand, though Trusty needed more confirmation than that to believe the preacher was who he was showing himself to be. He let his mind wander to the two hired men who had showed themselves after the hanging and let himself connect the two men in front of him with those two. He eased his hand to his side and restrained his fingers from unsnapping his holster. The air was unsettling.

"Some folks think there should be four graves instead of three," the preacher finally said, joining in the conversation.

A sudden reach of wind swirled through the cemetery, kicking up a small dust devil beyond the graves. Amelia lowered her head, refusing to offer an "I told you so" to Trusty, though that's what he would have said aloud if he were her.

"You fellas should get on with your business," Trusty said. "Don't pay us no mind. We're all mourners, and nothing more. One for each of the Darbys. You'll see no trouble from us. Not on this day."

"They don't deserve no mourners, them Darbys. None of 'em." The Teamster glared at Trusty as he settled the wagon's reins and hefted himself down from the seat.

"Doesn't matter what you think a man deserves or not, now does it," Judge Hadesworth said. "Every one of us has our judgment to face on our last day. This was theirs. Do you know when yours will be? Will you be welcomed or turned away at the gates that await you? No, I don't think you do know. Perhaps you should show some decency and respect to the dead and to the living. You'd be reminded to mind your manners to this woman. You know nothing of her trials. She deserves a mourner's respect, not a chide and the foul demeanor you have shown her."

The Teamster started to say something but swallowed his words when his eyes met the judge's. It didn't take a smart man to know that Judge Gordon Hadesworth was not the kind of man to be made an enemy of. Trusty had seen the same kind of behavior from the judge when he'd held court. There was no question that Judge Hadesworth was always holding court of some kind. These two men had failed to consider that there might be a time in the future when the learned old man's favor was needed. Instead of accepting the unsolicited advice, the Teamster walked to the back of the wagon and waited on the preacher to join him.

The hawk had flown off, leaving the sky barren of life, with only a few wispy clouds to be seen. Trusty was glad there was no weather coming their way. One less thing to worry about as he watched the hills around them for any sign of the hired men taking up a spot to cause trouble. There was none of that, either, so Trusty dismounted and joined the Teamster. "You look like you could use a hand."

"I thought you was a mourner?"

"You don't need to worry about what I am. Do you want my help or not?"

The Teamster shrugged and grabbed the closest coffin, while the preacher waited halfway to the grave with a relieved look on his face. Trusty grabbed the other side of the coffin and slid it out from the wagon's bed with the help of his newly found partner. They made quick business of dispatching each coffin to the open graves.

Judge Hadesworth dismounted, walked over to Amelia, and offered her his hand.

"No," she said. "I don't wish my feet to touch the ground until I am far from this forsaken place. That I am even here, in a place I am not welcome, even under the shadow of death, is more than I can bear. I will wait here, thank you very much." There was a finality to her words that was obvious enough to thwart the judge from arguing her off the back of her mount. Her attempt succeeded.

Judge Hadesworth walked away, came to a stop in front of the graves, took off his hat, and lowered his head in respect.

Trusty smirked silently, tried not to show what he was thinking: *Judge Gordon Hadesworth has met his match. Something to consider on the ride home.*

The preacher stepped up and read from the Twenty-Third Psalm. "The Lord is my shepherd; I shall not want. He maketh me to lie down in green pastures: he leadeth me beside the still waters. He restoreth my soul: he leadeth me in the paths of righteousness for his name's sake." He waited a second or two and let the wind carry the words away, then asked if anyone had anything to say.

Everyone looked to Amelia sitting on her skinny horse, all covered in her black garb, looking like a lone, frail crow waiting for the rest of its gang to show up. She shook her head no, then changed her mind and said, "I hope they rot in hell. All of them except Rascal. It wasn't his fault that he was stupid and needy. Momma always said he had a hard birth and was destined to be a half-wit the rest of his life. Some things can't be helped. Cleatus and Horace didn't have no excuse for their meanness. Rattlesnakes don't know they're nothin' else, but them boys had the choice to be human, kind or mean or not. They chose to be mean. I don't know why. I never asked them. They would have hit me with no thought given to what they'd done if I had questioned them one more time. They drank trouble like it was fine whiskey. Thrived on it. Created it. Couldn't get enough of it. They made their misery everybody else's. Some men can blame it on the war, but those bloody days are faded and long gone.

A man has to face that damage, come to terms with it after a while. You can't make war your excuse like Cleatus and Horace tried to. They ruined my life. Made a mess of everything. I hope they rot in hell is what I got to say again. Those are my words from my mouth to God's ears, and I ain't ashamed of any of 'em. Not a damn one of them." And with that, Amelia Darby spit at the graves with the same intensity as the Teamster had when he'd unloaded his tobacco juice, leaving all four men slack-jawed with nothing to say. Even the wind had stopped to listen, took a breath, was shocked at the words, too, which lingered in the air before echoing across the hills.

Another gust of wind pushed up the hill, causing Trusty to look away from the graves. His line of vision fell on the rising hill across the way, no more than thirty yards. A man was standing atop it. The man, like Amelia, was dressed in all black, but not in riding pants or well-worn boots. His footwear could not be seen, covered up by a long, flowing cassock. A wide-brimmed padre's hat sat on his head, and in the distance, the man, a papist priest, looked vaguely familiar, though Trusty was sure he'd never seen him before. With the wind as riled as it was, and the man's position on the open hill, he looked like a dark angel descended from the heavens; his arrival quiet and concerning to Trusty, who had let his eye off the ridge to consider Amelia Darby's harsh words. If the priest was a sniper, he would have had a clear shot at any one of them standing around the graves, including the judge.

Trusty thought it was odd that a priest would choose

such a distant spot to attend a funeral. "Are any of you papists?"

The question got Amelia's attention. She had not been aware of the priest's presence any more than Trusty had been. Her demeanor changed instantly. She became more tense, more brittle, if that was possible. Her face looked like it was made of glass, about to shatter into a million pieces. "My mother was a papist, but her associations with that religion were not passed to those of us who lived under my father's roof." Her eyes narrowed, and the two, Amelia and the priest, made eye contact across the expanse of the hill and the cemetery. They were the only two humans in the world at that moment; their gaze a battle of will, of good and evil, or evil and evil, for all Trusty knew. He didn't like what he was seeing, was more fidgety than he already was to get on the trail.

Once he had been noticed, the priest turned slowly and walked away, the cassock fluttering behind him like the broken hem in an unrestrained dress, dragging along the ground like a broken wing.


Judge Hadesworth fancied himself a whistler. It wasn't like the judge took to bird whistles or impromptu strings of notes. He whistled full songs, one after the other, "Camptown Races," followed by the well-worn Foster tune, "Oh! Susanna." Trusty in particular hated "Camptown Races," but he held his tongue and didn't offer the judge any criticism. He knew better. The judge had thin skin when it came to any commentary on his abilities— of any kind.

The three of them were riding in single file—the judge in the lead, Amelia Darby in the center, with Trusty bringing up the rear—through a shallow glide of head-high boulder and rock formations as Lost Mountain welcomed them on its rocky bib. With Amelia riding at a decent pace in the center, protected as a woman should be, Trusty was cut off from the judge, and he didn't like that, not even for the short time it would take for them to come outside of the narrow, unnamed pass. This, along with the fact that he didn't know Amelia's true intentions, was one of the reasons that Trusty had been opposed to Amelia's position on the ride. But the judge had insisted, just like he had insisted on placing the girl between them. Gordon Hadesworth was too used to getting his own way.

The sky overhead remained clear, blue as an expensive jewel, void of any predatory birds and their shadows. There had not been any other travelers on the trail since they had left the cemetery—or any sign of the priest. It was almost like the image had been a figment of Trusty's imagination, even though he knew better. And he was relieved to bid the preacher and the Teamster farewell and send them back to the stinking waters of Kosoma where they belonged. He hoped he never saw either man again.

"You spoke of your mother, Miss Darby," Trusty said to Amelia as they squeezed through the rocks, "but what of your father? Didn't he enforce any discipline to your brothers? Or was he just their maker, a mirror from which they grew, lived, and died?"

Amelia didn't turn to address Trusty, just kept her head faced forward, staring directly into the judge's back. "Haven't you had enough of my family woes today, Deputy? I would think you would have other things on your mind. Not the conflicts that might or might not have existed under the roof where I was raised."

"You sure don't make friends easy, do you?"

"Why on God's green earth would you think I would want to be your friend?" she said, turning around to glare at Trusty, all the while holding the reins to her horse steady.

Her hateful look almost knocked Trusty off of his horse, though he should have been accustomed to Amelia Darby's acid tongue. He wasn't though. It was difficult to recall a woman so enraged by her position. "I beg your pardon, ma'am. I was just passin' the time, tryin' to have a conversation with you is all. I don't mean no offense."

Amelia looked as if she considered his words poisonous, let her high cheekbones fall an inch, then cranked them back up. With that, she pointed her nose to the air, let out a "humph," and faced forward again, boring holes into the back of Judge Hadesworth's neck.

*I suppose that'll teach me*, Trusty thought to himself, allowing Horse to step off the pace and fall back a couple of lengths, just in case Amelia Darby had something untoward in mind. Lucky for all of them they were deep into the pass, otherwise he might have passed her up, taken ahold of Judge Hadesworth's reins, and left the spiteful woman in the dust—regardless of the judge's orders or objections.

It didn't take long to pad out of the pass, as a rocky expanse opened before the trio. Trusty remained eagle-eyed, perusing the shadows above and below with a slow, methodical gaze, seeing nothing that alarmed him. That didn't cause him to relax. That wasn't possible. Not with the company he had been forced to keep. A wiser man would have learned to ignore Amelia Darby, but Trusty didn't count himself among the sages. He left that to the judge. All he could do now was ride in silence, keep an eye out for trouble, find a decent spot to pitch camp, and get Judge Hadesworth back to Muskogee as quickly as possible.

It was almost like the judge could read Trusty's mind and sense the tension in the air. Hadesworth gave up whistling and began singing "Camptown Races" in a deep, cheerful voice—loud enough to scatter bobcats and birds and draw anyone with a threat on their mind closer.

"Camptown ladies sing dis song, doo-dah! doo-dah! Camptown racetrack five miles long, oh, doo-dah day! I come down dah wid my hat caved in, doo-dah! doo-dah! I go back home wid a pocket full of tin, oh, doo-dah day!"

The words and tune didn't improve Amelia Darby's attitude at all.

### *St. Louis, Missouri, winter 1865*

Even though he was just a seven-year-old boy, Sam knew the rattle in his mother's chest was getting worse. She refused to eat most days no matter how much he begged her to take a taste of food. He didn't want to have to lie to his father and he didn't want to lose his mother. He knew she had to eat to live. She was shrinking before his very eyes, finding her way quickly to the front stoop of death's door. Her voice was a whisper, more like the crackle of a dying fire, and she slept for long periods of the day. It was a reason to celebrate when Sam found his mother awake, looking refreshed, her face full of life and her eyes blue as a perfect summer day.

"Would you like some breakfast, Ma?" he said with a smile.

"Yes, that would be wonderful. I'm awfully hungry. I dreamed I was in a great desert left on my own. I prayed for an oasis, and here you are."

"I was here all along, Ma." Sam stood stiff in the middle of the bedroom. It smelled of sickness and dust. The windows were nailed shut and the thick draperies hadn't been opened in months. "Do you want some water before I get your breakfast?"

Mamie Dawson shook her head, turned it so she was facing Sam, and smiled broadly, as if it were the first time he had ever shown her such care. "That would be nice."

Sam hurried to the chest of drawers that sat opposite the iron-framed bed his father had built, and poured a glass of water from the pitcher that always sat there.

His mother tapped the side of the bed, inviting him to sit next to her. Sam hesitated. Any movement of the mattress usually caused her discomfort and unimaginable pain; he always treated her like she was made of fragile porcelain. "Are you sure?"

"Yes, of course." There was a brightness to Mamie that seemed unreal, conjured from a distant memory when Sam was much younger, and she was much stronger. Something felt off, but it was hard to figure out what.

Sam slid gently onto the feather bed and handed his mother the glass of water, holding the bottom of it as she tipped it to her mouth. She guzzled the water with enthusiasm. Drinking almost all of it in one gulp—like the dream about the desert. When he pulled the glass away from her mouth, he touched her forehead to make sure it was as cool as it looked. It was. Which was just as perplexing. His mother was usually feverish. In and out of consciousness.

"I want you to promise me something," Mamie said, wide-eyed with a peaceful look on her face, but with a solid demand in her brittle voice.

"What?" Sam said.

"You'll do what your father wants you to do. I know you think he is hard on you, and he is, but that is only because he loves you . . . wants the best for you. Be a nice boy and don't fight with him about the silly daily things."

"I hate the shop," Sam said, looking away from his mother. "I want to be outside with the other boys. They don't have to work as hard as I do."

"It won't always be like this . . . you'll see. You're a strong, smart boy. Promise me you'll be as good for your father as you are for me."

Sam looked at her, piercing the silence left by her plea. "I don't want you to go away."

"It's a journey, Samuel. I'm too weak for this world. But you'll always know I loved you. If you can't promise me anything else, promise me that you won't forget that no matter what."

"I promise."

"Good."

Sam leaned in and kissed his mother on the forehead, and heard the distant, familiar rattle in her chest. It sounded like the crackle of a dying forge. "I'll fry you up some bacon. How's that?"

"No, I've changed my mind, Samuel. I want you to go get the preacher for me. I need to talk to him."

"What about, Ma?"

"Don't you worry about it. Now, go on, do what I ask of you."

"But what about your breakfast?"

"I'll be fine until you get back."

"Are you sure?"

"Yes, of course I'm sure. Now go on."

Sam hesitated; knew he was supposed to feed his ma, then go into the shop to help his pa. But she asked. So he did what she wanted. He ran down the road to the Methodist church that he had been baptized in but rarely had seen the inside of since. It was hard for his ma to make the trip on Sundays. The preacher usually came by once a week on his own accord. It was one time when Sam was glad to stand in front of a pit of fire instead of having to listen to what was going to happen to him if he didn't walk the straight-and-narrow. His pa had no time for the preacher either; a commonality between the two of them that went unspoken. Hellfire and brimstone made their fortunes every day, no matter how meager. The preacher man had no idea how to survive the heat of a St. Louis summer day in a blacksmith shop—every day was an eternity stoked of fire and washed in ash. Sam knew more about hell than he wanted to.

The preacher, named James Brownly, a tall, middle-aged man with three daughters, seemed to understand what Sam's mother wanted right away and matched the boy's run home. But they were too late. She had taken her last breath alone. No fancy religious words or invisible god could save her or bring her back to life. His mother was dead, and Sam was sure his father would blame him for the loss. No matter the cause, her death would be his fault. But even if that didn't happen, something worse would: Sam would be left alone to fend for himself with his father. At least he didn't promise his mother that he would spend the rest of his life doing exactly what his father wanted him to.

# Chapter 5

*Paris, Texas, May 1888*

The room that any woman had given birth in might as well have been No Man's Land for Vance Calhoun. Not only was the room off-limits, but the entrance to such a sanctuary was undesirable even for Calhoun, who was not a man of normal reservations. Blood, feminine rules, and hidden mysteries held little sway over his thinking and actions. He hesitated a breath before he pushed inside the bedroom with the angry palms of both hands.

There was no knock, no light tap to gain permission for access, just a determined, dreadful walk with Sally Hoyle close on his heels. "Brother, you mustn't upset her," she was saying, trailing after Calhoun, grabbing at his thick, sweaty arm, unconcerned about being swatted away.

Jealousy and rage pulsed through every vein of Calhoun's body. A man's name, *Samuel*, bounced around in his mind like a bullet doing damage to every fiber of flesh and matter in his brain. His fists ached to hurt something. His ears begged to hear bones breaking. Instead, the door slammed hard against the wall; a loud bang shattering the silence of the interior room. The explosion of sound brought a sudden cry from the baby, accosting Calhoun's anger without raising any concern at all. He didn't know any man named Samuel that he could think of, not one that had come between him and Jessica and had relations with his wife. But then he hadn't known his wife all that long. Samuel could have been anybody from her past.

He stopped, standing tall, all puffed up, full of himself, his face red from whiskey and rage, his eyes blacker than normal. The putrid smell of birth, soiled sheets, and something vile that he recalled from the worst aftermath of wounds he had ever encountered in the war caused him to shield his nose. His stomach lurched unbidden. He wasn't prepared for what he saw, what he smelled, what he felt.

Maria, her white hair pulled back in a bun, short, squat, sat in a rocking chair next to the bed holding the screaming baby. Calhoun couldn't get a look at the face of the new baby girl to be able to judge the state of her health for himself. The little body was wrapped in a fresh blanket that made her look like a moth's cocoon instead of a swaddled child. The cloth wiggled and protested, and Maria did her best to shush the child. The effort was lost; the child didn't know how to respond to requests and demands. The Mexican woman's dark brown eyes were focused on Calhoun as he towered inside the door, fear painted on them by the sight and sound of him. A tremble rippled across Maria's weathered brown face.

Calhoun looked away from the child and Mexican woman to the blood-soaked bed. A motionless lump, the body of his young wife, lay pulled up in the fetal position, knees to her chest, blanket to her neck, eyes closed, hair twisted in a ratted nest. There was not enough breath in her lungs to move the cover. She was unrecognizable. Any beauty that had lit the room she had walked into the first time Calhoun had laid eyes on her was gone, expelled, drained away with the blood on the floor and the cocoon in Maria's arms.

Sally pushed up beside Calhoun and reached for his arm again to offer an anchor, a familiar touch of support. "I warned you about her, but you wouldn't listen. I thought she was hiding something from the start. If something's too good to be true, it usually is."

"Is she dead?"

"No, but I don't think it will be long before her battle to live is lost."

Calhoun looked over his shoulder to the open door that allowed fresh spring sunlight to penetrate into the house. "Where's Miguel and the doctor? They need to save her."

No one answered. A tall grandfather clock in the main room of the house ticked loudly, echoing into the vaulted ceiling, mocking him in his twisted, fearful, angry mind. The baby still wailed. The jealousy that had gripped his fingers and curled them into a fist had subsided the moment he had opened the door to see Jessica, or what was left of her, laying in their marriage bed.

The baby cried a different cry after gathering her breath, begging for food, reacting to the world she had found herself in, bright, mixed with strangers and foul smells. Every child longs for their mother's touch. This one seemed to understand that was not possible, that the opportunity was slipping away with every tick of the clock. Maria hugged the child, pulled her close to her withered breast, but there was no milk to offer the baby. That had dried up a long time ago.

"They should be here any moment," Sally said. She wore no worry on her face, only concern for her brother. There was no acknowledgment of the baby or her screams. Sally Hoyle stood straight as a broomstick, her jaw hardened in place, while her heart operated in slow, protracted, uncaring beats. It might as well have been any normal day.

"She'll be all right, then?" Calhoun said.

"You should prepare yourself for the worst, brother. I have seen this before, a woman struggling for her own life after bringing a child into the world. She was small in the hips to begin with, and the baby is large, though I fear that's not the whole of it. There's more going on that we cannot see. There is a smell of poison in her blood, and the afterbirth has yet to discharge."

Calhoun looked to Maria and the bundle. "But it's all right?"

"She, brother," Sally said. "The child is a girl not an it."

"What am I supposed to do with a girl? A boy I could have handled, bided my time until he could have walked and talked. You and Maria could have got the boy on his feet, and then I would have taught him what I know. I have always wanted a son."

"You don't get everything you want, Vance."

"I don't want this. A girl without a mother. This is not how this was supposed to go."

"Childbirth is difficult on some women." Sally maintained her grip on Calhoun's arm, steadying him as he returned his gaze to Jessica. "I knew my own body well enough to know that I might not survive the ordeal. It is why I lack a man in my life and live here with you."

"Spare me your sadness. I have heard your dreary stories more times than I can count. You are like our mother was, always looking for an audience."

"I am only saying what is the truth. You knew little of this girl, Jessica, before you took up with her. One minute you were a satisfied man, living your life as a rancher, and then another minute you were a schoolboy melting under the dress of this woman. Her family had influence, something you have always craved. I'm not the only one with desires beyond myself. I understand that part of you better than you think I do. But I have never seen you give away your will and everything else so quickly. Especially to a woman who most definitely had her own shadows and past to contend with. You barely knew her before you brought her here and commanded that I respect her as the lady of the house, give over what I had worked years for to a mere stranger. I was dirt swept under the rug, and now you want me to clean up this mess, and save her from death? I don't have that kind of wisdom or will of my own. She is your problem, brother. I can't fix this for you. Not this time."

Calhoun didn't hesitate. He reared back and slapped his sister across the face. The crack was as loud and damaging as the door slam had been, provoking another rise of screams from the baby. Maria hugged the girl even tighter, recoiled into the chair as far as she could without falling over. She whispered into the blanket. Unknown Spanish words of comfort. Calhoun had never learned the language. He didn't care to know what the Mexican said.

"She is my wife, sister," Calhoun bellowed. "And you will speak of her with respect while she's in this world and afterward, as far as that goes. Jessica is not some two-bit whore I brought home from the street. She is my wife. My one and only. Do you understand?"

The blow knocked Sally's grip on her brother's arm loose, separating her from him. The wall had stopped her from crumbling down to the floor. She touched the red sting on her cheek and her eyes flared with rage, anger, and tears that matched her brother's fury, allowing their Scottish similarities to shine in the glow of three hurricane lamps that lit the room.

"There is more, you idiot," Sally said. "You were so desperate to become what you think you are, a railroad baron and a greedy rancher, joining with that family in business and blood, that you failed to see what was right in front of you. If that child is truly a Calhoun I'll gladly give you my last dollar. You were tricked into that marriage bed, set up like the fool you are so that woman could bring a bastard child into the world and give it a name, a place, a father, instead of bringing shame on the high and mighty family you think you're connected to. You were tricked. Most likely by all of them, not just her."

"What are you talking about?" Calhoun arched his head backward like he had been hit himself, kicked in the nuts by an invisible horse. The air went out of his lungs as he considered his sister's harsh words.

Sally rubbed her cheek one last time, let a slight smile trickle across her face, then stood away from the wall, fully on her two feet, her shoulders squared, facing her brother without any fear in her eyes. "If you ever strike me again, I swear, I will walk out that door and I will never come back. You will be dead to me. I am not here for your money or whatever status you think you can achieve. I am here because you are the only family I have. But even I have my limits, brother. Don't test me. Not now. When you need me the most."

Calhoun was numb, didn't know what Sally was talking about, what was going on. The smell was over-whelming. The baby continued to cry. Jessica remained motionless, on the precipice, about to fall into the dark-ness of death, leaving this world and him, forever. He had never considered the possibility of loss—or that he had been tricked. He had been thrilled to find himself as an expectant father so late in life. He was hardly a young man, but far from old. He had given up on love a long time ago.

Sally smirked and turned her attention to the lump lying on the bed. "I have been in attendance at enough Calhoun births to know one of our own when I see it. Thick black hair, blue eyes, small at the start, then grows bigger as the days go by. This one has brown eyes, blond hair, and is bigger than any Calhoun baby I have ever seen," she said with an air of satisfaction and spite. "If I was you, I'd find out who this 'Samuel' is that your wife was crying out for in her time of need and delirium. My guess is that man has a story to tell you. One that involves a recent, broken relationship with the previous, and available, Jessica Marberry Tennyton of the fine Marberrys of Saint Louis."

"You're saying I am not the father of this child?"

"I can't prove it. I'm just telling you what I see. And I don't see one ounce of Calhoun in that child. We know our own, brother, and that baby is a stranger to me."

"Why should I believe you?"

"What do I have to gain by making up a story such as this?"

"You said yourself that you resented Jessica's position in the house."

"I would never punish a child of our own blood. You know me well enough to know that is true. That child is not a Calhoun. I am almost sure of it. Time will prove me right or wrong. I'm right. You'll see for yourself."

For a moment, Vance Calhoun forgot how to breathe. Not only was he faced with the death of his wife and bringing up a child on his own, he had to consider, if his sister was right, that he had been bamboozled. Once his lungs refilled, his fists returned to their default position, and he felt the need to hit something again. The math worked. They had been married less than nine months, and their whirlwind romance had started and ended a month prior. It was possible that Jessica had been pregnant before they had married. Slightly possible. But possible because Calhoun had had his eyes set on something else: the wealth of her father. Wealth that would come to him some day. He didn't grovel much about the pregnancy or count days when it arose. He saw an heir. A deeper path that led straight to the Marberry bank vault. He had dreams of being a rich man, and Jessica was his way to see his aspiration come true.

Calhoun didn't make the effort to look at the baby, to see for himself if his sister was right or not. The seed had been planted by the only person he could trust in the world. "Go through her things, Sally. See what you can find," he said, then turned and walked out of the room.

He didn't slow at the sound that escaped Jessica's throat, a wheeze and a gasp, the last attempt to hold on to life as death walked into the room and embraced her. Nor did he slow when Miguel and the doctor from town rushed in the door. Vance Calhoun stalked to the horse barn with his heart thumping inside of his chest, a plan and plot forming, two plus two that would turn out in his favor, so everything would add up, and he could still get what he had been after all along. Ownership of a railroad. That was the true road to riches. Buying and selling cattle and ranching was too much of a gamble, too much work. He wanted a wealth where everything was done for him. He wondered how much Theodore Marberry would be willing to pay for his dead daughter's baby. He jumped onto the saddle of the grullo and tore out of the barn, intent on sending a telegram to St. Louis to find out. The scream of an orphaned baby caught on the wind and followed him all of the way there.


A day later, the funeral coach stood waiting outside the door with a drab horseman sitting atop it, in the bench across the front, dressed in black from top hat to boots, staring straight ahead, waiting for the command to move forward. Two tall black draft horses stood still, swatting flies with their thick tails, breathing in the country air, snorting respectfully, preparing for the long journey ahead. They didn't know that their job was to carry sadness home. All they knew how to do was put one hoof in front of the other and pull the load that they were assigned to, that they were attached to. Work had no gauge of emotion or weariness to the horses. They had a reason to live when they were pulling; otherwise they were bored and waiting.

The coffin, simple, cut of freshly hand-hewn maple, sat unvarnished in the rear of the coach, only visible because the black curtains had yet to be pulled closed. A simple bouquet of delicate white flowers, lily of the valley, lay on the closed lid of the coffin, placed there by Jessica's father, Theodore Marberry. He stood on the front step of Vance Calhoun's ranch house, tall, withered with slumped shoulders, his head down, holding a brand-new brown leather satchel.

Vance Calhoun stood towering over the man, dressed in work clothes, his face cleared of rage and whiskey, his eyes as bright and sure as they were the day he had married Jessica Marberry Tennyton. Sally Hoyle stood at her brother's side, an apron bound across her waist, still dusted with flour from the day's bread; the emotion on her face deemed the event ordinary, just another day. Maria stood off to the right, cradling the baby girl in her arms, her own eyes streaked with red veins of sadness and worry. She rocked the baby with gentle hesitation in a clean white blanket. More Spanish whispers. More unknown words meant to soothe the baby girl who so far only knew good-byes instead of hellos.

"There you are, Calhoun, all of the shares I own in the

railroad. You still lack a majority, but something tells me that's your aim, and it won't be long before you attain your desire," Theodore Marberry said as he handed the satchel to Calhoun.

Marberry was Harvard educated, wore tailored clothes, had earned the gray hair on his head, and was known as a strict, savvy man with an eye for a deal, and a mind to make anything he took on profitable. On this day, he didn't look like any of those things. Marberry looked lost and weak, which is exactly how Vance Calhoun had hoped his former father-in-law would look.

Calhoun took the satchel without a smile or any show of emotion. It held a load of railroad stock giving him twenty-five percent ownership in the "Frisco" railroad. "This was never my intent, Marberry. I expected to live with Jessica happily ever after."

Marberry stood taller, stretched into his shoulders, and looked at Calhoun like he didn't believe a word he had said. "None of us believed that, but there was no stopping our Jessica once she set her mind on something. Well, until now anyway. I warned her that this matrimony would come to a bad end."

A flick of insult passed Calhoun's face and his lip quivered, holding back a slew of hurtful words. He restrained himself, knew he had to control his temper. There were too many riders about that he would have to consider if things got out of hand or if he had to kill Marberry. That would have to wait for another day, or another lifetime. If there was any hope in the day, then Calhoun hoped he would never see Theodore Marberry or any of the Marberrys, tall or small, ever again.

"Maria, hand over the child to Mister Marberry. I

have work to get to on the back forty. We've already lost enough time and effort on this day," Calhoun said.

The air didn't seem to be moving at all. No wind, no breeze, just an uncertain stillness that felt dry and uncomfortable. A carriage sat behind the funeral coach. More town coach than carriage, the top was up, shielding the occupants from the overhead sun—three females, Jessica's mother and two older sisters. Like the funeral coach, the women's transport was black and somber, but the team pulling it was a pair of tall Springfield mules—chestnut brown and proud as mules can be on such a sad day.

Maria nodded, nuzzled the swaddled child, offered another whisper, then did as she was told.

Theodore Marberry took the bundle, peered at the face, allowing a slight smile to cross his dour face; a deep reaction that he tried to fight away but couldn't. "She looks like her mother."

Maria backed away with her eyes to the ground, not able to watch the baby's departure.

"We left the naming to you," Calhoun said. He dug into his pants pocket and pulled out a piece of paper and offered it to Marberry. "This closes the deal. I agreed to your terms. I have no further legal right or attachment to the child."

"I expected more of a fight from you for your own flesh and blood." Theodore Marberry pulled the baby closer—who was quiet and calm—then took the paper from Calhoun and clutched it like it was gold.

"Believe what you will," Calhoun said.

Marberry cocked his head and a curtain of confusion fell over his face. To his credit, the educated man said nothing. Instead, he backed away from Calhoun, deposited the baby into its grandmother's waiting arms, stuck the paper in a pocket inside his coat, and said, "Good day, sir," to Calhoun, and climbed into the town coach and settled in for the long ride home.

Calhoun and Sally Hoyle stood and watched the two coaches depart, not moving an inch until they were out of sight.

"Go find Haden and Gladdy and tell them to come to my office. I have an errand I need them to run for me," Calhoun said.

Sally looked at her brother with a mix of dread and curiosity. "Be careful, Vance. Just because you cut the head off a snake doesn't mean it can't bite you."

# Chapter 6

*Lost Mountain, Indian Territory, May 1888*

By the time the trio reached the spot Trusty was aiming for, the rolling edge of darkness had caught up with them. Stars sparkled dimly in the west as the graying sky of the day surrendered to the black sky of night. Evening insects chirped and sawed without any nuisance or predator afoot to stop them. In the distance a flock of big birds, cranes, that Trusty had been told the French called horned screamers, lit onto the floodplain along the Kiamichi River, seeking shelter for the night. One of the four-and-a-half-foot-tall birds would have easily fed the three of them, the meat red and tasty, cooked over an open fire; it tasted more like beef than chicken. The thought almost provoked Trusty to go on a quick hunt, but that wasn't possible. He couldn't leave the judge alone with Amelia Darby. Trail food, jerky and beans, would have to do once dinnertime came along.

A breeze blew at their backs as Trusty eyed the familiar spot to make sure it was empty. They had been riding high on a bluff, facing a treeless clearing that was protected by a rise of boulders and stone that looked like they had grown out of the ground thousands of years before. A soft bed of grasses sat in the middle of the rocks, making the place perfect to camp. There was one way in, and one way out. The closest ridge was two hundred yards away, making it nearly impossible for a night shot to be accurate. The edge of the camp overlooking the river was almost straight down, rolling into a tumble of boulders, rocks, and opportunistic trees. It would be difficult for a man to climb up unheard or unseen. The two sides were stacked with pointed rock formations, rising to a curtain made of ancient granite. A fire could be hidden if it was built right, low and managed, not allowed to cast a blaze of light upward. The last thing they needed was glowing rock announcing their presence to anyone who might have a reason to care about where they were. Trusty would still have to keep watch, but the campsite was as secure as any he could find with only one man to defend. The hanging in Kosoma, along with the funeral and Amelia's presence, had left every ounce of Trusty's concern for a threat turned on high. Even the wind worried him. He wondered if their smell would carry.

"You always seem to know the best camps," Judge Hadesworth said, pulling his regal steed to a stop. Amelia followed suit, standing next to him. Both horses swished their tails as if they approved of the spot too. At least there would be something there for them to graze on.

Trusty's boots had already hit the ground. He was looking for a place to tether the horses. Then he'd worry about finding kindling to build a fire. "Lucky is all, Judge. I came upon this place a few years ago heading to Fort Gibson, and figured it would be a good place to stay safe if the need ever came up," he said as he pulled a long rope off the horn of his saddle. "Weather feels like it might kick up something undesirable though. Looks like you'll need to put your bedrolls under a lean-to. We've got a lot to do in a short amount of time."

Judge Hadesworth didn't answer. He was helping Amelia down from her skinny horse. The mount looked to be relieved from the burden of carrying a rider, even one as thin and light as Amelia Darby. Trusty was laying odds on whether the rickety mare would make it to Muskogee.

There was no acknowledgment by Amelia of her satisfaction or dissatisfaction of the stop. It was a welcome silence as everyone set about pitching camp. Trusty and the judge had traveled together enough to go about their own chores without saying much. Amelia's traveling skills were unknown. Trusty worried she would be inept, unable to find any comfort spending the night under the stars instead of under a roof. But like everything else he had assumed about Amelia Darby, it turned out that he was wrong. She seemed to know exactly what she was doing and didn't offer one outward comment or complaint about the spot, or the accommodations she had found herself subjected to. If anything, the farther away from Kosoma they traveled the lighter in mood she had seemed to become. Not quite likable, but less angry, less resentful, at least to Judge Hadesworth. The old man had charmed the Darby girl with his constant attention and soft, understanding eyes. She seemed flattered and unaccustomed to the thoughtfulness he paid her. If anyone could tame her, it was Judge Hadesworth. He could make a whipped puppy feel like it was the most loved dog in the world. Of course, the other side of him—the defender of the law, of right and wrong—could condemn a man, or three men, to death without the blink of an eye or the consideration of a tear. Ice tinkled in the judge's veins when he sat on the bench.

After helping Amelia finish building her lean-to, Trusty set about gathering kindling to build a fire. He also wanted to stake out the spot a little better, even though darkness had fallen completely. A puffy blanket of clouds had moved overhead and covered up the stars and moon, blocking out any helpful light. His eyes had adjusted so he could see well enough though. His ears were wide open, listening for anything unusual, out of place. So far, he hadn't even heard an owl hoot.

"I'll be close by if you need me," Trusty said to the judge.

"You have nothing to worry about."

"You know what to do if there's any sign of trouble."

"You're starting to remind me of my wife, Trusty. Go on, do what you need to do. I've managed to live this long; I think I can survive until you return with an armful of firewood."

Trusty just shook his head, smiled, and edged away from the camp, scouring the ground for any sign of wood to burn, of which there was little. The closest trees were down the ridge, clustered along the river in a thin line. If worse came to worse, he would have to make his way down to the water's edge, leaving the judge to truly fend for himself. Normally, straying from the judge by a hundred or two yards wouldn't have concerned Trusty too much. Judge Hadesworth carried a Henry rifle on his horse and was never without the Remington Model 95, a derringer, stuffed inside his coat. The little gun was hardly a threat to the men like Trusty had seen in Kosoma, but it was better than nothing. The judge had been urged over the years to carry a sidearm with more power, but he had refused, saying his protection came from words not bullets. There was no use arguing with the man, and Trusty knew it.

Trusty was under the assumption that Amelia Darby was unarmed, but that was a dangerous and unproven assessment. The woman hadn't been searched and he wasn't about to suggest such a thing. Still, he was bothered by the unknowns that accompanied her. The Darby Gang had favored a lot of firepower, wore their guns with honor and pride. Amelia had lived in a house where firearms were commonplace. There was no way she could have been ignorant of their use, unless she had naturally shied away from guns of any kind. For all he knew, Amelia had her own derringer hidden inside the black weeds she wore.

But they needed a fire.

The judge knew to put a shot in the air to get Trusty's attention if something was wrong. One crack of metal lightning and Trusty would have flown back to camp on invisible wings if he had to.

Every time the fire dared to rise up, Trusty tamped it down. The smell of coffee and beans drifted upward as both cooked, readying for a long overdue meal. A pouch of jerky had already been passed between the trio, and no one complained about the lack of flavor or toughness of the dried beef. There had been an acceptance of their accommodations, which made Trusty a little more comfortable. The weather had also cooperated. The earlier threat that had appeared overhead had passed on, blown away by the wind that had died on the tail of the turbulent clouds. Only a few dark gray puffs lingered behind, not in any hurry to catch up with what had abandoned them. A thumbnail moon hung crooked in the sky, and a dotting of silver stars pulsed beyond it.

"This reminds me of the time we were in Childer's Station, Trusty," the judge said, rising to pour a mug of coffee. He did so and offered it to Amelia. She declined. "Remember the contrariness of the weather then, clear one minute, then dumping a downpour the next?" He sat back down on a rock tall enough for him to stretch his legs toward the fire and warm the soles of his boots.

Amelia sat next to the judge, with Trusty on the other side of her. Judge Hadesworth always insisted that Amelia was in the middle of the two men, always protected, always looked after. That in itself had probably encouraged the change in the Darby girl's attitude.

"I do remember," Trusty said, helping himself to the coffee. "The Arkansas River was swollen out of its banks, and I wasn't sure if I was going to get you to court on time." He sat back down and tried to relax. "I heard they were changing the name of that town to Sallisaw."

"But there's a town fifteen miles north of there called Sallisaw," the judge said.

Trusty shrugged his shoulders. "I heard tell Willie

Wheeler has something to do with it. Got a new coffin shop there and all."

"Funny how things work out. Well, Childer's Station or Sallisaw, no matter what it's called. You always find a way to get me where I belong."

Amelia stared at the fire, oblivious to the conversation she was in between, and not part of.

"Got lucky is all," Trusty said.

Judge Hadesworth smiled. "Maybe everybody should call you Lucky instead of Trusty."

"Sam suits me just fine."

"You don't like your nickname?" Amelia said.

Trusty looked away from her and the judge, out past the fire, and into the empty grayness. Something had caught the attention of his ear, though he couldn't be sure what it was. Not a twig snap, or a slide on a rock. It was like flesh or fur rubbing its way down the mountain. Maybe a squirrel making its way home late. "If I'm being honest, ma'am, the answer would be no. But that's how folks know me. Strangers and friends alike. I can go into a town I've never been in before and the first person I meet calls me Trusty. I'm stuck with it, I suppose, for good or bad. There are things in this life that a person has no control over, so there's no use fightin' it."

"Like the family you were born into," Amelia said. "I'd trade my name for yours any given day."

"Trusty's name stuck because it's well-deserved." Judge Hadesworth smiled, then added a satisfied nod.

The sound again. Fur against rock. Movement. Something odd. Out of place over the crackle of the fire. Trusty set his coffee down and stood up. Both the judge and

Amelia watched him with uncertainty. The beans boiled in their pot.

"How is that?" Amelia said.

Before the judge could answer, Trusty put his index finger to his lip, signaling the two of them to be quiet.

Trusty dropped his right hand down to the ivory grip of his Colt and tugged the gun up a little bit out of the holster; far enough for him to be able to slip his finger onto the trigger. Then he backed away from the fire, eyeing the spot where he thought he'd heard the noise.

Judge Hadesworth let the uncertainty fall from his face and leaned over to Amelia. "This is why everyone calls him Trusty," he whispered.

Trusty ignored the comment but packed it deep in his pocket of accolades he'd been given by the judge. He kept backing away from the fire until he was five feet directly behind Judge Hadesworth.

Sure that he was cloaked in the shadows of the coliseum-style rock formations, Trusty stood opposite the fire, with his vision focused on a slight climb of rocks that looked much like the cairns he'd seen piled up on Poor Man's Hill in Kosoma. There was nothing there at first glance. No movement. Nothing to alarm him but the sound. Until he heard a click behind him—he was halfway in a spin to face whatever it was when the first gunshot rang out.

An orange flash, one that Trusty had seen more times than he cared to admit, came from the side of a rise in the rocks twenty yards away. A rifle crack, instead of short barrel, six-shooter explosions that were louder, more identifiable. Followed by the smack of lead against flesh, then a gasp and a surprised squeal, like a pig hit behind the head with a heavy, killing club.

The sound had come from Trusty's mouth as the bullet scraped alongside his arm, cutting through the cloth of his shirt and burning the top layer of flesh off as the bullet sped by.

Amelia screamed.

Trusty ignored the wound and returned fire. One shot followed by another. He stopped at three, then sucked in a slow breath full of gun smoke to calm himself. Something inside of him fell in place. That thing that had saved his life and those he had protected over and over again. He didn't panic. He never panicked. Not even when he was being attacked. The bullet graze didn't raise his heartbeat or push his adrenaline to its heights. A gunfight in the dark was a Sunday walk in the park as far as Trusty's body was concerned. His mind was another thing. It was scanning and calculating, doing its best to sum up the odds he was facing, trying to figure out the best way to save everyone's life. Somehow, someone had snuck up into his impenetrable spot while he wasn't looking.

"Get down and shut up," Trusty said. He might as well have asked someone to pass the salt at a proper dinner table. There was no need for an exclamation.

Judge Hadesworth understood completely what was going on. He pulled Amelia back from the fire, and they both scurried behind a stand of waist-high rocks. He pulled his derringer from inside his coat, while covering the girl's mouth with his other hand.

Another lightning crack shattered the night silence. A distant shot, a pulse of orange, but not from the same spot. Ten yards to the right. There were two of them. Trusty had assumed there were, that they were the hired men from Kosoma, the boxer and the bulldog. He wasn't sure of that, or that they were alone. There could be ten men for all he knew. He expected more shots from behind him, over the ledge that looked down onto the river, even though that would have been almost impossible.

Trusty dove farther into the shadows as the shot thumped into the ground next to his boot. He was close to the tethered horses; all three had started to stir at the sound of the gunshots. Horse was situated in the middle of the other two mounts, allowing Trusty to slide in and grab his Winchester out of the scabbard.

Another shot erupted into the air. Trusty wasn't the target this time. He didn't see where the shot had come from, didn't see any burst of light to accompany the sound. The two shooters hadn't fired. Amelia had popped up over the boulder that was covering her and the judge and fired off a shot from a six-shooter, an older Buntline Special with an eight-inch barrel that looked almost as big as Amelia herself. Trusty had no idea where the girl had been hiding the firearm, but its existence didn't surprise him in the least. He was glad to have some help from something a little more powerful than the judge's puny derringer.

The recoil of the shot was too much for Amelia, and she fell over backward, firing another shot off, straight into the air, as she crashed to the ground.

Judge Hadesworth reacted without thinking.

He stood straight up, turning to Amelia's aid.

It was obvious that he hadn't considered himself a target, in real danger, even though he should have.

# Chapter 7

*Paris, Texas, May 1888*

Vance Calhoun met Haden and Gladdy halfway to the horse barn. He was wearing his riding boots and was loaded down with a full complement of gun belts and pistols. His eyes were clear and focused, battle ready, and his stride was stocked with purpose. "I changed my mind, Haden. I'm going with you," he said.

Haden was about to slide his boot into the stirrup and pull himself up into the saddle. He stopped mid-pull on the horn and settled his foot back to the ground. "I thought you wanted this to be a two-man job. In and out, quick and easy."

Gladdy was already settled on his ride, a black mare with uninterested eyes and long runner's legs. The younger O'Connor was weighted down with enough ammunition to fight a small battle: two guns, two gun belts, and a taste for killing plastered across his face. Gladdy never backed down at the chance to take a life. He was good at it.

"I started to think about my plan, staying here and letting you two ride alone," Calhoun said to Haden. "Marberry is a smart man. Maybe smarter than I give him credit for. He might have protection riding with him, two or more men that hung back so we wouldn't see them when he came to pick up Jessica's body and the baby. I'm kickin' myself for not spying on them coming up the road, but I'm not myself right now. This whole thing with Jessica dyin' has knocked me out of my socks. I think you'll need an extra gun or two just in case I'm right about the feelin' in my gut about the old man. Miguel is joinin' us too."

Haden pulled himself into the saddle of his horse, a chestnut filly with a white diamond on her nose. The horse objected mildly to Haden's presence with a snort and slap of its lengthy tail. It was clear to Calhoun that Haden objected to his plan as much as the horse objected to be ridden, but that didn't matter to him. Both of them were beasts of burden.

"That Mexican can't hit the broadside of a barn with a scattergun, even less with a pistol when he's under duress," Haden said. His blue Irish eyes narrowed and looked beyond Calhoun for a sign of the Mexican. He hadn't arrived yet.

"Miguel's all we got. The rest of the men are out with the cattle," Calhoun said. "You know how spring is. Busy time. If there wasn't so much at stake, you two'd be out there chasin' down calves that got separated from their mommas too."

"You sayin' that funeral man ain't alone, boss?" Gladdy said, wiping his forehead with the back of his hand. It was hard for Calhoun to tell if the boy was hungry for more men to go after. Tryin' to read Gladdy was something he'd given up on a long time ago.

"I'm not going to bet against it. Marberry's a sly character. I'd have more guns on me than two coach drivers, especially with nothing but womenfolk inside, if I was him." Calhoun moved toward the stable where the grullo was waiting in its stall. The noise outside the barn had gotten the horse's attention. It looked more curious about food than anticipating a ride. "We need to get movin'. Those coaches won't travel fast at night, if they're travelin' at all. They got a long ride back to Missouri. We can cut across the north draw to intercept them as dark comes on if they ain't set up camp somewheres or taken rooms to let for the night in Paris."

"You think they're gonna travel all through the night?" Gladdy asked.

"What did I just say?" Calhoun said. "If Marberry feels like there's a threat, if he's got a good reason to get back home, then they might chance stayin' on the road with their wheels rollin'." He opened the stall door and took hold of the grullo's reins. "He'd be right to think like that. But you two need to remember what I done told you before we light out."

Haden nodded as he urged his horse out of the barn. "No harm comes to that baby. No matter what."

"That's right. No matter what Sally says that child was born under my roof and in my bed. She's mine to keep no matter what my sister says."

"That Marberry fella ain't gonna like that part of the deal, boss," Gladdy said.

"It won't matter if he's dead, now will it?"

"I suppose not." Gladdy smiled with his mouthful of ugly, brown rotted teeth, nickered his horse, and followed Haden out of the barn.

Calhoun prepared his own mount as quickly as he could, wishing like hell he had four or five more men to take with him that he could count on instead of having to rely on Gladdy. But as it was, he was stuck with the three men, Haden, Gladdy, and Miguel, to retrieve the baby girl and bring her home where she belonged.

The ride to the north draw didn't take long. There was a well-worn trail that Calhoun used to get to and from town in short order that he could've ridden drunk or blindfolded. He led with Haden at his side, while Gladdy and Miguel brought up the rear. Miguel wasn't happy to be included on the ride after already having gone into Paris earlier to fetch the doctor. He was short, squat, armed with two six-shooters and a scattergun in the scabbard. He wore thin wire-framed glasses, but they didn't do him much good, as was noted by Haden. Calhoun was sure Miguel would do whatever he had to to save his own life and pull off the job that needed doing. The old Mexican had never been much of a gunfighter. He'd always avoided violence whenever he could, preferring to use a hoe over a gun. Calhoun didn't care about Miguel's preferences. He needed an extra gun, and Miguel was the only man available to fill the spot. Either that or face the consequences of saying no. The Mexican knew better than to dig his own grave and refuse Calhoun's order to ride along.

Calhoun stopped on a rise that overlooked the empty road. Night had fallen, completely covering the fields and forest that lined the road. The moon, sliced like the curve of a thumbnail, hung crooked overhead in the center of a black quilt held together with silver pulsing star stitches. There was enough night light to see a good way in all directions; it was better than a full moon, which would have made hiding a lot more difficult. From the looks of it, they were all alone on the road. Crickets sawed their legs. A whip-poor-will hollered across the nearest field, repeating its song, which sounded just like its name, over and over again. Calhoun knew the night bird wouldn't be so vocal if Marberry's men were close by.

"Maybe they done went by," Gladdy said.

"They would have had to have been runnin' full out," Calhoun said. He wasn't quiet about his response. The whip-poor-will stopped in the middle of its song. "We need to separate. Haden, you and Gladdy take up a post up the road and me and Miguel will stay here. Hide your horses, but keep them close, be ready to run. Don't head back to the house. Go into the Territory for a few days. Hide out in our hunting shack across the river. We'll catch them in a crossfire, take out the drivers first. But wait for my shot first. Don't go gettin' an itchy trigger finger, Gladdy, you hear me?"

"Sure, boss. I ain't never in no hurry to get in a shoot-out in the dark of night," Gladdy answered. "But how do we know we ain't gonna shoot that baby?"

"Don't aim for the inside of the carriage, stupid." Calhoun shook his head in disgust and sighed heavily. "Go on, get to your places before they come along and we're not ready. I don't want to lose the opportunity to take what's mine."

"If you say so, boss," Gladdy said.

"You gettin' smart with me, boy?"

Haden and Miguel held back, didn't say anything. Miguel dismounted and towed his horse toward a thin stand of cottonwoods across the road. Haden slowly edged down the rise to the road, leaving Gladdy to face Calhoun on his own.

"No, boss," Gladdy said. "I ain't gettin' smart with you. I was mistook is all."

"Get the hell out of here. If it wasn't for your brother, I would have killed you a long time ago."

It was Gladdy's turn to shake his head. He wandered off, following after Haden, mumbling under his breath. "I know what the hell I said. One of these days, I'm gonna just up and leave. You wait and see. Don't matter if Haden goes or not. I hate it here. Him, too, and the horse he rode in on." He didn't think he was talking loud enough for Calhoun to hear him, but he was wrong. Vance Calhoun heard every word that Gladdy O'Connor had said and more.

The first two riders showed themselves ten minutes later. Calhoun was on the west side of the road, with Miguel opposite him on the east. Miguel's position worried Calhoun, and he didn't disagree with Haden's judgment, that the old Mexican was a bad shot. How could he not be? Miguel's yellowed eyes were as cloudy as a rainy day, and his hands shook when there was nothing to be afraid of. But Calhoun knew the Mexican would try his best, shoot in the right direction, do what he was told. Which was more than he could expect from Gladdy O'Connor.

There had been plenty of time for Calhoun to reconsider his plan, to turn back, and let Marberry take the baby girl to St. Louis. Life might have been easier and the risk lower to let it be, to be done with it once and for all. It didn't matter to Calhoun that Sally had found a small satchel of love letters to Jessica from another man—*that man*—the Samuel she had called out for in her hour of need and pain. Samuel Dawson. Calhoun knew of Trusty Dawson, had heard of him. A fine shot, reliable, a good deputy, but a prowler when it came to women, which surprised Calhoun that Jessica Marberry Tennyton would be drawn to such a man. The letters bore dates before the wedding, before Calhoun had met Jessica. He hadn't read them all. He didn't need to. From what Calhoun could tell, Jessica loved this man, but her father didn't approve. No surprise there. Theodore Marberry was a shrewd man, only agreeing to the wedding between Calhoun and Jessica if a dowry was paid, which Calhoun had done, signing over five hundred head of cattle to Marberry. Calhoun wanted that money back and had made it clear to Marberry in his wire announcing that Jessica was dead—which is what had led to the railroad stock deal. A surviving granddaughter and a body to bury had to be worth something more than the dowry.

What mattered now, though, was the baby. As far as Calhoun was concerned, she was still his. Or at least, she had been born to him. Whether she was of his blood was another question. A question that he didn't know the answer to but was determined to find out. There was no way to do that if Marberry held possession of the child. Sally had objected to Calhoun's plan. She had told him that he was playing with fire, that he didn't know what he was starting with Marberry, or the man, Samuel Dawson, who claimed to have been Jessica's love. Dawson, she argued, was a Deputy U.S. Marshal. Sally had warned Calhoun that the last thing he needed was to make an enemy of a wealthy man and the law, to boot.

Calhoun wasn't afraid of either man. He was surprised to find himself in a situation that he could profit from, all without any of his own doing, other than allowing a woman into his life. If he had known it was going to be that easy to make money, he would have gone looking for an endowed woman long before now. Sally was over-protective, always looking out for her own interest, and most generally wrong in her assumptions about business. Even if she was right, Calhoun was sure he could handle whatever came his way. He had been successful so far. There was no reason for him to believe otherwise, that his quest to retrieve the baby would turn out the way he thought it would.

The two riders were pacing slow, watching the side of the road carefully. There was no way to tell if they were riding for Marberry or not, so Calhoun held back, didn't fire on them as soon as he saw them. He let them pass by him, getting a good look from his hiding spot. They wore dusters, covering their sidearms, so it was hard to tell in the dark of night what they were carrying or how heavily armed they were. But they looked like serious men. Riders that Calhoun would be glad to have at his side if he needed protection. He was a little concerned about what he was up against, all things considered.

The funeral coach appeared as the two men rode on, unaware of the crossfire they had just rode out of. The two black draft horses pulling the coach were almost invisible, as was the driver, who sat alone at the helm, lurched forward, his head down and eyes on the road. Lanterns burned at every corner of the hearse, and another hung out front, attached to the shaft that linked the pair of horses together. The coach was well lit, making it possible for Calhoun to see in front of it as well as all around. All of the shiny black lacquer paint seemed to glow, making the sight surreal . . . not unexpected but an odd sight. The curtains were closed and Jessica's coffin was hidden inside. Both draft horses kept an easy pace, not brisk or in a hurry. No one seemed worried too much about being attacked.

The other coach, carrying the baby, womenfolk, and Marberry, was close behind the hearse. It was lit up in the same way as the funeral coach, allowing a clear sight of the elaborate carriage. The curtains were drawn as well, not allowing Calhoun a look inside. All he could see was the single driver atop the coach.

To Calhoun's surprise there was no rear guard, no protection that he could see other than the two riders in the lead. He'd been half right. Or at least it appeared so at the moment; he had imagined there would be four riders. He had to think fast, change his plans a little bit.

Time ran out and someone else made the decision for Calhoun to act.

A gunshot cracked into the night from behind the family coach. Followed by another and another, garnering the attention of the two riders and both of the drivers of the coaches.

Stunned for only a second, Calhoun felt a pulse of anger rise up his neck, then pushed it back down. Whoever shot first would pay later, but his bet was on Gladdy O'Connor for whatever the damned reason.

The protectors had circled back and were riding straight for the hearse. Calhoun shot the closest one, knocking him from the horse. The other rider fired in Calhoun's direction, unloaded six shots from one pistol, then shot two more rounds from another.

The night was suddenly full of orange and red blasts as the shoot-out grew from front to back, from Calhoun to Haden and Gladdy. Gunpowder stung Calhoun's nose as he hit the ground, avoiding being shot as best he could.

The lone rider was Calhoun's main concern. He was still atop his horse, aiming a Winchester in Calhoun's direction.

One easy shot, with help from the coach lights, from Calhoun took the rider down. He tumbled backward on the horse, sending the mount into a run. The man fell the rest of the way off of the horse and was dragged along behind it into the darkness.

Calhoun had wanted to yell at Miguel, tell him to take the man out, but he knew better than to give away his position. He didn't know why the Mexican wasn't shooting, covering him. Haden had been right. The old man was worthless.

A bullet pinged the ground six inches from Calhoun's

head, sending him scurrying backward toward his horse. He didn't know where the shot had come from until another came. The curtains on the hearse were open, and two men were inside, firing at him with rifles. They were better armed and determined to kill him. Another pair of men started firing from inside the family coach. Gladdy and Haden quickly silenced their shots. They were either hurt, or regrouping—which they were going to have to do without orders from Calhoun. He had problems of his own.

Calhoun got the picture real quick, figured out that he wasn't going to be able to hold off the rider much longer. He ran back to his horse, shooting over his shoulder as he went. He grabbed his Winchester out of the scabbard once he reached his horse and started firing as he mounted the saddle. The spot gave him clear sight of what was going on out on the road. He had been tricked. There was no coffin in the hearse. Theodore Marberry, the womenfolk, and the baby were nowhere to be seen. They had traded out their rides somewhere between the ranch and this spot in the road. Calhoun was impressed and enraged. He had no idea where the baby was. But his main concern at the moment was staying alive.

There was no time to rage. All Calhoun could do was save himself and run. He urged the grullo to speed away and the horse obeyed, hightailing it back the way it had come, with Calhoun shooting when he could, doing his best to get away from the setup with his own life. Miguel, Haden, and Gladdy were on their own.

One of the men from inside the coach took a fallen rider's horse, mounted it, and gave chase to Calhoun.

He'd escaped the road unscathed, not confronted by any of Calhoun's men. They had gone completely silent.

Calhoun headed to Indian Territory as fast as he could. He wasn't sure he was going to make it.

The rider wasn't giving up. He was chasing after Calhoun, determined to finish what he had started. Fleeing for his life hadn't been part of the plan.

The old hunting shack stood waiting for Calhoun like a palace on top of a mountain made of gold. He had been afraid that he wouldn't make it, that the rider would catch him and spare him no mercy. Not that Calhoun would have given up easily, but he wasn't used to being on the run, being the hunted instead of the hunter. The rider had been called off by a distant gunshot, turned back a few miles before Calhoun had crossed the Red River into Indian Territory, giving him room to breathe. But his heart still raced fast. He didn't like being afraid for his life. Or being outsmarted by Theodore Marberry.

"Damn, it. That was one hell of a double cross by Marberry," he said to no one as he dismounted the grullo and made his way inside the shack. "There's going to be hell to pay for that. Come hell or high water, I'll get that baby back. You wait and see."

Not even a coyote answered. The night was so silent it was like it had been reserved for the dead.

There hadn't been anyone at the shack in months, but there were still a few hurricane lamps with enough oil in them to light the darkness. Calhoun needed to calm down, gather his wits, and wait on the rest of the men to come and find him. If they had survived. There was a good chance they hadn't. Losing Gladdy and Miguel wouldn't have been a big loss. But Calhoun hated the thought of something happening to Haden. The elder O'Connor brother was a good hand. Trusted more than most. Hard to replace. If that were possible at all. They went back a long way.

"Damn it." Calhoun scowled, kicking at nothing, making the light in the lamp dance with the sudden movement. Shadows swayed on the wall, and for a second he thought there was someone else inside the shack with him. Calhoun wasn't used to being afraid—or alone. He usually had a man with him. Or Sally and Jessica hovering over him trying to tell him what to do and how to think and behave. He hated that. Which was why he had ridden off before Jessica had given birth in the first place. She'd overstepped her boundaries. Pushed him harder than she should have about one thing or another. With all that had happened since, he couldn't even remember what that overstep was. The pit of his stomach felt odd, and his heart still ran fast. If he were a crying man, he might have let loose and howled right then and there. Instead, he punched the wall, cracking the wood, stinging his knuckles, bringing him back to reality.

*Calm down, you fool*, he said to himself. *Calm the hell down.* Hitting something always made him feel better, always made him lose a little bit of anger. The timber he'd hit didn't bare a scratch, but his knuckles had begun to bleed. He double punched the timber again as hard as he could. There was no flesh to give way or bone to shatter except his own. He screamed in pain as blood from his hands dripped to the floor. Then, Calhoun exhaled as deep as he could, bounced back, and found himself in the center of the small shack. He wasn't expecting anyone to knock on the door, hadn't heard anybody ride up. He about jumped out of his skin when a fist banged against the door, announcing a presence outside with thunder and surprise.

"That you in there, boss?"

Sure as shit, it was the last person Vance Calhoun wanted to see or hoped would come to his aid. It was Gladdy O'Connor outside the door.

# Chapter 8

*St. Louis, Missouri, summer 1874*

Sixteen-year-old Sam Dawson wondered sometimes if people ever slept in the city. It seemed like there was a train coming or going at all times of the day and night. Wagons pulled into the city and joined others, parading west for a new life, an adventure, a chance to start fresh, one right after the other. There was a constant, endless supply of dreamers and risk-takers flooding in from the East. Sam hung on to the words of the men who came and went from the blacksmith shop, listening to their tales, their woes, and their hopes, as their wagons were either repaired or outfitted for the journey they were embarking on. Customers were never in short supply, which was good for his father. But for Sam there was little time for anything but work and school.

Sam was especially keen to hear stories about the Indians. There was always a war to consider, to hear about. The Red River battles with the Comanche, Arapaho, Kiowa, and the Southern Cheyenne seemed to be on the tip of every man's tongue of late. The attack on

Adobe Walls had started the fight, bringing the army up against the four tribes in the upper reaches of the Texas Panhandle. Five columns of soldiers had converged on the area, encircling the Indians. The newspapers were full of fighting accounts, but the reading of them was slow. Information was better passed from man to man. Sam was looked upon as invisible in the shop, unless, of course, the accounts became too violent, then decent manners dictated that the men restrain themselves. Sam didn't mind. The bloodier the better. The stories helped him take his mind off his dead mother.

"I'm tellin' you, none of this is gonna end," the portly man said to Markum Dawson as he looked at the wobbly wagon wheel, "until that Quanah Parker is put out of our misery. My wife's kin had a run-up with his kind. Survived with their scalps they did, but only because they got lucky and a battalion of Texas Rangers wandered by at the time of the attack."

Sam was bending eyes on handles like usual, listening to the man in between pulls and strikes. His father stood from a crouch and faced the talkative man with a worried look on his face. "Much as I hate to send you to Martin Fuller, the wheelwright, I have to admit that I can't help you. The rim's cracked and needs replaced."

"Well, hell. One more expense I wasn't countin' on," the man said. "I've already lost my cow and two goats. By the time I reach Texas I ain't gonna have a silver left in my pocket."

"You wouldn't have to worry about that Quanah Parker fella," Markum Dawson said.

"He ain't no fella. He's a scoundrel redskin is what

he is. But you might be right. That's not my fight. I'm hopin' it'll all be over with soon."

"I can't imagine the West without Indians," Markum said. He glanced over to Sam, who had stopped working, was listening to every word spoken between the two men. "Get back to work," he ordered Sam.

Sam hurried away from the anvil and stuffed a few rods into the forge. He could barely hear the two men over the roar of the flame and the screaming inside his head. But he knew better than to disobey his father in front of a customer. There'd be a price to pay later. At the end of the day when his father turned to the whiskey bottle to help him sleep. If Sam breathed wrong, he'd get a backhand to the face, or worse, depending on his father's mood. Sam had learned to avoid conflict as much as he could—his only escape was dreaming at night of being a hero in an Indian fight. He'd be worthy then, and not have to worry about facing his father's rage.

### Lost Mountain, Indian Territory, May 1888

The air hung heavy with the smell of spent gunpowder and death; acrid, metallic, bloody. A thick wall of angry clouds had pushed in from the west, covering the moon and stars with the promise of a violent spring storm. A strong breeze made sure that nothing lingered, smells, clouds, or otherwise, over Lost Mountain too long. The only light that offered any help to Trusty was the dying flame of the campfire. A flickering of warm orange fell on the heels of Judge Hadesworth's motionless boots. There was no sign of Amelia Darby; she was lost in the darkness to either death or fear.

There was nothing Trusty could do to help either one of them other than catch the attackers, stop them before all three of them were dead. An exhale restarted the push to slow Trusty's ramping heartbeat. He knew he had to keep his head about him, knew that he had to rely on the skills and knowledge that had kept him alive so far. This wasn't the first time he'd been ambushed—but it might be the last time if he didn't walk away from a blindsided attack and if he allowed his emotions to run over his fighting sense. The sight of the judge shot, falling to the ground, had staggered Trusty, stopped him in a way he had never been stopped before. If he lost Judge Hadesworth, everything was over. He was finished.

Trusty swerved away from fear and hoped he held the advantage of knowing the lay of the land better than the shooters. He had an idea what they looked like, but didn't know where they were from or why they had come after him and the judge. Any speculation that they were the hired men, the Darby sympathizers from earlier in the day in Kosoma, was just that, speculation. And there wasn't time for that. Not now.

There was only one way up to the spot that the shooters had taken. Whether they knew it or not, they had pinned themselves. There could be thirty men for all Trusty knew, but he doubted it.

An arete, a sharp edge of the mountain, jutted up the opposite side of the camp with an accessible terrace through a narrow crease in the rocks. Trusty counted on the shooters holding their position, even though the gunfire had been quiet since the judge fell forward and Amelia had answered with a surprise shot from her

Buntline Special. He hoped confidence had trapped the shooters, leaving them to face him, armed with his Colt, Winchester, and Bowie knife, if it came to that.

He edged along the cool, wet rock deliberately, hugging the mountain as if he wanted to melt into it, taking advantage of the shadows, with his ears open for any sound that was out of place. A spit of rain hit him on the cheek, and thunder rumbled in the distance. But he was focused on small sounds, like the one he had heard before the first shot rang out. Fur rubbing on rock, or fabric, as he knew now—a man shimmying up the rock slow and easy. There was nothing to be heard, not even the drawing of his own breath. The breeze had ramped up to a wind. The storm was determined to arrive sooner rather than later. Nature shouted at him from the heavens, overriding the simple movement of the men below.

Trusty held the Winchester in his right hand, while the pistol and knife remained holstered. His finger hugged the trigger, ready to pull for the slightest reason. He raised the barrel as he crept slowly around a soft curve in the rock. There was no worry about anything being above him. The rock face was rugged, sharp, almost straight down. A man would have to tie himself up in ropes to be able to stand on the top and shoot down at him.

A shot fired off as soon as Trusty eased around the curve. He drew back right away, committing to memory the location of the flash from the gun. The shooter was thirty feet away from him. The Winchester could hold fourteen rounds and the pistol six. He had twenty shots at the ready to defend himself.

Trusty rounded the corner, firing the Winchester, one

round after the other, his eyes scanning the darkness for anything that moved. One more shot came his way, pinging off the rock above his head. Gravel rained down on him, but Trusty didn't do anything to avoid the harmless avalanche. He fired seven more rounds toward the shooter. Most of the bullets ricocheted off of granite, but a few hit soft tissue, bringing with it another thud. A body hitting the ground; flesh hitting rock. There was no cry for help. Just a final gasp and nothing more.

Trusty fired off two more shots to make sure he'd hit his target, then made his way forward cautiously, eyes and ears on alert for the other shooter. He reached the body right away and could see clear enough in the darkness that it was a face that he recognized: It was the boxer from Kosoma just like he had speculated. The bulldog was still out there somewhere. He had been right to go in shooting. The judge had fallen, been hit with a shot. This was no time to ask questions.

Rain began to fall, and the wind whipped through the crevices and escarpments of the mountaintop. The darkness grew deeper, was as black as Amelia's mourning cloak, making it harder to see anything move. An occasional streak of lightning, sharp and pointed, flashed overhead, allowing Trusty a moment of clear vision.

"Drop it," said a man's voice from behind Trusty. "Then put your hands up where I can see 'em."

Trusty froze, then moved slowly, doing what he was told. He eased the Winchester down to the ground, then stood back up, fingers reaching for the clouds as a steady rain began to pat the top of his Stetson. The last thing he wanted to do was die from getting shot in the back. He wanted to see his attacker. Wanted to know for sure it was the bulldog. He hadn't given up, knew one way or the other that there had to be a way out of the jam he'd gotten himself into. He breathed deep, calmed himself, and opened his mind, searching for an escape route even though he knew there wasn't one. He was trapped in the tightest reach of Lost Mountain.

"Now what?" Trusty said.

"Now you die," the man answered.

"You're not gonna shoot a man in the back, are you?"

"Don't matter, does it? The reward is the same as long as you're dead. Head, back, belly, it don't matter where I shoot you. All that matters is that I put an end to you and serve you up dead for the world to see."

*That I'm dead?* Trusty thought but didn't say. He would have bet steaks and beer that their target was Judge Hadesworth, not him. "You know there's gonna be more law on your tail after today if you're the only one to walk away from here alive, don't you? If the judge is dead, that's a federal crime. Army'll be on you like flies on shit."

"Ain't so Trusty now, are you Dawson?" There was a tremble in the man's voice that wasn't there before.

"What are you waitin' on? You never kill a man before?" Trusty said. His voice was even, his mind back on that perfect summer, keeping his blood flowing as calm as possible. He had given up being afraid to die a long time ago. There are undeniable risks a man assumes when he puts on a badge, and dying for the cause of good over bad is one of them.

Lightning fingered across the sky, allowing Trusty to see the dead man before him. The boxer, eyes wide open with a bullet hole in the center of his forehead.

He wouldn't get so lucky again, shooting in the dark. He'd have to take the bulldog out some other way.

"Drop the gun belt too," the bulldog said.

"I'm gonna move slow-like," Trusty answered as thunder boomed overhead, following up on the brief explosion of lightning. The sky looked like a broken puzzle of angry, swirling clouds, the kind that could spawn a twister. There wasn't nothing worse than a twister on the ground at night—other than being held at gunpoint with nowhere to run.

"That's a good idea."

Trusty unbuckled the belt and let the weight of it sag in his hands. "If there's a price on my head, a man's got a right to know how much his life is worth."

"A thousand dollars, all in silver."

"That's a fair amount." Trusty still held on to the belt. "I got to wonder who can pay such an amount, and why they want me dead so bad."

"Seems like you made an enemy of a rich man, don't it? Now, go on, drop the belt before I shoot you and put an end to this conversation."

"You could have pulled that trigger long before now. I'm a dead man talking is all. Wouldn't you be long on making a conversation last?"

The bulldog took a deep breath. He was afraid. Didn't want to shoot a lawman and face the wrath, but would anyway. Trusty figured he must have got the man's attention by pointing out that the army would get involved if Judge Hadesworth was dead. This wasn't a simple bounty kill. Murdering a federal judge and a Deputy U.S. Marshal would provoke a manhunt like no other. The bulldog must have known it, must have put two and two together, equated his own fate with the Darby brothers in Kosoma, toes dangling, drenched in piss, with a rope tight around their necks.

Trusty couldn't wait any longer. A thousand dollars in silver was a lot of money to provoke a man to do something he didn't really want to do. Instead of dropping the gun belt, he spun and threw it as hard as he could in the direction of the bulldog.

The man wasn't expecting the move, or for Trusty to finish the spin, rush in low, and tackle him at the waist.

Both men crashed to the ground. The rock underneath their feet was wet and slippery, easy to lose their balance on. Thunder boomed overhead again. Lightning flashed and Trusty was left with no weapons but his fists. He pummeled the man in the face with all he had before the bulldog worked up enough rage and energy to raise a knee and push it into his stomach with the force of a fence post knocking down a door. Trusty rolled to the side and the bulldog jumped to his feet, almost falling, until he gained his footing on the wet rock. His rifle had been knocked from his hands when he had been rushed.

Trusty jumped to his feet, stepped in, and threw a hard-right punch. He had the favorable reach of a tall man, but the bulldog had the low advantage of a short, scrappy man and swayed right, avoiding the hit. Then he ran up on the inside of Trusty and delivered a punch of his own, landing it squarely under his right eye. Fist against the face, the taste of blood exploded inside his mouth.

Trusty staggered backward and the bulldog followed, staying up close to him, throwing one punch to the face after another. Stunned, doing his best to keep his footing,

Trusty took more hits than he had in a long time, but he was able to gather himself, seeing the bulldog's bloody face in the flashes of lightning that continued to stretch out in the sky. With all of the might he could muster, Trusty retaliated, punched the man in the nose as hard as he could, then followed that hit with an uppercut, sending the bulldog reeling backward. A couple of teeth flew to the ground; tobacco-stained ivory pebbles chinking against granite as they disappeared into the darkness.

The short man stumbled far enough backward for Trusty to reach a rifle on the ground—the bulldog's—grab it up and aim it straight at his attacker's head. "You move another inch and I'll finish you. I'll blow your goddamned head clean off your neck."

The bulldog was on his back, propped up, wiping his mouth of blood. "You ain't half bad, Dawson."

"Spare me the niceties," Trusty said. "I want to know who sent you after me and the judge."

"The judge don't have nothin' to do with this."

"He does now. If he's hurt or dead. He took a shot, so either way you got more of a storm comin' toward you than what's over your head right now." Rain washed down Trusty's face, mixing with sweat and blood. All he could taste was salt, anger, and gunpowder. His tongue felt double its original size in his mouth.

"You're the one with the storm comin' after you, Dawson. If I don't kill you, somebody else will be comin' behind me to do the deed. That much silver will get a lot of desperate men's attention. You got to know that. You had it right a little while ago. You're a dead man talkin', even if you ride away from here. If I die, you're not done lookin' over your shoulder. You're a marked man."

*What the hell did I do?* Trusty thought but didn't say. "Who put the bounty on my head?" He wanted to ask *why*, too, but he didn't.

"A man like you, with your reputation, along with the number of men who have seen the rope on your behalf shouldn't be surprised to find himself with a price on his head. You think that badge protects you? Makes you invincible? It don't. That storm is here for you. Don't matter who set the bounty. You stirred up a twister of hate for one reason or another."

"Then take me, and not that old man," Trusty yelled, his voice rising up to meet the thunder and a downpour of rain. "Get Judge Hadesworth help if he needs it."

Lightning flashed again. Darkness surprised by hot, white light. Trusty stood rigid with his finger on the trigger, rain running off his hat like it was a rotted eave, his eyes focused on the bulldog's head—a target he didn't dare miss if he took the shot. The bulldog stared back, unafraid as he reached for the gun in his holster. He struggled to defend himself to the very end, not giving up the fight. It was his final attempt to kill Trusty Dawson.

Trusty pulled the trigger and hit his target dead on. The boxer and the bulldog were a matched pair. Two head shots and a lot of questions left in their wake. Lady Luck had left the bulldog high and dry. He should have given up when he had the chance.

Hoping that the boxer and the bulldog were the only two men on his tail, Trusty grabbed up his gun belt and rifle, then hurried back to the campsite as fast as he could. The rain blew sideways as he went, doing his best to stay upright, not to slide down the path he'd come up on. He slipped and fell a couple of times.

There was no fire, no light to help guide Trusty back to the campsite. He let his instinct and memory lead him to the judge—who, to his surprise, wasn't lying face-down dead, like Trusty had expected to find him. Judge Hadesworth was sitting under a lean-to, nursing a wound to his side. It had looked like he had been shot in the back to Trusty. "I thought you were dead," he said.

The judge smiled as he put more pressure on a blood-soaked rag. "It'll take more than a shot out of the blue to end me."

Trusty was standing in front of the lean-to, doing his best to consider the judge's condition as well as the fortitude of the shelter he was taking refuge under. "Where's the Darby girl?"

"Your guess is as good as mine."

"I saw her pull a Buntline Special out of that garb she was a wearin' and fire toward the shooters. To be honest her shot barely missed me. That's way too much gun for such a little lady."

"Toppled her over is what it did," the judge said, pulling the rag off his shoulder and looking at it. "I think the bullet's still in there. You any good at surgery, Trusty?"

"Can't say that I am. You don't think you can make it back to Kosoma?"

"What, through this storm? Do you have nighttime traveling skills that I'm not aware of? Even on a good day, I think I'd be in trouble. I think that bullet sliced through something important. I can't get the bleeding to stop. A slow death is worse than a quick one as far as I'm concerned."

"Let me take a look," Trusty said as he moved into the lean-to.

"I've got some matches in the satchel there."

Trusty nodded and found his way into the judge's satchel of papers and dug out a box of matches. He struck one, bringing a flash of consistent light to the tiny shelter. Judge Hadesworth's gaunt, pale white face stared back at him. Blood had soaked his white shirt, and his right hand looked like it had been dipped in red paint. If desperation had a smell, then the mix of blood, confinement, and fear would have filled out the recipe.

The tip of Trusty's tongue tasted coppery, and he tried to ignore the implications, but he couldn't. He knew them too well. Death had stalked him as a scout in the cavalry, and even before, at a young age. But this was no illness. This was a gunshot wound. One that Trusty only had the basic knowledge to attend to.

"You're right, that doesn't look good," Trusty said. "We need to get that shirt off you and tie off the blood flow if I can. All I've got is my carryin' knife, so it'll have to do. If I can get the bullet out, I'll cauterize the wound, then we'll head back to Kosoma and get you to the doc as quick as we can."

"In this storm? I don't mean to be redundant, but this one looks like it has some staying power behind it, has probably driven even the most stubborn predator into a cave to ride it out."

"I don't think we have any choice."

Judge Hadesworth grimaced with pain, then nodded. "I'll do whatever you say, Trusty. My life is in your hands."

Trusty started to help Judge Hadesworth take off his shirt, but he stopped as soon as he heard someone approach.

"Don't move, neither one of you."

Trusty knew the voice. It was Amelia Darby. He looked over his shoulder, the match still burning in his hand. Another flash of lightning reached across the sky with prickly veins that lit the camp like it was daylight, but only for a second. He saw Amelia standing twenty feet from him, still dressed in all black, bound up in widow's weeds that she had no right to claim, her face twisted into a hateful stare, with the Buntline Special held securely with both hands, pointed straight into the lean-to at the judge. Then she disappeared into the darkness as the lightning snapped away. Trusty let the match fall out of his hand, and it spiraled downward like a falling star. He reached for his Colt, but he was too late.

Amelia fired the Buntline and hit Judge Hadesworth in the chest, putting a quick end to any hope of saving him and any doubt about what Amelia's true intentions were.

The Darby girl followed the first shot up with another one in quick succession. This bullet hit its target, too, sending Trusty tumbling backward into a ragdoll pile of pain, blood, and surprise.

The darkness reached out and welcomed Trusty, offering him no final moment of heroics or a chance at redemption. The Colt slipped from his hand, and any reaction was lost in the fall to a spindly girl who had spit on the grave of her brothers and family name, perhaps in truth or in deception, to convince him and the judge that she was honest in her attempt to leave the Darby way of life behind. It was a lie. Death had come to visit Trusty by way of an angry young girl, wild as a wolf and mean as a stepped-on snake.

Trusty had no choice but to shake death's hand as everything around him folded into the most frightening color of black he had ever seen.

# Chapter 9

*Lost Mountain Pass, Indian Territory, May 1888*

There was no otherworldly light, no dreams of angels lifting Trusty to a greater height into heaven. There was nothing that Trusty could remember of leaving the waking world, if that had actually happened. By all accounts it didn't. He woke up with a start and a cough, opening his eyes to a funny smell in the air. The odor was something unknown, sweetness and an odd medicine smell, mixed with wood smoke and the aftermath of rain. Definitely not coffee or breakfast. He had to wonder if this was hell.

The harshness of daylight forced Trusty to squint. His body felt like every inch of it had been attacked by fire ants. His skin stung, and he ached from the inside out. He closed his eyes again and concentrated on breathing, on being awake and alive. Whether he was safe or not was the last thing Trusty was concerned about. At least he wasn't dead—which was what he expected to be.

"I knew you would live," an unfamiliar man's voice said.

Trusty summoned what strength he could find to open his eyes again. "Who are you?" Even his eyelids hurt. The sun was an unwanted enemy that persisted whether he liked it or not. The image of a man was a blur; black and white paint strokes smeared in sharpening oil. "Where am I?" He reached for his gun, but it wasn't there.

Trusty struggled to focus on the man sitting across from him. The man was dressed in black from head to toe and looked like he was glowing; the sun was behind his head. The stranger's face was distorted, not kind or angry. The face seemed familiar, like Trusty had seen it before, but he couldn't put a name to it.

His weapons had been taken from him. It was an assumption, a reason to be fearful, but he didn't overreact. If the man wanted him dead, he wouldn't be awake. He'd already be six feet under. "Who are you?" he said again.

The man didn't answer. Just stared at Trusty with a blank face and uninterested eyes.

"What do you want?" Trusty tried to sit up, alarm rising from the usual places when something was out of sorts. A sharp jolt of pain forced him back down to the ground. He was lying on a soft bedroll, but the ground was rock-hard underneath him. He was still on the mountain. Still in the camp from the looks of things. It was past morning. Tilting toward late afternoon. The sun was dropping in the west, but that didn't matter much to Trusty. He was more interested in the man sitting across from him.

"What's the last thing you remember?" The man was

on his feet now, walking toward Trusty. He offered him a mug with steam rising out of it. The sweet smell grew stronger, comforted him with the remembrance of an elixir his mother had given him when he was a boy, stricken with an ongoing cough. Nothing brought fear to his mother's eyes like a cough that wouldn't go away.

Trusty took the mug, helped himself to a sip, then spit the liquid out as soon as it touched his tongue. "What the hell is that? That's the worst thing I've ever tasted."

"It's not coffee. It's water, honey, prairie herbs, and a dose of laudanum. Drink it. Your pain will go away."

"I've never had such a concoction. You got any coffee?"

"That's all I have."

"Thanks just the same." Trusty set the mug down on the ground. More pain arrived with the movement and he flinched and moaned unconsciously.

"Suit yourself, Dawson," the man said as he moved back to the other side of the campfire.

"You know me, but I don't know you."

"Everyone knows you, or have you forgot who you are?"

"Where's the judge?"

"Dead. Don't you worry about him. I wrapped him up in a blanket so nothing can get to him. There's a shallow cave a hundred yards down the mountain. I tucked him away until you're able to ride."

"I know the cave."

"It'll keep the body from stinking too bad."

"He's really dead."

"That's what I said."

"No, it wasn't a question. I was letting it sink in. She really did kill him."

Amelia Darby's face flashed in Trusty's mind, surrounded by black, lit up by a wicked jab of lightning slicing the sky in half, a satisfied sneer on her face, with the Buntline held confidently in her hands. Her eyes were as black as her cloak and as angry as the stormy sky. There was no way Trusty was ever going to forget the sight of that girl as she pulled the trigger. Not until the day he died. She had tricked him and the judge, gained their confidence, encouraged them to let their guard down and feel sorry for her. "I'm such a fool," Trusty said to himself, under his breath too soft for the stranger to hear.

"Yes, she killed him," the man said. "She meant to kill you too. I arrived too late to stop her."

Trusty tried to get up, but the pain forced him back onto the bedroll again. "Where is she? Where is Amelia Darby?"

"I don't know, but I have my thoughts where she might be headed," the man said. "We had an exchange and she got away, rode out, and disappeared."

"She ran off into the night?"

"Into the storm. But that would be Amelia's way. She wouldn't let anything stop her once she has her mind set on something. Rain, lightning, a twister, or a deep darkness wouldn't dare stand in her way. My guess is she knew exactly where she was heading and had an escape plan, a place to run to until things quieted down. She played with you like a big cat smacking around its prey for the fun of it, then ran off after the kill. The only spoil she took with her was the satisfaction of revenge."

"Revenge. It was always about that, wasn't it? I failed to trust my gut. I knew I should have never trusted her. I didn't from the start, but the judge warmed to her."

"Amelia loved her youngest brother, Rascal, more than she let on I would imagine."

"She said she hated them all."

The man shrugged, then grabbed up a cup of coffee and took a sip of it himself. Trusty couldn't imagine that it was the foul-tasting medicine that had been handed to him.

Trusty didn't feel threatened by the man, but he wasn't comfortable either. The man's voice was soft as butter and his eyes and body movement were hard to read. The stranger was stiff, uncomfortable in his clothes. Denim trousers. A chambray shirt with a defined yoke. Boots with a new shine on them. All black, like Amelia Darby in service of mourning or something bad.

Trusty's vision was clear now, but he still didn't know who the man was. He was still a stranger, the face more familiar than the voice. "You sound like you know her pretty well." Another pain exploded inside Trusty's body as he moved to get comfortable on the hard ground. His vision paled white and for a second he was blind from the hurt. Another moan escaped his lips even though he fought against it.

"You should drink from the mug that I brought you."

"How do I know that I can trust you?"

"You don't know. But you have my word that it will ease your pain and not bring any harm to you. That's all I can offer you. The risk is yours to take."

The tincture of laudanum took Trusty into a deep, fit-filled sleep. Pain crashed into hazy dreams that left him floating in a known, but unknown world. As suddenly as he had woken, alive, next to the campfire with certain knowledge that Amelia Darby had killed Judge

Hadesworth, he had been transported into a drug-induced stupor that left him lost and afraid, a place he was unaccustomed to visiting.

Trusty opened his eyes to see stars overhead. The campfire burned steadily next to him, offering the comfort of warmth and the pleasant odor of hardwood burning slow. There wasn't much pain in his body, but his head felt funny . . . achy like he had been drinking, but different. It must have been the laudanum. He was able to move this time, prop himself up and see clearly.

"Who are you?" Trusty said to the man opposite the fire.

"Amelia Darby is my sister," the man said, letting the truth of his words dawn on Trusty.

Trusty sat up, relieved for a moment from the pain, and reached for his gun—that wasn't there.

The man stood up as well. "You have nothing to fear . . . relax. If I was like the rest of my family, you'd already be dead."

"I've heard that song and dance before and look where it got me."

"I assure you that I mean you no harm."

Without any weapons to protect himself with, and his current state of injury that disallowed for a successful outcome of a fistfight, Trusty relented, scanning the ground for a rock that might be useful. "What's your name?"

"Father . . ." he stopped as soon as the word dropped off his tongue. "Michael. Just Michael now. Michael

Darby." He made his way over to Trusty and offered his hand.

Trusty took it and allowed himself to be pulled upward onto two feet. Pain revisited his torso, radiating from his shoulder, from the bullet wound that had been bandaged with the skill of a doctor. He was wobbly and weak, but determined to stand, to face Michael Darby. The pain was distant for the moment. The tincture offered relief, but Trusty was troubled by how it made him feel, not to mention the distant dream he tried to repel and capture at the same time.

On closer inspection there was no question that the stranger was a Darby. He had the same birdlike features as Amelia: a beaky nose, wide-set eyes, and narrow face. His hair was shorn short, recently cut, and black as crow feathers. His clothes looked new, store-bought, not home-made, not worn out. He looked uncomfortable in the black getup, like the material itched or didn't fit right. Something about the man didn't seem right about him, but Trusty couldn't put his finger on what that something was.

"You did this?" Trusty said, pointing to his shoulder.

"I had no choice. You were going to die if I didn't do something. I could have left you and gone after Amelia, but that didn't seem to be the right thing to do. I couldn't leave you to the wolves."

"You have skills."

Michael Darby nodded. "I had some training on the battlefield. Blood and stitches are hard to avoid in this world."

"Thank you," Trusty said. "You saved me."

"That used to be my business." Michael let go of Trusty, allowing him to stand on his own.

"I don't understand."

"Why don't you sit back down. You're not strong enough to stand very long. I'll make us some dinner. You're lucky this mountain is home to a good population of rabbits."

Trusty didn't have to be told twice that he was still weak. His bones felt like they were made out of paper. He settled down onto the spot where he had slept. "How long have you been here?"

"A day."

"A day?" A rush of panic plowed through Trusty, almost propelling him back onto his feet. "We were supposed to be in Muskogee by now."

"I'm sure someone has already noticed that you're late." Michael had produced a pan and a tin drum canteen from somewhere. He set the pan on a grate over the fire and poured water into it. He was not troubled at all about Trusty's concerns. He was as calm as Trusty normally was—which comforted and bothered Trusty in a way he didn't understand.

"Judge Hadesworth is a federal judge," Trusty said.

"*Was*. He was a federal judge."

"I don't want to think like that."

"You can't bring him back."

"I wish I could."

"We all wish we could change the past, but we can't. I thought you would have learned that by now."

Trusty didn't like the change in Michael's tone. It was condescending, like a teacher who had no right to grade him. He wasn't sure he liked Michael Darby at all. "You need to explain to me why you're here, sir," Trusty said. "I appreciate it that you helped me, but my experience with the Darbys hasn't been positive of late, so I can't exactly say I'm real comfortable right now. Especially when I consider that Amelia said she was the only Darby left in Kosoma. She said she was the last of the Darbys. How can that be if you're a Darby too?"

"Believe it or not, she was telling the truth. There are no other Darbys living in Kosoma. I was living in Krebs. I was a priest at Saint Joseph's. My family had long given me up for dead, or hoped I was dead."

"Dead?"

"Figuratively. I chose a different path than what they wanted me to. One that involved learning, reading, and giving my life over to the way of the Lord. They were ashamed of me, wanted nothing to do with me, and I felt the same about them. I found refuge in the church, but the church did not find refuge in me. The trials and tribulations caused by my brothers continually reached the ears of my superiors, and I was continually looked upon with suspicion. The curse of being a Darby. The recent killing spree in Kosoma cast a bad light on me, and instead of being cast out, I walked away, took off my collar, and left it behind. I had no choice and nowhere else to go. I was tired of living under the roof of people who did not trust me, that judged me for the actions of others. I couldn't do my job."

"I saw you when we were on Poor Man's Hill."

"Yes, I regret not coming to your aid then. If I had known who you and the judge were, I would have warned you of the danger that you were in. But from a distance, it was hard to tell if you were of her ilk, if you were part of the Darby gang or just bystanders. It didn't matter much. I had no desire to see Amelia. I was always her least favorite brother."

"Why's that?"

"I could always tell when she was lying."

"How's that?"

"Because she never told the truth. She would have made a wonderful actor in one of those traveling shows."

"And you don't have that skill?"

"I assure you, Deputy, I have no reason to lie to you or bring any harm to you. If I can, I hope I can help you."

"Help me do what?"

"Bring Amelia Darby to justice. I hope to see her hang for killing Judge Hadesworth."

# Chapter 10

Vance Calhoun eased along the trail with his head down, allowing the grullo to make his way home pretty much on his own. The reliable horse had made the journey and delivered a drunken Calhoun to his doorstep more than once. The vast darkness of the night had wrapped Calhoun in a black blanket; a stunned look had settled on his face after discovering the bullet-riddled bodies of Haden and Miguel. The extent of Marberry's rouse was undeniable to acknowledge. Not only had Calhoun been outsmarted, but he had lost his most trusted man in Haden. Sally and Maria would be stricken with the loss of Miguel, and Calhoun was certain that his sister would take him to task for the loss. Walking into the St. Louis railroad man's trap would be all his fault. And maybe Sally would be right in her attack, in her grief, in her fear. Calhoun knew he had reacted and not thought out his actions. Just like now, plodding along, not paying any attention to what was around him. He could have been riding into another ambush. Marberry was certainly capable of such a thing, finishing what he started. At that thought, Calhoun raised his head, took a deep sniff of the air, and realized that Marberry had the upper hand, that for whatever the reason—whether he blamed Calhoun for Jessica's death or feared that Calhoun would take the baby—he wouldn't stop until Calhoun was no longer a threat. A war had been started. A deeply personal war that could only end in the man's death.

Gladdy O'Connor followed close behind Calhoun, keeping pace but giving the man some distance. "I got your back, boss," Gladdy had said once they headed for home.

There were two other horses tied behind Gladdy's ride, Haden's and Miguel's—both had stayed close, weren't taken by Marberry's raiders. The horses wore lifeless bodies draped over their saddles, heads to the ground, dead as dead could be, shot and killed by Marberry's men.

Calhoun could barely contain himself as he looked behind him and caught the silhouette of the death parade in the dark. Rage and the desire for immediate revenge bubbled under his thin skin. His sore fingers wrapped around the grullo's reins so tight that he could feel his heartbeat inside his fingernails. The *boom*, *boom*, *boom* told him that he was still alive, still capable to retaliate, to rise up against Marberry and take back what was his. "You have no idea who you are dealing with," he said under his breath.

Gladdy sat stiff in his saddle, shoulders square, eyes and ears peeled for movement of any kind, his right hand close to his six-shooter. He sat taller in his saddle, not at all beset by any emotion over his brother's death; he looked like he was in charge of something new.

Calhoun thought Gladdy was acting a little odd, but he was more concerned about Marberry. He figured that the old man and his thugs were long gone, well on their way back to St. Louis with the baby girl stored somewhere safe. Or as safe as possible. It wasn't until he smelled smoke that he thought any different or was concerned about his own well-being.

Calhoun slid up in his saddle, relaxed his grip on the grullo's reins, and took in everything around him. It was like he had awakened, suddenly opened his eyes after a long sleep or snapped out of a self-induced trance. His rage and concern about the future—payback—slipped away and the present was his only concern.

The grullo, being a decent and instinctive horse, felt the change in Calhoun's attitude, the release of tension, and slowed its trot to wary steps.

Gladdy caught up without having to try. "Everything all right, boss?"

Calhoun flinched at the words. He didn't like the way Gladdy called him boss. He didn't like Gladdy at all and wished it was him tossed over the saddle of a horse instead of his brother, Haden. He was going to miss Haden, as much as he hated to admit that. He didn't want to be the kind of man who would miss any man after they died. That kind of thing was a weakness, made for bad decision making in times of war and battle. The last thing Vance Calhoun wanted anyone to think of him was that he'd gone soft.

"You smell that?" Calhoun said, bringing the grullo to a full stop.

"Smoke."

"Doesn't smell like a campfire."

"I suppose not."

Calhoun looked at Gladdy, sitting next to him on his horse with the other two in tow behind him, with a sneer, like he had expected an argument. "Smells bitter. Like old wood." He looked up then, in the direction toward home, toward his ranch. The blackness in the sky had changed, grown lighter, edged into the color of a sunset instead of the cover of night. Time had suddenly flipped around, turned upside down, and of all of the things Vance Calhoun had expected to feel on the ride home with two good men dead, panic wasn't one of them. But that was what hit him with an unexpected suddenness. Pure panic. The kind he had felt in Shiloh, knowing that all was lost, another defeat, lost in smoke and blood.

"The ranch is on fire," Calhoun said aloud, not to Gladdy but to himself and to the world. He couldn't believe it, but he knew sure as anything that was what he was looking at. Fire at the ranch. It smelled like Marberry's work. An attempt to finish Calhoun once and for all. Kill him and burn everything he owned down to the ground. Punishment enough for allowing Jessica to die.

The sky turned orange, then red, glowing with anger and spite, the wind fanning the flames, pushing the smoke deeper into the Red River Valley until it surrounded Calhoun completely, choking him with the acrid smell of death and destruction.

\* \* \*

Calhoun's worst fears were realized as he pushed the grullo to run faster and harder than the gelding had ever run before.

Flames jumped upward out of the windows of the ranch house without any inhibition or sorrow at all. The wind pushed them upward to the roof, where the flames continued to eat the available rafters, continuing their angry path, determined to cover the entire house. Some of the roof had already collapsed, leaving a gaping opening over what once was the bedroom. The same room where Jessica had given birth and died. Like her, the room no longer existed—which at any other time might have been a favor to Calhoun. He didn't care to reenter that room anytime soon and revisit the events that had taken place there. The bedroom was a den of deception, the place where Jessica had tricked him into thinking that he was her man, the father of their child—a second chance for him that he didn't see coming at this stage in life. He had been duped. The daughter was just like her father. The house could burn to a cinder—under different circumstances. Vance Calhoun knew in his bones that this fire was no accident, that he was right in his assumption that Marberry had set the fire.

Calhoun left Gladdy in the dust and pushed forward, his head down against the wind, next to the grullo's neck. His face was pressed hard against the horsehair, and he could feel the horse's sweat against his cheek and taste the smoke from the fire on his tongue. The heavy smoke and wind created a coating of ash that wouldn't go away no matter how many times he spit.

The grullo rode hard as Calhoun scanned the land for any threat, for any sign of help. It was a contradiction of need. He wanted to kill Marberry with his bare hands and needed someone to help him put out the fire. Instinct and pride demanded that he save what was his, even if he couldn't stand to look at it, bear the memory of Jessica alive or dead. The ugliness of her betrayal wrenched his stomach.

At first Calhoun didn't see anyone. Not only was the house on fire, but both barns were alight, too, flames reaching into the calm night sky and spoiling it red. Frightened horses rushed outward, fleeing burning straw and timber; they were running as if their lives depended on it—because it did. Smoke rolled across the ground like fog, enveloping everything in its path, obscuring full sight of the ranch.

The closer he got, Calhoun saw shadows of men dancing in the smoke, trying to douse the fire with buckets of water. Cowboys from the range. Most likely one was Denton Hobbs, Haden's right-hand man, as good a cowhand as could be found in Texas, or anywhere else for that matter. He was shouting instructions to no one in particular. Other cowhands had joined in. Men from all around the valley had come running at the first smell of smoke. Four thousand head of cattle was a big operation and required a good-sized crew. It looked like they were all in, doing their best to fight the fire. Help was there. A need fulfilled. Revenge would have to wait.

Smoke burned Calhoun's eyes, but he kept searching for another familiar face, a familiar form as he drove the grullo forward as fast as he could. But no matter how deep into the smoke he looked, he could not find Sally.

\* \* \*

Maria held Sally in her lap, limp and twisted like a sooty ragdoll tossed down a staircase, her face marked with black streaks of ash, her eyes closed. There was no sign to Calhoun that his sister was breathing, was alive. As much as she had tested him, rose up against him, demanded that he be better than he was, she had never feared angering him. Calhoun had never considered his life without her. Sally had always been by his side, a surrogate spouse for more years than either of them ever wanted to admit—without the intimacy—but unbreakable in their connection to each other. It was an unspoken marriage that had been taken for granted, and at any other time Calhoun might have acknowledged the loss with a broader show of emotion. But this day had taken its toll. He had nothing left to offer, not even a kind word of inquiry. He walked over to Maria and Sally and took the handkerchief that Maria had been using to wipe Sally's forehead. He stuffed Sally's handkerchief in his pocket as a keepsake—so he wouldn't forget this moment—then turned away from Maria, who like Sally was singed and soot-covered, and walked back toward the burning house. He didn't have to ask if Sally was dead. He knew just by looking at her.

"What of Miguel?" Maria said, her voice brittle, like the inside of her throat had been burned to a crisp.

"He's dead," Calhoun said. "What happened here?"

Maria breathed her first breath knowing for certain that her husband no longer shared the living world with her. She didn't seem surprised as grief fell over her face, gray and smoky, in a veil of black ash and anger at death that promised to never wash away. Her pale, red-rimmed eyes faded into a distant point past Calhoun that didn't exist on this earth; her emotions were tangled up in the past and the future. She was deaf to his request as her round body started to quake from the toes up.

"What happened here, Maria?" Calhoun insisted, grabbing her wrist, forcing her back to the present moment. "I need to know."

A gasp escaped the Mexican woman's mouth and the pupils of her brown eyes pulsed in recognition. "They waited until you left. Four men. They rode in quietly, lit torches, then started to throw them on the roofs. I do not think that they were expecting a fight, but Miss Sally put a rifle in my hands and we started to shoot. One fell. The others rode off. But it was too late to stop the fires. When Miss Sally ran out to gather the pails for water, one of the men shot her. He was waiting on the edge of the darkness, just out of sight. I tried to save her, but I let the house burn." Maria's voice quavered and broke as tears rolled down her cheeks. She hadn't let go of Sally for one second.

Calhoun shook his head, flexed his fists as he digested the woman's words, and envisioned the scene that Maria had just described to him. He wasn't surprised that Sally had died defending the ranch. But she had been tricked as much as he had by Marberry and his men. A deeper revenge began to tingle in his heart, and there was no stopping it from growing from there.

Calhoun pulled away from Maria without offering any words of condolence or comfort.

Maria and Miguel had been with Sally longer than Sally had been with Calhoun. He heard the old Mexican woman's whimper turn into a mourning wail, but kept on walking, every part of him numbed, weakened, broken, burned down, enraged, looking to settle a score.

The sun rose over the farthest ridge to the east of the ranch, casting soft white light down onto what remained of Vance Calhoun's empire. Only one barn stood intact. The rest had burned to the ground. Timbers smoldered. Cows were lowing in the distance; a herd had gathered on a hill as if to bear witness to an unspeakable human tragedy. The ground was scarred black where the house and other barns had once stood. An outline of the buildings was definable to Calhoun as he stood in what was once a corral. He was alone, the only one awake as far as he knew, surveying what once was his pride and joy.

The Bar-C-Bar Ranch had been his hope and dream, his power and his wealth, something that in the beginning of his life he did not possess but wanted desperately. He would do anything to be rich, to be a man of means, to have the money to do whatever he saw fit. And he did do anything. He had cheated and stolen and lied and bullied and killed; whatever it took, he did it. To which he felt no remorse. Until now. Until there was nothing left. And that emotion only lasted a moment. Revenge was never far away from Vance Calhoun's mind. There were no walls or faces to hit. No bones to break. No lives to snuff out. It would take more than that to extinguish the fire that had been set inside of him. Theodore Marberry needed to lose more than Calhoun had. He needed to suffer. Slowly. The why of it was clear. The how of it, though, had yet to reveal itself to him.

"I'm sorry about all of this, boss." Gladdy had walked up beside Calhoun unannounced.

"Save your sorrow for another day." Calhoun turned so he was facing what was left of his house. A charred chimney jutted up from the black ground, purposeless, unable to contain any fire inside the hearth.

"Hobbs is getting some men together to dig the graves for Haden, Miguel, and your sister," Gladdy said.

Calhoun nodded. "I suppose it has to be done. You tell him to do that?"

"Nope. He told me he was doing it. I ain't got the right to pass out orders."

"Remember that." Calhoun sighed and turned his attention to the younger O'Connor. "Seems to me you got reasons to be angry this morning yourself."

Gladdy bit his lip, nodded, then eyed the muddy tips of his boots. "Haden was a good brother. Me and him didn't always see eye to eye, but we was there for each other. He didn't deserve to die by no ambush."

"No, he didn't. We have to avenge his death. Sally's and Miguel's too. Marberry has to pay for this, for all that he took from me." Calhoun's eyes narrowed as he studied Gladdy's worn Irish face. None of them had washed the residue from the fire off of their skin or clothes. Calhoun's nose had become immune to the smell. He expected it now, didn't know what it was like to encounter air not tainted by fire. "And what he took from you too."

Gladdy nodded, then twisted his face curiously. "What do you got in mind, boss?"

"Not sure. Not yet. All I know is that Theodore Marberry is gonna suffer. Whatever I decide, it's gonna be slow and painful. You can count on that." There was no more to explain than that, not to Gladdy O'Connor. The Mick wouldn't understand what had been lost to Calhoun. The house and everything inside it—including the railroad stock that had given him the twenty-five percent of the "Frisco." He had to wonder if that was Marberry's intent on setting the place on fire, destroying the railroad stock certificates, or if it was something more. His own strike of revenge for the death of his daughter. "An eye for an eye," Calhoun said. "An eye for an eye."

# Chapter 11

*Lost Mountain Pass, Indian Territory, May 1888*

Michael Darby stood on the precipice of Lost Mountain, looking toward Kosoma with his back to Trusty. The former priest looked like he was about to jump, standing so close to the edge like he was, but that didn't seem to be the man's intent. There were no cassocks ruffling in the wind this time, no offer of imaginary wings or a vision from another world or a nightmare. All Trusty could see was a skinny man dressed in black with a pensive look on his face, tight, drawn-in shoulders, squared and lean, ready to face whatever the world had in store for him. The black outfit did little to provide the man with a good look or any assurance of genuine kindness. But it wouldn't have mattered to Trusty if Michael had been dressed in all white with gilded seams, he wouldn't have trusted the man any farther than he could throw him regardless.

"There's riders coming," Darby said.

Trusty stood up as tall as he could, trying his best not to move too fast. He didn't want to irritate his bandaged shoulder. It didn't matter whether there was any question of Michael Darby's motives or reasons for helping out in the time of trouble; there was no question about his surgical skills. The bullet from Amelia's Buntline had been removed, the wound cauterized, sewn up, bandaged, and cleaned regularly with whiskey from Michael's own rations. Trusty hadn't questioned the man about the acquisition of his skills, or why an ex-priest had whiskey with him.

"Probably the Tenth Cavalry," Trusty said, "coming to look for me and the judge."

"Buffalo Soldiers?" Darby turned away from the vista and eased his way back down to the camp, or what had been the camp. Everything had been packed onto the horses, including Judge Hadesworth's body.

"Out of Fort Gibson," Trusty answered. "For now, until next year. Once they open the Territory up, there'll be no need for the fort. That's the word I heard. Muskogee's not going to be the same."

"Nothing is going to be the same."

"I can't argue with that."

"You want to wait here?" Michael Darby walked up to his horse, who carried a light load, two small panniers and no scabbard, ready to mount. A single-action Colt .45 sat securely in a holster on the man's right hip, the only showing of a weapon that Trusty could see. That didn't mean there wasn't something else hidden in the garb the man wore or stuffed inside his packs.

"It's time to go. I can't stay here any longer," Trusty said, hesitating to mount his own ride. Horse stood waiting, with the judge's mount tied behind him. Trusty wasn't sure he had the strength to pull himself up onto the saddle, but it was more than that. He didn't want to face what awaited him in the world beyond Lost Mountain even though he knew he had to. There would be questions. An inquiry. A lot to face and a lot to answer for. He had failed to do his duty. He hadn't protected his charge. He had lost a judge—all because he hadn't trusted his own instinct about Amelia Darby. He had read the tea leaves wrong, assumed it was the boxer and the bulldog who were angling to kill the judge, and he had killed those two men—dead and buried by Michael Darby. But he had been wrong about that too. The two men were after *him*. There was a price on his head. He had his own secrets from Michael Darby. But there was no escaping his failure. Judge Gordon Hadesworth was dead and Trusty Dawson had blood on his badge. He couldn't hide out on Lost Mountain forever. He had to face the consequences of his actions, answer for his failures. Running away from responsibility had never been his way, and he wasn't going to change now.

Trusty and Michael Darby met the 10th Cavalry at the base of Lost Mountain. The procession of Buffalo Soldiers was led by Colonel John J. Mizner, a short white man with wavy black hair and a thin mustache that rode high on his tight lip. Beyond Mizner was a troop of ten men, all black, either former slaves, freedmen, or sons of slaves. The 10th had a long, valiant history fighting in the Indian Wars, and Trusty held them, and their reputation, in high esteem. He had mixed with Mizner a few times at Fort Gibson, but those meetings had been a few years ago as the cavalry passed through the Territory on their way to Arizona. He didn't know Mizner well at all.

The colonel put up his hand to stop the troops behind him, then rode to face Trusty and Michael Darby. His horse was a tall chestnut gelding without any white marks showing on the muscled body at all. The horse held its head proud and looked to be a steed worthy of a man like Mizner. The colonel sat straight in the saddle and wore a blank, unreadable expression on his face.

"I feared we would find you in trouble, Dawson," Mizner said to Trusty. He looked Michael up and down, judging him, calculating the threat level from the look in his eyes, then turned his attention to Judge Hadesworth's body. "You're known to be as reliable as a clock."

Trusty's mouth went dry. He didn't like the taste of failure, especially when it was coupled with grief for a man he cared about and respected. "We were ambushed, then tricked by a woman who was riding with us. She shot Judge Hadesworth and fled." He looked away, cleared his throat, and tried to find an explanation for his failure. There was nothing more than the truth. Embellishments and suppositions would only lead to trouble he didn't need.

"And you took a bullet as well," Mizner said, noting Trusty's bound left arm.

Trusty nodded. "I'd likely be dead or in worse shape if it wasn't for this man here."

Mizner turned his attention to Darby with squinted

eyes and glared at him as if he was an unsatisfactory recruit. "And who would you be, sir?"

"Michael Darby." There was no hesitation in his voice, no previous claim to being a priest. The answer was confident, short, and nonchalant. Darby and Mizner didn't look to know each other—or be impressed by each other's position.

Before Trusty could fill the colonel in, Mizner said, "I thought all the Darbys were hanged in Kosoma?"

"My brothers, sad to say." Michael adjusted himself in his saddle. He sat atop a sturdy gray mare with a gentle face that he called Spirit. "I found my calling early in life was a much different path than anyone in my family. I went to seminary and became a priest."

"Your garb suggests differently," Mizner said.

Trusty was glad to sit back and let the two men do the talking. He was trying to find his own comfort in the saddle, along with his balance and comfort in his own skin. Thankfully, the shot from Amelia's Buntline had pierced his left shoulder, missing bone and anything vital to his circulation. The chance of infection still worried him, and, of course, his own future wearing the badge, which would be at the hands of William Grimes, the U.S. Marshal of Indian Territory.

There was also the prospect of higher authorities weighing in on whether Trusty was guilty of neglect or deserved to remain in the marshal service. All logical concerns, but Trusty was more concerned about Amelia Darby's whereabouts by the minute. Every second that was wasted was one more second that she was farther down the trail, riding scot-free, uncharged for the murder of Judge Hadesworth. If there was anything Trusty could find to be thankful for in that moment it was the use of his right hand, his gun hand. His shooting ability was unhindered since the shot had pierced the muscles in his left shoulder, albeit untested. He would need the use of both of his hands if he was going to bring Amelia Darby to justice, which he knew he had to do as he sat there, staring at the colonel and his troop of Buffalo Soldiers behind him.

"I walked away from the church," Michael said. "It was time for me to leave. I served my duty and now see another calling."

"And what is that, if I may ask?" Mizner's horse swished its tail and cocked its head, pulling against the bite. The colonel loosened his grip on the reins, relaxed his arms, if only a little. "I find it odd that a family of outlaws can produce a man of God, and then, when they are set off to meet their maker, probably at too late a date from the sound of things, you give up the cloth and take up a righteous path. You would assume any man would be suspicious of your name and your actions, wouldn't you?"

"Any man is free to think what he may."

"I suppose that is fair," Mizner said.

"My decisions are my own," Michael answered, "but it was the only way I could see fit to stop my sister, Amelia, from doing something destructive and lethal. Unfortunately, I was too late. She is the one who killed Judge Hadesworth."

"I see," Mizner said. "You are certain she is the killer? A woman? Another Darby."

"Yes," Michael answered. "A woman with a score to

settle. She was fond of our younger brother, Rascal, and sought to gain revenge for his death. I assure you that my sister and I are the only two remaining Darbys."

"This sister did not want to avenge the other two Darby brothers?"

Trusty had steadied himself on Horse and felt himself growing stronger as he sat there. The sun beat down on his face from a cloudless sky, allowing clear sight of the land in all directions. There was no sight of Amelia, but that didn't mean she wasn't close by, lurking about, waiting for an opportunity to complete the task she had set for herself. Or someone else, someone who had taken the bounty on his head just like the boxer and the bulldog had. In all of his years as an army scout and a Deputy U.S. Marshal, Trusty had never found himself to be a defined target, felt like a crack of a rifle could erupt at any second—from anywhere around—and snuff out his life. Living like a wary rabbit was going to take some getting used to.

"I do not know Amelia's full intent, sir," Michael said to the colonel. "But she is a Darby, and that makes her as dangerous as any man. To underestimate her is a mistake that will only be made once."

"Rest assured that there will be Wanted posters plastered across the Territory with a high reward, portraying your sister as the dangerous animal she is—if what you say is true. You are a Darby too." Mizner stared at Michael, doing his best to make the man look away, to break his confidence, but that didn't happen. Michael stood his ground and held the colonel's gaze.

"And so I am," Michael said. "I can ask for your trust and faith, but that doesn't mean that you will give it to me. My actions will be proof enough. I am here to help bring in Amelia and hold her to account for the crime she has committed."

"Well," Mizner said, "a federal judge has been murdered. That is no small crime. She will most likely hang if she is found guilty."

Michael still held the colonel's gaze. "She is guilty. I saw her pull the trigger. Trusty did too. His wound is evidence enough, but the judge's body is proof of her misdeed."

"That's for a judge and jury to decide," Mizner said. He studied Michael for a long moment, letting his own words echo away on the wind. "How did your sister escape so easily? Did you let her escape?"

"No," Michael said flatly, not breaking the colonel's hard gaze. "I am riding alone, and I made the choice to try and save Trusty. By the time I was sure that the marshal was going to live, Amelia had vanished. I am aware that Amelia has a lot to answer for when she stands before her maker. As do we all."

Mizner twisted his horse's head to the side and looked behind him. He judged the two rows of black soldiers quickly, obviously found them to be in order, then faced Michael Darby again. "How did you come about being here, Darby?"

"I was on the trail of the three riders. I was sure that they belonged to the deputy, my sister, and the judge. I heard gunshots and was close enough to pursue the sound."

"You arrived too late," Mizner said.

"By seconds."

Trusty knew this story to be true. At least the timing

of it. When he opened his eyes, Michael Darby was standing over him, tending to the gunshot wound.

"But like you said, your sister was able to flee," Mizner said.

"You don't believe me?"

"Just trying to understand the sequence of events. I'll have a report to write."

"I fired a shot in her direction, heard her flee on a horse. But I also saw the deputy injured, shot, bleeding in a bad way. If I chased after Amelia, he would not have recovered as he has now. I had a choice to make. Let Trusty die or go after Amelia. My choice was clear," Michael said. "I don't think I can make it any clearer than that."

It was Trusty's turn to grip the reins with tension. He urged Horse to move forward toward Mizner so that he was a head's length in front of Darby's gray mare. "I'm going after Amelia Darby myself, Colonel. I'd be obliged if you would escort the judge's body into town and relinquish it to the undertaker."

Mizner's blank, pasty white face twisted curiously as he considered Trusty's request. "What makes you think you're in any shape to go after a murderer, Deputy?"

"What else am I to do? Amelia Darby is a cold-blooded killer. Every second we sit here, she gets farther away, closer to freedom, wherever that may be. I can move faster than you can with ten men, and travel undetected, while you and your men will bring attention to your cause by your mere presence. That, and I've got reason to want to be the one to bring her in. She killed the judge. He was a fine man, not only in stature but as a friend. I failed him, and seeing Amelia to the gallows is the only way I know to repay him."

Michael Darby had traded places with Trusty. He held back, put in his place by Trusty, and for the moment looked comfortable with staying there.

Mizner moved his chestnut gelding forward, close enough to touch noses with Trusty's horse. "Your right to duty and continue to wear the U.S. Marshal's badge will come into question, Dawson. I suppose I have the power to deny your request on a federal level."

"I am more than willing to face whatever may come from this incident, sir," Trusty said. "But even without a badge, I would go after Amelia Darby, even if it took every ounce of energy and life that had kin to me. I'm not asking for your permission, Colonel. If you want my badge you can take it, but that won't stop me from riding out of here."

"I'll be going along with him," Michael said. "I don't think either of us will rest until Amelia is captured."

Trusty shot a sideways glance toward the only surviving Darby brother that could only be interpreted as "I don't need your help." He didn't say a word though.

"I know Amelia better than anyone," Michael went on. "Her habits are not that unusual. I expect to find her in a town taking a rest, most likely Enid by the directions of her tracks. And I can aid the deputy, who is clearly not whole in his physical ability."

Mizner looked at both men and shook his head. "You can keep your badge, Trusty. That's not mine to take from you. But I would warn you that coming into Muskogee empty-handed would not be advised. If you fail to bring in this Amelia Darby, your days in the marshal service are surely over with."

"I'll wire Marshal Grimes the first opportunity that I get."

"See to it that you do that. I will need a description of this Amelia Darby. Is there anything else that needs added to the report?" Colonel Mizner said.

"No, sir," Trusty said, fighting off the pain in his shoulder and in his heart. "Please convey my regrets to Judge Hadesworth's family if you don't mind."

"That's your duty, Dawson. Not mine. You need to look his widow in the eye and tell her what happened to her husband under your watch. No one else can do it for you."

# Chapter 12

*Leaving Lost Mountain, Indian Territory, May 1888*

The 10th Cavalry kicked up a cloud of thick brown dust as they marched north. Mizner led the troops with a strict face forward without any kind of good-bye. He had said all he was going to say to Trusty.

Two perfect lines of soldiers, their skin black as the soles of their boots, looked like they were caught inside a faded sepia-toned photograph from Trusty's vantage point. He sat atop Horse on a craggy rocky ridge with his left hand cupped over his eyes, trying to keep the sad parade in sight for as long as possible. He lacked a decent set of binoculars and made a note to purchase a pair the next time the opportunity arose. As it was, he had lost sight of the judge's body, but the tether of failed duty and regret still pulled at his heart. Trusty knew deep in his bones that he should have been the one to escort the judge into Kosoma. It should have been him to show the world and all its critics and judges his worst failure. Instead, he had conscripted the task to Colonel Mizner and his Buffalo Soldiers—for a good reason, if it could be argued. And it would be, most likely beyond the newspapers of the Territory and all the way to Washington. It wasn't every day that a federal judge was murdered.

Trusty sat alone for a long moment, facing north and inward at the same time, lost in judgment of himself and his future, if there was one to be had. He had faced hard times in his life before, but this one felt like the earth under his feet was about to shatter like a glass thrown against a wall. He hoped he had made the right decision, was doing the right thing pursuing Amelia Darby. It was the only way he knew how to clear his name, or at least, take away the taint on it. He likely wouldn't be known as Trusty any longer. The well-worn moniker had turned out to be as fragile as the soil under his feet.

Michael Darby rode up alongside Trusty a minute or so later, uninterested in the cavalry's departure. "I found her tracks easy enough," he said. "She's headed west. Like I said, I think she'll hide out in Enid, but my guess is she's ultimately heading for No Man's Land. I'm none too thrilled at riding through the Seminole Nation or paying a tax for the pleasure of crossing into their land, but that's the way of things these days, if they will allow us entry."

Trusty dropped his cupped hand to his side and fought off a shot of burning pain that radiated from the wound. "You're riding with me, Darby. I don't pay a traveling tax to any of the Five Civilized Tribes for the right to travel through their land. You might want to keep your past occupation to yourself though. Religion, especially yours, provokes suspicion and anger that we won't want or need to face. You know how it goes. Some of them found salvation in the presence of the missionaries, while others found hate and torture."

"My religion is my business. You don't wear a magic shirt that wards off bullets, do you?"

"The Ghost Dance is troubling. I'm surprised you've heard of it," Trusty said.

"I heard a lot of things as a priest. I agree, the idea that spirits of the dead would help the living and rid the Indian world of white people is dangerous. It can only come to a bad end."

Trusty wondered about Darby's beliefs, if he still believed in the church and all that it stood for. One set of magic stories didn't sound too different to him from the other if he thought about it long enough. But he didn't. There were other things on his mind. "Why do you think Amelia will go to No Man's Land? She told me that she wanted to be a milliner in Muskogee."

"She told you what she wanted you to believe is all. She had her story all thought out, practiced if I know her like I think I do, so she wouldn't slip up. It was all a lie. But she has good cause to head up to the strip. Her common law Choctaw husband, David Folsom, squats a piece of land there and collects buffalo bones and sells them for fertilizer. At least that was what he was doing when I last heard. It might have been no more than a ploy to look respectable. That could have changed. Folsom has been on the run for one thing or another for as long as he has been alive. He's a confidence taker, a liar, and a thief who would steal the nickels off his mother's eyes."

"And he's married to a woman who is a killer."

"Sounds like a match made in heaven, doesn't it?" Darby said.

"That would be your line of work, not mine."

"Not anymore."

"I suppose not. I have to say, your sister is full of surprises. I wouldn't have thought she'd associate with a Choctaw in that way." Trusty knew of more white men who lived with and considered themselves in a common marriage with an Indian woman than he did the other way around.

"Marriage to the Indian is much different than it is to us, Trusty," Darby said. "There's no obligation of fidelity, or a sharing of property, or acting in a manner that pleases the Lord in any way. It is most likely for that reason that my sister took up with David Folsom when she was thirteen. So she could live her life the way she wanted to, and he could live his. But now she needs him. I'm certain if we find Folsom, we'll find Amelia close by."

"And I should trust you on that?" Trusty said, turning his attention back to the cloud of dust the troop had created as it settled back to the land. The 10th had ridden out of sight, were nowhere to be seen, leaving Trusty on his own to face his own destiny and to answer for his own shortcomings. The fact that he still wore the badge and wanted to keep wearing it, at least until he was able to capture Amelia, then stand up in his own defense, kept him settled in the saddle. It would have been easier to ride with the Buffalo Soldiers and turn in his badge along with Judge Hadesworth's body.

"You don't have to trust me at all," Michael answered. "All you have to do is follow Amelia's trail. You'll end up in the same place as I will, but you might be too late to catch her. We can either ride together or alone. It doesn't matter to me. She won't be expecting either of us. She saw me wearing my priest garb at the cemetery in Kosoma, and most likely has assumed that I retreated back to the rectory where I belong after seeing me on Lost Mountain. And you know nothing of David Folsom as far as she knows. Amelia is smart, but she won't be able to hide out long on her own. She'll need David Folsom and whatever crew he associates himself with these days. No Man's Land might be far enough away for her to drop her guard, relax after a time. That's my hope anyway."

"I usually ride alone," Trusty said. "There'll be other marshals on the lookout for your sister. The Guardsmen, Chris Madsen, Heck Thomas, and Bill Tilghman, will stop what they're doin' to bring a judge's killer to justice. It won't just be us that will be after her. Her face will be plastered all over the Territory in a matter of a day or two once Colonel Mizner translates the description we gave him. I doubt she'll have time to relax anytime soon."

"Maybe you're right. But what about the men who are coming after you?"

Trusty looked at Darby with another side glance, another question of the priest's motive. "There will be that. Just like the two that you buried. They weren't out for the judge. I was their quarry. I told you what happened to me after I was able."

"A man should know what he's getting himself into," Darby said. "If you're a target, then so am I by association. We both take a risk by riding together to bring in Amelia."

"I suppose that's true. It seems to me that you've given up a lot to go after your sister, and for reasons I still don't fully understand. I have a duty, a name to clear, redemption for the judge, who I respected as a friend and a man. I couldn't walk away from that even if I didn't wear a badge, or if it was taken away from me. I would still go after her. But what of you, giving up a calling? Even if you were judged? Aren't there other churches in other territories, far from here, far from the Darby reputation, that would welcome you?"

"I suppose so, but I am seeking my own freedom. This land is my home and I'm obliged to it. Maybe things will be different for me if I could bring in Amelia. We both have a lot riding on this. You see that, don't you?"

"I suppose I do. What will you do once this is finished? Can you go back to being a priest?"

"Sometimes situations change in life," Darby said. "One phase ends and another begins. I was getting anxious inside the chapel, bored in the confession booth, and uncomfortable in my daily shoes. I was feeling confined in a way that I never thought possible. When word of my brothers' deeds fell on my ears, I knew there was more trouble coming. I knew Amelia would retaliate. If I didn't stop her, no one would. When I saw her riding with you and the judge, I was sure of her plans and I knew I had to lay down one cross and pick up another. That's as clear as I can make it for you. You know where I'm heading and why. I know I'm a Darby and that would give any man cause for doubt and mistrust. Do as you will, but I'm going after my sister. I hope you'll ride with me. I can promise you that I'll cover your back, and I'll hope that you'll cover mine. I have no currency to offer you other than my word. You can take it or not. The choice is yours."

Trusty studied Michael Darby's face, digging into his dark blue eyes as deep as he could. There was nothing that set him to wonder inside, to doubt what he said, but Trusty reminded himself that he had fallen for Amelia's story. He had believed her, to an extent, one that allowed her to ride alongside him and the judge. He had a choice to make, and he hoped he didn't regret this like he had the last one. "I'll take a chance on you, Darby. But you're gonna have to earn my faith in you."

"I've been doing that all of my life," Michael Darby said with a nod, then nickered his gray mare and pointed her head west. "We best get going, the sun's falling faster by the second, and Amelia will be closer to No Man's Land, if we sit here and jaw all day."

"Let's ride," Trusty said.


The two men traveled as darkness fell, forcing them to slow their horses. The night had become darker as a thick blanket of clouds covered the sky, obscuring the moon and stars. Michael knew the trail, had ridden it more than once, as they headed for a Choctaw town, Atoka, to spend the night in. Trusty was less familiar with the ride. He had only been to Atoka once or twice in his travels.

"We'll take refuge at Saint Patrick's once we arrive," Michael said. They rode side by side at a lope, with both of them able to keep an eye out for holes in the ground or any threat that might present itself in the black of night. "Father Smyth will welcome us no matter the hour. It was the first Catholic church in Indian Territory and remains the heart of the faith for the area."

"You'll be welcomed even though you are no longer wearing the affiliation and collar?" Trusty said.

Michael's skin was pale white, and his face easy enough to be seen from where Trusty sat atop Horse. The man flicked a smile. "I am a strayed sheep now. A challenge to the father. You and I are not so different in that way, are we?"

"I guess we're not."

"We will be welcome, but only if we lay low and don't cause any trouble."

Trusty shook his head. "No whiskey or women for me. Not until this is over. And maybe not then."

"That's a disappointment."

"You sound like the judge."

"I'll take that as a compliment," Michael said, then urged his gray mare forward, leaving Trusty a few strides behind to consider what lay ahead, and what he had left behind.

### Atoka, Indian Territory, May 1888

By the time Trusty and Michael reached Atoka all of the proper businesses had shut down for the day. Every building on the main street was dark, shades pulled, with CLOSED signs turned out for the world to see. There wasn't a saloon to be seen, lit up with piano keys tinkling into the night air—those types of establishments didn't exist in Indian Territory. The town was silent as midnight even though it was hours earlier.

"I should check in with the Union Agency," Trusty said. "And let them know I'm in town."

"You think that's a wise idea?" Michael stopped his gray mare and Trusty followed suit.

"The Agency and the marshals have an agreement of assistance. It's the right thing to do to seek out the Indian police."

"And if they are also aware of the price on your head?"

"You don't trust the Choctaw or the Agency?"

"I'm just wondering why you should. You don't know who wants you dead, or why. Not that you've mentioned it to me. If I were you, I wouldn't be too trusting of anyone right now."

Trusty shot Michael a surprised look and said, "You included?"

"That goes without saying. I wouldn't trust anyone named Darby if I were you. But here I am."

"I've been thinking about that, about who's after me," Trusty said. "It could be anybody that I've sent to jail. Maybe even a family member. That's all I can think of. I don't go out and wrong folks without any regard."

"You don't seem the bullying type to me."

"I guess I should be happy about that."

"A thousand dollars in silver is a hefty price. That rules out a lot of men."

"I suppose it does. I'll think on it some more, but until then, I'm going to let the Agency know I'm in town."

The Union Agency had been created in 1874 after individual agents for the Five Civilized Tribes had been eliminated. Trusty, and the rest of the marshal service, worked with the Agency from time to time expelling intruders, settling land disputes, and helping out with crimes committed in the nations when they were asked. But Trusty had no relationship with the Agency or its members in Atoka.

"The hour is late," Michael said. "Wouldn't it be best if you waited until morning?"

Trusty looked up and down Atoka's dark and deserted main street again. Nothing moved. Not even a rat. He wondered for a moment if there was anyone alive in the town at all. But he knew better. There was enough fresh horseshit in the street to confirm the day held some movement and traffic for one reason or another. "All right, it's late. I can wait until tomorrow."

Michael nodded, then urged his gray mare to move ahead.

Trusty followed along, keeping his eyes and ears open along the way. He had no idea where they were going but didn't expect the church to be too far once they crossed the railroad tracks that belonged to the M-K-T Railway. The Missouri-Kansas-Texas Railway had put the small town on the map, bringing with it the headquarters for the Choctaw and Chickasaw tribal grounds.

The town remained eerily quiet. Not even a dog barked. A cool breeze, gentle in its touch and intent, pushed down from the north, and the clouds remained overhead, prohibiting any light of any kind, star or moon, to fall to the earth. Michael was almost impossible to see, dressed in all black and riding his gray horse. He looked like a shadow moving ahead of Trusty instead of riding beside him.

As they turned a corner, Trusty laid eyes on a white clapboard church with a tall bell tower jutting into the darkness. The glow of a lamp burned behind a stained-glass window; shimmering blues, reds, greens, and whites, all combining into a scene that depicted lambs on a hillside.

Michael rode up to the church, reined in his mare, and dismounted. Trusty pulled up alongside him but hesitated before he moved off the saddle. A shiver ran up his back, curled around his neck, then exited the top of his hat-covered head. He had no fear of hallowed ground, but he had no pull to it either. The law and the natural order of right and wrong had always been enough for him. Especially after his time in the army, and even now, most recently with the killing of Judge Hadesworth. It was hard for him to believe that a man like the judge who had lived a righteous and productive life deserved to die at the hand of an angry woman seeking revenge. Where was the redemption or the salvation in that?

# Chapter 13

*Paris, Texas, May 1888*

Vance Calhoun stared out over the emerald-green paddock, leaning forward on the cross-cut fence, watching the rising sun lay golden fingers on his land. No matter the direction he turned, he owned everything he saw. The grass, the trees, the mountains, and in the distance, the herd of mooing cows that worried over their young; only the sun belonged to someone else. The ranch had been full of promise, everything he had ever wanted, until he had it, and then it wasn't enough. Then he wanted more. A bigger house. More gold. A beautiful wife. Ownership in her family's railroad. Even a child or two, an heir to pass his riches on to after he was worn out and had left this world once and for all. His ambition to make a name for himself, to see men cower to his presence when he walked into a room, could never be satisfied. He never dreamed someone would come along, burn down his house, and kill the only surviving family member he had. He could hardly believe that Sally was dead. He rubbed his pocket where he kept his sister's handkerchief as a keepsake. It was all that was left of her. It seemed like his whole life had been burned to the ground in the blink of an eye.

When Calhoun turned and saw the reality of what was left of his dream and hard work, that it was nothing more than a pile of ashes and three fresh graves, he could see nothing but gray ashes strewn like a tornado had tossed them about—touched with the same golden sunlight that made the paddock glow green.

Calhoun's head screamed with pain so badly that it felt like he was being hit in the head with a hammer. He had never been so mad, but even with that, he knew that striking out, moving quickly, was the worst thing he could do. He kept his boots firmly planted on the ground even though that was not his nature, his inclination. He wanted to finish the fight that Theodore Marberry had started.

"Mornin', boss," Gladdy said as he walked up next to Calhoun. The Mick propped his elbows on the fence and looked out at the land with the same look of ownership that Calhoun had on his ash-smudged face.

Calhoun hadn't heard Gladdy come up behind him. He didn't have time to prepare himself for his least-favorite O'Connor. "What do you want?" He was as startled as he was annoyed by Gladdy's appearance.

A slight breeze pushed across the paddock, depositing the acrid smell of ash and burned timbers on Calhoun's upper lip. He licked it off, tasted defeat and death one more time. It didn't improve his state of mind at all.

"The boys want to know what to do," Gladdy said.

"Cows don't care what happened here. You go tell Hobbs he's the lead man now and get back to work. This is just another day on the ranch, you hear?"

"Yeah, boss, I hear you. I'll tell Hobbs. But what about me? I don't know what to do without Haden tellin' me what to do neither. He's always done that. I woke up this mornin' and he wasn't there to wake me up, to rustle me out of bed, and tell me to cook his breakfast. I had to put the coffee on without bein' told. There's half of it left 'cause I made some for him. You want some coffee, boss?"

Calhoun clenched his fist and fought off the urge to backhand Gladdy O'Connor. He'd had his own unsettled morning, waking up in the barn instead of his own bed. Maria had been wrapped up in a blanket, whimpering, hugging herself to hold in her grief, in the next stall. Sally wasn't there to snap Maria out of it, to put her boots on the floor, and get things moving in the house. The house didn't exist anymore and neither did Sally. Another lick of the lips reminded Calhoun of what had been taken from him. Things he could see and things he couldn't imagine being gone. He didn't know what all had been taken from him yet.

"No, I don't want any goddamned coffee," Calhoun said. "I want to be left alone. I need to think things through, build a plan, and try to anticipate Theodore Marberry's next move. Surely there will be something else comin'. He'll know that I've survived the attack on the road, and that I wasn't in the house when it was burned to the ground. He meant to kill me. To keep the ownership of the railroad to himself. To raise Jessica's girl without the threat of me comin' after her. He meant to kill me is what he meant to do. Marberry started a war. I just have to figure out what to do next so I can win that war."

Gladdy stood back and wiped his chin with his right

hand, leaving a streak of black ash across his smooth face. "Well, why don't you burn down his house and show him how it feels?"

Three recently closed graves sat in a small cemetery overlooking the Red River. The spot was on a rise free of floods in the spring, dotted with enough cottonwoods, oak, and hickory trees to provide a shady, peaceful resting place for the dead. Squirrels were plentiful, and the outskirts of the family plot had provided dinner to the ranch more than once. The cemetery had been there when Calhoun had taken ownership of the land, and it seemed as decent a place as any to bury Sally, Haden O'Connor, and Miguel.

The day was early and light, and both Calhoun and Gladdy sat on their horses—Calhoun on his grullo and Gladdy on Haden's mount, a tall black gelding called Ben. The black horse looked oversized with Gladdy atop it, skinny and short as he was, but the rider didn't seem intimidated by the horse or the fierceness it bore in his eyes. Both men were ready to ride, saddlebags packed, black dusters on even though the weather didn't call for them. Their weapons were polished and loaded with enough ammunition to shoot through any kind of trouble that showed itself. All they were waiting on was the preacher to finish up his duties, say his peace, offer whatever grace he could, and talk the deceased through St. Peter's gate if that was possible.

The preacher, a man named Abel Fielding who Calhoun did not know but Denton Hobbs did, was a Methodist man from Paris, Texas, who had offered his services. Fielding had a booming bass voice and wore shoulders that looked broad enough to carry a barrel of beer. Calhoun had never set foot in the man's church but offered him twenty dollars to say the necessary final words needed.

Maria, dressed in black weeds with a veil to cover her face, clutched a rosary of old beads and knelt at the foot of Miguel's grave, not objecting to the sermon or the difference in religion from hers to the Methodist preacher's. A few of the men, including Hobbs, had come from the ranch for the funerals, while the rest continued to work the cattle. There was no one else. No society of women from Paris. No men of equal to Calhoun, because there weren't any—at least in his eyes—or town officials come to offer their condolences and be a party of mourners. If Calhoun had friends or family other than Sally, they either hadn't been notified of the tragedy or had been made enemies like everyone else left in Calhoun's wake.

"Ashes to ashes, dust to dust . . ." Abel Fielding said, his words disappearing on the breeze. He looked more like a hunchbacked undertaker than a preacher. A cap of thin snow-white hair topped his bare head, and a drift of flakes of dried skin sat on his shoulders.

A cardinal sang in a tree branch high above the funeral, the red bird's song happy and boastful, contradicting the human mood underneath it. The day belonged to the bird and he was letting everyone know it.

The grullo danced back and forth, anxious to make a run on the trail that led away from the cemetery. Calhoun let the horse do what it wanted to within reason, holding the reins lightly in his hands. He was just as anxious to get on with the ride as his horse was.

Gladdy sat solemn in his saddle, his hat held to his chest and his back straight as an arrow, his eyes glazed with wetness that took a twist of his chin and some effort to fight away tears. "I guess I'm really all alone now," he said under his breath, staring at Haden's grave.

"You've always been alone." Calhoun urged the grullo to stop fidgeting. He was head to head with Gladdy's horse. They looked like they were about to start a race. "We're all alone from the day we're born till the day we die."

"What about afterwards?"

"Dead is dead."

"I hope you're wrong."

Calhoun turned his head to Gladdy with a quick snap, like he'd been punched unawares. It was a reaction to being countered, to being questioned, especially from a man like Gladdy O'Connor, slight and stupid as he was in Calhoun's eyes. Under normal circumstances, Calhoun would have taken Gladdy off his horse and beat him until he begged for forgiveness. But this day required restraint not only because of where he was—on hallowed ground of sorts—but in a small crowd of people who probably would have interfered. Even Calhoun had some respect for the dead and the natural order of things, funerals and such, but he was beyond antsy. He had waited long enough to get on with his plan for revenge.

"That is all," Fielding said. "You are all free to leave and live your life with the blessings you have."

Calhoun rolled his eyes, and thought, *Finally*.

The preacher walked over to Calhoun's horse, stopped at the grullo's side, and looked up. "Thank you for sending word for me, Mister Calhoun. I appreciate your generous patronage of my church."

Calhoun sat in the saddle unmoved and stared down at the preacher, trying to figure out what the man had just said. It took him a second longer to realize that what Fielding really wanted was payment for his services. The man of God was a businessman just like any other that Calhoun had encountered. In the end, all that concerned Fielding was the jingle of coins in his pocket. A smile came to Calhoun's face at the realization. He dug into his pocket then and paid the preacher what he had been promised. He hadn't expected to find a kinship with the Methodist.

Fielding took the money, tucked it inside his coat, and said, "I'm sorry for the loss of your sister, Mister Calhoun. If there is anything else that I can do for you, don't hesitate to stop by the church and ask."

Calhoun nodded. "I'll keep that in mind. I never know when I'll need a favor from a man like you."

It was Fielding's turn to look a little stunned, like he didn't understand what had been said. He shook his head and walked off toward his horse and buggy.

Hobbs walked over to the grullo, taking the preacher's place. "I suppose you're off now, boss," he said.

"We are. You need to get a crew to clean up the remains of the house while I'm away."

"What'll I pay them with?"

"The banker in Paris has been given instructions that you are in charge. He will keep track of every bit of what's withdrawn from my account and you will have to answer for all that you take. You understand what I'm sayin', Hobbs?"

"Yes, boss, I think I do."

Calhoun nodded, then looked over to Maria who was still crumpled at the foot of Miguel's grave. "Take Maria back with you. Put her to work as soon as you can. She needs something to do. It's the only way she'll stop that incessant sniffling."

Hobbs didn't answer straightaway. A concerned, conflicted look fell across his face. He started to say something but obviously thought better of it and nodded instead.

"I'm hopin' to be back in a week, Hobbs," Calhoun said. "I don't want to see sight of a piece of charred wood on my return." Calhoun squared his shoulders and didn't wait for an answer. He pulled in the grullo's reins, nickered, punched the horse in the side with his boot heels, and headed away from the cemetery as fast as he could.

It took Gladdy a long second to realize what was happening. He looked to Hobbs, shrugged his shoulders, then took off after Calhoun and doing his best to catch up, settling himself into Haden's saddle, which from the looks of things was a little too big for him.


The best way to get to St. Louis from Paris, Texas, was north through Indian Territory, then all the way east from one corner of Missouri to the other. By horse, it would be a long, treacherous ride. One that would require Calhoun and Gladdy to be on a constant lookout for Marberry's men and other trouble that showed itself in Indian Territory. The alternative to the trail ride, and all that came with it, was to take the trip by train. The only problem with that was Marberry again. The St. Louis businessman still maintained a portion of the Frisco line from Paris to Fort Gibson—it was likely Marberry would have eyes out for Calhoun in Paris and on the railroad. Up the line? Maybe not so much. That was the plan. Ride north and catch the train in one of the small stops, in a town like Kosoma. No one knew who he was there.

Kosoma was about fifty-five miles north of Paris, and with good weather and some luck, Calhoun figured they could get there by nightfall. His plan was to stable the horses, spend the night in a decent hotel, then catch the train the next day and head north. He expected to be in St. Louis a few days beyond the trip to Kosoma. That was if he and Gladdy could travel undetected by Marberry's men along the way. Calhoun was prepared for trouble at every stretch, but for once, he hoped for a quiet ride to his destination. All hell could wait to break loose until then.

Gladdy kept a couple of lengths of distance between his horse and Calhoun's horse, and that was just fine with Calhoun. He was in no mood for conversation of any kind with the younger O'Connor. Any word from Gladdy would only bring home the truth of Haden's demise. Calhoun still couldn't believe that Haden was dead. Or Sally for that matter. Both had been trusted companions in one way or the other. Now he had no one to rely on.

The silence of the ride and the wind rushing at Calhoun's face appealed to his glum mood. No matter that the ride north was for revenge; it was what the revenge was for that rubbed Calhoun's craw. It was one thing to try and kill him. More men besides Marberry had tried that and failed before. But to burn down his house and kill his sister and his lead man, well, that was something else. That act required retribution. To his surprise, Gladdy's suggestion of burning down Marberry's house hadn't been a bad one. It wasn't the end though. It was only the start. In Calhoun's mind, the only way to satisfy the feud was to kill Marberry himself, as slowly and painfully as possible. He knew that wasn't going to be an easy thing to do. Every mile that was ticked off gave Calhoun the opportunity to consider ways to make sure that Marberry suffered painfully and slowly before he died.

Night had already arrived by the time that Calhoun and Gladdy rode into Kosoma. Most of the businesses had gone dark, and the boardwalks were clear of people. All that mattered to Calhoun was finding a decent stable, then a soft bed to fall into. He hadn't had a bath or a good night's sleep in days.

"Boy howdy, boss, it sure does stink here, don't it?" Gladdy said. "Smells like rotten eggs. You think it's like this all of the time? I don't know how people live here. I know I sure wouldn't want to."

Calhoun shot Gladdy a look that clearly said *shut up*, but he didn't say it. He had been through Kosoma a few times but had never stayed there for a length of time. He knew the smell, and didn't like it, either, but that didn't matter to him. It was a stop along the way. Calhoun remained silent, and surprisingly, Gladdy took the hint and didn't pursue the conversation any further.

The two men rode silently down the middle of the main street in Kosoma at an easy pace. Calhoun watched the shadows, looked to the rooftops for a sight of a rifle barrel or a man on watch. He was relieved not to see anything out of the ordinary.

The livery was easy enough to find, and after rousing the stable boy, Calhoun and Gladdy dismounted their horses. Both men tried to get their bearings.

The boy carted off the horses, and an older man appeared out of nowhere to settle on terms. He was older than Calhoun, with gray frizzled hair and had whiskey breath that smelled more fresh than foul. "I'm Amos Parker. I run this establishment," the man said, extending his hand to Calhoun. "How long you in town for?"

Calhoun shook Parker's hand quickly. Gladdy stood shoulder to shoulder with him, quiet, his hands stuffed in his pockets and his mouth sealed shut, fully aware of his place.

"We're leaving tomorrow by train. I'll need to board these two horses for a week, maybe more. It depends on how long my business takes me."

"And what kind of business would that be?"

"Personal business."

"I see," Parker said. "I can make you a fair deal." He hesitated and looked past Calhoun into an empty stall. "You're lucky you got here when you did. Any earlier, there wouldn't have been room for you anywhere in town."

"Why's that?" Calhoun asked.

"There was a hangin' in town. Three Darby brothers met their much-deserved fate, God rest their souls. Folks came from all over to see that through. Hangin's is good for business, I can tell you that. I've been celebratin' my good fortune a little more than I should have." Parker's words were a little slurred, and he smiled.

Calhoun was starting to get impatient. He wanted a meal, a bath, and a good night's sleep. He wasn't in the mood to have a conversation with a half-drunk stable man. He started to ask how much boarding the horses was going to cost him, but Parker didn't seem interested in concluding the business deal. He kept on talking.

"And then there was that bad trouble up on Lost Mountain," Parker said.

The word *trouble* got Calhoun's attention. He had to wonder if it had something to do with Marberry's men. If so, that would change his plans. "Trouble?" He tapped his pocket, felt for Sally's handkerchief. It was still there.

Parker leaned into Calhoun, was about six inches from him. Good thing the man was shorter than he was, or his breath would have been intolerable. "Bad trouble. The Tenth Cavalry rode through."

"Buffalo Soldiers. The army?"

Gladdy stood still next to Calhoun, silent but intrigued, just like his boss.

Parker nodded. "Yes, sir. That's what happens when a federal judge gets killed. In comes the army to clean things up."

Calhoun had been immersed in his own troubles and hadn't heard a word about a judge being killed. In normal times, he was sure he would have been made aware of such a thing. That was big news and would spread fast. "How'd that happen?"

"It was Judge Hadesworth. He presided over the trial of the Darbys. Word is it was retribution for the hangin'. Not unexpected, and we was all surprised that there was only one deputy marshal to escort the judge back to Muskogee, even if it was Trusty Dawson."

Calhoun's mouth went dry. "Dawson? Sam Dawson?"

"Yup. Most folks call him Trusty though."

"What about him? Is he dead or alive?" Calhoun said, rummaging through his memory back to the moment that Sally had told him that she had found letters from a man named Sam Dawson in Jessica's things. This was the same man he had heard of, womanizer, good shot, a reliable deputy. But maybe not so much anymore.

"Last I heard," Parker said, "Trusty's still alive. Wounded, but on the trail of the person who killed Judge Hadesworth. That's all I know. Like I said, big trouble. The judge's body is at the undertaker's now and will be transported back to Muskogee on tomorrow's train. You might have a problem gettin' a seat north, now that I think about it."

"Well, that's all right," Calhoun said. "I think our plans just changed."

# Chapter 14

Trusty and Michael arrived at St. Patrick's well past dark. The sky was black as coal and all the lamps in town were extinguished. If Trusty were a hard-drinking man, he would have found himself a bootlegger, but he was on a mission not a pleasure trip. He shied away from bootleggers, who were usually able to easily outwit the Indian police but not the marshals. Deputy U.S. Marshals like Trusty were paid a fee per arrest, and it was easier to arrest a drunk Indian than it was a white bootlegger. Trusty preferred escort duties over alcohol arrests—at least until now. Most towns like Atoka were usually quiet after dark.

The front door to the church was unlocked and a candle burned in the window. Instead of walking inside, Michael knocked loudly, banging a patinaed brass knocker with a rare display of urgency. The bang echoed up and down the empty street. Both men had tied their horses to a hitching post and were the only rides in sight. Horse and Michael's gray mare seemed to tolerate each other.

Both beasts were good natured, which had made the trip to Atoka easier than it might have been.

Trusty stood back, weakened by the ride from Lost Mountain Pass to Atoka. His entire body ached, and pain pulsed at the site of the bullet wound. He couldn't forget what Amelia Darby had done to him—or the judge—if he wanted to. "Maybe there's no one here," he said, clutching his shoulder. He felt paled, hungry, like his body would shatter into pieces if he took another step. Even breathing hurt.

Michael turned away from the door. "Father Smyth is here. He is always here. Are you going to be all right?"

"All right as I can be. Don't worry about me."

"You should have gone back to Muskogee with the Tenth and put yourself in the care of a doctor. I'm capable of bringing in Amelia on my own."

"It's my job."

"I'll remember to say that you were dutiful at your funeral."

"I would appreciate that, but I'm determined to bring in your sister."

"You're in no shape to travel. You need to rest and regain your strength."

"I appreciate your concern, but I'll be ready to continue on in the morning." Trusty coughed and an avalanche of pain cascaded from his shoulder to his toes.

Michael nodded and sighed, was about to knock again, when the door opened. A tall, thin bald man with a chest-deep frazzled gray beard stood hunched in the doorway. Dim light wrapped around him, making his black cassock look even blacker than it was. The man's eyes were hard and gray as granite, tinged with a little annoyance. He looked to be in his mid-seventies, maybe older. "The hour is past respectable." If his voice had been any sterner it would have broken into an angry yell. Even the horses looked up, paid attention to the man. Trusty didn't want to get on his bad side.

"Hello, Father Smyth," Michael said as calmly as he could. There had never been any sweetness in Michael Darby's voice, just the opposite; his tone was hard and direct. But in this instance, his voice was smooth, a combination of butter and honey. Even Michael's face looked different to Trusty. His jaw had softened and his eyes twinkled, though that could have been caused by the flickering candlelight.

"Is that you, Michael Darby?" Father Smyth said.

"'Tis."

"I heard you walked away from your calling. I didn't expect to see you again anytime soon."

Trusty remained quiet, fighting off pain, thirst, and the hunger he felt.

"News travels fast," Michael said.

"You know it does." Father Smyth eyed Michael as if he were seeing him for the first time, head to toe, from the top of his cowboy hat to the soles of his shiny new boots. "I wouldn't have recognized you if I saw you walking down the street." His eyes stopped on Michael's gun belt. Father Smyth shook his head, then looked to Trusty. The air was thick with disapproval. "And who is this man?"

"Sam Dawson," Trusty said, hoping to lose the nickname now that he had failed to live up to it. "I'm a Deputy U.S. Marshal in pursuit of a woman who killed Judge Gordon Hadesworth."

"My sister," Michael said.

"We've always worried about the state of your soul, Michael, and that of your family. I assume your sister's crime is what prompted your departure from our brotherhood and caused you to pick up a gun?" Father Smyth said.

"I tried to stop her, but I was too late," Michael said. "Words wouldn't have convinced her."

"I heard of the judge's demise. A sad day for the Territory. I have lit a candle for him." Father Smyth looked past Michael again and made direct eye contact with Trusty. "Nice to meet you, Deputy. Aren't you the one called Trusty?"

Trusty's shoulders sagged and he lowered his head. "I am."

"I see," Father Smyth said. "Well, I assume that you both are in need of lodgings. I can't imagine that either of you have come to pray at this hour."

"Yes, Father," Michael said. "I was hoping we could rest here for the night. Trusty was injured in the melee and needs to regain his strength before we move on."

The elder priest stiffened and took hold of the door handle. "You are welcome to the barn. The both of you. I'm sorry to say that you've lost any privileges, Michael, since giving up the collar. We do not welcome weapons of any kind in our house. Please be mindful of where you are. Have a good evening." And with that, Father Smyth closed the door to St. Patrick's. It wasn't a slam, but there was a finality to the close that suggested neither man knock again and argue with the decision that the old priest had made.

"Sorry," Michael said, "I had counted on a kinder

reception, but I should have known better. Come on, we can be comfortable in the barn. It's not the first time I've slept there." He walked past Trusty, untied his mare, Spirit, and headed toward the barn.

Trusty had little choice but to follow Michael. He didn't like that fact, but it was where he was. Dependent on a Darby for a roof over his head and food in his belly. There was no way that he couldn't wonder if he would wake up alive in the morning.

### St. Louis, Missouri, fall 1874

Eight years had passed since Sam's mother had died. Somedays the moment she died felt like yesterday to him, and then other days, it felt like she had been gone for a hundred years. Not much had changed in the mean-time. Sam and his father still lived in the shack behind the blacksmith shop, spending day after day in hot toil over the forge and quench, bending iron and seeing to every customer's needs. The work lasted from sunup to well past sundown. There was always a demand for a blacksmith in St. Louis. At least, when Sam wasn't in school. That was about to end. He was going to graduate from eighth grade, and his father had already made it clear to Sam that a further education wasn't required. He was needed full-time in the shop. Business was increas-ing and Markum Dawson had no intention of hiring a man that needed to be paid.

Sam liked school. It was time spent away from his father and the shop. And he was good at it. Numbers came easier to him than letters, but he was a capable reader when it was required of him. He could memorize poetry and sonnets, and his marks were always good. His teachers encouraged him to work harder, to think about continuing his education, going to college someday, but Sam knew that would never happen. There was no use trying. He did what he had to to survive in school so he wouldn't get sent home. His father believed that the blacksmith shop offered the only education Sam would ever need. There was no arguing the point. His father's mind was made of will forged from iron and money. Markum Dawson couldn't be broken. Sam knew that. He had tried and paid the price for the attempt.

It was on a cool fall day, toward the end of school and after passing a final test, that Sam found himself in the midst of standing up for what he really wanted. As he walked home from school, he was working up the courage to tell his father that he wanted to go on to high school, that he wanted to continue his learning. He hurried home, noting the familiar smell of smoke chugging out of the smithy chimney as he rounded the corner, not paying too much attention to anything else, just focused on getting home. Sweat beaded on the back of Sam's neck, and the tips of his fingers trembled as he rehearsed the speech to his father over and over in his head. *I want to go on to the ninth grade, Pa. Mrs. Abernathy says I'm smart, that I can handle it, go on to college if I apply myself. I want to do this, Pa.*

The shop was in a busy part of town, next to the livery and a few hotels. The train station was two blocks away. There was always a need for his father's services from one source or another, especially in the garage that housed locomotives in need of repair that sat adjacent to the station. Markum had picked an opportunistic location for his business and had benefited from the decision greatly. But there was starting to be talk from the city politicians of building a grander, more fitting train station for the gateway to the West several miles north. That would change some things for the shop if it happened. It was just talk. The first brick had yet to be laid. But there was an extra layer of worry in Markum Dawson's smoke-stained furrowed brows.

Sam hurried to the shop, sweating, reciting his silent speech as he followed the smoke, knowing full well that his father had some chores for him to do once he arrived. He planned on being more agreeable about the chores and talking to his father over dinner about further schooling. But he stopped short of running into the shop. A fancy Rogers & Co. carriage, shiny with black lacquer paint that reflected the overhead sun like a mirror, was parked in front of his father's business. That was not so unusual. Carriages, wagons, and carts of all kinds came and went every day. Most of them had problems with their axles if they were made of iron. But on this day, there was a girl close to Sam's age, standing outside of the carriage and looking to the sky, with the late afternoon light bathing her completely in a golden hue that lit up her hair like it was straw set afire. She wore a long dress without the bustle that a lot of older, high-class women were wearing; it was made of a light blue material and matched her curious eyes.

Sam approached the girl slowly. His speech to his father was lost, replaced by a dry tongue and an urge to know who this beautiful girl was. He had never seen her before.

The girl was smiling at nothing that Sam could tell. He stopped when he got across from her and looked up to the sky to see what she was fascinated with. That, and to be close to her, to say hello if he could get his tongue untwisted in his mouth. The girl was pretty. Prettier than any girl he had ever seen before. At least that's how he felt at that moment.

"Hello," the girl said, dropping her gaze to Sam with the same smile that she had been looking at the sky with. "Did you see the chimney swifts?"

Sam followed the girl's gaze to the sky, then looked into her eyes for the first time. Spring went on forever inside them. They were a deep pond he could fall into, that he wanted to fall into. "No," he answered. He had no idea what a chimney swift was.

"My mother is from England and they have swifts there. She says they sleep while they are flying. Can you imagine such a thing, sleeping on air instead of a feather bed?"

"I can't imagine flying. I'd be scared I would fall to the ground and die." To his surprise, Sam found the words easy to say.

"I hadn't thought about that." There was no judgment in the girl's voice and no pretense in her stance. If she thought she was better than him, richer, more worthy, she didn't let on. The girl laughed, then jutted her finger up into the air, pointing at a bird that chirped as it flew by. It looked like it was flying on one small wing instead of two. Both wings flapped so hard that it was hard to tell that the bird was really flying. "There," she said, "that's a swift."

"It's awfully small," Sam said. "How can it sleep while it flies?"

"I think it glides, but I'm not sure that the swifts here

can do what they can in England. Mother makes her home country seem so magical that I never know whether to believe everything she says about it or not. Have you ever been to England?"

"No," Sam answered, "I've never been anywhere."

"Me either. I hope to go there someday. Then to Paris, and all around the world. Wouldn't that be grand to see how other people live? Hear different languages? Taste foods that you've never tasted before?"

Sam's father was good at cooking beans. Meat for dinner was a rarity. Someone had to trade a leg of beef for an axle repair for that to happen. A trip to the butcher's didn't occur at Christmas. Nothing happened at Christmas. It was another working day in Sam's house. "I suppose that would be nice," he said. "I'll probably spend the rest of my life here."

"That's sad."

"I don't think so," Sam said. "I think that's just how life is for some people." The world around him had disappeared. There was no traffic on the street in front of the shop that took his attention away, or any clangs and bangs from inside. The sun continued to beat down from the sky like one bright light focused solely on the girl. He believed she would see the world beyond St. Louis. She had the kind of eyes that agreed with her words; she meant what she said. "What's your name?' he asked, being bolder than normal, not concerned about the difference in class. It was obvious that the girl came from wealth. She was proper in a way that only wealthy people could be. Training from an early age was apparent, but the girl seemed unaware of it. At least at the moment.

"Jessica," she said. "My name is Jessica Marberry."

*Atoka, Indian Territory, May 1888*

The night was filled with fits and starts of sleep for Trusty. He had found it more difficult than usual to get comfortable on a bed made of straw. This wasn't the first time he had slept in a barn, but it was the first time he had been shot, wounded, and put to the ground to rest. His luck had finally run out. There had been no dodging Amelia Darby's bullet, though he would have gladly taken two, especially the one that had found its way to the judge's body. He kept seeing the sight in his mind over and over again. Blood splattering in the light of the fire. Certain death coming to the judge. The thump, then silence, then another shot with lead burning through his own skin and muscles. If Amelia's aim would have been a little better, he'd be dead, too, instead of weakened and in the care of another Darby. A Darby that there had been no sight of when the shooting had started. Michael Darby had been there when Trusty awoke—after the smoke had cleared. He had to take the man's word that he'd come to stop Amelia. There was no more proof of that than there was that Amelia had fled, disappearing into No Man's Land if Michael was to be believed.

Trusty's ear had been cocked toward Michael most all night, snoring peacefully in the stall next to him, waiting for the man to stir in the middle of the night and betray him. Run off, leave him, or worse, finish what his sister had started. He didn't trust Michael Darby and had fully expected him to shoot him in the head sometime during the night, but that obviously didn't happen. He awoke in the morning as alive as he was when he'd taken to the straw bed the night before.

Michael was standing at the gate of the stall, dressed in the same clothes he'd worn the day before, drinking a mug of coffee and smoking a cigarillo. The gun belt hung comfortably on his hip. Dressed all in black like he was, Michael Darby looked more like a hired gunfighter than an ex-priest. "I wondered if you were going to sleep until noon," he said.

"I don't feel like I slept at all," Trusty said, sitting up and wiping bits of straw from his own shirt. Pain still thundered through his upper torso, especially at the wound, but it was a little less intense than it had been the day before.

Michael set down his mug of coffee, disappeared for a second, then returned with another mug and offered it to Trusty. "Father sent the cook out with a pot of coffee and some warm bacon."

"That was kind of him," Trusty said, taking the mug. He stayed seated and took a sip.

Michael stood back and smirked. The smoke from the cigarillo in his other hand twirled upward and caught a drift of air pushing through the barn. "He also told the cook to tell us that we needed to move on. He didn't want any trouble. We're not welcome to stay any longer."

Trusty struggled to stand up, but finally did so by pulling himself up on a slat of the stall. "Suits me. I'd rather ride than stay where I'm not welcome."

"You don't look like you're in any shape to put any miles behind you."

"Doesn't matter. I'll stop off at the Union Agency and send a wire to Marshal Grimes and let him know where I'm heading. I'd like to know where I stand, and where the Guardsmen are at."

"That's a formidable crew."

"You know of them?"

"Who doesn't? Their names are as well known as yours in the Territory. I was a priest, not a prisoner locked away in a prison cell. I heard tell of crimes, captures, and shootings like that of Bill Doolin's just like any other normal man."

"I'm sorry," Trusty said, "I've not spent a lot of time around papists like yourself. I'm ignorant of your daily life."

Michael had grabbed up his own mug and took a drink of the coffee. "Amelia's gone and done it this time. There's no saving her if the Guardsmen pick up her trail."

"Is that your intention? To save her?"

"It is my training to save everyone, Trusty, but I have learned the hard way that some people can't be saved and must face whatever they bring on themselves on their own."

# Chapter 15

Vance Calhoun stood at the registration desk of the Hobart House Hotel anxious as a two-year-old filly ready to start a race. His jaw hurt from clenching his teeth so hard. He tapped his fingers on the mahogany counter in an annoying unison. The call bell rattled from the vibration, and in it he kept hearing the words *Sam Dawson* bounce around inside of his head. The two had nearly crossed paths. Calhoun had only been a couple of days too late. The only problem was that he didn't know that he'd had anything in common with the Deputy U.S. Marshal before then. Or more frankly in his mind, that Jessica had known the man, cared about him enough to stow his letters to her in a secret place. Sadly, those had burned too. Any hard evidence that Jessica Marberry Tennyton and Sam Dawson had had a relationship of any kind had been destroyed. Unless he could find Dawson and learn the truth of what he knew. Tap, tap, tap. *Was the baby girl really his, or was Trusty Dawson the father?* A man had to wonder; all things considered. The baby girl had value to him either way.

Gladdy stood off to the side of Calhoun, unsure of what to do with his hands. He kept shifting his weight back and forth, but kept quiet, seemed to know his place. The décor and the hotel looked like it overwhelmed the Mick, like he had never been in a place like it before. And that was probably true. At least as far as Calhoun knew. It had always been Haden who had traveled with him.

"There you are . . . two rooms, Mister Calhoun," the short, white-haired clerk said as he handed Calhoun two brass skeleton keys. "If we had known you were comin', we would have made the Ambassador's Suite available for you, but it is occupied until tomorrow."

Calhoun stopped tapping his fingers and took the keys from the man. "I would appreciate it if you kept my stay here to yourself. I'd rather no one know that I am in Kosoma."

"As you wish, sir. Is there anything else I can provide for you? A girl, perhaps, to help with your bath and any other aches that might need tended to?"

Calhoun leaned forward and stopped himself from saying yes. Normally when he was out of town he welcomed an adventure between the sheets with a local girl, but as things were, being in mourning for one thing or the other, having a girl underneath him was the last thing he wanted to deal with at the moment. "I can take care of myself, thank you. So can he." Calhoun motioned toward Gladdy, quelling any speculation that a girl was needed for him. "I'd be glad to have a drink after I get settled though. That sure would relieve an ache or two from the ride."

"This isn't Texas," the clerk said.

Calhoun reacted before he talked himself out of it, reached across the desk, and pulled the little man to him so they were face-to-face. "Do I look stupid to you? I know this isn't Texas. And I also know that places like this have bootleg rooms for men like me who are willin' to pay a robber's fee for a taste of Indian whiskey. Are you tellin' me that don't exist here, little man?"

"Garland Faulks. The name is Garland Faulks. Hanford Hobart is my father-in-law. He owns this hotel."

"I don't care if your father-in-law is the king of Spain, that don't give you the right to get smart with me."

"I beg your pardon. Mister Calhoun, that was not my intent. Could you let me loose, please?"

Calhoun stared into Faulks's faded blue eyes and smiled. He saw fear swimming inside the old man, and it made Calhoun feel good. The only thing that would make him feel better would be to squeeze the life out of the desk clerk. But there was no need for that. Not now. He needed to get settled and get a drink, so he pushed the little man away from him.

Garland Faulks gasped for air like a dying fish, then said, "Check in with me when you're ready and I'll make sure the door to the back room opens for you, Mister Calhoun."

"That's more like it," Calhoun said. "Come on, Gladdy. I can smell you from where I stand. The foulness of you is about to turn my stomach." Then he stalked away from the desk and headed to the hallway of rooms on the first floor.

Gladdy O'Connor followed the raging bull of a man

he called boss like he was a puppy still sucking on the teat. "I sure wish Haden was here," he said under his breath.

The whiskey burned the back of Calhoun's throat as it went down. Not the best he'd ever drank, but not the worst either. Gladdy sat across from him, hair slicked back, still wet from the bath he'd given himself, still dressed in his riding clothes, but his face and hands were free of dirt from the day. Calhoun was in the same shape. Clean of trail dust, but in a new set of clothes that hadn't dried stiff with sweat. He would have preferred to have some sweet young thing wash his back and beyond, but he knew himself well enough to know that was a bad idea. One wrong word from the girl and he would have pulled her head into the water and drowned her right then and there. Just the thought of complicating the ride any more than it already was didn't seem like it was worth the minutes of pleasure the girl would have offered him.

Night had fallen outside, but it was impossible to tell that from where Calhoun sat. There were no windows in the hidden liquor room at all. Just a door to go in and out of and a pantry that stood behind the ten-foot-long bar across the back wall. Four tables dotted the room, but Calhoun and Gladdy sat at the only one that was occupied. A lone bartender stood behind the bar. The air had the smell and taste of stale cigar smoke, mixed with the yeasty aroma of beer bubbling to life somewhere out of sight. There was no piano playing or pretty girls fluttering about like horny butterflies to add to the mood of a normal saloon. Happy drinking places like that were hard to come by in Indian Territory, which suited Calhoun just fine. He had nothing to celebrate. The weight of everything he had ridden away from and what he was riding toward had caught up with him. He was tired and warmed by the whiskey. A good night's sleep wasn't far off.

"We still headin' to Saint Louis, boss?" Gladdy said after finishing off two fingers of whiskey. His smooth face flushed red and his dim eyes glazed over, then dropped to the table. He was talking to make conversation, which seemed as awkward to him as finding someplace to put his hands when he wasn't doing something useful.

"Things have changed," Calhoun said as quiet as he could, leaning forward and eyeing the bartender, a bored square-head who had said his name was Johann. Calhoun didn't trust anyone, especially in such close quarters. The square-head was tall, blond, and had a set of ears the size of batwings.

"I suppose that's fine with me," Gladdy said. "I ain't got nowhere to go but where you tell me to now that Haden's not around to do it for me."

"It is fine, O'Connor, or you're on your own. You like that room I got you? Then you'll go where I go, and I'll take care of what you need from now on. But here and now, I need to figure out what happened in this town and how we can find the marshal who was in the middle of it."

"That Dawson fella?"

Calhoun nodded and leaned back in his chair as he watched Johann disappear into the pantry. "Yeah. We need to track him down. I got some questions for him that I need answers to in a bad way."

"I thought we was gonna burn down the man's house who kilt Haden and your sister?"

Calhoun clinched his fingers into a fist. "We are, you idiot. But in due time. Now that I think about it, tracking down Dawson plays better to that plan. The longer we take showin' up in Saint Louis, the more slack Marberry's men will take in the rope they put my name on. He might underestimate me and think that I'm not going to retaliate. They'll all relax day after day, get on with their lives, and that's when we swoop in for revenge. Once I know whether to save that baby or not."

"Maybe Marberry thinks you're already dead," Gladdy said. "It was an easy ride here. If someone was after us, they didn't show themselves in no way."

Johann walked back into the room from the pantry. He was carrying a stack of glasses that clattered and clinked inside the small room. The bartender paid no mind to Calhoun and Gladdy.

Calhoun leaned forward toward Gladdy, only this time he had a smile on his face. "You know, that's not a bad idea now that I think of it, O'Connor. I'm gonna need you to send a wire to the newspapers in Paris and Saint Louis that says I died from injuries that I got tryin' to put out the fire and that you buried me along the trail."

"But you ain't dead, and that man at the front desk knows who you are."

The air escaped out of Calhoun's chest so loud it caught him by surprise. "You're not as stupid as I thought you were. Maybe Haden was right about you all along. He said I should bring you along on my trips so there'd be three of us instead of two. Okay, you're right. We'll have to take care of that man before we leave, but we can't be sloppy about it and get caught. From the sound of things, the law's been thick around this town lately."


Calhoun took another drink of whiskey, then sent Gladdy to his room. He was going to do this deed himself, make sure it wasn't messed up by the Mick. It felt good to have a plan, a release, something to track down. That had always been the thing about killing that he liked the most. Not the reactionary fights when his temper took over and released itself with a fist to flesh and the crack of bone, but the ones that took time to plan, to think out; killing a man slowly was like eating a good meal. This one had purpose, had reason, and there was nothing better than that.

Calhoun liked the idea that no one could know that he was still alive. Once the wire was sent and the news of his pretended death hit the newspapers, then he would have the freedom to pursue his revenge however he wanted to. The more he thought about the plan, the more he liked the idea that Gladdy had given him. Everything that had happened in the last few days, from the birth of the baby, to losing Jessica, then being outsmarted by her father, combined into something that he had not even considered that he needed: a fresh start. The ranch was a lot of work. Being a landowner didn't suit him. Freedom did. He hadn't felt so excited about life since the war.

Calhoun slid out of the bootleg room and made his way into the lobby of the Hobart House Hotel. The room was cavernous with eighteen-foot ceilings, dominated by a river stone fireplace that climbed up the wall. The windows were covered with thick red draperies, and the wood plank floor was warmed by hand-woven rugs large enough to cover the roofs of normal-sized sod houses. The furniture was covered in tanned leather, giving the room a comfortable feeling rather than a pretentious one like so many hotels that Calhoun had been in aspired to. Candles burned dimly in sconces that lined the walls, and an ornately carved grandfather clock ticked toward midnight. The desk clerk was nowhere to be seen. Even the mice in the place were quiet. It was just the way he needed it to be.

A thin glow of yellow light escaped from under a door behind the registration desk. There was no way for Calhoun to know whether the door was locked or not, but he was betting it wasn't. He unsheathed his knife, then carefully slid it up his sleeve, balancing the point in between his fingers. All he had to do was open his hand and the hilt of the knife would slide out. Firing a shot would alert everyone within earshot, awake or asleep, that something had gone wrong, that there was a threat about. Calhoun didn't want that. He hoped Garland Faulks was in the office and would be relieved by someone in the morning, putting enough space between the killing and the shine of discovery.

Calhoun eased behind the counter, making sure not to creak a floorboard and give away his presence. He stopped next to the door and gave a listen. At first all he could hear was his own heartbeat, ramped up by the prospect of killing the desk clerk and getting caught. It was a thrill that made the tops of his ears tingle with excitement. Once he got past the sounds his own body was making, Calhoun heard a soft snore and knew that Faulks was sleeping, relying on someone to ring the bell on the counter to wake him up. A smile crossed Calhoun's face, but he didn't make a move. Not yet. He was plastered up against the wall like a moth trying to blend in and disappear into tree bark. It was the lobby and what was outside it that interested him now.

The hotel was silent and so was the street outside. All of Kosoma slept under the cover of darkness, immune to the smell of the sulfur, and snuggled in safely behind their doors, just like Garland Faulks.

Vance Calhoun knew the only thing that could trip him up was a traveler coming in seeking a room for the night. Even though that seemed unlikely, it was possible. But the possibility didn't stop him. He pushed inside the office slowly, leaving the door open for a quick exit.

A small oil lamp burned on a desk at the back of the room. The desk clerk, Garland Faulks, sat in a chair with his head down, comforted in a triangle made of crossed arms. He slept peacefully, unaware that anyone had come into the room. A ledger lay open on the desk with a pencil next to it. The only available weapon that Calhoun could see for the man to defend himself with was a silver letter opener a few inches from his head.

Calhoun slowed himself down, opened his ears in search of any sounds behind him, and let the knife drop into his grip when he was about a foot behind the sleeping man. There was no turning back now. Get it over quick and get out. That was always the plan, and most of the time it worked.

In one swift motion, Calhoun grabbed the man's head and pulled it up so he was staring at the wall before him straight on. Faulks didn't have time to scream out or question what was happening; he was barely awake. Calhoun sliced the man's throat from ear to ear deep and fast, then let his head fall forward in a bubbling plea for help that couldn't form into words. To make sure no one could hear a thing, Calhoun ground the clerk's face into the desk, held it there with all of his might until the shaking, gasping, crying man went still.

Blood dripped off the knife, and the familiar smell of the life fluid hit Calhoun's nose with a welcoming lick of the lips. The killing had been the meal he had been hungering for since the moment he figured out that Marberry had called his bluff and come after him, taking the things that meant the most to Calhoun.

To make sure the deed was done, Calhoun raised the knife high above his head and drove it down with as much force as he could muster. The steel point sliced through Faulks's neck, just under the skull, not stopping until it came out the other side, through the man's throat. The blade drove two inches into the desk, echoing inside the small office like a head hitting a board. The sound stopped Calhoun. He had to listen hard over his racing heartbeat, over the thrill of the kill. All he heard was the ticking of the clock in the lobby. He smiled, pulled out the knife, wiped it on the clerk's back, sheathed it, and disappeared out the door, doing his best not to be seen or heard.

If he was lucky nobody would find the dead man until the morning. Calhoun planned on being long gone by then—and dead himself, at least to the rest of the world.

# Chapter 16

The man at the Western Union office was drinking his morning coffee when Trusty walked in the door. Soft golden light pushed through the window that fronted the main street of Atoka, making the small office glow like everything in it was gilded with gold. The smell of paper and ink hit Trusty's nose as his eyes dropped from the man to the telegraph machine on the desk before him. It still amazed Trusty that words could be sent over a wire hundreds of miles away with the punch of a few buttons. "Mornin'," he said to the operator.

The thin, young man stood up, holding on to his coffee, suddenly aware that his tie was not pulled tight or that his cap wasn't on his head where it was supposed to be. He was a Choctaw with light brown skin, looked to be in his mid-twenties, still wet behind the ears but old enough to facilitate a job as important as the one he held at the moment. "Good morning, sir. I beg your pardon for not bein' ready."

"Not a problem." Trusty stopped at the counter. A newspaper was laying on the man's desk. The headline did not surprise Trusty. It read: FEDERAL JUDGE MURDERED IN KOSOMA. KILLER STILL ON THE LOOSE. "That's bad news," he added, nodding to the paper.

"It is." The operator set his coffee mug down, wrestled his tie tight at the neck, and popped on his Western Union cap. "How can I help you?" Once he was settled, he looked Trusty up and down and let his eyes rest on the badge. There was still a smear of blood on it. Trusty hadn't bothered to wipe away the tragedy and bring a shine back to his badge.

"I need to send a wire to the U.S. Marshal, William Grimes, in Muskogee. Can you do that?"

The operator nodded, sat down, picked up a pencil, and prepared to write what it was that Trusty had to say. There was no mention of the man's name anywhere to be seen, and Trusty wasn't concerned enough to ask. He had a task to do and a horse to ride after the wire was sent.

"What's the message?" the operator asked.

"Write him that Deputy U.S. Marshal Sam Dawson is on the trail of Judge Hadesworth's killer. Stop. Was wounded as reported, but capable of riding. Will check for further orders in prescribed locations. Stop. Will not be attending the judge's funeral unless the assailant is apprehended or am ordered to. Stop. Best regards, Deputy Sam Dawson."

The operator kept on writing after Trusty stopped talking. Once he was finished, he looked up at Trusty and said, "You're Trusty Dawson."

The only answer that came to his mind was that *I used to be*, but he didn't say it out loud. He just stared at the operator. "Do you need anything else?"

"There's no charge."

"Of course." Trusty turned and started to walk to the door. The telegraph machine started tapping and at first, Trusty thought the man was sending the message, but it turned out that a message was coming in.

"You better wait to hear this, Marshal; it's a telegram for the Agency," the operator said, calling after him.

Trusty had his hand on the doorknob, ready to pull it open to leave. His mouth was dry, and the taste of sadness and failure was thick on his tongue. Pain from the wound throbbed a bit, but the pit of his stomach hurt more. He didn't want the operator to catch sight of his sad, glazed eyes. "What is it?" he said.

"Looks like there was a murder in Kosoma last night. A desk clerk at the Hobart House Hotel."

The machine kept tapping and the operator was scribbling as fast as he could, trying to keep up with the message.

Trusty headed back to the counter. "What else does it say? Did they catch the person who did it?"

The operator shook his head. "No, the killer wasn't caught. The Indian police are speculating that it was the same person who killed the judge."

"Why is that?"

The operator shrugged his shoulders. "Doesn't say. But the reward for Amelia Darby's capture has been upped to five thousand dollars."

### St. Louis, Missouri, spring 1875

It seemed like every time Sam looked up, Jessica Marberry was standing in the doorway of the shop, or waiting for him when he returned home from school. He didn't mind. His heart skipped a beat when he saw her—even from a distance. But his father had warned him there was no place for Sam in the life of a girl like Jessica Marberry. She was "out of his league," Markum Dawson had said more than once. "A man like Theodore Marberry wasn't gonna tolerate a lowlife blacksmith's son to be seen with his one and only daughter." Like everything else his father said, Sam tried not to listen. But he couldn't help but believe the words, because he felt them when Jessica was around. He knew he wasn't good enough for her.

It was no surprise then, that on a fine spring day that Sam rounded the corner to see a familiar Marberry carriage parked in front of the shop. A pair of black, shiny horses stood rigid, at military attention as if they had been transformed into onyx statues. The carriage, a two-door cabriolet, held an equal amount of gleam and polish. There didn't seem to be anything wrong with it that Sam could see. Jessica was nowhere to be seen. Nor was the driver, a thin black man called Earl Handsome, who usually eyed Sam with suspicion and acted as a quasi-chaperone or guard for Jessica.

Sam had been on an errand, sent by his father to purchase a load of wood for the declining stack. Business in the spring seemed never-ending. Wagon trains and fortune seekers had insatiable needs of iron and metalwork that his father was more than happy to provide.

When Sam walked into the shop, he had expected—hoped—to see Jessica waiting for him. But she was nowhere to be seen. The only visitor in the shop was Jessica's father, Theodore Marberry.

Theodore Marberry was cornstalk tall and dressed by the finest tailors in St. Louis. He wore gray tweed suits, perfect white starched collars, and boots that shined like the horses and carriages he rode in on. Sam could only imagine the cost of the clothes the man wore, and like he was when he was in Jessica's presence, he felt less than, dressed in working rags as he was.

The shop felt like a living being, breathing fire and exhaling smoke. Grit and dust floated through the air from one end of the wide-open room and back again until it found a place to light. Everything in sight was smudged black with soot. Cleanliness was not a consideration. There was no point—or time—for such effort. Orders were stacked up for weeks on end. Theodore Marberry looked out of place, perfectly creased and put together, standing in the middle of the shop with his jaw set hard and his eyes narrowed with a hint of anger. Sam's father stood before the man with his head down, eyes to the floor, shoulders dropped in submission.

Both men looked relieved when Sam hurried into the shop. They looked at him in unison, while Sam continued to search the room for a beam of blond sunshine.

"She is not here," Theodore Marberry said in a proper, harsh way. "And she will not be returning to this establishment for any reason, ever again." He looked to Markum with the expectation that the man would reinforce the words that were just spoken.

"And you are not to go anywhere near Miss Marberry, Samuel," his father said. "Do you understand me?"

Sam had stopped ten feet from the men. He jammed his hands into his pockets. "I didn't do anything wrong."

Markum Dawson sighed, looked at Theodore Marberry with disdain, then said, "Do as you're told, Sam, and there will be no trouble. Mister Marberry doesn't want you associating with his daughter."

Sam wanted to ask why but knew better than to disobey his father openly in front of another man. He looked down and stared at the toes of his boots, wondering what had happened. He had seen Jessica a week prior, had spent a half an hour talking to her. They didn't hold hands, and they had never kissed. Sam was aware of his place in the world, even if he'd gotten the feeling more than once that Jessica wanted him to kiss her.

"Yes, sir," Sam said, still looking at his boots.

"Look me in the eye when you say that," Marberry said.

Sam looked up and made eye contact with the wealthy man. He couldn't see a thread of Jessica's beauty in the man. The man's face was twisted in bitterness and ownership in a way that Sam didn't understand. "Yes, sir," he said again, boring through to the back of Marberry's head with his eyes.

"Good. As long as we're understood." Marberry began to walk away from Sam's father without the offer of a good-bye or a handshake. "I never want to step in this place again." And then he walked out, leaving a breeze behind him that kicked up old dust.

Sam waited until Marberry was gone before he said anything. "What did I do?"

Markum Dawson had been waiting for the man to leave too. He walked up to Sam and backhanded him with all of his strength. The blow surprised Sam. He hadn't been ready for it, even though he should have been. He tottered to the right, almost lost his balance as his hand found his cheek, trying to relieve the pain.

"You lost us a paying customer is what you did. A good one. I don't want you talking to anyone ever again. Especially no girls who come in here. Am I clear?"

"Yes, sir," Sam said, all the time wondering what mistake he had made. His face stung like acid had been thrown on it. One of these days he would defend himself, stand up to his father and fight back. But today was not that day. He was too upset about Jessica.

Two days later while walking home from school, a carriage pulled up alongside Sam as he meandered down the sidewalk, taking his sweet time.

"Hey there, boy," a familiar voice called.

It was Earl Handsome. Sam stopped and smiled slightly at the sight of the colored man. "I didn't think I would ever see you again."

"Missy sent me to find you and give you this note." Earl Handsome dug into his fancy black coat, pulled out a piece of paper, and handed it down to Sam. "Don't you tell nobody, now, you hear? Mister Marberry wouldn't like it."

Sam took the paper, looked at it like it was unexpected gold because it was, and said, "What did I do wrong?"

Earl Handsome shrugged. "Don't you worry none about that, boy. You didn't do nothin' but be kind to a lonely girl. Ain't no harm in that unless a rich man has cause to worry that kindness will lead into somethin' else. That man ain't got a nice bone in his body. You do as you're told now. I gots to go." And with that the carriage hurried off, leaving Sam to consider the paper in his hand.

He smelled it and found himself lost in a violet perfume. Spring. Beauty. A reminder of Jessica. After a time, he opened the letter. The words were simple and direct: *Meet me at the corner church, a block from my house, after dark. I'll explain everything then. Jessica.*

A smile grew on Sam's face as he stuffed the letter in his pocket and hurried home, anxious for once for the sun to drop and the moon to rise. He knew, though, from that moment on that anything that had to do with Jessica Marberry had to be a secret. He couldn't tell anybody a thing about her. Not his father. Not anyone. Jessica was his own special secret.

### Atoka, Indian Territory, May 1888

There was no need to stop in to see the Indian police before leaving Atoka. Trusty knew as much as they knew or would know. He figured the best thing to do was to get moving. It was a long ride to Enid from Atoka.

"I don't think it was her," Michael said after Trusty recounted the wire to him.

"Why's that?"

"She wouldn't have backtracked to Kosoma. That's the last place she would have gone. She hated that town."

They rode their horses, Spirit and Horse, side by side with Atoka disappearing behind them. The ground was as flat as the bottom of a frying pan, but not as hot. The morning was still cool, filled with the soft gentle sounds of happy birds celebrating a new day. Blue sky reached out for as far as Trusty could see, dotted with puffs of clouds that held no threat in them at all. It was a comfortable ride, and both horses kept a steady pace, allowing the men to talk. They had yet to break into a full run, but it was easy to see that Horse and Michael's mare were champing at the bit to break free of the tight reins that held them back.

"You can't be sure of that," Trusty said. "Amelia might have had some business to finish. Maybe the man at the hotel knew something that he shouldn't have. Seems to me that Amelia will go to any length to protect herself and pursue her plans."

"She would have taken care of that before she left town. I don't know, it doesn't feel right, like it is something she would do," Michael said.

"Regardless, a five-thousand-dollar reward will put a lot of men on her trail that weren't there before."

"That kind of money could change a man's life."

"I suppose so," Trusty said. "If a man could capture me and her in the same place, it'd be a double payday, wouldn't it?"

Michael stopped his horse and Trusty followed suit. Darkness came to the ex-priest easily, especially dressed all in black like he was, his eyes shielded from the sun by the Stetson. "There's a lot more men that know the value of my sister than they do of yours, if I understand your situation like I think I do. If you're insinuating that my aim is to collect both rewards, then you are sadly mistaken."

"I didn't say that," Trusty said. "I don't know who put a price on my head or why."

"And neither do I."

"But I want to find out. I don't like livin' like this, lookin' over my shoulder every ten seconds to see if a rider's coming up on me, or worse, settin' up on a ridge somewhere aiming to take a long shot at my head."

"The hunter becomes the hunted."

"Something like that, I suppose. I wasn't suggesting anything. Just sayin', is all, that me and Amelia have something in common."

"Only she knows why she's on the run, and where she's going."

"You're sure that she killed the judge for revenge and nothing more?"

"If there's any other reason, it hasn't revealed itself to me yet. I'll let you know if something comes to me." Michael hesitated, looked over his shoulder, making sure the way behind them was clear. "If you want to ride ahead, I'll cover your back. That might be a better plan, all things considered."

"No," Trusty said, "I don't think that matters. Let's go." He let the reins go slack, nickered, and urged Horse to a run with the press of his knees. It wasn't long before the wind pushed at his face, and the way before him seemed clearer than it had before they'd arrived in Atoka.

### *Wapanucka, Indian Territory, May 1888*

Trusty and Michael didn't stop riding until they reached the small town of Wapanucka. The name *Wapanucka* meant "Eastern Land People," and was given by the Delaware Indians who had arrived in the area before the War Between the States started, but it was populated with mostly Chickasaw and Choctaws. A massive two-story stone building sat off the main street, towering over the rest of the false-fronted buildings. It was a well-kept building that immediately looked institutional, surrounded by a wrought iron fence that caught Trusty's eye. The decorative ironwork was puddled iron like his father worked with. Whoever had put the fence together knew what they were doing.

"Presbyterian missionaries built that as a school for girls," Michael said, nodding toward the building. "But it's been a mix of boys and girls since the end of the war. Locals call it Allen's Academy after the man who built it."

Trusty was still focused on the fence, riding slow, though he did wonder how Michael knew so much about the building. It had something to do with religion, so that probably explained it.

"We rode out this way with regularity," Michael continued on, "to give sacraments to the true believers. I've always liked this part of the Territory."

Trusty nodded, then turned his attention away from the fence and the life he used to know as much as he could. He had to consider that his life might have turned out differently, better, at least at the moment, if he would have done exactly what his father had wanted him to do instead of running off and joining the army, then going on to becoming a Deputy U.S. Marshal. Life as a blacksmith would have been a simple, safe way of making a living without the threat of being shot. Instead, Trusty would have died from boredom and old age. He wasn't sure which he preferred at the moment. The pain and constant throb of the bullet wound was a reminder of his mortality, that he had missed meeting death face-to-face by only an inch or two. It was as close as he'd ever come to meeting his final end.

The late afternoon sun was starting to dip onto the horizon, emitting a warm golden light that covered everything in its path. Wapanucka looked like every other town in the Territory: quiet, a little run-down, and full of people who cast the two riders a glance of suspicion—even in light that looked soft and peaceful.

"There's a livery at the end of the road here," Michael continued, "next to what used to be the post office. Word came in that the railroad was going to be built between Haileyville and Ardmore so they moved the post office to Button Springs." Michael pulled the reins a little tighter and pulled back Spirit's head. "Looks like we're getting more attention than I thought we would."

Another group of onlookers had formed in front of an empty store. Three men, two women, and a little boy without shoes, who stood caged behind his father's arm. Brown-eyed, brown-skinned, concern and wonder was evident without the utterance of one word.

"You're used to leading with a cross around your neck," Trusty said, trying his best to ignore the stares.

"True. But I'm riding with a deputy that everybody knows about and the trouble that he brings with him. You don't ride into a town without reason. Even that child knows that."

Trusty didn't say anything. His eyes fell to two Indians standing outside of a mercantile staring at him as he rode by. He didn't like the feeling he was getting on the ride in any more than Michael did. From there, he broke his gaze from the Indians and scanned the upper reaches of the buildings on both sides of the street.

"We might have to sleep with the horses," Michael said. "There's no hotel here. That would have changed if the railroad would have come through. If it wasn't for the academy this town would dry up and die now that it's going to be off the beaten path. At least there's a café we can grab a meal in."

Trusty took in the street, noting the empty storefronts, looking for shadows moving inside them. There was no threat that he could see, but his gut told him to be careful. The air was thick, and the eyes cast on him were clouded with disrespect. He was relieved to see the livery come into sight.

The liveryman welcomed the two riders with the same judgment that the rest of the citizens of Wapanucka had: disdain and earned suspicion. He was a grizzled Indian who looked old enough to remember when the range was free to ride, and the white man's laws and ways hadn't been imposed on him and his tribe. No matter the badge that Trusty wore, there was still distrust and anger over the past to face in the Territory.

Both Trusty and Michael dismounted. The liveryman took hold of Michael's gray mare first. "For the night?" he asked. His two front teeth were missing, and his dark, leathery face was wrinkled by the sun and time spent in it.

"Both of us," Trusty said.

The man nodded and pulled Spirit inside the barn, leaving the two men alone.

Trusty watched the old Indian disappear inside, then said, "I've been in friendlier towns."

"You've never been here, then?"

"Can't say I've had any reason to."

"Well," Michael said, "that's a good thing, I suppose. We need to ask the liveryman if Amelia has been through here."

"You think she'd be so bold as to stable her horse in town, in plain sight of everybody?"

"You see any Wanted posters of her yet?"

"No," Trusty said.

"There's no wire office here either. Her bet would be that nobody had heard about what she did."

"But she has to know somebody would be comin' for her."

"Probably, but Amelia likes her comforts. Once she steps foot into No Man's Land, she'll vanish, but you have to consider that she's married to a Choctaw. She knows how to speak to them and how to ask them to hide her. David Folsom casts a long shadow. My guess is she holed up along the way with folks who were kin to him, or associates in one way or another. If you're thinking that Amelia is a typical white woman, then you're underestimating her in the worst way."

Trusty rubbed his shoulder and said, "There's nothin' typical about Amelia Darby. I appreciate the enlightenment. You're right; I failed to consider that she knew the way of the Indian as well as she does the way of the white man."

"She's good at making that happen," Michael said. "She always has been. Don't be too hard on yourself for falling for her lies."

The liveryman returned and took hold of Horse's reins. "I take?"

Trusty nodded and watched the old man lead his mount into the barn like he had Michael's. He had to

seriously consider that Amelia might have already been
to Wapanucka and left it behind in the dust. He didn't say
so, but he was starting to be glad for Michael Darby's
company. Even if he didn't trust the man, he was worth
listening to. There was no way that he wasn't going to
be hard on himself though. Judge Hadesworth was dead
because of his failure to tell the difference between the
truth and a whole bunch of lies.


  The café in Wapanucka was a little hole in the wall
that sat in between two vacant stores. There were six
rickety tables, with a long bar across the back of the
room. The air smelled of fresh baked bread, pig grease,
and a bubbling spice that Trusty had never smelled
before, pungent and sweet at the same time. The walls
were bare of pictures, but a few sconces were scattered
about, dousing the gray, lackluster room with flickering
light. A water-powered fan turned overhead, distributing
the smells and moving the air lazily. Three of the tables
held patrons: a family of four, two men, and an older
couple. Michael and Trusty were the only white-skinned
men in the café.
  A middle-aged woman walked out from the back
room before the bell on the front door quit tinkling.
"Hello, strangers," the woman said, coming to a stop at
the table Trusty and Michael had helped themselves to.
"We're about to close. My name's Mae if you need to
know. All we got left is some bean soup and bread. That
suit you?" Her hair was piled up on top of her head,
mostly gray, with a few brittle strands falling across her
blue eyes. She was short and robust, her skin brown but

bleached enough to make a man wonder if she was mixed or full-blooded. The front of her body was covered with a dirty white apron, and a sheathed knife hung from a rope belt at her ample waist. This Mae didn't look to have a lazy bone in her body and left no doubt to anyone paying attention that she was the person in charge of the café. Pots and pans rattled from the back room.

"That'll be just fine, ma'am," Trusty said.

Michael nodded when Mae looked to him for his approval. "I'll be right back," she said, then hurried back to the kitchen, the floor creaking under her steps as she went.

Chairs scooted across the dry floor, drawing Trusty's attention to the two men. They both stood up, the food on their plates half-eaten. One of them, the taller of the two, glared at Trusty, tossed a few coins on the table, and walked out the door, followed by his partner. The rest of the patrons watched but said nothing. The café had been uncomfortably quiet from the moment Trusty and Michael had walked in the door.

It didn't take long for the woman to bring the food to the table. She set down two bowls of thin soup in front of Trusty and Michael, along with the bread, and started to turn away.

"You haven't seen a white woman come through here, have you?" Trusty said.

Mae stopped and faced him. Michael took a taste of the soup, watching her reaction closely.

"We don't get many travelers through here. Most folks go through Button Springs these days," Mae said.

"So, no one's come through here then?" Trusty held the woman's attention, searching her face, like Michael was, for any sign that she was uncomfortable or forcing an answer. It'd been his experience that people fidgeted one way or another when they lied or were trying to hide something.

"That's what I said," Mae answered. "You lookin' for someone in particular, Marshal?"

"I am. A petite woman by the name of Amelia Darby. She's wanted for the murder of a federal judge."

Mae shook her head. "Don't know a soul named Amelia Darby, and no woman on her own has been through here of recent. A judge, you say. I'm surprised I ain't heard of such a thing."

"Been recent," Michael said.

"I suppose that explains it then." Mae's feet were planted firmly on the floor. Trusty's question had piqued her interest.

"What about with another man? A Choctaw maybe?" Trusty said.

"Well, I'm sure I'd remember that, wouldn't I, if you're suggestin' what I think you are?"

"Just askin' questions," Trusty said.

"There's been no one here like that, Marshal." Mae didn't wait for Trusty to say anything. She spun around and disappeared into the kitchen.

"You don't believe her, do you?" Michael said as quietly as he could.

Trusty shook his head no, then spooned up some soup. It was cold to the taste, but that didn't stop him. There wasn't any place else in town to get a meal. He'd have to eat what was given to him whether he liked it or not. The beans were sparse, but the stock held some chicken flavor.

Both men ate in silence, sharing the bread, drinking

water from a pitcher that had been sitting on the table. Mae remained distant, if not hidden, and Trusty didn't try to start another conversation with her again. By the time they paid for the meal, the café was empty and darkness had fallen outside.

Michael stopped on the boardwalk just outside the café door and pulled a cigarillo from his shirt pocket and lit it. "I have to say, that was one of the worst meals I've had in a long time," he said, exhaling a puff of smoke.

Trusty didn't have time to say anything. A rifle shot rang out from across the street. The bullet thumped into the wood next to his head, sending splinters flying. Both men figured out what was going on real quick, backed their way into the café, pulling their guns from the holsters as they went.

One shot was followed by more. Glass shattered, barely missing Trusty. They returned fire without regard to Mae, who had rushed from the kitchen at the first sound of trouble.

Trusty paid the woman no mind. Both he and Michael were focused on the roof across the street and the sniper who had taken a position there. Trusty was glad the café was empty. He wasn't ready to carry the responsibility for another senseless death. One was enough to last him a lifetime.

# Chapter 17

Mae picked up a lever-action scattergun and chambered a cartridge, getting Trusty's attention. "Friend or foe," he said without taking his eyes off the roof across the street.

The shotgun was aimed at Trusty's head. "You'd be dead if I thought I had a good reason to pull the trigger," Mae said. "I've got five shots to deal with you both if I wanted to."

Another shot punctured the front door from the shooter on the roof. The bullet skidded across the floor in between Michael and Trusty, giving them both reason to pause and take a deep breath. *Shit, that was too close.* They looked away from Mae, to each other, then took up spots opposite the shattered front window. Hopefully the beams to support the building were thick enough to stop any bullet that might penetrate them.

"You're welcome to join in," Trusty said to Mae. His Colt was leveled at the roof across the street, poked through a section of broken window . . . jigsaw puzzle pieces sharp as knives that would come in handy if one of the intruders wanted to go hand-to-hand.

The woman didn't move an inch. "I'll stand right here. If they do away with the two of you, I got a business to protect if'n they're after more than your hides."

"If they kill us, they'll be gone," Michael said.

A smirk crossed Mae's plump face. "You're pretty sure of yourself even for a white man."

Another shot blasted through what remained of the window, sending shards of glass flying into the café. Mae ducked, but Trusty didn't see whether or not she was hit. He had a target in sight, had caught the silhouette of a man as he'd popped up over the roof and fired. Trusty fired back, knowing full well that his chances of hitting the shooter were slim. He needed his rifle, but it was stowed with his travel bags back at the livery.

"You think you can keep him busy?" Trusty said to Michael.

"Sure . . . what do you have in mind?"

"I'm going out the back and sneak up on him. Get him in range. We're dropping lead into the air and nothing more shooting back and forth. They're just trying to run us out of bullets," Trusty said.

"You think he's the only one?"

Trusty looked to the table that still held two plates of half-eaten food on it and said, "Nope, my guess is there's two of them."

"You need to start traveling without that badge on your chest," Michael said. "It's a target as soon as every desperate man in the Territory figures out who you are and what you're worth dead."

Trusty glanced back at Mae to see if she understood

what Michael had just said, then turned his attention back to the roof across the street. "That's never gonna happen, and you know it. The only way I'm taking this badge off of my chest is if somebody takes it from me."

"Or you're dead."

"Well, there is that, but I'm not plannin' on dying anytime soon."

The gloom of the dark evening held fast overhead. A wall of gray, foreboding clouds had rolled in from the west, promising a fresh drench of spring rain. The cover between the earth and the stars was so thick that the clouds looked stationary, like the movement of the earth had been halted by a giant, invisible hand. Lack of light helped Trusty more than it hurt him as he edged across the back of the café. His Colt was loaded, barrel pointed to the sky, but he wished he was dressed in all black like Michael. It would have been easier to vanish from sight. He needed all of the advantages that he could get.

The echoes of shots volleying back and forth continued between Michael and the roof sniper. A crack in the air like weak, man-made thunder echoed down the empty street. So far, the noise hadn't attracted any kind of notice; if there was some Indian law around, they had chosen to ignore the shoot-out, or were deciding whether or not to join in themselves. Michael's reminder of the price on Trusty's head was an easy explanation for the sudden attack, but it wasn't proven yet. Being hunted was going to take some getting used to.

Trusty made his way along three more buildings,

stumbling over a sleeping cat as he went. He hoped he was far enough along to cross the street unseen.

The existence of a conflict, of gunshots ringing out into the night, had left the main street of Wapanucka void of any traffic. It was like a storm had arrived and sent everyone scurrying inside to weather whatever was to come.

Trusty stood in between two buildings and was about to crouch down and tear out across the street in a fast run, when he heard someone say, "Stop right there, Dawson, and drop your gun," from behind him.

There was no way he was going to die by getting shot in the back. Trusty knew he had no choice but to move one way or the other. In a split-second, he dove to the right, onto the boardwalk fronting the local bank. A bullet thudded into the ground inches from his boot heel.

Trusty had no time to consider the pain in his shoulder as he rolled to a stop and jumped to his feet. He plastered himself against the bank, knowing full well that he had exposed himself to the shooter on the roof. He hoped Michael wasn't running low on ammunition.

"That was a big mistake, Dawson," the unknown man said, unseen from inside the alley.

"So I was just supposed to stand there and let you shoot me in the back?"

"You might as well get it over quick."

"Today is not the day I die," Trusty said as he made his way to the side of the building. An overhang kept him in the shadows. "How do you know who I am?"

"You're not one of the Three Guardsmen, are you? I know those faces. Then you must be Trusty Dawson."

The exchange of shooting from the café and the

rooftop had stopped. Trusty spoke only loud enough for the man to hear him. From the way he could figure it, the man was at the back end of the bank. He needed to draw him out into the open, so he had a clear shot.

"So that makes me a Deputy U.S. Marshal with a price on his head?" Trusty said.

"You got a reputation for bein' untouchable, but that seems to have changed."

A rifle shot cracked in the air, and it didn't take much to know that the rooftop shooter had seen Trusty. The bullet pinged off the hitching post in front of the bank. Returning fire wouldn't do him any good; it'd just waste more of the cartridges that remained in his belt. He needed to keep the man talking all the while staying alive.

"What am I worth alive?" Trusty said.

"Nothin'."

"Dead?"

"A thousand silvers."

"I must have really gone and done it this time."

"Seems like," the man said.

Another rifle shot rang out. This time the bullet hit the boardwalk. The darkness was making it difficult for the rooftop shooter to sight him in. That and Michael returned fire, only this time the shots sounded different. The blasts from the café were from a scattergun. Vengeance boomed from down the street, matching another boom from overhead. The fury in the clouds had held back long enough and let loose with a drop of hard rain as the approaching storm arrived over Wapanucka.

Trusty was protected from the downpour, but he didn't know if the man in the alley was getting soaked or if the coming storm would run him off. He hoped not.

"Who gets the honor of paying for my empty boots?" Trusty said, only louder this time to compensate for the rain. The rooftop shooter hadn't responded to the scatter-gun blast, so Trusty figured the man was on the move or had been stopped one way or the other. Stopped would be good. One less shooter to worry about. He hoped Michael had finished the man off.

"You don't know, do you?" the man said.

Trusty didn't wait. He reached around the side of the building and fired a shot, hoping the man was looking to do the same thing, hoping to wing him at least.

The man laughed after the reverberation of the shot drifted away. Rain continued to fall steadily, making the dirt street a long ribbon of mud. Water splashed off the street in big, brown drops. The sound of the wind, rain, and rumbling thunder made it hard to hear as the man's laughter joined the chorus. It made Trusty feel like the entire world was laughing at him, condemning him for his failures—but even worse, for something he didn't know he had done, or who to. He'd had enough of trying to figure out who had put a bounty on him. Losing the judge and nursing a bullet wound was one thing, but car-rying around a target on his back without knowing who put it there was another. Trusty had been off balance ever since he figured out the bulldog and the boxer had come to kill him, not Judge Hadesworth.

"Show yourself," Trusty said. "Step out on the count of ten, and I'll do the same. I'll give you your shot at me, and I'll take mine at you. But only if you tell me who put the price on my head. Your partner's gone silent. You hear that? Nothing. I'm not riding alone either. But I suppose you know that if I'm guessin' right and you're one of the men who walked out of the café once you recognized who I was."

"You got that right," the man said. "We knew who you was straightaway. Trusty Dawson, the marshal who went and got a judge kilt by a woman."

"So that's the story," Trusty said.

"It is."

"Come out on the count of ten."

"Ain't gonna happen."

"Oh, yes, it is." It was Michael's voice. "It's your turn not to move. Drop your gun. Then face the man and answer his question. Simple as that. Do as I say, then you live. Be stupid and you die."

Trusty stood with his back against the wall, staring out into the street through a sheet of rain. It was dark, wet, and cold. He had never felt so alone in his life. Everybody in the Territory knew what had happened at Lost Mountain Pass. He was a laughingstock. For a brief second he considered putting himself in the line of fire, telling Michael to stand out of the way and let things happen as they may, but that wasn't his way. That would be the easy way out. His reputation would be forever ruined, but he knew that. Bringing in Amelia was the only way to stitch that wound, but even capturing her wouldn't get rid of the scar.

"You're clear to come out, Trusty," Michael called out.

Trusty took a deep breath and peered around the corner of the bank. He saw Michael standing behind the man, one arm wrapped around his throat, the other with his six-shooter pointed at his head. Even from a distance, there was no mistaking the man from the restaurant.

With his Colt leveled at the man's head, too, Trusty made his way down the alley. "Where's his partner?"

"Pleading for his soul at the Pearly Gates," Michael said. "Mae kept him busy while I made my way up behind him."

"You're a dead man too," the man said through gritted teeth to Michael.

Michael pressed the barrel of his gun harder to the man's head than it already was. "One more word from you and it'll be your last."

Trusty stopped before the man. "The way I see it, the only thing you've done wrong is shoot at a U.S. Marshal unprovoked. Now I can be a generous man, or I can take offense to your indictment of my character and see you locked up." Rain splattered off his blue Cavalry Stetson as the water from the sky continued to fall in buckets. Thunder rumbled overhead and the wind continued to push up the street and through the alley, making all three men uncomfortable—but Trusty wasn't going anywhere. "You in a deal-makin' mood, mister, or are you gonna play tough on me, spit nails, spread lies, and entertain your chances in a jail cell for the next year or two? All you got to do is tell me who put the price on my head, and you're free to go."

"Why should I believe you?" the man said.

"I give you my word. It's all I have left to offer you."

The man was soaked to the bone. His face was dark and his eyes hard to read. A short stubbly beard looked like a waterfall. "The order comes out of Saint Louis. A big man there. Markerry or something of the like. He don't want you alive. Dead with proof is the only way he'll pay. No sweat off my back to tell you that one more man in the world hates you enough to put a price on your head."

"Marberry?" Trusty said as everything inside of him went dry. His throat crackled and his heart slowed a beat.

"Yeah, that's the name. Never met the man myself. Picked up the bounty in a Texas saloon. Word on you is far and wide, Dawson. It ain't like I'm the only one on your tail."

"You're sure it's Marberry? Theodore Marberry?"

"I done told you that's the man. Now, let me go."

Michael pressed into the man and ground the barrel of his gun even harder into the man's temple. "Not until you give the marshal your word that you'll be on your way."

The man squinted his eyes as a flash of lightning streaked across the black sky. "I've had about enough of you, mister." With that, he jammed his elbow into Michael's stomach as hard as he could. Michael hadn't been expecting the blow and stumbled backward, loosening his grasp enough for the man to break free. In a matter of seconds, he produced a knife and was about to throw it toward Michael, but Trusty stopped the action mid-throw. He pulled the trigger of his Colt, adding an explosion of gunpowder and the sound of a shattering skull to the stormy weather. The bullet caught the man square in the forehead, sending him sprawling backward into the mud. He was dead before he hit the ground.

All Trusty could do was stand there in disbelief as he played the conversation over and over again in his head. *Marberry? That is the last name I had expected to hear.*

*Why in the hell would Theodore Marberry put a bounty out on me?*

### St. Louis, Missouri, spring 1875

Jessica Marberry stood in the doorway of a monolithic four-story limestone church, the dim light from inside glowing behind her like the sun showing itself for the first time among a gathering of gray, smoky clouds. There was no announcement or need of service for the Marberrys that Sam knew of. She stood framed in the door like a statue made to praise a goddess in Rome, Greece, or some other faraway place that Trusty had only heard of in books. She was a myth, maybe a fragment of his imagination; he couldn't believe she was standing there waiting for him. His heart beat fast not only from the sight of her, but at the prospect of getting caught.

Jessica was dressed in a loose-fitting blue aesthetic dress and wore a smile that Trusty had come to know and dream about when she wasn't nearby. But the smile was sadder than normal. "I was afraid you wouldn't come," she said.

"I'm not supposed to be anywhere near you." Sam looked up and down the empty street. He didn't like the light emitting from the church, and did his best to find a shadow to stand in. Two towering oak trees hovered over the entrance of the church, creating an arch of thick leaves that filtered the grayness of the night.

"I know," Jessica said. "That's my fault."

Sam wanted to be closer to her, breathe her toilet water, but he held back, stayed three feet from her. "How can that be? We haven't done anything wrong."

Jessica smirked. "You don't know my father."

"I'm starting to."

"I'd rather you not."

"Me too."

"Our maid, Lilty Best, found my diary and read it. There seemed to be some things there that alarmed her. She gave it to my father."

Sam looked at Jessica confused. "I don't understand."

"I've been writing how I feel about you."

"Oh," Sam said. He wanted to ask: "And how is that?" but he didn't. He thought he might have an idea what she meant. His stomach flipped and his heart clapped with happiness.

"I knew better. I knew my father would never like any boy I liked unless he picked them for me. But . . ."

"But I'm a blacksmith's son," Sam said.

"I wish that didn't have anything to do with it." She stepped forward, closing the distance between them.

She didn't stop until her face was inches from Sam's face. He was uncomfortable, but he wasn't moving, wasn't going anywhere.

"Do you want to kiss me?" she said.

Sam didn't answer with words. He leaned in and kissed her like he had wanted to from the first time he had seen her—except he never thought it would ever happen. Jessica returned his kiss and the world around them both disappeared for a long moment. When they pulled apart, life as they had known it before had changed forever. Sam knew little of love, but he was certain that this was what it felt like.

Jessica looked sad instead of happy. "What's the matter?" Sam said.

"Father is sending me away," she said.

"Where to?"

"England."

"Why aren't you happy? You've always wanted to go to your mother's home country."

"Not to stay. Not to go to school. To visit. To see the castles and moors. I don't want to live there."

"Oh," Sam said.

"He says it's for my education, but I know it's not about that. He wants me to be more refined so I can meet a better man. I am not interested in suitors of any sort, and he was already starting to suspect I've already given my heart to someone. The diary proved it. I'm such a fool." Jessica stared at Sam, her eyes boring through his head like beams of the sun.

He didn't understand what she was saying—or didn't want to. All he could think about was that she was leaving. "Will I ever see you again?"

Jessica reached out and took Sam's hand. "Let's run away."

"Together? Me and you?" Something triggered in Sam's mind. His schoolteacher, Mrs. Abernathy, encouraging him to continue his education. That didn't happen. His father wouldn't allow it. Sam was stuck in the fiery hell of the blacksmith shop for the rest of his life. He envied Jessica and her opportunity. He couldn't believe that she didn't want it. He would have given anything to be in her shoes.

"Sometimes I think your brain is made of iron. Of course, me and you. We can go anywhere we want to."

"With me? You want to run away with me?"

Sam stared at Jessica dumbfounded. "I can't do that," he said, looking over his shoulder to the big houses that lined the street opposite the church. "I can't leave my pa, and you can't leave yours. I can't take care of you like you're used to bein' taken care of. I wouldn't know where to start. I can't, Jessica. Not now. Probably not ever. You deserve to have a better life than I can give you. You deserve to have a good education. I can't take that away from you. No matter how much I want to run off with you, I just can't."

A tear streamed down Jessica's cheek. She sighed, then walked right by Sam without saying another word to him. He watched her disappear down the street, into the darkness, all the while fighting off the urge to go after her. But he didn't. Sam didn't see Jessica again for another eight years, and that was only by chance—or fortune, depending on how you looked at it.

# Chapter 18

"We're losin' daylight," Vance Calhoun said to Gladdy O'Connor. Calhoun was standing in the shadows of the alley, next to the Western Union office, out of sight, as the sun started to dive toward the horizon. "What'd you find out?"

"The man at the mercantile was a little bit of help. Buffalo Soldiers rode through escortin' the body of the judge that was kilt. Word is a woman shot the man. Her brothers was hanged a few days before. The order was given by the same judge, so everybody seems to think that it was nothin' but a revenge killin'. The thing is, this woman, Amelia Darby, rode out with the marshal and the judge. No one trusted her, held a low opinion of her and her brothers, so they weren't too surprised by what happened. Meaner than a skunk with a toothache is what the merchant said they was. All of them. The town was better off without them all."

"What about Dawson, the marshal?" Calhoun looked past Gladdy, up and down the alley, keeping track of everybody that was coming and going. So far, he hadn't drawn any attention to himself.

"Here's the thing," Gladdy said. "They suspect that this same woman is behind the killin' of the clerk at the hotel."

Calhoun hadn't been expecting to hear that. "I still need to get out of this town as soon as possible without being seen, but that's good news, Gladdy. You done good."

"Thanks, boss." Gladdy tried to smile, but he couldn't quite manage it.

"Now, what's the word on Dawson?"

"Him and the Darby woman's brother headed west after her. He's shot up though. They won't be gettin' anywhere fast, but he's not givin' up goin' after her."

Calhoun nodded. "Good to know. How many of these Darbys are there? They sound like a bunch of rabbits."

"Papists is what the man at the mercantile said. The one brother was a priest but walked away and went after his sister."

"To save her?"

Gladdy shrugged. "Man didn't know more than what he told me. He said no one ever trusted the sincerity of the brother's callin'. He figures the priest is after the reward money on his sister. His words, not mine. I don't even know what a callin' is."

"I'm sure you don't. Did this fella have any idea where this woman might be runnin' to?"

"Not really," Gladdy said. "They fear she might still be in town, lurkin' about to take revenge on the people who treated her bad. The hotel wouldn't give her a job, and the man at the mercantile wouldn't extend credit to her. He said everybody in town was nervous. His shotgun was loaded under the counter. He said she could probably find an offense taken to her by everyone in Kosoma."

"That doesn't help me. Dawson and the brother had to have a reason to head west. We need to find out what that reason is."

"Now?"

"Yes, now, you idiot. Go back out there and start askin' questions. See if you can find out if this Amelia Darby woman has any ties west of where she killed the judge. Maybe she's on the run. But I doubt she's here in Kosoma. They're lookin' for the wrong killer. That's good for me, bad for her."

"You gonna be here while I go?"

Calhoun shook his head. "I'll be at the livery waitin' on Hobbs and the rest of the men to get here. We're gonna need a gang of men to go after this Dawson fella. We wait. You hear?"

"What about burnin' down the man's house who killed my brother?"

"In due time, Gladdy. Now go on. See what you can find out about this Darby girl. Don't bring no attention to yourself and try to stay away from any conversation about that hotel clerk who was killed. You know too much about that. I don't want you to slip up and tell anyone what you know."

"You're safe with me, boss. I know you had to kill that man so he wouldn't tell anybody you was still alive."

"Go on. Daylight's burnin'," Calhoun said as he watched Gladdy slink out of the alley. He couldn't help but wonder if he could trust the younger O'Connor brother as much as he trusted the older O'Connor brother. If not, he'd have to kill him too.

* * *

The livery was dark, and Calhoun was propped up in the corner of a horse stall, half-asleep, half-awake, waiting on Gladdy and Hobbs to arrive. Like planned, Gladdy had sent a wire out telling everyone that Vance Calhoun was dead to all of the newspapers. One in St. Louis, Paris, Texas, and Dallas, so the word would get out to everyone that mattered. He also sent a wire to Denton Hobbs at the ranch, requesting the foreman to gather a group of men to come and take Calhoun's body back home. That was a lie, but Gladdy couldn't wire Hobbs and tell him the truth.

Gladdy was still trying to find what information he could about the Darby woman. Calhoun was relieved to have some time to himself to think things through without Gladdy interrupting his thoughts every ten seconds. There was a lot to consider, especially since his plans had changed so drastically. When him and Gladdy had rode out, all Calhoun could think of was exacting his own revenge on Theodore Marberry—after he made off with Jessica's baby girl. But that changed when he had learned that a marshal named Dawson had been in Kosoma. It had to be the same man in the letters Sally had found in Jessica's room. Calhoun wished he could have read those letters before they burned up, so he would know the nature of the communication, but he'd had no choice but to take Sally's word for the implications she'd divined from reading them. Jessica and Trusty Dawson had had some kind of intimate relationship, recent, right before Calhoun had met Jessica and got caught up in her whirlwind. A relationship that, according to Sally, was close enough to put doubt on who the baby's father was. That in itself was enough to change his plans for. He needed to know the truth. And if, in fact, Trusty Dawson was the child's father—then Calhoun swore right then and there that he would finish what the Darby woman had started. He'd kill the son-of-a-bitch himself.

A collection of loud voices woke Calhoun from his half-sleep.

"He's over here, I swear." It was Gladdy O'Connor's unmistakable voice. He was as shrill as a pigeon-toed schoolgirl when he was excited.

Footsteps thudded on the hard dirt floor of the barn, and before Calhoun could rub the sleep from his eyes and knock the straw from his sleeves, he was staring at a bewildered Denton Hobbs.

"So it is true," Hobbs said.

Calhoun struggled to his feet and furrowed his brow, looking into the gray light of the barn for more of his men. "Get in here and keep your voice down, you fool. Of course, I'm alive. I've got my reasons to make the world think I'm dead."

Hobbs did as he was told, edging past Calhoun's grullo. The horse looked annoyed at the prospect of sharing his stall with so many men.

"Where are the rest of the men?" Calhoun asked. The sight of Hobbs, who he'd last seen as he'd rode away from the Bar-C-Bar Ranch, brought back the memory and rage of the fire that had set him off on this journey in the first place. He tapped his pants pocket nervously. He carried Sally's soiled handkerchief as a reminder of what Marberry had done to her and his life.

"You've got to give me a minute, boss," Hobbs said.

"I ride all the way to pick up your dead body. I wasn't expectin' to find you wakin' up from a nap."

"I'm not gonna die in a stinkin' place like this," Calhoun said.

Gladdy stood by the half-door of the stall, knowing without being told to act as a lookout for anyone coming. Calhoun was surprised the man was trained enough to take on the task without being told. His brother must have had something to do with it. He sure did miss Haden.

"All right then, boss, I suppose you got a plan of some sort, or you wouldn't have had me ride all the way up here."

"Of course, I got a plan. The first thing we got to do is get me out of this town without bein' seen. Then we need to head west and pick up the trail of Trusty Dawson."

"The marshal?" Hobbs said. "I thought you was goin' after that Marberry fella for killin' your sister and O'Connor's brother."

"He burned down my house," Calhoun said.

Hobbs tried to wipe the confusion off his face, but it wasn't going anywhere. "That too. What's Dawson have to do with all of this?"

"That's not your concern. How many men did you bring with you?"

"Four," Hobbs said.

Calhoun nodded with approval. "That's seven of us against two of them. Gladdy, you find anything else out about this Amelia Darby woman?"

Gladdy tore his attention away from his watch duty and said, "She's married to a Choctaw. His name's David Folsom. Word has it, we find him, we'll find her. Last anybody heard, he was off in No Man's Land collectin' buffalo bones and sellin' it for fertilizer. But I was also told not to underestimate the Indian. He's smart, good with a gun, and sly as a fox. Them two together is supposed to be a good team. So there's that, boss. It's all I could find out."

"You continue to amaze me, O'Connor. No Man's Land explains why Dawson is headin' west."

Hobbs scratched his head this time. "No Man's Land is a long ride, boss."

"You got a problem with that?"

"No, sir, just sayin' is all. We're not geared up to ride that far."

"Well," Calhoun said, "you best make sure and take care of that before we ride out. We're leavin' after the clock cracks midnight. Everybody that matters should be asleep by then."

"I sure wish we didn't have to ride at night," Gladdy said.

Calhoun sneered at Gladdy, then spit to the straw. "You can stay here or six feet under. Your choice. Now get out of here. Both of you. Keep an eye out and make sure nobody stumbles onto me, you hear?"

Both men nodded and made their way out of the stall. Silence returned after a minute. Even the grullo seemed to calm down. Calhoun was left with his thoughts and had time to reconsider his plan, even though he didn't think it was necessary. Being dead was hard work at the moment. Hiding out. Making sure he wasn't seen. But it would get easier once they were out of Kosoma. It might be a good thing. A fresh start. Telling the world that he was dead is something he should have done before now.

If he had, none of the mess he was knee-deep in would have happened. No Jessica and her lies. No baby to question or retrieve. No double cross from Marberry. Sally would still be alive, and the ranch would still be standing. Things had changed so fast for him—alive or dead—that he could barely grasp ahold of everything that had happened. But he knew one thing for sure. Somebody was going to pay for his pain and his troubles. That would start with Dawson and end with Marberry. After that? The world was his to do with whatever he wanted to. He could be anybody, go anywhere, and not be beholding to anyone. He liked that thought, that image of his future. It had been a long time since Vance Calhoun had felt so free. And he was going to remain that way. No one was going to stop him. Only a fool would try.


The seven men were saddled up and ready to ride out of Kosoma. Gladdy, Calhoun, and Hobbs rode in the middle of the pack with two men in front and two men behind. Calhoun was settled in the middle of Gladdy and Hobbs and wore a cloak with a hood over his head instead of his Stetson. The night air was cool, and the sky overhead was bright with stars and a descending thumbnail moon. Everyone, it looked like, in town had gone to bed hours earlier. There were no lights burning anywhere to be seen. The cover of darkness was what Calhoun needed to get out of Kosoma unseen. All seven men kept a steady pace, doing their best to make as little sound as possible.

As they rounded the last corner before leaving town, a light in the mercantile snuffed out, and a short, rotund older man walked out the door, locked it, then stopped in surprise when he saw the troop of seven men. The man recognized Gladdy right away. "Hey there, friend," he said, trailing after the men. "Where are you going at this hour?"

Calhoun whispered, "Stop." A bead of sweat appeared on his upper lip. This was not in the plan.

The lead horseman, a fella called Blake, raised his hand and motioned everyone to do as Calhoun had ordered. All of the horses pulled against their bits; a few danced, annoyed at Calhoun, while others dropped their heads and waited patiently.

"You should go on home, mister," Gladdy said to the mercantile man. "What are you doin' out this late anyways? You should be home in bed."

"I was balancing the books," the man said. "Time got away from me." He looked past Gladdy to Calhoun and let his gaze linger on his face a little longer than he should have. "I heard one of your crew was dead. Looks like you're here and accounted for to me."

Calhoun sighed. Gladdy stiffened. Hobbs spit a thick stream of tobacco juice to the ground.

"You should have gone home before now," Gladdy said. His voice was sad, and his words fell to the ground just as Calhoun pulled his sidearm out of the holster, cocked it, and pulled the trigger. The shot echoed up and down the street, erupting overhead like thunder from an invisible cloud. A gathering of sleeping pigeons was awakened from their roost on a roof and lit into the air with a flutter and slap of wings, adding to the noise.

The bullet thudded the mercantile man straight in the chest, driving him backward with a shocked look on his face. His calves caught the boardwalk and he tumbled onto the wood planks. Another thud echoed into the night. A horse pranced. Another whinnied softly. Calhoun stuffed his Colt back into the holster and stared at Gladdy for a long minute, trying to decide whether or not to kill him too. If they got caught it would be the Mick's fault and there'd have to be a price to pay.

None of the men said a word. They waited for Calhoun to move next.

Instead of shooting Gladdy, he reached into his pocket and pulled out a soiled woman's handkerchief and handed it to Gladdy. "Here," Calhoun said. "Toss that on the ground at his feet."

Gladdy took the piece of cloth and said, "What's this?"

The temptation to backhand Gladdy coursed through Calhoun's veins, but there was no time for that. "It was my sister's. A keepsake so I wouldn't forget what Marberry did to her and my ranch. But I don't need trinkets as a reminder of that night. I'll never forget what's been done to me. Not even after I exact my revenge. Do as I told you. We've got to ride now. Whoever finds this fella will think the handkerchief belongs to that Amelia Darby woman. They think she's here, so it won't be a stretch. Nobody'll miss us."

A light flickered on two buildings down from the mercantile. All of the men saw the glow reach into the street. "Ride now," Calhoun said. "Ride now."

Blake lurched forward first, then they all broke into a run, pushing out of sight as fast as they could.

Gladdy tossed the handkerchief as he went, watching it fall to the ground over his shoulder like a snowflake drifting down from the sky in a season it didn't belong.

The white tatted piece of cotton, soiled from the fire, landed in the muddy street not far from the dead man's feet. What happened after that was anybody's guess, but Calhoun figured the people in Kosoma were scared enough of the Darbys to believe the handkerchief belonged to Amelia without asking one question. If a posse came after them, they'd be ready—but Calhoun was betting they'd get down the trail just fine. One step closer to Dawson, to finding out the truth about Jessica, then on to St. Louis for the real victory. He could taste the ash on his lips from handling Sally's handkerchief, and Calhoun knew he would never forget that taste.

# Chapter 19

Trusty settled into the livery stall, taking in everything that had happened at the café and beyond. He sat in the corner, so he was as far away from the door as possible.

"Why don't you get some shut-eye," Michael said. "I'll keep watch for three or four hours, then we can switch out. I think it's going to have to be that way until this is over with."

Trusty looked up at Michael. Even in the darkness of the barn, he could tell the man wore a troubled look on his face. "You sure about that?"

Michael nodded, then pulled a cigarillo out of his pocket and rolled it between his fingers. "I don't mind first watch. I've got some things to think about that'll probably keep me from sleeping for a while."

Trusty understood that. He had a lot to mull over too. His own attempt to sleep would be difficult. He was still shocked to learn that Theodore Marberry had put a bounty on him. Putting a price on a man seemed like a dire thing to do, out of character for a man of Marberry's stature. Or maybe not. Trusty didn't know Marberry, or his personal ethics, very well at all. Some men would do anything to be successful—or protect their name and reputation. Even have a man killed if such a thing was deemed necessary.

"This was your first time killing a man, wasn't it?" Trusty said.

Michael nodded. "Something like that."

"And you're struggling with 'Thou shall not kill'?"

"Yes, there's that Commandment." Michael produced a match, struck it, then stared at the small orange flame as it erupted to life. The light was welcome in the dark barn, allowing Trusty to see Michael's face more clearly. The ex-priest was pained; his face tight and his eyes red-lined and weary. "But," Michael said, "it's more like *John 3:12*. 'Do not be like Cain, who belonged to the evil one and murdered his brother.' Now, I am no different than any of my brothers—or my sister, as far as that goes. We are all killers. Every single Darby has taken a life. I am a bad seed, born and bred, and no matter how much I tried to avoid that, change that about myself, I couldn't. I am a killer and nothing more. The fires of hell await me." Michael moved the match to the cigarillo that dangled from his lips and lit it, taking a long draw as he shook out the flame, extinguishing the light in the barn. Michael's face was nothing but a shadow now.

Trusty let Michael's words fall away before he said anything. "I'm sure there are more passages that you could quote about forgiveness. You only took a life to save your own life. You had no choice but to defend yourself and me. Is there no room for that in your beliefs? Does a man at war face these fires of hell you speak of?

We are seekin' to deliver justice by findin' a killer and stopping her before she kills again. That is pure goodness. Not evil. The men that died came after us to kill me. We survived and can continue on to find Amelia. Isn't that enough to set your mind at ease?"

"I have no idea what the judgment of God will be." Michael smoked and exhaled again, as silence fought to surround the two men.

The smell of tobacco burning hit Trusty's nose, and it was a reprise from the straw and shit smell of the barn. He resettled himself, leaned back against the wall, and stared up at Michael, coming to the conclusion that he knew little of the man before him. Time had eroded his distrust of him, but there was still something about Michael that caused Trusty to look over his shoulder, not rely on his words or his actions. Both were too smooth and calculated. There was no way to shake the feeling that Michael Darby was up to something. And Trusty couldn't figure out what that something was.

"I've assumed all along that you were not a believer," Michael said.

Trusty shrugged. "There was only one book in our house. The family Bible belonged to my mother. It helped me to learn to read, along with the schoolin' I got, but none of the words stuck much. Especially after my mother died. I didn't find any comfort in the promises made there."

"I'm sorry about your mother. How old were you?"

Trusty cocked his eye up at Michael and examined his face again. It was easy to see that Michael was trying to change the subject. Trusty didn't blame him. Killing a man was never easy no matter the reason. Especially the first time.

"I was only a boy," Trusty said. "It was me and my father after that. My father owned a blacksmith shop in Saint Louis. I was his indentured servant from the time I could stoke the fire in the forge."

"It was just you then?"

Trusty nodded and looked away from Michael. "My mother had consumption, was always frail and weak. Birthin' me nearly killed her. There was no riskin' another child."

"You ride comfortably alone for a reason."

"I suppose I do. No offense to you."

"None taken." The cigarillo was squeezed between Michael's fingers like he had been smoking for a long time.

A priest that was comfortable with tobacco and whiskey didn't live up to Trusty's image of a perfect man of God. Maybe he was looking for a reason not to believe Michael had his best interest at heart, was always on the lookout for his Darby-ways to show themselves.

Trusty stood up and walked over to Horse. He opened his traveling bag, pulled out some cartridges, and started to reload the empty slots in his belt.

"You have your own reasons to be a little unsettled," Michael said. "But at least now you know who put the price on your head. What do you know of this Marberry fella? I've never heard of him."

Trusty stopped, sighed, and lowered his head. He really didn't want to talk about Theodore Marberry or the possibility that the man wanted him dead. "I suppose you're accustomed to people tellin' you their private moments."

"It was part of my day. I had to learn to listen," Michael said.

"I'm not used to talkin' about the past. I'd rather take a joshing from the judge about my appreciation of whorehouses, which although it may be true that I like the company of a woman from time to time, I think my reputation as a womanizer was more for the pleasure of gossip than the truth."

"It's not a bad reputation to have, I suppose."

Trusty eyed Michael and wondered if women were an addition to his appreciation of vices like whiskey and tobacco. Whether one was forbidden over the other was unknown to him. As far as Trusty knew, women were off-limits for the padres. "I suppose not, but rumors of the off-color variety can complicate a man's life in proper company."

"I'm assuming you're speaking of this Marberry fella."

Horse swished his tail and let out a snort. He hadn't been offered a bucket of oats yet. Trusty ignored the beast's demand. "I most likely am. I've known of Marberry since I was a boy. He would bring his carriages and buggies into my father's blacksmith shop for repair. Or send a man to do it. The first time he came in an axle or wheel needed repaired, I don't remember which. That was when I met his daughter, Jessica. We became fast friends then, Jessica and me. Every time there was a need for a visit to the shop, she found a way to come along and see me. Jessica was good at that, getting her way, doin' what she wanted to regardless of her father's wishes."

Michael nodded and said, "Let me guess . . . this Theodore Marberry didn't approve of the friendship."

"No matter how hard I tried I was never gonna be good enough for Jessica Marberry. I figured that out early on, but she was such a beauty, such a breath of fresh air in the hot, fiery smithy shop, it was like a visit from an angel to hell every time she walked in the door. She liked me too. Maybe too much. She wrote in her diary about her feelin's and her father found out. He forbade me from seeing her ever again. That was fine when we were young, but he couldn't stop us when we were older."

"You loved her," Michael said as he took a slow draw off the cigarillo. He exhaled, then tapped the hot ash into a pail of water next to the horse's bucket of feed.

Trusty didn't answer. It had been clear to him that Jessica was in the middle of this from the moment he heard the Marberry name, but he had no idea what he had done for Jessica's father to want him dead. "I'm glad I know who set the bounty in motion," he answered, ignoring the comment from Michael. Jessica Marberry was the only woman he had ever loved. "Once I've set your sister to rights, then I suppose it's time to go home, knock on the man's door, and find out what the hell's goin' on. He's going to answer to me."

"A thousand silvers is a lot of money to men who have nothing to lose." Michael stared at Trusty, searching, it seemed, for a crack in his demeanor.

"I'll have to get used to lookin' over my shoulder. You don't have to. You're free to ride off on your own anytime. You know that. We have no contract with each other. Like you said, I'm used to riding alone."

Michael stood rigid. "My interest is seeing to it that

Amelia is stopped from killing another man and nothing more. You know that."

"I think I do."

"I'm not going anywhere. I don't mind riding with you."

"Even if it means killin' another man?"

"If I have to, I will. I can't do anything about whatever awaits me in the afterlife. I can only hope that I have done enough good in this world to warrant a moment of mercy and salvation. If not, then I will face that fate when I must."

"I suppose we all will," Trusty said. "But I'm not ready to die just yet."

### Fort Reno, Indian Territory, fall 1877

A cold rain drizzled down from the gray morning sky. The air was cold, threatening to turn the rain to snow. Twenty-year-old Sam Dawson, tall, full-bodied, and mus-cled more than most of the men in the army, stood out-side a whitewashed wood-frame barracks, looking up at the sky, amazed at the open vista beyond the fort's build-ings. There were no high-picket walls surrounding the fort for protection like Sam had imagined there would be. Instead, there was a scattering of methodically built structures, mostly white with red roofs, organized to pro-tect and control the Cheyenne and Arapaho after their surrender. The fort was five years old and continued to grow. The smell of fresh-cut lumber perfumed the air with permanence and possibility even though neither of those things could be seen in the eyes of the Indians. There were about a thousand Northern Cheyenne living at the fort, and none of them were as happy as Sam was about being there.

It didn't take much to amaze Sam Dawson. Only months before he'd felt like he was serving a life sentence inside the blacksmith shop from sunup to sundown with no hope of parole or escape. His eyes had been irritated by the smoke, his arms constantly sore from swinging a hammer, and his throat raw; he sounded like he'd swallowed a comb when he talked. Sam feared his lungs were congested and would solidify from the soot that was as common as dust in the air of the shop. He knew if he had stayed inside the shop for the rest of his life he would die at a young age. He might not have had consumption like his mother, but he had felt the wear on his body from the work his father forced him to do day in and day out. There was no promise in the future. No hope to hang on to. Jessica was long gone, still in England, still being educated in ways that were unimaginable to Sam. A letter would arrive from her from time to time, but even those were getting less frequent. It seemed like she was never coming back, and even if she did, her father would never permit a courtship between the two of them. Sam knew he should give up hoping that they could be together someday, but his heart wouldn't allow it. No girl had ever captivated him like Jessica Marberry had. If he was ever going to have a chance at winning Jessica's hand, he was going to have to make something of his life, be more than a blacksmith. So one night, after a particularly hard day when his father could do nothing but scream at him, Sam snuck out of the house with a small pack of clothes and what money he had managed to save and joined the army.

After training and finding his way into a uniform—that smelled as fresh and new as the lumber in the fort—he had been sent to Fort Reno in Indian Territory. Now, on that gray morning, he was about to go on his first expedition, and he was starting to wonder if he had made the right choice. Death would come slow in the darkness of the blacksmith shop, but it could come quick at the hands of an Indian armed with a rifle as powerful as the one he carried. This was a lot different from the tales the men told in the shop; this was real. Still, it was a chance to prove himself, to become someone, who might just impress Theodore Marberry enough to allow Sam to court his daughter. Being a hero in the Indian Wars was the only way Sam knew to make himself respectable. He was never going to be a banker or businessman worth anything. He was determined to be the best shot, best soldier the army had ever seen.

"Dawson," a familiar voice demanded, taking Sam's wonder away from the sky. "You need to head to the armory, secure your weapons, and fall in with the rest of the men. We ride in ten minutes." The voice belonged to his captain, Joe Timberlock, a grizzled veteran of the 7th Cavalry and the Little Big Horn campaign. Timberlock had the look of an angry dog even when he slept, but for some reason the captain had taken a liking to Sam, saw something in him that he didn't see in the other new recruits. Sam had figured this out pretty quickly upon his arrival, when the captain judged him to be a fine new recruit, just what the company needed. Sam hadn't wanted to disappoint the captain from that moment on.

"Yes, sir." Sam snapped to attention and focused on Timberlock, doing his best to hide his doubt and fears.

"This'll be a hard ride, Dawson. I hope you're ready for it. We're heading into battle for certain. Dull Knife and his gang of escapees are intent on joinin' with the Southern Cheyenne and returnin' to the Black Hills. I always knew it was a mistake them Indians was allowed to keep their mounts and weapons. I knew this would happen. Shouldn't be no laws applied to their terms of surrender, if you ask me, but no one did. This is what you signed up for. I hope you're as keen under fire as you are on target practice. You've got one of the best eyes for shootin' that I've seen in a long time."

"I'm ready, sir." Sam tried to sound as confident as he could, but deep down, he was still a little bit nervous. He'd never been shot at before—or had to shoot to kill another man. Indian or otherwise. The thought gave him a tremble that he'd never felt before. He wasn't sure he could kill another man unless he absolutely had to.

Sam's commander, Lieutenant-Colonel William H. Lewis, was no stranger to battle. Lewis had been a military man from the start. After graduating from West Point, the colonel fought in the Seminole Wars, took part in the Utah Expedition against the Mormons, and fought in the Navajo Wars, all before the War Between the States began. After the Civil War, Lewis stayed in the army, fighting the Indians again, ending up in Fort Dodge, Kansas. It was there that Sam and the men of his troop, led by Captain Timberlock, had joined up with Lewis to pursue Dull Knife. A group of armed citizens had also joined the troops, helping sniff out Dull Knife's trail.

Sam rode close to the front of the troop, always keeping an eye on Colonel Lewis and Captain Timberlock. The positioning was Timberlock's choice, and it gave Sam a feeling of confidence and importance that he had never felt before. Timberlock was counting on Sam's shooting ability to keep him and the colonel safe, and to bring an end to Dull Knife's run.

Sam would have never experienced such a thing in his father's shop. He couldn't hold a hammer the right way or breathe right as far as his father was concerned. At the moment, riding in a long string of armed men, Sam felt more alive than he had ever felt before. His fear of dying hadn't gone away, but he knew he wouldn't have wanted to have missed a second of life as a man in the army. He kept Jessica's most recent letter hidden inside his shirt as a piece of luck and a reminder of why he was doing what he was doing.

Six days into the ride, they caught up with Dull Knife and the rest of the Indians the chief was riding with. The Indians had set camp deep inside a thick grove of hardwoods alongside a shallow creek with a steep ravine. An escape plan had already been established by the Cheyenne, because the encounter resulted in a small skirmish, an exchange of long-range gunfire and nothing more. It was good practice for Sam, targeting shadows, firing under pressure, processing rapid orders from Captain Timberlock, and the watchful eyes of Colonel Lewis. Sam was determined to hit his target—which for him was a more tasteful way of thinking than of killing a savage Indian. It wasn't until the fire was returned that

Sam lost any concern about the human beings at the wrong end of the bullets. He had to protect the colonel and his fellow soldiers.

Dull Knife fled and Colonel Lewis with the rest of the troop and armed citizens chased after the Indians with a resolve and quiet certainty that Sam admired. It wasn't long before they crossed the Smoky Hill River into Kansas and followed a mass of Indian tracks down Punished Woman's Fork, where they found Dull Knife and his warriors dug in and waiting for them.

Bullets flew back and forth, and Captain Timberlock called Sam forward to take a shot into a clearing where another flank of Indians were preparing to engage the infantry. Sam took his spot, found a target that he thought he could hit—an Indian crouching low to the ground, joining the flank—and sighted the man in. He pulled the trigger without thinking and easily hit the man square in the head, sending him sprawling to the ground in a splatter of blood. There was no time to consider what he had done. It was war. It was his life or the Indian's simple as that. This wasn't about being a hero. It was about staying alive. It was about doing his duty.

More gunfire was exchanged, and an unfortunate bullet from the Cheyenne side of the river found its way into Colonel Lewis's leg. Stricken, but not dead, the colonel continued to shout orders and fire into the collection of holed-up Indians. The colonel's orders reached out to the rest of his men, including Sam, with the intent of surrounding the Cheyenne. It didn't take long, with Captain Timberlock in the lead, to capture the Indians. The first thing Timberlock did was take away their guns and horses.

Colonel Lewis was in bad shape and sent by wagon to Fort Robinson for care—but he didn't make it. Lewis died on the way, casting a pall over the troop's victory celebration. Sam didn't have time to confront his feelings about killing a man, an Indian, with the colonel's death at hand. The Cheyenne had got what was coming to them.

### *Wapanucka, Indian Territory, May 1888*

Trusty didn't sleep well in the barn. Every little noise caused him to stir awake, flitter his eyes open to check on Horse and Michael, who had taken up watch at the door of the stall. Once in a moment of brief wakefulness, Trusty heard an owl hoot not too far away. Then thunder rumbled and rain began to fall, lulling him back to sleep. Another time he woke, drenched in sweat like a fever had broken. Whenever he was sick as a boy, his mother hovered over him, fearing that he would be taken by consumption, suffer like she did. His father would rage against his mother, but that didn't deter her. But this sweat was from no illness. Trusty was sure it was from the gunshot wound in his shoulder. If there had been any fever, it was gone, along with a good portion of the pain that had been provoked by the shoot-out in the café. Sleep came in a deep drop after that, but it didn't last. Horse woke him snorting and dancing around in the stall, pulling at the lead bar he was tied to.

Trusty wrestled awake, not too happy about being awoken, rubbing his shoulder to make sure it still didn't hurt as bad, then clearing his eyes. Daylight was start- ing to breach the slats in the stall from the open front door. The light was soft, making it easy to see as Trusty stood up.

There was nothing else to see. No one was around. Just Trusty and the horses. His hand slid down to his gun belt just to make sure his Colt was still on his side. All things considered he wasn't going to sleep without it close by. The gun was there—but Michael Darby wasn't. There was no sign of the ex-priest. Not even a whiff of tobacco smoke lingered in the stall. It was like the man had been gone for a long time. Or was never there at all. Though Trusty didn't believe Michael was an aberration. He was a real man with problems, secrets, and an agenda of his own.

# Chapter 20

*Wapanucka, Indian Territory, May 1888*

Trusty walked into the café, scanning the tables for a familiar face. There had been no sign of Michael Darby in the barn. No note left behind, no word with the livery-man, nothing. The café seemed the next logical place to look for him, even though something gnawed deep in Trusty's mind; a voice telling him that a Darby was a Darby and the man had made a run for it—for whatever the reason. Regardless of the cause, Trusty was on his own, left to wonder why Michael left in the middle of the night. But there was more than that. There was the worry of the ex-priest's motivation. Trusty was concerned he was going to have to look over his shoulder for Michael coming after him too. He had trusted one Darby—Amelia—tepidly, with reserved judgment, and that had not turned out well at all. There was even more reasons not to trust Michael, regardless of his previous vocation as a priest. Maybe even more so. Something about the man didn't seem to fit the cloth or the collar that he had once worn. But there had been, Trusty reasoned, more than one opportunity for Michael Darby to kill him. If that was the man's intent, then why wait until now to show himself, to leave? It didn't make sense to Trusty unless he considered that something was wrong, something had happened to Michael. If that were the case, then he owed Michael the same kindness he had been shown at Lost Mountain Pass. He had to try and find out what had happened to him.

Mae looked up as Trusty made his way to her. The café was about half-full of patrons. The air smelled of frying bacon and coffee boiling on an unseen stove. "I didn't expect to see you this morning," the Choctaw waitress said. "Where's your partner?"

"He's not my partner."

The mumble of conversation in the café dropped to a level just above silence. A piece of thin wood had been nailed over the shot-out window, causing any noise to ricochet to the back of the little restaurant. A cook continued to work in the kitchen, shifting pans, shuffling around. That was the only noise Trusty could hear.

"You could've fooled me," Mae said. "Looked like you two had a working relationship."

Trusty almost said that he always rode alone, but he restrained himself. He didn't know if there were any opportunity-seekers in the café. Wearing the badge and revisiting the scene of the shoot-out was enough of a tell about who he was to folks. He didn't need to advertise his name. Funny how that changed once there was a price on his head. Trusty would have given anything to have walked into the café and everyone know his name as soon as he did. Even Trusty instead of Sam. It didn't matter. Not now. That would have meant that all was well with the world. That Judge Hadesworth was still alive, trailing after his wife in Muskogee from one shopping spree to the next, dispersing justice like he was meant to, angling toward the final, doting years of his life. And Trusty would have gone on with his own life as a marshal doing whatever needed done. But that was not to be. Now he didn't even dare to mention his name aloud. Amelia Darby had changed everything for him.

"So, you haven't seen the man I was with?" Trusty said. "Michael Darby. His name was Michael Darby."

"Not a shadow. I ain't never heard of no Darbys."

"You're too far away from Kosoma, I suppose."

"Toughs, uh?"

"They were until they met the end of the rope."

"I suppose there is justice in this world."

"You didn't see anybody leave town?" Trusty said.

"Kind of hard when there's no window, ain't it?"

"Yeah, sorry about that."

Mae smirked a little bit and relaxed her broad shoulders. "Don't worry about it. You didn't start the shootin' now, did you?"

"No, we were leaving if I remember right. That was a right fine meal, at least up and until then."

Mae studied Trusty's face, then looked past him to a man sitting alone at a table in the corner, soaking his eggs with a piece of toast. "You're a bad liar. What are you gonna do once you find this man?"

"I need to get on the trail," Trusty said.

"Where are you headin'?" Mae returned her focus to Trusty.

He almost answered her again, told her exactly where he was going, but he restrained himself for a second time.

It was time to leave. Michael was nowhere to be found here. "Parts unknown, ma'am."

"Well, you be careful out there."

"Thanks for your hospitality, ma'am." Trusty smiled, doffed his hat, then turned to leave. He found the man with the eggs staring at him as he went for the door. The man had dark, penetrating eyes, stringy black hair, and a face that looked like it had been used to rake gravel. Trusty did his best to memorize the man's face in case he saw it again—and continued walking until he was out of the café and free of stares.

Horse stood tied to the hitching post, waiting patiently. The saddlebags were packed full, and Trusty's Winchester angled out of the scabbard. Nothing looked disturbed or out of place. He relaxed a bit, glad to be out of the café. A quick glance across the street to the rooftops seemed a prudent thing to do, all things considered. He didn't have Michael to help if another round of bounty hunters were lying in wait for him. There was nothing to alarm him or cause him any concern.

The street was a little busier, but Wapanucka was not a thriving city. It was a lazy town that relied on an academy and surrounding homes to keep it alive. Even the trading post looked worn and tired. A few Indian men on horses trotted by as Trusty mounted Horse, not paying any attention to him. He settled into the saddle and took another deep look around, hoping for a sight of Michael, but there was nothing to see. Michael Darby had vanished into thin air.

The sky was clear of clouds and the sun was rising in the east, behind him. Beyond the men on horses, Trusty scanned what little walking traffic there was on the boardwalks. Three women, one man, and a lazy spotted dog were all he saw. Still no sign of Michael Darby, adding to the unsettled feeling that had appeared in his stomach as soon as he realized that he was on his own.

There was nothing to do now but head north into what was known as the Unassigned Lands. In a year, the land would be opened up for settlers of all stripes, and life in the Territory would be changed forever. Trusty had mixed emotions about the change that was coming. There was bound to be conflict and violence, but that was nothing new. Only now there would be more people. More reason to need U.S. Marshals. Which would be a good thing for him if he wasn't in the position he was in, trying to redeem himself, trying to reason with himself and the rest of the world why he should continue on and be a man who wears a badge. He didn't know if he would have a job in a year or be alive for that matter. Not with every gun in the Territory pointed at his head.

No Man's Land was a three-hundred-mile journey northwest, and there was no guarantee that Trusty would be able to find Amelia Darby once he arrived there. Having Michael with him had given him a modicum of confidence that they would be able to find Amelia. But with Michael gone, so was the help—and the confidence.

Trusty had learned a few things from riding with Michael though. Amelia was married to a man named David Folsom. He was a bone collector, which was not so unusual, unless the fertilizer scheme was a front. Or Michael was lying. Everything the man had said was always strained through a sieve of distrust by Trusty, but even more so now that he was gone. He had to consider that everything Michael had said could have been a lie. David Folsom could have been a made-up name, and a reason to head to No Man's Land could have been nothing more than a rouse or a trap. For all Trusty knew, Michael could have been helping Amelia all along, diverting attention from her, sending Trusty in the opposite direction, and keeping him away from her so she could do what? Hide out forever? And as Trusty reasoned as he rode free of Wapanucka, if that were the case, then why didn't Michael just kill him in the first place and collect his thousand silvers from Theodore Marberry? The more he thought about it, the more Michael's disappearance didn't make sense, and he continued to wonder if he had made a mistake. Or maybe he should have looked for Michael Darby a little harder. The man could have been in trouble. Needed his help instead of his judgment. Michael could have fended off a bounty-seeker, been hurt, or worse for all Trusty knew; he could be dead. Sadly, he had to consider that he might be wrong about Michael, about leaving him. For all Trusty knew, he had failed Michael too.

The thought forced him to bring Horse to a stop. Without allowing another thought to stop him, he turned around and headed back to Wapanucka, kicking up dust, pushing Horse as hard as he could. Michael deserved more of Trusty's time—even if he was a Darby. It was the right thing to do, no matter the risk of drawing bullets to himself. Michael had fended off Amelia, saved his life more than once. Trusty owed him the same in return.

\* \* \*

Allen's Academy seemed the most logical place to start looking for Michael. The building, a sight to behold upon arriving in Wapanucka, was easy to find. The massive, redbrick institutional building stood on the outskirts of the main street town, casting a shadow on everything within sight. After hitching Horse outside the building, Trusty made his way inside a tall double-door entrance. He found the school office right away and came face-to-face with an older Choctaw woman. She was two heads shorter than him, twice as wide, wore a serious look on her face, and was leaving the building as he was entering. Her thick, light brown arms were loaded down with a bundle of papers. "May I help you?" she said.

"I'm looking for someone. I'm hoping you can help me."

"A student?" The woman wore thin gold wire-frame glasses and her eyes were a little foggy. She strained upward when she looked at Trusty's face. Her brittle gray hair was tied back in a bun, and the pressed expression on her face made her look severe and angry.

"No, I'm not looking for a student. I'm looking for a man who was riding with me. Have there been any strangers come in since this morning?"

"Oh, you'll need to speak with the supervisor, Mister Hoarsley. I'm sorry, I have to get these papers upstairs. You tell him that Hilda Lowwater sent you. He's in the third office on the right." The woman, Hilda, started to walk away, then stopped and said, "You're not here to cause any trouble, are you?"

"No, why do you ask?"

"Because you're Trusty Dawson, that's why, and you've got a gun on your hip and a knife in your belt.

And there was trouble in town last night because of you. I heard tell two men found their way to the grave this morning, may they rest in peace, and there's more death east of here. Bad news travels fast, you know."

"I know how that goes." Trusty shook his head. He almost smiled at the mention of his name but didn't. "I promise there's no trouble here to cause that I know of. I'm just tryin' to find a man is all."

"Okay, then. Mister Hoarsley will help you." Hilda stared at Trusty for a long second, then hurried off with her arms full of papers.

Trusty watched her go, then made his way to the supervisor's office. He found it straightaway and was surprised that there was no one else to speak to that allowed entrance into the office. He knocked on the door with a gentle rap.

"Yes," a man's voice answered.

"Trusty Dawson, Deputy U.S. Marshal, Mister Hoarsley. Hilda Lowwater sent me. I was hopin' I could ask you a question or two."

"Come on in, Marshal Dawson, I've been expecting you."

Curious, Trusty pushed inside the small office to find a Choctaw man with thin white hair shorn short on the sides, with a long beard the same color flowing over from his chin to his chest. He wore glasses, too, and was dressed in a black suit that made him look more like an undertaker than an academy supervisor.

"Expectin' me?" Trusty said.

"Yes, I assumed you would come here looking for Michael Darby."

"He's been here?"

"He's here."

"Where?"

"Why don't you sit down, Mister Dawson," Hoarsley said, peering up through his glasses. He wore the same serious, severe look as Hilda. Trusty wondered what they taught in this school and who they taught it to. Most likely Indians, trying to convince them that the white way of living was the right way of living.

"Is Michael all right?"

"Physically, yes. Please sit down." The supervisor changed the tone in his voice to make his words sound more like an order than a request as he swept his hand toward the chair that sat in front of the desk. He settled back in his own chair and wore the confirmed look of an administrator.

Trusty did as he was told. "What's the matter with Michael? I thought he took off on me, or worse, found trouble at my expense."

"I can assure you that he didn't take off on you. Just the contrary. He came here for help. We may not be of the same faith, Mister Darby and I, or share the same tenets of that faith, but we are a place of refuge as well as a place of learning. He knew that and sought out permission to rest here."

"He could have told me."

"I can't speak to anyone's actions but my own."

"He's okay, then?"

"No, I don't think so. Michael Darby is a broken, conflicted man. He needs some time to himself to consider his path in this life."

Trusty sighed and settled back in the chair, lowered

his head, then looked back up to the elder supervisor. "This is about the man he killed last night, isn't it?"

"Yes, I suppose it is, though that was the breaking point, I suspect. His spirit has been under a lot of stress. Do you understand what I'm saying, Mister Dawson?"

"Yes, I think I do. Can I speak to him before I leave?"

"Of course. Michael Darby is not a prisoner here. No one is. He's free to leave or do whatever he wants. He is in the sanctuary at the end of the hall."

Trusty stood up and headed for the door.

"Mister Dawson?" Hoarsley said.

"Yes?" Trusty stopped and turned his attention back to the supervisor.

"Not all wounds and scars are visible to the eye."

Trusty nodded and walked away, digesting what he had been told.

The sanctuary was a large room with a three-story ceiling, filled with long wood pews that faced a solid wall with an oak-carved cross mounted on it. Tall, narrow windows lined both sides of the room allowing soft morning light to filter inside the room in long, defined golden shafts. Dust, floating like diamonds, dangled in the air, twinkling on and off as they moved in and out of the light. Michael was sitting in the front pew, bent over, his elbows propped up on his knees, his head down, his hands cupped at his forehead.

"I thought you ran off," Trusty said. His voice had an echo that reached the ceiling. "I rode out of town looking for a sign of you but doubled back."

"You should have kept on riding."

"I owed it to you to find out if you were alive or dead."

Michael sat up and looked forward. Trusty had stopped

halfway up the aisle. "I should have let you know that I left, but I went out into the night chasing shadows and ghosts and ended up here. You know how hard it is to find whiskey in an Indian town in the middle of the night?"

Trusty stood still as a rabbit with a hawk circling overhead in the sky. He didn't know what to say, what to do. Now that he knew Michael was alive, he wanted to walk out the door, get on Horse, and ride to No Man's Land as fast as he could. But he couldn't do that. Not yet. He needed to know if Michael was going to ride with him or not.

"Somehow, I found my way here," Michael continued. "I figured I would. I couldn't outrun what I had done, what I had become. There is no repenting for killing a man, for shedding my collar, and for picking up the gun. I should have known my true blood would prevail. You were a fool to allow me to ride with you."

"I would likely be dead if it wasn't for you," Trusty said. "You saved my life. There has to be something to account for in that."

"I lied to you too. I have betrayed you as much as I saved you."

Trusty walked up to Michael then and said, "What are you talking about?"

"My sister was never heading to No Man's Land."

"Where is she heading then?"

"Oklahoma Station. She's meeting up with her husband there."

"How do you know this?"

"She told me, Trusty. She told me exactly what she was going to do, and then she went and did it, that's how I know. Amelia told me."

# Chapter 21

*Atoka, Indian Territory, May 1888*

Vance Calhoun and his six riders rode into Atoka as the sun fell below the horizon. The sky burned red, lighting puffs of clouds with tips of invisible flames, pulsing the outside of the cotton balls like they were on fire. The burning sky was a reminder to Calhoun of all that had been lost to him, but he didn't dwell there for long. Gladdy had tracked Trusty Dawson and another rider through Lost Mountain Pass to the small town of Atoka. They were closing in on Dawson, or at least it felt that way. Calhoun looked forward to looking the marshal in the eye before he killed him.

Gladdy was riding ahead of Calhoun, already at the livery, dismounting from his horse. The rest of the men rode two abreast, with Denton Hobbs riding alongside Calhoun.

"I know this town," Hobbs said, looking around. "I thought the lay of the land looked familiar about five miles back."

"How so?" Calhoun wasn't really interested. He was

looking for a decent hotel or a restaurant to fill his empty belly. He didn't see either with an open sign obvious, but that didn't mean anything in a town like this. Hotels were always open, and if the price was right, grub could be rustled up. The only thing that looked lit and welcoming was a papist church, which held no interest at all to Calhoun.

"There was an outpost here in the war," Hobbs said. "Federals came down from Fort Gibson with the intention of breaking the hold on Indian Territory. There was over a thousand of 'em. Phillips, I think that was the colonel's name was that led that charge. You know of 'im?"

Calhoun shook his head no and continued his disappointment with the town. He missed the comfort of what had been his home . . . his soft, warm featherbed, a known woman, and a meal cooked by Maria that would satisfy any man. But that world didn't exist anymore— or a world with Vance Calhoun in it. As far as everybody was concerned, he was dead and buried. The last thing he should have been concerned about was his comfort, but he was. He had to wonder if this whole thing hadn't been one big mistake.

"About ninety of us Rebs took on about a thousand of the Federals," Hobbs continued once he figured out that Calhoun wasn't interested in joining the conversation. "We was out by the Middle Boggy River. Outnumbered ten to one. Lost nearly fifty men that day. It was bloody as hell, and with over half of us dead, we had no choice but to make a run for it or die. I ain't no runner, boss, you know that, but we had no choice. Not one of them Federals died."

"What's your point, Hobbs?" Calhoun said as he brought the grullo to a stop in front of the livery.

"I don't have no point, boss. Just sayin' I remember this place is all, and I don't have good memories of it." Hobbs looked to the fiery red sky, then lowered his head as he stopped his horse next to Calhoun's grullo. "All I got is bad feelin's about this town. I think we should be careful is all I'm sayin'."

Calhoun stared at Hobbs for a second, then glanced over his head, back to the burning sky. "If I believed in ghosts coming for me, Hobbs, I'd never get out of bed. How many years ago was that battle—if you want to call it that—comin' up on nigh on twenty-five years or more?"

"Somethin' like that. I ain't no good at math. Sometimes in the middle of the night it seems like I'm still there. Ain't it that way for you? The war never seems to go away."

"I don't think about it." Calhoun took his attention from the sky and studied Hobbs's gray, haunted face. He made a note to himself not to trust the man in a gun battle. Not only was Hobbs a runner, he carried fear with him for more years than he should have.

Gladdy O'Connor walked out of the livery as Calhoun dismounted from the grullo. "Man says there's a restaurant alongside the hotel. Says not to expect much more than beans and cornbread, and no back room for liquor that he knows of. But he's an Indian and he looked at me with suspicious eyes like they all do. Especially seven of us lookin' for lodgings. He didn't ask no questions, though, boss. I say we have a man stand watch, or we'll be needin' to sleep with one eye open."

Calhoun nodded and turned around to survey the other riders, all doing the same, climbing off their horses, looking relieved to be out of the saddle—all of them but Hobbs. It looked like he was trying to decide to stay or go. If he decided to ride off, Calhoun didn't figure he had any choice but to shoot the man. Hobbs knew his true identity, that he was still alive. That might be some valuable information for Hobbs to barter or sell to someone. This wasn't the time to take any chances.

Hobbs pulled himself off the saddle and settled his feet on the ground, allowing for his life to continue a little longer.

Calhoun relaxed as much as that was possible, then turned his attention back to Gladdy. "Get the rest of the horses settled and meet us at the hotel."

"Which one?" Gladdy said.

"You think there's ten to choose from in this flea-speck of a town?"

"No, boss, I guess I don't."

"Then use that goddamned brain of yours and find us when you're finished up here," Calhoun said as he walked off. "Find out what you can," he added over his shoulder.

Gladdy stared at the man for a long second, took the grullo's reins, shook his head, then headed into the barn.

The sky faded from red to pink, finally giving up the fight for color to gray, then to black. Clouds dissipated and pinprick stars pulsed in silver specks overhead. Somewhere in the distance, an owl hooted and a dog barked. Other than that, it was quiet in Atoka.

* * *

The restaurant was the usual fare found in small Indian Territory towns. Not much more than an alcove filled with tables and chairs, offering little or no atmosphere like a big city restaurant might. Calhoun longed for a Delmonico steak, but knew he was going to settle for beans or something worse. Gladdy had already warned him about that.

The air smelled of grease and smoke, and there were no patrons in the restaurant. A short, overweight Choctaw woman looked up from sweeping with a broom when Calhoun and his crew walked in the door. Only Gladdy was missing. He was still at the livery seeing to the horses.

"We're closing," the woman said.

Calhoun led the pack of hungry men, breaking away from them with long strides, and said, "No, you're not. My men have been ridin' all day and need fed. And you're gonna feed them because there ain't nowhere else in this poor excuse for a town that I see to do that."

"We don't have enough food for all of you." The woman had stopped sweeping. Her round face was expressionless, and the skin was loose around her eyes, showing no tightness or fear. Her words were matter of fact, steady.

The men had stopped behind Calhoun. All of their eyes were on him, tired, hungry, worn out by the ride and in no mood for any kind of resistance. They looked like they could turn into a raging mob at the drop of a penny and tear the place apart for nothing more than the fun of it. Their dusters draped off their shoulders. Dirt had settled in the crevices of their hats, and their spurs were quiet. Every man wore a sidearm within easy reach. There was always the suggestion that more weapons were hidden under their riding clothes, but none of this seemed to intimidate the Choctaw woman.

"What's your name?" Calhoun said. In an odd way, she reminded him of Maria. He hoped she could cook as well as the Mexican woman had.

"Talli. What's yours?"

Calhoun almost blurted out his name, almost said Vance Calhoun without thinking about it, but he stopped the words halfway up his throat. He drew a breath and hesitated. The truth was he hadn't thought about what to call himself. He hadn't thought that far ahead of his decision to tell the world that he was dead. Whether he had believed the plot would work or not wasn't important. It had been a quick decision, an easy fix to a big problem that had seemed to have worked—until now. "Joseph Jones," he said. "My name's Joseph Jones. Ain't it, boys? The one and only Joseph Jones from Montgomery, Tennessee."

"Whatever you say, boss," Hobbs answered back. The rest of the men nodded, grumbled under their breath, shrugged their shoulders or looked to the muddy toes of their boots.

The Choctaw woman didn't seem to notice or care about the gang's reaction. "Well, Mister Jones, I can ask our cook Randolph what he can feed you, but it might not be much if you're gonna insist," Talli said.

Calhoun smiled. The woman hadn't flinched at the lie, had believed him straightaway. He liked that. It made him feel good. The name had stuck. "Tell Randolph I'll pay extra," he said. "To him and you, Talli. Tell him to find enough food for my men and it will be worth his while." Calhoun dug into his pocket, pulled out two bits, and handed the coins to the woman. "There's plenty more where that came from."

This time it was the Choctaw woman's turn to smile. Her front teeth were missing but that didn't seem to matter as she took the money, tucked the coins into a pocket in her apron, and hurried off to the kitchen. "Ain't closin' now, Randolph. We got payin' customers, you hear?" she called out as she went.

The smile hadn't left Calhoun's face. "Sit down, boys, and make yourselves comfortable."

No one moved. They waited for Calhoun to sit down first, which he did at the closest table. Hobbs joined him, but no one else did. The remaining four men, all cowboys from the ranch who had been loyal to Haden O'Connor, sat at a table behind Calhoun, leaving two empty seats at the boss's table.

"I wonder what's takin' Gladdy so long," Hobbs said.

"Gladdy's a curious kind. He's asking around to get a feelin' of the town."

Hobbs looked at Calhoun like he didn't agree with him about Gladdy, but didn't say so, at least not out loud.

Talli hurried out of the kitchen carrying a pot of coffee in one plump hand, and three mugs, grasped with her fingers wrapped through the handles, with her other hand. The smell of fresh brewed coffee followed her as she stopped at the table. "Randolph says there's tomorrow's bread you have for tonight," she said as she set the coffeepot down in the middle of Calhoun's table, followed by the mugs.

"I appreciate that," Calhoun said. "And so do my boys."

Talli smiled as she poured a mug of coffee for Calhoun and handed it to him. "It's a might strong."

"Just the way I like it." Calhoun took a sip of the coffee and watched as Talli poured Hobbs a mug. She was close enough to smell of flour and grease from the day spent in the restaurant. "There haven't been any strangers through here in the last few days, have there, Talli?" Calhoun set the mug down and stared at the Choctaw with his cold, hard eyes.

Talli froze, going from Calhoun's table to the next one with the four cowboys. "Strangers? In here?"

"Anywhere." Calhoun didn't take his gaze off Talli's face. She twitched. Had to catch her breath. It was obvious she hadn't been expecting the question. "In town. I figure you hear everything that happens around these parts, now don't you?"

"Yes, Mister Jones, I usually do." Talli broke the stare-down between the two of them and looked away to the door that led outside. Randolph banged some pots and pans in the kitchen. The smell of warm bread replaced the smell of the Indian woman and the coffee.

"Well, has there been any strangers in town?" Calhoun persisted. His voice was edged with the tone of a threat that silently said, *don't make me ask again.*

"There was a couple of riders who took refuge at Saint Patrick's church for the night." Talli moved to the table and put the remaining mug down. She filled them both, eyeing the mugs, then turning her attention back to Calhoun, then back to the coffee. She was suddenly as nervous as a rabbit on the run. "Then there's always the train that comes and goes. Not many folk stay here. They're usually on their way to Oklahoma Station or parts farther north, Kansas, you know." Talli paused, then turned her attention to the cowboys. "I'll be right back with three more mugs."

None of the men said anything. They all stared at her, not interfering in the conversation she was having with Calhoun. Talli started to head toward the kitchen, but Calhoun grabbed her elbow and stopped her mid-stride.

"Tell me about these riders. Was one of them a marshal?" Calhoun said.

Talli didn't try to wriggle out of Calhoun's tight grasp, but her brown skin turned a shade lighter. "Yes," she said. "I think so."

"What'd they do while they were here?" Calhoun asked, tightening his grip a little harder. He was starting to enjoy himself, could see the discomfort on the woman's face. She wasn't hurting . . . yet.

"I don't know. Word was the other one used to be a priest, but he wasn't allowed in the church. They left out the next mornin' and headed west. Neither man came here for a meal, I don't know any more about them than what I done told you."

"West? Where west?" Calhoun loosened his grip, then let go of Talli. All he wanted her to know was that he could hurt her if he wanted to. He didn't want to spoil his dinner and cause her to run off.

"I don't know," Talli said, stepping back, rubbing her

arm. An impression of Calhoun's fingers was left behind. "I swear, I don't know, Mister Jones."

"Okay. Go on, get us our food and coffee. We ain't got all night."

Talli didn't need to be told twice. She hurried off and disappeared into the kitchen before Calhoun could say another word.

All the men remained quiet. The mood didn't lighten when Gladdy finally walked in the door, followed by a burst of cool night air. Oil lamps flickered in his wake as he made his way to Calhoun's table. His spurs jingled, and his boots thudded on the wood floor, echoing throughout the restaurant. He stood for a second and waited to be told what to do.

"Go on, sit down," Calhoun said. "What'd you find out?"

Gladdy took the empty seat across from Calhoun and looked at the empty coffee mug. "I was right to think we was on their trail. Dawson's been through here. Ridin' with another man. A priest who wears a gun."

"I already know that." Calhoun glared at Gladdy, then looked over his shoulder to the kitchen and tapped his fingers on the table at the same time.

"Word is the priest is kin to the woman who shot that judge that Dawson was escortin' back to Muskogee."

"Kin you say?" He had Calhoun's attention now. "That's news."

Gladdy smiled, then said, "They're not far off that woman's tail. She was through here, too. Outrunnin' Wanted posters before they hit the nail and everybody knew her face."

"Where was she headed?" Calhoun said.

Gladdy didn't answer. He watched Talli make her way to the table carrying two bowls of steaming soup. The smell of sweet broth permeated the room, reminding Calhoun and every other man in the café how hungry they were. Talli was followed by an Indian man who it was assumed was Randolph the cook. He was thin as a rail with thick black hair cut square around his head like a bowl had been used as a guide for the scissors. Randolph carried two bowls of the soup and a loaf of bread. The Indians distributed the soup, serving Calhoun first, along with giving him the bread, then headed back into the kitchen.

Calhoun didn't wait and slurped up a helping of the soup. To his surprise, the broth tasted of fresh chicken, and there were some carrots and beans mixed in with a little meat. He only stopped to break off a bit of bread, then went on eating. Talli and Randolph returned with the rest of the bowls, then again to serve the remaining coffees. Randolph headed back to the kitchen and Talli stayed behind.

"Good?" she said to Calhoun.

"Yes, it is. We had jerky on our ride here. This'll be a fine meal," he answered.

"Save some room for some huckleberry pie." Talli smiled and started to walk off.

"You didn't tell me there'd been a white woman through here too," Calhoun said. He'd dropped his spoon on the table and glared at her.

Talli looked to Gladdy and put two and two together. "You asked if any men had been through. I thought you were only interested in the marshal and the man he was ridin' with." Her response was too quick, tinged with a nervous crack in her voice.

Calhoun stood up, towering over the Indian woman. All of the men except Gladdy stopped eating. He dipped at the soup like a dog who'd been deprived of food and water for a month. His slurps filled the small café with a disgusting sound.

"Would you stop it, Gladdy," Calhoun demanded. "You got the manners of a cow."

"Sorry, boss. I was hungry."

"You think this here woman is tellin' the truth, Gladdy? That white woman's a killer. Why do you think nobody would tell us she was through here? Why would they hide a white woman?" Calhoun held Talli's gaze even though he was talking to Gladdy.

"Don't know, boss," Gladdy said. "Other than she's married to an Indian."

"An Indian, you say?" Calhoun crossed his arms, doing his math about the situation he'd found himself in. "A Choctaw?"

"Yes, boss? How'd you know that?" Gladdy said.

"Lucky guess." Calhoun stepped forward so he was within inches of Talli. She didn't move, didn't step back. A line of perspiration bubbled on top of her forehead. "You want to tell me what this is about, Talli? I ain't in the mood to hurt no one. You and Randolph have showed us a kindness, and that soup was awful tasty. I'm hopin' that huckleberry pie tastes just as good. But I need to know everything you know about this woman, you hear me? I ain't gonna hurt you unless you lie to me, then I'll kill you right here and now. You best believe that, woman."

Talli trembled and nodded. "I believe you. I do. But I don't know the woman you speak of. I know her husband, David. David Folsom. He's got kin here."

"In this town?" Calhoun said.

Talli nodded again. Her eyes were glazed, watery; she was on the verge of tears.

"Is he here? This David Folsom?"

"No," Talli said. "He's been up in No Man's Land for a spell, but word is he's on his way to meet up with his woman."

"Where?" Calhoun said.

"I don't know." Talli sucked in a deep breath of air. "My guess is Oklahoma Station."

"Why?" Calhoun sighed and looked to the ceiling. "I hate that town."

"I heard unfinished business is all."

"What kind of unfinished business?"

"Something to do with the white woman's brother. It's all I know," Talli said. "I swear. Please don't kill me, I've got children at home."

"I ain't gonna kill you," Calhoun said. "You gave us some good soup. Best food I've had since I left home. Is there anything else you ain't tellin' me? The marshal and that priest, they were on the white woman and Folsom's trail?"

Talli nodded as the color came back to her face and the fear of dying seemed to subside. "I think so. But there were other men askin' questions about that marshal too. Said there was a bounty on his head and they aimed to get it."

Calhoun cocked his head and tapped his ear to make

sure it was working properly. "A bounty you say? On Trusty Dawson?"

"That's what they said. Come from a man in Saint Louis willin' to pay a thousand dollars for the kill."

"Well," Calhoun smirked, "ain't that somethin'. You hear that, boys? Looks like there's gonna be a payday for your troubles. Dawson's got a price on his head." Put there, he went on to think, but didn't say, by Theodore Marberry. It had to be. That sure would clear things up for Calhoun. There was only one reason Calhoun could think of why Marberry would want the marshal dead: Jessica and her baby daughter. If it was true, Calhoun wouldn't have to wonder or not if he had been bamboozled by Jessica Marberry Tennyton. He would know for sure. "Hurry up, boys, we got a ride to make and some money to collect."

# Chapter 22

A cold hard wind blew out of the north, sweeping across the Platte River with a freezing bluster that only January could bring. From Sam's saddle the ice on the river looked flat and solid. A drift of snow had piled up a foot high on the opposite bank, sweeping the flakes from the surface of the frozen water. The Platte looked like a melancholy gray ribbon of a road snaking to the east and west. The grayness of the ice was a reflection of the sky and Sam's mood. Being out in the weather was reason enough for the misery he felt, once again on the trail of Dull Knife, who had escaped with most of his captive band of Cheyenne from Fort Robinson. It should have been easy enough to track over a hundred Indians on the run in the winter when the flat land was covered with snow and ice. And there were unmistakable signs to follow, but with his eyes glazed over, watered from the blustery cold, and his heart and mind a thousand miles away, he could have ridden straight into an ambush without seeing it coming. Minutes before the call came for him to ride, a letter had arrived all the way from England. Jessica's letters were usually thick, at least ten pages long full of captivating descriptions of her days, of her learning, of the events and sights she had gone to see, but this letter was thin; one page and half of it was blank. The only sentence that mattered was the one that Sam carried with him, and repeated over and over in his mind as he searched for Dull Knife:

> *I am getting married to a man named Bower Tennyton on the thirtieth of March.*

Even in the blinding push of wind, Sam could see the words as plainly as if they were written on the river's ice. He sat motionless on the army mount, a staid chestnut gelding who moved to Sam's commands like one of the best soldiers in the military, staring into the distance but not really seeing it. The horse was as leery of the river as Sam was.

Another rider joined Sam on the bank of the river, a female Apache, an Indian scout called Woman's Clothes, wrapped in a hooded buffalo coat and leggings, her hands covered in rabbit fur mittens. It would have been almost impossible to know the rider was a woman with the way she was dressed, but Sam knew. He had ridden with Woman's Clothes before. Her scouting and tracking skills were unequaled, even if she was a woman—which as far as Sam was concerned gave her the advantage of low expectations and the element of surprise. Woman's Clothes could go places that some would not have dared. Sam had learned a lot just by riding alongside her since he had taken the role of scout in the army. Most of the time, the Apache was quiet, listening to the world around her, and spoke little. Her discomfort around white men was obvious, and Sam had wondered more than once why the woman had agreed to scout for the army. He didn't know her story, and he had never asked. The discomfort worked both ways.

"You were right to stop," Woman's Clothes said. "The ice thins in the middle of the river and the current runs fast underneath." Her English was perfect, suggesting she had been schooled at an early age, most likely by missionaries.

Sam didn't turn to her, didn't acknowledge her arrival. He stared into the blurry nothingness of his broken heart—but with a few blinks, banishing Jessica's words for the moment, he could see hoofprints descending off the bank like they were going across the river. The wind had blown the snow from the ice, and all of the tracks vanished. "Where did the horses go?" he said, waiting for a gust of frigid air to die down before he spoke. The cold reached down his throat and added to the ice that was already forming around his heart.

"It is a trick. I have shown you their ways before if you cared to see," the Apache said. She seemed unperturbed by the weather or the cold. Her eyes were black, focused on the ground as she dismounted her paint mare. "They edged along the bank until the river bends at the stand of cottonwoods. The water is shallow, but the ice is thick there. There were three of them. Two women and one man; two mares, one stallion. I think they are heading to the Hat Creek Bluffs. Little Finger Nail is leading this band. They will dig in along the creek and wait for us to come to them."

Sam stared at Woman's Clothes unsure how she knew so much from seeing so little, but he didn't question her judgment. Sam would have normally dismounted and tried to eye the tracks himself, not only to learn, but to come to trust her any way he could. He had been shot at by too many Indians to take the word of one, especially a woman.

"What is the matter?" Woman's Clothes asked, staring at Sam. "You do not seem like yourself."

Sam shook his head. "We should head back and tell the captain."

"Yes." Woman's Clothes looked down the winding river, then made her way back to her horse. In one easy pull up, she settled in the army saddle as comfortably as she could, sitting next to Sam. "Are you sure?"

"It's best. There are more of them than there are of us."

"But yet you do not ride."

*I could stay right here forever*, Sam thought but didn't say. He didn't know why he was surprised that Jessica was getting married. She was beautiful, smart, and from a well-to-do family. She was most likely pursued by a lot of men. A catch that would have made their mothers proud. He knew he never had a chance at winning her hand. Their fates were too different, but there had always been a token of hope stuffed deep in Sam's pocket that could only be spent on Jessica and what they had shared together. Sitting in the middle of Nebraska in the winter was as far away from London, England, as he could get. There had been no apology, nothing other than a statement of fact, and Sam had to wonder if the love he had felt for Jessica Marberry had been one-sided. Perhaps it was merely a schoolboy crush that he had carried into manhood, keeping him distant from available women, who would have married him at the asking long before now. Something felt broken inside of him. It was a feeling he had never felt before. Like the past and the future had been taken from him in one fell swoop.

Woman's Clothes sat staring at Sam with a look of concern on her face, but he ignored the suggestion of emotion. He was probably mistaken. Indians had always been hard to read. He finally nickered the army gelding and turned away from the river, intent on rushing back to camp.

"Whatever it is that is bothering you, you should leave it here," Woman's Clothes said.

Sam held fast to the horse's reins. He didn't know what to say, other than he wasn't surprised that the Indian woman could decipher his mood; she could see horse tracks that were invisible to most everyone else. "It's nothing."

"Thinking like that will get you killed." Woman's Clothes didn't wait for Sam. She kneed her paint mare and rushed off, leaving him behind. He knew she would deliver the news of Little Finger Nail to the captain, but he had to consider the woman's words.

He didn't know how to leave his love for Jessica behind. On a normal day, he would have screamed from the bottom of his lungs—but that would have gotten him shot, given away the location of the troops to Dull Knife and his own scouts. Sam couldn't do that. All he could do was ride away, and whisper "Good-bye," as he went.

* * *

It turned out that Woman's Clothes was right about Little Finger Nail. Captain Henry Wessels led four companies of soldiers, one hundred and fifty men, including Sam, into the Hat Creek Bluffs. Thirty-two of the Cheyenne were holed up in a dry creek bed: men, women, and children. Twenty-four members of the tribe were killed, including Little Finger Nail in a long battle that was bloody and brutal. Wessels was wounded, and eleven soldiers, plus one Indian scout were killed: the scout was Woman's Clothes. Sam came out of the fight whole, congratulated on helping find the band of escapees, his reputation growing, but he had lost something more than he could share. He would always remember the Fort Robinson Massacre as one of the worst days of his life.

### *Wapanucka, Indian Territory, May 1888*

"When did Amelia tell you that she was meeting her husband in Oklahoma Station, Michael?" Trusty said, hardly able to believe what he had just heard from Michael Darby. If there was any leftover pain in his shoulder, Trusty didn't feel it. A rage ran through his entire body as he stared at Michael with more than a mounting case of distrust.

The two men were standing a few feet apart. Close enough for Trusty to reach out and punch Michael if he took the notion. He sure felt like it.

"In Kosoma, before the hanging," Michael said, his eyes to the ground, his voice fragile as window glass in a hailstorm.

"Before the hanging?"

"Yes, I sought her out. I knew she would take the death

of Rascal hard. I intended to console Amelia if she would have it, but as I suspected, she didn't want to have anything to do with me or the promise of faith and subservience that I offered her."

"What do you mean?"

"I suggested Amelia join me at the church, give up her selfish ways and serve the rest of her mortal life as a nun and ask for forgiveness for all of her sins. She laughed at me, of course, swore that she was already poor and refused to be poorer, that there was no such thing as salvation for a woman like her. She is probably right about that. I knew about David, that their marriage was a common-law marriage, so I didn't think it was a problem. I was wrong about her devotion to him. I was wrong about everything when it came to Amelia. I always have been, but that is nothing new."

"Something we share," Trusty said. "What did she tell you she was going to do, Michael?"

He sighed, then ran his right hand across his throat, where he once wore a collar, but only found bare skin. "She swore she would get revenge on every man and woman who saw to it that her brothers were hanged. She knew she couldn't do it alone. She needed David and whatever gang he could round up to do any real damage. I thought there was time when I saw her at the cemetery with you and the judge. I knew then I had to give up my calling and do what I could to stop her."

"Why didn't you tell me where she was going?"

"We would have gone through Oklahoma Station on the way to No Man's Land," Michael said. "But if I had told you that was where she was headed, you would have rushed straight there and most likely met your death in the shape you were in when I found you. I thought you needed time to heal. I'm sorry. My intentions were to look after you, help you stay alive. I was going to tell you once we got to Oklahoma Station. I hadn't counted on killing a man, of having to face the worst part of myself. I am a Darby. I am a killer. I'm not sure how to live with that, but I've told you that." Michael took a deep breath and looked away from Trusty. "You should ride on without me. That's what I hoped you would do. But don't go to Oklahoma Station."

"Why not?" Trusty said.

"I doubt she will be there now. She's had time to meet up with David. My guess is they are heading back to Kosoma to finish what she started."

"You're sure of this?"

"As sure as I can be about anything right now." Michael sat back down on the academy pew and looked to the window and the golden light that was flowing through it. "The people of Kosoma are in danger. Even if I ride with you, you'll need more gun power than I can offer."

"What are you suggestin'?" Trusty said.

"I don't know. What do you do when you need help?"

"I ask for it."

Trusty walked out of the Western Union office and wasn't surprised to find Michael saddled on his gray mare, standing next to Horse, packed and ready to go.

"I expected you to stay at the academy, or at least find your way back to your church," Trusty said.

Michael didn't flinch. He sat straight-backed with his

shoulders squared like he was about to ride into battle. "I figured if Amelia was going to finish what she started, then it was time for me to do the same if you'll have me on the ride."

Trusty didn't imply one way or the other how he felt about Michael's request. "I sent a wire to Marshal Grimes and asked him to send along the Guardsmen. I can't say that all three of the marshals will join me, but one or two of them will depending on where they are in the Territory. With the killin' of Judge Hadesworth so fresh, I got a feelin' it won't take them too long to catch up with me. I can use another gun since I don't know what I'm ridin' into, how many men Amelia and this David Folsom will have with them, but I don't want to ride with a man who lies to me or holds back information that might cost me my life—or someone else's. You swear you've come clean on all that you know, then I won't tell you no to your request, but I won't say yes neither. You make up your own mind." Trusty paused and stared Michael in the eye with an unwavering look of determination. "They'll be more killin', you know that, don't you? If you ride with us, I'll expect you to shoot to kill no matter who it is if it comes to it, includin' Amelia. I can feel the pain of her rage every second of every day."

"You want your own revenge?"

"I only want justice for what she's done."

Michael sighed and nodded. "Killing is the way of this world no matter how much I dislike it or try to hide away from it. I'll do whatever I have to to stay alive and make sure I'm on the right side of the fight."

Trusty didn't say anything else. He mounted Horse,

settled himself in the saddle for a long ride, then pointed his horse's head east and urged him to a quick run.

The street was still damp from the rain the day before, not allowing any dust to kick up but a sling and shower of heavy mud in Trusty's wake—along with Michael Darby—followed him out of town.

*Fort Robinson, Nebraska, winter 1879*

Weeks after the massacre, Sam found his way into one of the many makeshift saloons that edged the grounds of the fort. Whiskey had never been a refuge for him, but the burn on the back of his throat and the warmth and numbing on his brain seemed to help ward off a fatigue and cold that had followed him since the last battle, and the arrival of Jessica's letter. He couldn't shake a hopelessness that had overtaken his mood in waking moments and sleep, when it came. The grayness of winter seemed stalled overhead; dark skies, frigid nights, a bashful sun, all contributed to his sour mood.

A piano tinkled a slow rhythm as Sam walked in through the tent flap of the saloon. Ten tables had been set on the hard, worn-down ground. Almost every chair was full of off-duty soldiers from the fort. Poker and faro games were in full swing. Laughter and conversation were constant. Life had gone on for most of the soldiers, or they were in the midst of seeking the same kind of relief Sam sought.

A bar, crafted out of fresh-cut pine, had been erected at the back of the tent. Shelves full of bottles stood behind the bar, and a six-by-six-foot picture of a naked woman lounging on a sofa hung centered over the bar. She wore a bored look on her face, and a ribbon of green cloth was draped across the plump woman's privates. One bartender, a short, stocky, bald-headed German, worked feverishly to keep up with the demand for beer and whiskey. Three women worked the floor, taking drinks to the men, flirting, smiling, playing along any way they could to fatten their purses from the generous, drunken soldiers. Two of the women were older, hair piled high, their ample bodies stuffed in velvet dresses with cleavage overflowing without concern or bashfulness. The other woman was closer to Sam's age, blond, petite, shaped like a dream, her dress cut low, too, but not in a dire way. He stopped at the sight of her. She looked enough like Jessica Marberry, or Jessica Marberry Tennyton now, to take his breath away, to take him right back to the memory he was trying to escape. He was starting to doubt whether that was possible.

Sam made his way to the bar, never taking his eyes off the girl as he went. He quickly found an empty stool and waited for the bartender, who answered to Hans, to take his order. But the short German ignored Sam. He was too busy pulling drafts and wiping counters to care about a new customer. There seemed to be an endless supply of soldiers from the fort wandering inside the tent.

The girl tapped Sam on his shoulder, causing him to jump unexpectedly. She laughed and said, "Oh, I'm sorry. I didn't mean to scare you silly." Her voice was as smooth as her red velvet dress, tinged with a hint of Southern honey on the tip of her tongue.

Sam smiled for the first time in weeks. "You snuck up on me." He stared into her eyes—brown instead of blue like Jessica's—then looked her up and down, casually, not in a horse-buying way. She smelled of jasmine and looked prettier close up, even though on closer inspection, the girl really didn't look anything like Jessica at all. It had been Sam's imagination, or hope. He wasn't sure which.

"You seem to like what you see," the girl said.

Sam swallowed hard. He wasn't expecting her to be so forward, but he shouldn't have been surprised. More than one of the saloon girls had fluttered their eyes at him in the past, suggesting some fun could be had—for a price. He'd never been interested before. But that was before. This was now. "Thanks, I'll have a whiskey," he said.

"Is that all?" The girl didn't break eye contact with Sam and put her hand on his knee. "I get off work in a half hour if Hans'll let me out of here."

"Well," Sam said, doing nothing to dissuade the girl, "it looks like the whiskey is just a start to the rest of the evenin', then, isn't it? I'll sit right here and wait until you can get away."

"I was hoping you would say that."

# Chapter 23

*Leaving Wapanucka, Indian Territory, May 1888*

Trusty was in no mood for conversation as he rode away from Wapanucka. Horse ran at a steady pace on the trail, and Michael and his gray mare followed, keeping a respectable distance. The land was flat and open, and the sky was clear of any threat. New grasses pushed up from the soil and leaves on the trees were almost fully fledged. The air was sweet with the nectar of fruit trees and wildflowers that were in full bloom. There was nothing to hinder Trusty's vision, which at least was one less thing to be concerned about. Not only was there the realized threat of Amelia and her husband to be on the lookout for, but he was looking over his shoulder for the bounty hunters sent by Theodore Marberry. The two concerns put together spelled trouble from all directions, added with the distrust Trusty held for Michael Darby, especially now. Still, Trusty was glad that Michael was riding with him—instead of joining those that were on the hunt for him. Every rider they encountered had to be viewed as a threat, as somebody who was out to do him harm.

He would feel a little better once he was able to join up with the Guardsmen.

They rode through the day, stopping only to water their horses when the opportunity arose, and tend to their own quick reliefs. It wasn't until the sun started dipping to the horizon that Trusty started to think about setting up camp for the night. There had been no sign of the Guardsmen, Heck Thomas, Bill Tilghman, or Chris Madsen. Of the three, Trusty knew Heck the most and Madsen the least. He'd rubbed shoulders with Bill Tilghman a few times, rounded up a couple of outlaws in pursuit of the Dalton Gang, but didn't know the man well enough to call him a friend. All three of the marshals were held in high esteem, not only by Trusty but by most of the citizens of the Territory. They all three shared the same kind of recognition that Trusty did; everyone knew their names and what they were capable of doing. Only their names weren't tainted like his was now.

A creek lined with towering hardwoods presented itself just before darkness fell, offering as decent a place to stop for the night as any. The creek water ran fast from the recent spring rains, and the collection of trees promised game of some kind for dinner; squirrels or rabbits would do. Trusty set about gathering firewood while Michael tied a picket line to secure the horses for the night. Sleeping on the ground presented no problem for Trusty. He liked being out in the open air, especially in the spring when the days were warm and the nights were cool. But he wasn't going to make the same mistake he had last time when he'd set camp with Michael in Lost Mountain Pass. He was going to take first watch.

After a dinner of beans and jerky, Trusty stood up and started to walk away from the fire.

"You sure you want first watch?" Michael said, washing out his bowl with canteen water.

Trusty nodded and kept on walking, embracing the darkness that waited for him beyond the reach of the campfire. He didn't stop until the light of the small blaze escaped the heels of his boots. He was glad to be alone, in the darkness, away from the possibility of conversation.

The night passed without incident, or visitation from anything other than an owl who had swooped low to the ground in front of Trusty, chasing a rabbit that had stirred from the brush. Michael took his turn at watch in the middle of the night, walking the perimeter of the camp, while Trusty slept fitfully on the ground, awake at every little noise. He felt a battle coming, a fight for his life— which was nothing new but had been a rarer occurrence since he'd left the army and became a deputy marshal. Duties like escorting a federal judge, adding manpower in local strikes, chasing down bootleggers, or arresting Indians for drinking was miles away from the bloody days in the Indian Wars when one fight led to another. Becoming a marshal hadn't been easy, but it was calmer, less threatening than being a soldier and scout. Or, at least, it had been.

What lay ahead was personal. Amelia Darby had intended to kill him and had inflicted more damage to Trusty's reputation than he had ever thought possible. Judge Hadesworth was as much a friend as a charge, and his death demanded justice. And Theodore Marberry, a man Trusty had known of for most all of his life, had put a bounty on his head for no apparent reason. The last time he had seen Theodore Marberry was years before, and only in passing then as his carriage turned away from a bank in St. Louis. Jessica, on the other hand, was a different story. Trusty had encountered her almost a year prior, and that had been a brief, unexpected reunion in Muskogee that had ended in a sad, permanent parting of ways. The last he'd heard Jessica had given up her widowhood to the Englishman, Tennyton, and married a man who owned thousands of acres of land and ran cattle in Texas. Trusty had had no contact with Jessica since Muskogee; no letters, nothing. He was still confounded by the bounty—but not enough to disbelieve it. Four men had come after him in hopes of collecting a thousand silvers. All of this weighed on Trusty, along with the grief over losing Judge Hadesworth, as he tried to prepare himself for what was to come. Sharing his concerns with Michael was out of the question. He still wasn't sure what side of the fight the man would end up on. Sleeping with one eye open had become a necessity.

After cleaning up breakfast and hiding the ashes of the fire the best he could, Trusty wandered out to the road while Michael packed his horse. The road was nothing more than a path of dirt worn down by wagons and horses heading east and west. Grass still grew between the wheel ruts, which were thankfully dry.

Trusty stood on the side of the road, looking east across the flat land. There were a few struggling trees and no sign of human or animal life at all. Green met blue with a sprinkling of white puffy clouds. It would be a good day to ride, but that wasn't Trusty's concern. He turned his focus to the ground and started to walk slowly away from the camp, away from Michael, looking for any sign of recent travelers.

It wasn't long before he came across the signs he was looking for: a pile of day-old horse manure followed by an almost invisible line of urine, there for him to see with his eyes trained by the army and the Indian scouts he had ridden with. The line was made by a male, a stallion if it was an Indian horse, urinating as it trotted. The tracks were mixed up with some other hoofprints, making it impossible to tell how many riders there were at one time, but following the tracks and his instinct, Trusty found another sign of discharge of urine, only this wasn't a jagged line cut into the dirt. It was more of a puddle, more of a squat from a mare who had stopped. Most Indian women rode mares, and the men rode stallions. If he was seeing things right, then Trusty could surmise that the riders were one man and one woman. There was no way to know for sure if the riders were David Folsom and Amelia Darby, but it was likely they would travel this way if what he had learned was true, that they were heading back to Kosoma. Then again, it could have been any Indian couple on their way east. Amelia and David might have taken a less visible trail or could have been riding with more riders. There was no way to know for sure, but the signs gave Trusty a little confidence that he'd made the right decision to return to Kosoma—after asking for help from the Guardsmen.

Trusty stood up and looked east, toward Kosoma, and saw nothing that concerned him. The tracks continued on at a steady pace. The pair, whoever they were, were a good way down the road. He held on to the assumption that the riders were Amelia and her common-law husband. He knew better than to think that Amelia would do what was expected, that she might not be hiding in wait for him along the road, knowing full well that he was coming for her. She wasn't stupid. And Trusty doubted that the man she rode with was either. David Folsom had surely seen his fair share of trouble before, knew how to survive a gunfight and stack the odds against his opponents. He was, after all, married to a Darby.

Trusty turned around and started to walk back to camp but stopped a few strides in. The reach of his vision was long, without anything to hinder it, and there was no mistaking a group of riders on the western horizon. A small cloud of dust followed the fast-moving group, and there was no mistake that they would be upon him and Michael before they could make a run for it. If that was the right thing to do. The riders could either be the Guardsmen, come to help him, strangers on the way east on business of their own, or a group of men set on collecting the bounty on his head. There was no way to know for sure.

Trusty didn't hesitate. The first thing he did was whistle, doing his best to capture Michael's attention. Then he pulled his Colt from the holster and ran toward the camp.

Michael had spotted the riders at about the same time that Trusty had noticed them. The picket line was down, and he held the reins of both horses in his hands. He hurried away from the stand of cottonwoods and met Trusty halfway to the road. "Looks like company," he said, handing over control of Horse to Trusty, while he maintained a grasp on Spirit's reins.

"It's a solid group of six or more men," Trusty said as he pulled himself up onto the saddle.

"Not the help you were expecting?"

"I don't think so." He knew his fellow marshals were much like him. They usually rode alone.

"The creek looks like it runs into a thicker grove of trees," Michael said. "We can find some protection there." He was settled in his own saddle, pulling his mare's head away from the road.

"It's too late to hide," Trusty said. "They've already seen us."

Both men looked down the road to see two of the riders break away from the group of men and push toward them at a higher rate of speed.

"If we're gonna go, we better go now," Trusty said. "If we get separated, meet me in Lost Mountain Pass."

Michael nodded and urged his horse into a run. Trusty did the same thing. The quick push off from the two horses was met by another sound, a crack in the air that was familiar to both men. A gunshot echoed across the open sky, following them as they made their getaway.

*Muskogee, Indian Territory, September 1887*

Taking leave for a few weeks, Trusty decided to stay in Muskogee instead of returning to St. Louis. His father still worked the blacksmith shop meeting the demands of a growing city and the constant flow of visitors, just as he had when Trusty was a boy. There had been little communication between the two of them. Sam had grown into a man of his own—earning a nickname that separated him from the boy that he was at home—seeking adventures as a soldier, then on to becoming a deputy marshal and leaving the world of smithing in the past. His life stuck in the dark, fiery shop was a memory gilded with a golden edge: He had escaped and lived a life on his own, free of hammers, smoke, and boiling rage that could never be quenched. There was no reason to return to St. Louis for the rest and Trusty wasn't sure that he would be welcomed if he did show up on his father's doorstep in the first place. Instead, he had decided to spend his short window of respite in Muskogee and enjoy the sights, sounds, and the comforts of a city that he knew little of. Home was in the saddle, sworn to duty, pursuing whatever wrong that needed righted. He had afforded himself a soft bed and fresh sheets at the Muskogee Hotel, one of the finer places to lay his head in Indian Territory.

A cool push of air was not unheard of in Muskogee in September, announcing the change of seasons. The air grew colder in the winter, but not Dakota Territory cold, and Trusty had decided that a new fur-lined coat would be a necessity for duty in the winter. Trusty had found himself lacking of a warm coat; his only coat was a worn duster that had protected him from the weather since his army days. He'd visited a shop on Main Street but had not found a coat to his liking. He left out of the store casually, walking on the boardwalk, eyeing the sturdy redbrick buildings that lined the street, letting his mind wander since he was trying to encourage a calm, state of relaxation. But the ease of his walk and mood changed immediately as soon as he saw a woman crossing the street who looked familiar. He stopped mid-stride like he had run into an invisible wall. The last time he had received a letter from Jessica Marberry she had still been in England. *It can't be her*, he thought to himself. *Not here*. But the more he watched her, the more he was sure that the woman was the Jessica he knew.

Something in his mind and heart wouldn't allow him to add the Tennyton to the end of her name. She would always be Jessica Marberry to him.

The woman wore a flowing emerald-green dress that reached to the ground. A high collar made of rabbit fur was turned up to ward off the cool, autumn wind, covering the back of a matching green hat that only allowed a peak at the woman's golden hair. Her profile was regal, straight nose, high cheeks, rosy from the chill, with a thinker's forehead. She had the smooth gait of a woman full of confidence and good breeding. If she were a horse, there would have been no mistaking her for a thoroughbred. There was no way not to watch her cross the street, adding a much-needed dose of color to the drabness of the day—gray clouds that restrained the sunlight and promised rain at any moment. The entire city street seemed to be wrapped in a gray blanket that betrayed Trusty's relaxed spirit. Everywhere he looked he saw life going on with the normal drudgery of a regular day. No one was on a holiday except him.

Trusty followed after the woman, who it appeared was alone, crossing from one side of the street to the other unaccompanied by a companion or chaperone, man or otherwise. She dodged piles of manure with hardly a bobble or notice. A matching green purse hung comfortably from her left arm, and she stayed focused on the way ahead of her. She stopped once she reached the board-walk and dusted off the front of her dress, giving Trusty the opportunity to catch up with her. She didn't seem to notice when he came to a stop before her. She was bent forward but caught sight of his boots and stood up slowly with a perturbed, unapproachable look on her perfect porcelain face. The annoyed look vanished as soon as she recognized that the man before her was Trusty, not anyone intent on doing her harm.

"Sam? Sam Dawson? Is that really you?" Jessica's voice sounded different. She'd always been well spoken, speaking every letter clearly so she wouldn't be misunderstood, but there had never been an accent of any kind attached to her voice. Now there was. Not quite British, but the effect of living in England, drinking the water, breathing the air, participating in years of conversations had had an obvious physical effect on her. Closer up, it was easier to see that Jessica had aged, matured from a perfect girl into a beautiful woman. She was more perfect than she had ever been.

"It is, though hardly anyone calls me Sam these days." Trusty felt more aware of his worn duster and boots than usual; he regretted not buying a new coat. If he'd spoke the truth aloud, he would have said that he had always felt less than worthy in Jessica Marberry's company. Not because of anything she said or did. She never acted like she was better than anyone that he'd seen. But the difference in their status had been obvious from the first day that he had met her outside of his father's blacksmith shop.

"And what do people call you these days?" Jessica had not let her gaze break away from Trusty's warming eyes.

"Trusty. Trusty Dawson."

Jessica nodded, then smiled. "That has a nice ring to it. How'd you come across that name?"

"In the army. From a fellow scout. An Apache woman. She called me that one day after I fired a shot that saved her life, said I was trusty with a gun. It stuck. Folks have been callin' me Trusty Dawson ever since."

"I think she saw what everyone who knows you sees. You're as reliable a man as they come. I could always count on you."

"Almost always. I wouldn't run away with you, if I remember right."

"That was probably for the best. I was angry at Father. I was always angry with him, or him with me. We're too much alike, I suppose. That wouldn't have turned out well for you if you would have joined in my madness. I should have never asked such a thing of you. I was only a girl then. I didn't know any better. What happened to the woman who nicknamed you Trusty?" Jessica asked, changing the subject.

"I couldn't save her," Trusty said, lowering his head at the thought of Woman's Clothes. "She was killed in a massacre not long after. To be honest, I've never cared much for the name. I think it's a little too boastful, but when I hear it I think of her, so it's not all bad. I've been called worse things over the years."

"I can't believe you're here," Jessica said.

"I was about to say the same thing about you. I've thought of you often, but I never dreamed that I would see you again. At least, out here in the Territory."

The world went on around them. People passed by on the boardwalk. Wagons carted their loads past them unaware, pulled by bored horses that either knew the route or weren't going to be bullied to go any faster than they wanted to. Small drops of rain started to fall from the graying sky, disappearing as soon as they hit the ground.

"I'm glad you thought of me," Jessica said. "I thought about you too."

Trusty lost track of how cold it was outside. They stood under an overhang and had no worry of getting wet. "That's nice to know." He smiled, pulling his shoulder as straight as he could, starting to wonder if it was going to be possible to spend any length of time with Jessica. "Your last letter came from England. You didn't say anything about coming back to the States."

"I've been home for a month. My husband died unexpectedly, and I needed to be on familiar ground."

"I'm sorry, I didn't know."

"I should have written to you."

"It's okay," Trusty said. "I was out on a ride one way or another. All of the letters pile up for me at headquarters."

"Do you have a home here?"

Trusty didn't understand what Jessica was asking him at first. He had to think about it. His finger was free of a wedding band, but that didn't mean much. Most men like him didn't wear a ring whether they were married or not. "Um, no. I'm stayin' at the hotel. I'm just here for a little while, takin' a rest for a few weeks. I'm here alone, if that's what you're askin'."

"Oh." Jessica's face blushed red, pulling a curtain of warmth and embarrassment across her face, adding to the rosiness of her cheeks. No matter the color, her face still looked fragile to Trusty, like she could break apart at any second. "I guess that's exactly what I was asking. You always were able to understand what I meant, even if I didn't know myself. You were a good friend, Sam, or Trusty. Can I still call you Sam?"

He felt himself shrink at the mention of being a friend. Jessica had always been more than that to him. He had thought she had felt the same way about him at one time, but maybe he had been wrong all along. "You can call me whatever you want."

"I like Trusty now that I think about it. It's a fresh start. Something new for us. I like that," Jessica said with a smile, pushing away the blush.

Trusty looked away from her, down the street. "I'm staying at the hotel. There's a restaurant inside. Maybe we could get something to warm us up. A cup of coffee or a bowl of soup?"

"That'd be nice. I'd like that." Jessica hadn't taken her eyes off of Trusty. She slipped her arm through his, and they both began walking slowly toward the hotel, dodging raindrops the best they could. "You have just made a gray day much brighter, Trusty Dawson."

All he could do was smile.

Time ticked away. Trusty learned that Jessica was in Muskogee with her father, who was finishing up a business deal before winter set in. She hadn't spent much time alone since being back in the States and was only in the early days of mourning her dead husband. She had been shopping for more black clothes; she didn't have enough to wear for a year. When it was time for them to part for the evening, neither one of them could bring themselves to say good-bye to each other. So they didn't. Trusty found out that he was more than a friend to Jessica Marberry after she joined him in his room.

### *Little Boggy Creek, Indian Territory, May 1888*

Trusty and Michael split up. Michael cut across the flat land and headed west at an angle, running full speed toward a thick stand of trees. Trusty headed south along the creek, pushing Horse as fast as he could. The relationship between man and beast was the most consistent relationship Trusty had maintained over the years, and Horse seemed to have enough sense to know they were being chased, were in danger. Trusty had given Horse his head, let him run with the reins slack as he looked over his shoulder and readied his Colt to fire.

Michael had vanished from sight. Three men on horseback were riding hard, a good quarter of a mile behind him. Three against one. *I've faced worse odds than that*, Trusty thought. Another gunshot rang out, but the bullet didn't hit close. Oddly, it looked like the man had fired his rifle into the air. A warning shot. Not a killing shot. That didn't make sense. For a second, he wondered if he had made a mistake. Ran at the first sight of the riders instead of determining if they were friends or foe. He knew they weren't the Guardsmen. He would have recognized those three men from a distance. But Madsen or Tilghman could have sent help in the form of men closer to Trusty when he'd asked for assistance. That didn't seem likely. These three men were running too hard and shooting to be friendlies. He had to wonder at the second shot where the other men were. At first sight, it had looked like there were six or seven riders. Now there were three.

Trusty didn't have to wonder long. When he looked forward again, three men on horseback stood a hundred yards in front of him with their rifles aimed straight at him.

# Chapter 24

Vance Calhoun sat in his saddle with his Henry rifle sighted on a man that he believed to be Trusty Dawson. The sun glinted off the U.S. Marshal's badge on the man's chest, making Calhoun almost sure he'd captured his quarry. "Might you be Trusty Dawson?" he said, making sure before he went and killed a man innocent of being anything other than a marshal.

Gladdy and Denton Hobbs sat on their horses off to the right of Calhoun with their hands on the butts of their guns. Gladdy wore his holster on the left, but Hobbs wore his on the right, with the butt backward so he didn't have to reach across himself like a lot of ex-cavalry riders did. They knew to let Calhoun take the lead.

"Who's askin?" the man with the badge said.

Calhoun wouldn't have known Trusty Dawson close up if they were shoulder to shoulder in a saloon. One thing was for sure, this man didn't shake or shy away from trouble. He didn't look scared at all even though he was staring down the barrel of a rifle.

"I am," Calhoun said. "Now, I figure the first thing you ought to do, Deputy, is toss that sidearm of yours to the ground, then follow that up with that Winchester pokin' out of your saddlebag, then you and I will get along just fine for the time bein'."

"You might want to reconsider your position," the man said, "threatening a Deputy U.S. Marshal with a firearm is an offense you'll have to answer for."

"So, you are Trusty Dawson. Or should I say Sam. It is Samuel, isn't it?" Calhoun didn't waver his aim. The barrel of his Henry was still pointed confidently at the man's badge. He liked having a target.

"Deputy Dawson is just fine with me."

Calhoun wasn't convinced that was true. Dawson had flinched at the call of his real first name. He seemed surprised to hear it. "Well, Trusty Dawson, why don't you go ahead and do what I tell you to do now that we've got our familiars out of the way."

"What do you want? And who are you? This introduction seems a little one-sided to me."

"I'm the one askin' questions," Calhoun said. "And holdin' the gun on you. I get to say what's what, now don't I?"

A gunshot in the distance captured all four of the men's attention. They looked to the east, almost in unison. Calhoun returned his attention back to Dawson quickly, not wanting to give him a chance to pull his gun. He'd heard that Dawson was a sure shot but didn't know the truth of that tale. Some of the marshals had myths built around them that seemed unlikely, but worth taking note of.

Silence followed the gunshot, which Calhoun took as

a good sign. He hoped the other four riders in his crew had taken Dawson's partner with ease. That would give him more of an advantage. Not that he needed it.

"I figure there's more to this than you're sayin, mister," Dawson said. "If you wanted me dead, you've already had a decent chance at pullin' the trigger and the deed would be done. Did Marberry send you? Or are you set on collectin' the bounty on my head. I heard I was wanted dead. Not alive. So I'm a might confused about what it is you're after. If this is a robbery, my coins are few. If it's the bounty, then why am I still talkin' to you?"

"You're a smart one," Calhoun said. "I'll give you that. You can rest assured that me and Theodore Marberry have got some business to do in the near future, so not all of this has to do with you, Samuel Dawson. That man, no matter how rich and proper he might seem, is a deceitful bastard who's no better than a common thief and liar. I don't care what the social pages say. He's lower than a snake's belly, that one."

"Something we can agree on," Dawson said. "I have a low opinion of the man myself."

He cocked his head like he didn't understand. "What kind of business do you have with Marberry if it isn't the bounty?"

"I said, I'm the one askin' questions. Now you're pushin' my patience. Drop your guns." Calhoun paused. "Don't worry, I ain't gonna kill you at the moment. I'm a fair man. You'll have a chance to save yourself. You just need to answer some questions for me. If you tell me what I want to know, then me and you are gonna go at it with our fists. You game for that?"

"And what happens after I bring you to your knees?"

"I like your confidence, Dawson," Calhoun said. "Gladdy and Hobbs will see to your end if I can't. But they won't take to a fight. They'll fill you with lead, won't ya, fellas?"

Both men nodded. Gladdy smiled, pulled his six-shooter from his holster, aimed it at Dawson, then acted like he shot him like the little boy he was. Calhoun wasn't entertained, but he let Gladdy have his fun. Hobbs just sat still as a mountain lion ready to pounce when the time was right.

Calhoun leaned forward in his saddle, examining Dawson as close as he could. "Looks like you're favorin' that right arm of yours. I know pain and discomfort when I see it."

"I took a gunshot, but don't think that'll give you an advantage against me. I'm not sure I like those odds if I take you down," Dawson said. "I'm happy to take you one on one, but I don't care for the outcome if I win."

"You're not gonna win," Calhoun said.

"Then shoot me now." Dawson sat in his saddle with a straight face and squared shoulders. He didn't look afraid to die to Calhoun. He liked that about a man.

"All right." Calhoun tipped the barrel of his Henry to the ground. "You answer my questions and give me the answers I want, I'll set you free if you give me a lickin'. Otherwise, I win, and that means I ain't gonna stop beatin' you till you're dead, broken wing or not. Just so you understand the stakes."

"I think I got a clear idea of what's goin' on." Dawson nodded, then tossed his Colt to the ground, followed by the Winchester.

"I don't think you do," Calhoun said. He glared at the man before him, then closed his eyes briefly and remembered what was left of his home, of his ranch. Nothing but cinders. Sally was dead. Miguel was dead. Haden was dead. And Jessica was dead. The railroad certificates had been burned up in the fire set by Marberry's men—if they had been real in the first place. Calhoun had nothing left, all because he had been deceived by Jessica Marberry Tennyton and her father. But there was another player in the deception, and that man was finally standing before him. Trusty Dawson himself. Calhoun had to wonder if the deputy knew what had happened to Jessica and her daughter. Their daughter if the man confessed to being with the woman in a biblical way. The memory of the ranch was followed by the memory of Sally telling him that she'd seen Calhoun babies born before, and the one that Jessica had brought into the world was not a Calhoun at all. Was she a Dawson?

"Go on," Calhoun said to Gladdy. "Get his guns."

Gladdy jumped off his horse, hurried over to the Colt and rifle on the ground, and picked them up. He dropped them in front of Calhoun's horse, then looked up for his next set of orders.

"Now, get off your horse, Dawson," Calhoun said.

"Why don't you ask me your questions?" Dawson answered. He didn't budge.

Calhoun didn't like it when a man disobeyed him, but he expected it from Dawson. This man was no simpleton or a cowhand easily pushed around. "All right. You need to know what you're in for. When was the last time you saw Jessica Marberry?"

Dawson stiffened in his saddle. "What does Jessica have to do with this?"

"Everything," Calhoun said.

"How do you know Jessica?"

"She *was* my wife."

"Was?" Dawson asked. His voice sounded weak as tin all of a sudden. Calhoun smiled. Dawson was smart, and this was going better than Calhoun had hoped. He'd had no idea that the man was physically wounded. That was a help in itself, but if he could wound his spirit, then that would make his plan all the easier.

"Yes, was," Calhoun said. "She's dead."

Dawson's face paled and he looked away, gripped the reins of his smart roan gelding tight with a clenched fist. "How? When?"

Calhoun smirked and said nothing. He sheathed his Henry and dismounted from the grullo. "Don't think about doin' anything stupid like makin' a run for it. Hobbs is a fine shot and he'll blow your head off before you can count to two."

"I can see that," Dawson said.

Hobbs smiled and set a round in his Peacemaker, cocked it, and pointed it at Dawson's head without being told. Gladdy mounted his horse and sat back to watch the spectacle unfolding before him.

"Come on," Calhoun said. "Get down."

"You didn't answer my question. When did Jessica die?" Dawson didn't flinch. He locked in eye to eye with Calhoun. His face was still pale from the shock, but Calhoun knew fury and anger when he saw it, and that was exactly what was brewing in Dawson's eyes.

Calhoun lunged at the side of the roan horse, reaching

for Dawson's leg with the intent of pulling him out of the saddle in surprise. But the deputy had been expecting a move of some kind. Calhoun's chin met the swinging toe of Dawson's hard-tipped boot, sending him spiraling backward with blood filling his mouth. Pain and a couple of broken teeth rattled inside Calhoun's head, igniting a familiar rage. He never felt more alive than right after the moment of taking a punch to the face. His rage had only needed a spark, but the kick from Dawson was more of a torch set on a pile of dry tinder than a nudge.

Dawson jumped off his horse and rushed after Calhoun, diving on top of him, hitting him in the face with the fist of his right hand. Calhoun took it for a second, laid on his back allowing the pain and the attack to settle into that place of fire and hurt that had always encouraged him to fight back. Then he fought back with a knee to Dawson's midsection, sending him flying to the side.

Before Dawson could catch his breath and react, Calhoun had straddled the big man and pinned him down at the shoulders. That move obviously sent another shock of pain through Dawson's body as he yelled out in pain. Must have been from the gunshot wound.

The salty, metallic taste of blood filled Calhoun's mouth and he had to spit before he could speak. The ground turned red to his side. "Now tell me, Dawson, when was the last time you saw Jessica."

"What business is it of yours?" Dawson said, catching his breath.

"I done told you. She was my wife. I got a right to know."

"She wasn't your wife the last time I saw her."

Calhoun slipped his right hand from the man's injured

shoulder and gripped Dawson by the throat, threatening to strangle him. "Tell me when that was, and you'll live."

"If you kill me, you'll never know."

Blood dripped from Calhoun's mouth, and his head still felt like he'd taken a hit from a ball-peen hammer. Frustration boiled beyond the pain. He was close to tossing aside any concern whether Sally had been right about the baby or not. Calhoun knew the truth deep in his bones. A woman like Jessica Marberry Tennyton would have never been interested in him if she didn't have something to gain from being with him. He'd never felt any love from her. Not that he had ever known the truth of such a thing. Even in their marriage bed. She was cold as a frozen pond in the winter and just as slick. She was always in a hurry to get away from him, like his touch repulsed her. There was no mistaking that. The truth was, Jessica knew she was pregnant when she had married Calhoun, and she was either hiding the fact of it from her father, from society in the distant hills just beyond the Red River, or Theodore Marberry knew about her condition too—and had seen Calhoun as a pawn that would help him save face. Calhoun didn't need Dawson to tell him what he already knew. It was easy to see that man cared about Jessica from the first mention of her name.

Dawson must have sensed a moment of hesitation, and arched his torso, rolling his body like a caterpillar trying to escape the grasp of a bird's beak with all of his might. Calhoun was knocked off balance, sending him tumbling to the side.

The marshal kneed Calhoun in his rib cage, adding another shot of pain to the building storm. Something cracked. Calhoun had heard it, then felt the reverberation through his entire body. He was injured, wasn't going to be able to recover quickly from this bout. They were on even footing now, him and Dawson. Both broken. All because of a woman.

Dawson was on his feet, his fists clenched, feet planted, ready to continue fighting. "Muskogee last fall," he said between pants. "I don't know why that's important to you, but we parted ways on bad terms; not that it's any business of yours."

Calhoun pulled himself up, clutching his side, trying to ward off the pain of the rib hit the best he could. He could still count inside his head and figured from the fall to the spring was enough time for the baby to be Dawson's. "Bad terms," Calhoun said, standing as tall as he could and casting a glance to Hobbs while taking a deep breath, readying a signal to end things once and for all.

"She wanted to run off with me," Dawson said. "I told her no for the second time in our lives, and that was that. If you married her after she left Muskogee, then she must have found what she was lookin' for."

"And what would that have been?"

"Someplace, some man, far, far away from her father. I refused to be her reason to wage a war with the man. I have a life to live."

Calhoun smirked and felt the pain of his body go away. He had Dawson now. He just needed to hear the truth before he ended things with the man. "But Theodore Marberry put a bounty on your head and not mine. You ever wonder why that was, Dawson?"

"You sound like you know."

"I got an idea. Me and Marberry are at war ourselves except I got one advantage that you don't."

"And what's that?"

"He thinks I'm dead. The whole world thinks I'm dead. Imagine that. Vance Calhoun is dead, but here he stands." Calhoun caught himself and stopped talking, but it was too late. He had given Dawson his real name, not Joseph Jones, the moniker he had come up with on the fly in the Atoka café. He'd never liked that name anyway. It was a risky admittance, sharing his real name with Trusty Dawson, but Calhoun was certain that the marshal wasn't going to live to tell anyone about this encounter, so he let any worry of it pass.

"That is an advantage, I suppose, Mister Calhoun." Dawson hadn't moved, was standing in a fighting stance, ready to take on whatever came his way.

"If I know anything, Marberry'll keep comin' for you until you're dead. Jessica cared about you," Calhoun said. "Saved all of your letters. My guess is, if she was capable of lovin' a man, then you might have been it. You should have hung in there. She would have given you something no one else could have."

"And what is that?"

"A ticket to the kingdom of gold. More wealth than you can imagine. Something her father covets and will do anything to protect."

"Quit toyin' with me, mister, or I'll finish what I started."

"You don't want to die before I tell you what you need to hear."

A confused look crossed Dawson's face. "I ain't got nothin' that Marberry could ever covet."

"Yes, you do. A child. Jessica died giving birth to a

child. A child that looked nothin' like any Calhoun my sister had ever seen. Now, if there's a chance you and Jessica spent some private time together last fall, you might have your answer why me and Theodore Marberry want you dead."

All of the color drained out of Trusty Dawson's face. He looked like the brush of a feather could have knocked him over. That was all Calhoun needed to see. He nodded to Hobbs to shoot the man. But he was too late.

Seconds before, Dawson dove forward, toppling Calhoun at the hooves of the standing horses. Gladdy's horse spooked, reared up, and sent the Mick toppling off his saddle. Hobbs fired, but the bullet hit dirt and he was knocked to the side by Gladdy's horse. Calhoun was on the ground before he knew it, moving slow, unable to overcome the pain. When he cleared his vision, Trusty Dawson was standing over him with a gun in his hand, staring down the barrel, surprised by the recognition of defeat.

"You're under arrest, mister. You move another inch and I'll put another hole in your head," Dawson said.

Before Calhoun could call out to Hobbs or Gladdy for help, the air cracked with another gunshot, met with the thundering hooves of approaching horses. Calhoun could see the men clearly enough to know they were not riders from his crew. The horses belonged to three men, two of them wearing badges on their chests, with serious looks on their faces and rifles in their hands pointed at Gladdy and Hobbs. Calhoun wasn't going anywhere—unless he wanted to die. The men were not his. They were the law come to help Trusty Dawson.

# Chapter 25

Trusty didn't relax the grip on his Colt. He held the gun tight, aimed at Vance Calhoun's head. The pain and rage somersaulting inside of him could have tricked him into pulling the trigger with justification and more than a dose of satisfaction. Three men against one, assault, confinement of a U.S. Marshal; the list giving him permission to shoot the man was long. But this Calhoun fella had just shook Trusty to the core. First by telling him that Jessica was dead, and second that she'd had a child. A child that Calhoun implied Trusty had fathered. *It was possible*. He had spent the night with Jessica in Muskogee. Everything that had happened, that he had learned, was more than Trusty could put together into one finite decision: *Pull the trigger, damn it. Pull the trigger and end this man and his meanness.*

What Calhoun had said made sense, though, including the reason that Theodore Marberry had put the bounty on Trusty's head. There had never been any love lost between the two men. The attack by Calhoun had been fortuitous, but dangerous. Trusty had to wonder what else the man on the ground before him knew. Especially what *else* the man knew. Where was the child now? Did it live or die? Was it a boy or a girl? Did it matter? The last thing Trusty had been expecting to hear was that he might be the father of a child.

The man on the horse, the one Calhoun had called Hobbs, had regained control of his steed, took in the coming riders, and decided to lower the barrel of his weapon in surrender. The other man, Gladdy, the one that had been thrown from his horse, recovered, stood up, and put his hands up into the air, offering the same surrender as the three riders came to a stop. All three men were held at bay, something their defeated faces showed in droops, resignation, and surprise.

"Looks like you found yourself in a bit of a pickle, Trusty," Bill Tilghman said. Tilghman was a fellow Deputy U.S. Marshal, most often associated with the Guardsmen. The help that Trusty had sent for had arrived in the nick of time.

Tilghman, in his mid-thirties, had been a marshal in Dodge City, and had had a hand in ending the Kansas County Seat Wars. A longtime friend of Wyatt Earp and Bat Masterson, Tilghman was a marshal through and through. Trusty looked up to the man, even though Tilghman was only a few years older than him.

"Good to see you, Bill. Thanks for coming out. You got here just in time," Trusty said. He tipped his hat to Chris Madsen, the other Guardsman. Michael Darby sat alongside Madsen with a glum look on his face and offered nothing. There was no sign of Heck Thomas, the other member of the trio either. Trusty assumed the two marshals had dispatched the other riders one way or another. "Everything's all set, then?"

"It is now," Tilghman nodded. He held his nickel-plated .45 with pearl handles straight at Vance Calhoun's head. "Any of the three of you move an inch, that'll be the end of you, you hear?" He wore a Colt SA .38 with a five-and-a-half-inch barrel on the other side of his gun belt for backup if he needed it.

Calhoun was still on the ground, his eyes searching for an escape, his body as still as a turtle soaking in the sun. "Nobody's gonna take on the Guardsmen," he said. "Not today or any day."

Tilghman, with his eyes shielded from his Stetson, and the bottom half of his face covered by a thick, black mustache, nodded. "Two of your compatriots are dead, and the other two took to the wind, running away from your trouble like scared rabbits. Now if they decide to circle back and attempt a rescue, well, I'd be surprised about that. They didn't seem to be the kind of loyal riders willin' to put their lives on the line for the likes of you. They ran pretty easy. Cowards I'd say."

Calhoun didn't say a word; all he could do was glare at Tilghman with hate and frustration.

Trusty knew better than to get in between Bill Tilghman and his position of control upon arrival. The man didn't wear any sergeant stripes. None of the marshals did. But there was no mistaking who was in charge when Bill Tilghman was around. Trusty stood back and let the smell of spent gun smoke drift past him and mix with the opportunity of the spring day that surrounded them. Bees went about their business on wildflowers, paying no mind to the humans or the aim of their guns.

Chris Madsen inched his horse a little forward. He held a Winchester on Hobbs, the man on the horse who was still holding his gun, albeit pointed to the ground. Madsen wore a similar thick mustache as Tilghman only it was brown as fresh-cut wheat instead of black as coal. He was shorter, had a rounder face than Tilghman, making him less serious looking. Only a fool would have judged Madsen a lesser marshal than Bill Tilghman, or Trusty himself for that matter. Born in Denmark, Madsen had had a lengthy career as a fighting warrior from the time he could serve. He'd dedicated himself as a young man to duty in the Danish Army, fought in the Franco-Prussian War, then joined the French Foreign Legion. From there he came to the United States in 1876 and joined in the U.S. Cavalry, where he crossed paths with Trusty on more than one occasion fighting in the Indian Wars. Of the Guardsmen, Trusty knew Madsen the least; they weren't close friends, just trustworthy acquaintances.

Madsen continued to hold the Model 1886 Winchester on the man on the horse. He carried a nickel-plated Colt .45, without pearl handles, with a four-and-three-quarter-inch barrel and could match shooting skills with Tilghman or any man in the Territory. Both men were not to be dallied with, allowing Trusty to breathe a long sigh of relief. "If'n I was you, mister, I'd toss that gun to the ground and join your partner with your feet on the ground and keep your hands up in the air," Madsen said.

Hobbs smirked, then spit to the ground. "Not today," he said. He flipped his six-shooter up, popped his finger on the trigger, and flat-handed the top of the gun with the obvious intention of fanning the hammer. His hope of taking out the gathering of marshals was thwarted; he was too slow.

Tilghman fired first, followed by Madsen. Both men pumped three pieces of lead into Hobbs, knocking him backward off the horse. He was dead before he hit the ground.

Calhoun and Gladdy didn't move, went from petulance to shock.

Once the gun smoke cleared, Tilghman said, "Either of you try such a thing, the result will be the same. You want to live, you do as you're told. You want to die on this fine spring day, go ahead and point a gun at any of us and see what happens. I've already been shot at today, and there ain't much that gets my ire up more than that, other than a foul-mouthed snake talkin' bad about my mother, may she rest in peace."

Madsen nodded and climbed off his horse with ease, holding his aim on Calhoun. "You need to stand up slowly with your hands up in the air and do as Marshal Tilghman says." There was a stilted, detectable Danish accent on the end of each of Madsen's words. The difference in speech had caused the man some trouble in the past, but he didn't seem too worried about being overtaken by discriminating thugs at the moment.

Calhoun stood up and did what he was told. "Now what?"

"Go join your partner," Madsen said. "We'll bind you together so we don't have to worry about you doing anythin' stupid."

"He's not my partner," Calhoun said. "Not now, or ever."

\* \* \*

The man said his name was Gladdy O'Connor, but Trusty didn't know whether to believe him or not. Regardless, the two men, O'Connor and Calhoun, sat back to back, bound by a thick rope, their feet and hands manacled in irons while their fate was being decided. Neither could cause any trouble. The dead man, Hobbs, with eyes wide open to the heavens, was already drawing flies. He wasn't going to cause anyone any kind of trouble ever again.

"Where's Heck?" Trusty asked Tilghman casually. They were standing over an easy fire waiting on a pot of coffee to boil.

"Broke off to Kosoma. There's been a couple of killin's startin' two days prior with a hotel clerk, then the next day another fella who ran the mercantile. Folks are all up in the air as you can imagine. They thought this kind of thing was behind them with the three Darby brothers seeing the end of a rope, but that wasn't to be. No surprise, if you ask me. Rumors point toward the Darby girl you're a trackin' after to be the one that did it, but there was no witness of that, just a woman's handkerchief found near one of the bodies. No sightings, no nothing. Pure speculation. Heck's got as good a nose as any of us when it comes to rootin' out the truth. He'll figure it out by the time we get there. You can count on that. But the rumors don't settle well with me. That girl was on the run after killing Judge Hadesworth. Seems unlikely she'd risk a killing spree of some kind in a town where everybody was on the lookout for her."

A studious look crossed Trusty's face as he held Tilghman's attention. Madsen was twenty yards away, close to the road, keeping an eye out for anything that moved and making sure the two errant riders didn't surprise them. Michael stood with the picket of horses on his own. He had been quiet and reserved since arriving with the two marshals.

"According to Michael, the Darby girl's brother," Trusty said with a nod toward the man, "she was intendin' on meetin' up with her husband, a Choctaw called David Folsom. The timing doesn't seem right to me either. I wouldn't rule it out, because she's the vengeful type, and it's said she is headin' to Kosoma to finish what she started when she killed Judge Hadesworth."

Tilghman stiffened and looked to the east. "That makes our next move all the more obvious then. We need to head back to Kosoma to help out Heck. He can handle a man and his wife, but if there's more riders with them, he might be in a little more trouble than I thought."

"What about those two?" Trusty said.

"We'll drop them off at the jail in Atoka and check in at the wire office for any orders from Marshal Grimes. He'd like us to make a showing in Muskogee for Judge Hadesworth's funeral."

"I don't see how that's possible."

"We need to ride hard," Tilghman said. "Unless you got cause for not wanting to show face at the judge's funeral."

Trusty hesitated, then said, "The man is dead because of me."

Bill Tilghman stared Trusty in the eye, unwavering. "You've fought enough battles to know that war takes the best of men. You did all you could. I'm not the kind of man to tell you how to live, or what to carry with you, but if I was you, I'd pay that man and his family my respects and do my best to make sure something like that didn't happen again. Last I heard, nobody was asking you to take off your badge. If that was the case, Grimes would have made that clear from the first word of the killing."

"We're in no war," Trusty said.

"Sure we are," Tilghman answered. "We're always in a war of good and evil, right against wrong. There's no land to claim or a victory parade to celebrate our fight, but trust me, it's a war that all of us who wear a badge are fighting. That girl that pulled the trigger and killed Judge Hadesworth and wounded you is as bad and unjust as any of her brothers, or them Daltons. They're the enemy, and the bad thing is, once they're behind bars, someone else will take their place. The war will never be over. So what are you going to do? Give up the fight? Or keep on riding and paying heed to your calling? You're a good marshal, Trusty, just like you were a good soldier. You think about that. We got a battle ahead of us if you're right about this girl. She needs to be stopped and stopped soon before someone else gets hurt."

All Trusty could do was nod. He let Tilghman's words settle inside his heart and mind. The words were a salve, but he feared there was no cure for the hurt and doubt he felt about what happened to Judge Hadesworth. "Thanks, Bill, I appreciate your kindness."

"Ain't kindness, just the truth. You can't let this stop you. If you do, that girl killed the best part of you too.

You gonna let her win that easy? That's never been your way as far as I can tell."

Trusty made his way to Calhoun and O'Connor. "On your feet, Calhoun," he said, hoisting the rope at the man's back.

Bill Tilghman was two steps behind Trusty, but he stopped hard in his tracks. "Calhoun? I've heard that name recently. The rancher from Texas? Vance Calhoun?"

Calhoun looked away as if he was hiding his face, didn't want Tilghman to be able to see him clearly.

"That's the one," Trusty said. "At least that's the name he claimed himself to be."

"I heard he was dead." Tilghman allowed his hands to rest at his sides, within reach of both of his guns.

"I assure you, he's not," Trusty said.

Tilghman tried to take in Calhoun's eyes, but it was impossible. "Last he was heard from was in Kosoma, right before them two fellas were killed. One at the hotel. I'd guess a man like Calhoun would stay at a place like that instead of a flophouse. Then there's a newspaper story that claimed his death in Kosoma, but there was no body or evidence to show for it. Sounds like a convenient alibi to me, doesn't it to you, Trusty?"

"I'll believe anything these days. What say you, Calhoun?" Trusty said. "You told me everybody believes you're dead."

"I'm not the only Calhoun in the world," he said to the ground. "I'm an innocent man."

"An innocent man who came up on me shooting, then holding me to account for something that had nothing to do with you." Trusty stiffened and felt a bit of anger rising up that had been set aside from their first encounter.

"What are you talking about?" Tilghman said.

"Calhoun gave me the reason I have a price on my head."

Tilghman nodded, a little more clear-eyed than he was a second before. "I heard about that. Something for us all to be aware of."

"There might be more trouble waiting for us because of that," Trusty said.

Tilghman smiled and said, "We'll handle whatever comes our way, don't you worry about it."

Trusty turned his attention back to Calhoun. "I bet there's only one Gladdy O'Connor that rode with Vance Calhoun. Won't be too hard to confirm such a thing," he said. "If that's the case, then it might not be that difficult to put the two of you and your gang right back in Kosoma, responsible for those two deaths. That would be cause for another hanging in Kosoma if you ask me."

"We need to ride," Tilghman said. "The sooner we're free of these two, the quicker we can get to Kosoma. Best way's through Lost Mountain Pass."

"I was afraid you were going to say that." Trusty hoisted Calhoun to his feet, waited until Tilghman walked off before he said, "Me and you still have some business to conclude," as quietly as he could to Calhoun.

"We have no business to conduct," Calhoun said. "You're on your own now."


Trusty, Michael Darby, and Bill Tilghman sat on their horses with their saddles packed and their eyes on the trail toward Kosoma. Madsen was still on the ground, preparing to leave. The sky was blue in the east but starting to gray behind them with a wall of clouds building into a dark mood. Distant thunder rumbled and lightning jabbed down from the sky. The air smelled of another spring rainstorm, which could either be a swift drink of water or spiral into an angry twister set on destroying anything in its path. There was no way to know for sure what was heading toward the riders, or whether they could outrun nature's resolve. As far as Trusty was concerned there was no stopping them, no matter what. Especially now that he had a man to the right of him that he could trust. Michael, on the other hand, was as predictable as the swirling clouds. There was no way to know what to expect from him next.

"You got this, Chris?" Tilghman said to Chris Madsen, looking past him to the grumpy sky.

Madsen finished cinching his saddle, stood back, and looked to the two horses behind his. Calhoun and Gladdy were in their saddles, hands bound by manacles, their horses tied together with Madsen's ride in the lead. The two men had been stripped of their weapons along with anything that could be used as one, like a belt, if they somehow managed to free themselves.

"Sure, I got this," Madsen said. "Once I lock them up in Atoka, and drop off the dead body, I'll join you. No sense slowing you down. There's no time to waste from where I sit. If I can't escort these two thugs in on my own, I might as well give up right now and set myself out to pasture."

"I don't see that happening anytime soon." Tilghman

stiffened and looked to Trusty and Michael. "You two ready?"

"Let's ride," Trusty said, kneeing Horse, spurring the roan gelding into a run. A roll of thunder followed as all three men rode off. The rain and trouble held in the angry clouds promised to catch up, doing its best to stop them from getting where they were going.

# Chapter 26

Rain fell steadily from the sky, muddying the trail, forcing the trio to ride slow with more caution than they wanted to. Trusty led with Michael in the middle and Bill Tilghman in the rear. Once they got to the mountain, the trail would turn from thick mud to slick gravel, making the ascent through the pass even more treacherous than it already was.

Trusty wore his slicker like the other two men to ward off the rain and cold wind that came with it. With Lost Mountain in sight, he held back and paced abreast with Michael. "Anything that you can tell us to be on the lookout for when it comes to Amelia and David Folsom will be helpful," he said.

"You know as much as I do," Michael answered, allowing his horse to match strides with Trusty. "I've already told you everything I know about my sister's intentions. I left our home a long time ago, so her ways are little known to me. She's a Darby. Expect the unexpected.

Expect her to come at us with everything she has if she has reason to, if she is lying in wait."

"I know that." Trusty didn't have to say any more. The ache in his shoulder was enough of a reminder of what Amelia Darby was capable of. "You've said little of David Folsom."

"That's because I don't know him well at all. Amelia was young when I left home. I've been inside the church a long time. But I don't know of David being a killer. That doesn't make him any less dangerous. He'll do anything for Amelia. That's all I know. Any man pinned against the wall will defend himself or the one he loves."

"I can only hope they're in Kosoma."

"She knows we're coming for them," Michael said. "You can count on that."

"What happened back there?"

"I'd be a dead man if those two marshals hadn't shown up." Michael cocked his head back to Tilghman, who was riding steadily, eyes on the trail to avoid the rain in his face. Fighting men had a sense of trouble on the horizon and usually met it with a brooding silence. Trusty could tell that the conversation between him and Michael annoyed Tilghman, but he didn't care. He wanted to know what he was riding into. "I go from being a killer to almost getting killed in a matter of days. That's a far cry from my normal life inside the safety and quiet life of a priest."

"Maybe you're not cut out for life in the broader world," Trusty said.

"I wouldn't argue with that. We're both alive, though, because you had the foresight to ask for help. Most people don't get what they ask for—at least that's been my experience. Those men were bounty hunters then?"

Trusty shook his head. "I thought so at first. But the big Scot, Calhoun, he had a grudge to settle with me. It was personal, not about money. At least at the start. Once the fightin' got started, I think it was about jealousy and a woman we both knew. The encounter was a surprise to me, if I'm being honest."

"He tracked you down for a fight about honor and valor?"

"There's more to it than that."

"There always is when there's a woman involved," Michael said.

The mud started to shift to gravel and the grade of the land began to climb upward. There was no way for Trusty not to acknowledge what had happened the last time he was through Lost Mountain Pass, so all of his senses were on alert. He expected the shooting to start at any second.

### Muskogee, Indian Territory, September 1887

Soft morning light dappled across the bed. Jessica lay in bed naked, still as a mouse, her deep blue eyes focused on something past the ceiling, the past or the future. She might as well have been a million miles away, unaware of Trusty as he tugged on his boot and readied himself to go. Leaving so soon, with a cold silence settled between them was the last thing Trusty had expected to happen the night before. He longed to be under the covers with Jessica, his warm body next to hers, but that longing had been interrupted by the nothing talk, and whispers that came after . . . Intimate and innocent words had slipped from Trusty's mouth that he wished he could take back, but couldn't: *There's no future for us. All we have is now.*

He stood up and rattled his gun belt as he settled it around his waist. "I wish we were still kids."

Jessica's eyelashes flittered with life as she returned to the present from wherever her mind had taken her. "We should have gotten this out of the way then," she said.

"We were never alone."

"We could have made it happen."

"Maybe I was a scared little boy," Trusty said.

"Like now?"

"No. I'm a man with a life that can't be changed any more than yours can be. Our worlds are too different." He headed for the door, stopped and put his hand on the cold, brass knob. "That doesn't make leavin' you any easier. I'll regret it for the rest of my life."

"Me too," Jessica whispered. "Me too."

"Good-bye, Jessica. I hope you find what you're looking for."

### Lost Mountain Pass, Indian Territory, May 1888

The ground under the three men's horses' hooves became more unstable in the rain. Trusty powered forward with his head down, rain draining from his Stetson. Wind pushed down through the pass, slapping against the back of his neck all the while Horse responded with his usual obedience. The roan gelding had never seemed to mind the weather or tackling tricky terrain. At the moment, Trusty felt lucky to have such a steady mount.

Once they crested the top of the narrow pass, it was

easier to see ahead; down the trail to Kosoma and behind the three of them, the roiling storm clouds seemed to stretch all the way to California. Weather was their enemy at the moment, obscuring the way forward, covering the trail in late afternoon shadows that danced from one side of the rock to the other. The constant roar of thunder and fall of rain drowned out the softer sounds, making it nearly impossible to hear another horse or an unrepressed cough from a shooter doing their best to stay hidden. But that didn't mean Trusty wasn't aware of his surroundings. He was extremely aware, maybe too aware, dashing in and out of the past as he closed in on the spot where Judge Hadesworth had been killed and he had been shot, his eyes darting about with the expectation of an attack.

The trail narrowed and the rock rose up so the height of it was level with the top of Trusty's Cavalry Stetson. It was a dangerous spot. Michael was close on Trusty's tail, and Bill Tilghman had tightened his spot behind Michael's horse. Tilghman carried his Winchester across his lap. The wind calmed down as they descended on the other side of the mountain, but the rain still fell, unrelenting from a driving force splashing in the mud and gravel to a steadier downfall. Horse slipped a bit, causing Trusty to tighten his legs around the beast and pull the reins back a little tighter. He didn't want to stop the horse, just slow him down. His focus was lost on staying upright.

A crack of thunder drew Trusty's attention back to the trail, back to the distance. The sudden explosion wasn't the sound of one cloud butting up against another. It was a firing pin hitting the primer of a cartridge, sending a bullet into the air from an unseen gun. He reined Horse back the rest of the way and came to a stop. Clearing his vision, he saw a horse blocking the trail ahead with a rider cloaked in a slicker and black hat, pointing the barrel of a rifle right at him.

Another shot fired, hitting nothing but air, drawing a quick glance from Trusty over his shoulder, past Michael and Bill Tilghman. Another rider sat on a horse, his rifle like the other, pointed at Tilghman. They were trapped in the pass with nowhere to go. The sides of the rock were too steep to ride over, and there was no way to turn around or gather together any tighter than they already were. Trusty felt like a fish in a barrel.

Trusty reached for his Colt, but by the time his hand hit the ivory grip, three more riders had appeared. Two on one side of the pass and one on the other. Two of the three held rifles aimed at the trio, while one, a woman Trusty recognized straightaway, sat on her skinny black horse with nothing but a smug look on her bird-eyed face.

"Amelia Darby," Trusty said, wrapping his fingers around the Colt.

She ignored Trusty and looked to Bill Tilghman. "You just keep that rifle across your lap, Marshal, and nobody'll get hurt. We have no quarrel with you. Any of you move an inch, and we shoot you. Am I understood?" Amelia was dressed in black, protected by a rain slicker. Her pale white skin glowed bright in the gray shadows, allowing for her expression of seriousness to be seen without question of its intensity. "Now, there's a wide spot in the trail about twenty yards forward. I want you all to ride to it and stop. Then we can sort out our situation from there. Don't think you can escape, or do anything stupid, or you will die."

There was a strength in Amelia's voice that Trusty hadn't heard before. Her prior weakness must have been part of her ploy, an act to gain sympathy. There was no way he was going to underestimate the woman again. He let his fingers fall from the Colt and urged Horse forward.

As he rode forward, Trusty passed underneath Amelia and the rider next to her, a tall Indian man that he assumed was David Folsom. The man on the other side of the pass was white, not familiar to Trusty. Neither was the man who had been blocking the trail.

Both Michael and Bill Tilghman followed along without making a fuss or attempting to do anything that would draw fire from the four rifles that were pointed their way. Trusty was pretty confident that Amelia was armed, too, with the Buntline Special holstered and hidden somewhere inside her riding garb.

Under normal conditions, Trusty would have been more than a little concerned about the situation that he'd found himself in—but he'd fully expected to find Amelia Darby in Lost Mountain Pass no matter what he had said to Michael. All he had to do was stay alive, and keep Michael and Tilghman safe, too.


The wide spot in the trail gave everyone enough room to settle their horses, all the while preventing the three men from escaping. Amelia sat in the middle of the Indian and the white man, while the other remained on the left side of the trail, on the rock over their heads, as a lookout. The other rider remained on the trail, blocking it to and from, north and south, from any attempts to flee.

Trusty sat in between Michael and Bill Tilghman, all on their respective horses, hands in the air, assured that they would be killed on the spot if they made any move toward their guns.

The rain fell gently, and the spot was protected from too much wind. Thunder rumbled in the distance, and an occasional flash of lightning streaked across the sky, but there was nothing threatening about the storm at the moment.

"Well, brother," Amelia said, "you've done well." She smiled and nodded.

Michael lowered his head and urged his horse forward, breaking away from Trusty and Tilghman. He joined the three, settling next to the Indian. He didn't pull his gun, though, and offer a barrel toward the two marshals. The ex-priest looked to the ground, refusing to make eye contact with Trusty.

"Why am I not surprised?" Trusty said under his breath, loud enough for Michael to hear him.

Bill Tilghman wore a stern look on his face, his eyes focused on the guns pointed at him. It didn't seem to matter to him that it appeared that Michael had betrayed him and Trusty in one way or another.

"We meet again, Trusty Dawson," Amelia said.

"Let me guess. You heard there's a bounty on my head and you've come to collect." Trusty turned his attention to Michael and added, "Are *you* going to split it fifty-fifty with your sister?"

Amelia leaned forward in her saddle and turned her

lip up a little bit. "You don't worry about what's between me and my brother, Trusty Dawson, you hear me?"

"Why didn't you kill me when you had the chance?" he said. His voice bounced off the rock walls that surrounded them. Even tinged with rage, they sounded hollow as they mixed with the falling rain.

Trusty glanced past Amelia, down the trail, then to Bill Tilghman. The marshal sat still as a weary rat with the lights on, expressing no emotion at all. He was waiting just like Trusty was.

"I had to meet up with David, and I didn't know you were so valuable. I was only after the judge in the beginning, but them other men showed up in Kosoma looking for you and that sealed the deal for me. It would be enough money to get away from here once and for all. Start over and open that milliner's shop I told you about." Amelia glanced at the Indian, then back to Trusty.

"But you couldn't do it alone," Trusty said.

"What's it matter?" Amelia said. "Here we are with you caught and nowhere left to run."

"I wasn't running anywhere. Why the wait? Why not shoot me now and get it over with?"

"You in a hurry to die, man?" David Folsom said.

"Just curious is all," Trusty said, then followed their gaze to Bill Tilghman. "Oh, I see. You don't know what to do with him? Me, you can collect a thousand silvers for. Him? All you get for him is a rope over your neck. All of you." There was no hiding the clenched teeth, disappointment, and anger directed at Michael from Trusty. "But you kill two marshals, and all hell breaks loose and everyone is on your tail, putting an end to your happily-ever-after. It's a shame Michael couldn't get word to you and let you know what was comin' your way."

Michael finally looked Trusty in the eye. "I guess I am a Darby through and through. Sorry to disappoint you, Trusty. I told you who I was more than once."

"I never expected you to be anything else other than what you are. For a second or two, I thought maybe you were different, able to change your stripes. You broke away from the family and made your own way. I thought your vocation might be real, true. But I was wrong, one more time. You could have killed me anytime you wanted to and collected the bounty all for yourself. It would have saved you a lot of trouble."

"I gave my word to Amelia that we would split the bounty. Regardless of what you think, I keep my word."

"I usually admire loyalty in a man, but you can count me out this time, Michael."

The ex-priest looked to the ground again, breaking eye contact with Trusty.

Thunder clapped to the west, not overhead but almost. The intensity of the storm was picking up. Rain fell harder, but the pass protected them from the full strength of the wind. Trusty looked away from Michael, caught a glance of Amelia digging inside her slicker with her shooting hand. In response, he slowed down his breathing and relaxed his finger. He was still more than a little surprised that the Darbys hadn't ordered his weapons to the ground. Tilghman's too. That was the wild card he had been right about. Bill Tilghman's presence had muddied their plans. It was obvious that Amelia and David Folsom thought it would only be Trusty and Michael to confront—and with Michael on their side, that meant Trusty would have been on his own, an easy kill. Not so much now.

Lightning flashed again, casting daylight clarity down on the group for a split second, long enough for Trusty to see off in the distance. What looked like a wall of rock in the grayness of the storm was a line of armed men, called to the pass when Trusty had sent the wire to the Guardsmen asking for help. He had also wired Colonel John J. Mizner and asked for the 10th Cavalry to come to Lost Mountain. Buffalo Soldiers had circled Amelia and her gang, trapping them without warning. No one had seen them yet. Just Trusty. It was the sign he had been waiting on. Bill Tilghman too.

Amelia pulled out the Buntline Special and aimed it at Trusty. His mouth went dry, and he reached for his Colt as quick as he could. But Michael intervened. His gun was out, his finger on the trigger, and he pulled it without hesitation. The bullet slammed into Amelia's chest, knocking her back, turning her so she faced Michael. "You always were a traitor," she said as she fired the Buntline, hitting Michael at the base of the throat. He bounced backward on the saddle and fell to the ground.

David Folsom had his pistol out, but not raised before he could meet the barrels of Trusty's and Tilghman's guns. The tall Choctaw dropped his gun. It hit the ground at about the same time as Amelia did. He put his hands into the air and surrendered.

That left the men at each end of the trail and the man on the rise above the trail. Mizner and the Buffalo Soldiers made themselves known then, and it only took a second flash of lightning for the men to realize that they were surrounded and outnumbered ten to one.

\* \* \*

Amelia was dead and Michael was dying. Trusty cradled the man's head, protecting him as much as he could from the rain. There was no saving Michael, even though Trusty was putting pressure on the wound. Covering the bullet hole was the only way Michael could talk, and even then his voice was weak and distant.

"I couldn't let her do it," Michael said.

"I appreciate that, but help was already here." Trusty looked up to see Bill Tilghman in conversation with Colonel Mizner. A single row of Buffalo Soldiers went on for as far as the eye could see. "I'm sorry I didn't tell you, but I didn't think I could trust you."

"You were right about that." Michael grimaced and flexed his fingers, fighting off the pain the best he could. "What happened to you is no fault of your own. Greed is a powerful drive of human desires. I wish I could have been better." A tear slipped out of the man's eye—or it might have been the rain, Trusty wasn't sure.

"I'm sorry it turned out this way," Trusty said.

"I'll find out soon enough if there's more of a price to pay for my actions, for being a Darby."

"You couldn't help being what you are any more than a coyote can help bein' a coyote, and in the end, you chose to save a life instead of taking one. If there's comfort to be found," Trusty said, his voice cracking and almost as weak as Michael's, "I hope you find it in that. Maybe that's the only thing that will matter."

Michael urged a slight smile, nodded, then began coughing. His body convulsed a couple of times. The coughing stopped and his eyes set to the sky, wide open, without pain or fear.

Trusty stood up, his hands bloody from trying to ease the man's pain, took off his hat, held it to his chest, and showed the man and his death the kind of respect he deserved.

# Chapter 27

7

*Muskogee, Indian Territory, May 1888*

Trusty stood outside of Marshal William Grimes's office staring at the toes of his boots. Mid-morning light pushed inside the long hall through windows at each end. An empty bench offered itself for rest, but Trusty had been pacing for an hour as Chris Madsen, then Bill Tilghman had taken their turns at talking with the marshal, telling him their version of the incident at Lost Mountain. Trusty'd had time to write up a report and submit it so there would be documentation of his side of the story.

Trusty was dressed in his best Sunday-go-to-meetin' clothes, a store-bought black suit, white shirt, and a black tie. He wore his gun belt on his waist, and his boots were shined with a fresh coat of polish. His badge was pinned securely on his chest, cleaned and shined, too, with more than an extra rub. He wanted to look his best if this was going to be the last day he spent as a Deputy U.S. Marshal.

The only sound in the hall was the echo of Trusty's

footsteps. He couldn't hear any conversation taking place behind the closed door. He didn't want to snoop or pry.

The door opened after another long ten minutes, and Bill Tilghman walked out wearing his normal expressionless face. He left the door open behind him. "Marshal's ready to see you," he said to Trusty, not offering any hint of what was to come or what had been said.

Tilghman kept on walking down the hall, and Trusty watched him go, hesitating, doing his best not to feel like the cowering boy he once was when his father took him to task for one of his many failures.

"Come on in, Dawson." It was Marshal Grimes's voice from inside the office, distant like he was in the back of it. Which is just where Trusty found him, sitting behind a neatly organized desk that sat in front of a tall window, which almost touched the twelve-foot ceiling. "Have a seat," Grimes said. He was in his late fifties, his face free of a mustache or beard, his thinning hair cut short and graying at the sides. He wore a heavily starched white shirt and collar, gold wire-frame glasses, and a serious look on his face that had been there every time Trusty had encountered him.

Trusty sat down on the edge of the nondescript high-back wood chair. "It's good to see you, sir."

Grimes looked down at a paper in front of him, then back up, halfway, looking over the top frame of his glasses. "I wish I could say the same."

"I understand. I failed in my duty to keep Judge Hadesworth alive."

The marshal sat up fully in his chair and grasped his hands, resting them on the desk. "It was a rare lapse in judgment. I have to say that when the news arrived, I was a little more than surprised. How is the bullet wound?"

Trusty glanced to his shoulder, then back to Grimes. "Sore, getting better every day."

"You're lucky to be alive yourself. If you were a cat, I'd say you used quite a few lives on this trip."

Trusty didn't know whether to smile or nod, so he didn't do either. "If I would have told that woman no, none of this would have happened."

"Do you really believe that?"

"I do."

"After reading your report, and talking with the other marshals, I'm not sure that I do. It seems that there were men coming for you that you were unaware of. You were bound to encounter trouble with or without the company of Amelia Darby."

"The bounty," Trusty said with a sigh.

"Yes, that's an outstanding problem. I've sent men to St. Louis to speak with Theodore Marberry about the threat, to find out if it is true that he is the issuer of the bounty. He has not been found at this point. Just so you know."

"That I still need to look over my shoulder."

"And in front of you."

"It's personal between me and Marberry."

"So you believe he is the true source of the threat?"

"I do. It's something I'll have to deal with one way or another."

Grimes unclasped his hands and picked up a pen, dipped it in ink, then signed the paper before him. Finished, he put the pen back in the well. "This is a

U.S. Marshal problem, not just yours, Dawson. That kind of threat cannot be tolerated."

Trusty wasn't sure he understood what the marshal meant. "I'm being relieved of duty?"

"Not unless you want to be. Don't read into that as forgiveness of the judge's death. I am reprimanding you for allowing Miss Darby into your party. It will be in your permanent record. Another such incident will result in a more severe punishment. Do I make myself clear?"

"Yes, sir."

"Good. Now I need to know if it is your desire to remain a Deputy U.S. Marshal."

"Of course."

Grimes nodded and settled back into his chair. "I'm a firm believer in second chances, Deputy Dawson. I have an assignment for you if you're up to it."

Relieved, Trusty settled back into his chair—as far as he could go with a fully complemented gun belt and Colt in his holster. "I am."

"Good. I want you to go back to Kosoma and escort Judge Bartlett Tripp back to his home in the Dakota Territory. Judge Tripp is filling in for Judge Hadesworth. He lives in Bismarck."

The assignment wasn't what Trusty was expecting, but there wasn't any way he could say no. "I suppose I should be glad it's not winter."

"I take it that's a yes," Grimes said.

"Yes, of course. Thank you, sir." Trusty stood up but made no effort to head to the door before he was dismissed.

"Good. I'm glad to hear it, Dawson. I understand this whole thing could have turned out a lot worse for everyone. There was some luck to be had, but from what I've heard from Madsen and Tilghman, and read in your report, there was thought and foresight put into the outcome."

"I still regret the loss of Father Michael Darby."

"He set his course, and by stopping his sister, he stopped more bloodshed. Whether he saw himself as a hero or not is unknown, but it should be told that he acted bravely in his last moments."

"I told him the same before he died, sir."

"I'm happy to hear that."

"Will there be anything else, Marshal Grimes?" Trusty said.

"Yes, there's one more thing. When you get Judge Tripp home safely, you need to check in with Marshal Delaney in Bismarck. You'll be working out of that office."

"Temporarily?"

"No. You're being transferred."

"As punishment?"

"Call it what you want, Dawson, but the Dakotas are flat and open. You can see a man coming at you from miles away. Considering the circumstances you've found yourself in with Marberry, I think the Dakota Territory is the best place for you for now. Unless, of course, you would rather not take the order. That's always your choice."

"No, sir, I understand. The order stands and I won't refuse it," Trusty said.

"Good, glad to hear it. That'll be all."

Trusty nodded, and said, "Thank you, sir," then headed for the door.

"Dawson," Grimes said.

"Yes?" Trusty stopped in the doorway and turned back to the marshal.

"You're a good marshal. One of the best. Don't let this darkness cloud your capabilities. You've got a good future ahead of you."

"I appreciate that, sir," Trusty said. He walked out of the door into the empty hall with a mix of pride and dread settling under his skin.

### *Kosoma, Indian Territory, May 1888*

Vance Calhoun stood at the window, staring at the gallows that stood on the other side of the jail. He could hardly believe what he was seeing, along with the crowd that was gathering in the town square. He had forced himself to look away from the simple wood structure when he had been delivered to the town in the back of a barred wagon. He had screamed, "There's been a mistake made. Don't you know who I am?" But no one listened, especially after the snively little judge had delivered the guilty verdict and ordered him to be hanged.

Calhoun had never thought about his own death too much. Not that he thought he was immune to the end result of living a long life. He felt his body tiring, growing older, but that day was a long way off in his mind. Punishment for a deed, a murder—two in this case—was for other fools. Not him. He had always been able to buy or fight his way out of trouble. Why should this time be any different?

"Psst," someone said from below the window. Calhoun looked down the best he could to see Gladdy O'Connor crouched under the sill.

"What are you doin' here?" Calhoun sneered. He'd hoped to never see Gladdy again.

The Mick stood up and stared at Calhoun through the bars with hard eyes and a stoic face. He was fresh-shaved and wore clean riding clothes: duster, a brushed hat, and a shirt that wasn't stiff with trail dirt and sweat. "I wanted to see you before I rode out."

"How'd you get free?"

Gladdy didn't hesitate. "I told 'em what you did. Killed that clerk and the mercantile man for no cause other than your own purposes."

"It was you who turned on me," Calhoun seethed.

"Who's the idiot now?" Gladdy smiled, his teeth uneven and brown, still ugly, but there was no doubt he was proud of himself. He started to walk away, then stopped and said, "You got Haden killed. It's your fault he ain't here with me. What else was I supposed to do?"

The back of Calhoun's neck burned red as rage overtook him. He could hardly see straight. "Where are you going? Come back here. You've got to get me out of here!"

Gladdy kept on walking. "Can't, boss, I got a house I gotta go burn down," he said as he kept walking, disappearing into the crowd—who had stopped to see and listen to the verbal scuffle between Gladdy and Calhoun.

Calhoun screamed and started punching the wall. Pain erupted in his hand, warning him to stop. But he didn't, not until blood dripped to the floor and his knuckles broke apart like eggshells inside his skin.

A clatter of irons took Calhoun's attention away from the window.

He stood broken, bloodied, sweaty, and enraged. He

had no fight left inside of him and dropped to his knees in surrender.

An unnamed deputy stood at the cell door holding the chains that would prevent his hands and feet from any attempt at escaping. He'd already tried to bribe the deputy, and every man he had come into contact with since being pushed inside the jail cell.

"Time to go, Calhoun," the deputy said. He wore a thick horseshoe mustache and uninterested eyes. There was no obvious joy in the effort of his job. "I've seen men do worse than that to themselves before they're hung. Get up. You got no need for a doctor now."

Calhoun stood up. He looked back out the window, searching for Gladdy. Instead, he saw two men standing at the bottom steps of the gallows. The executioner, dressed all in black, holding a Bible in his hand. The other man was another deputy. He held a rifle in one hand and jiggled his other hand in his pocket, bored.

"I never thought it would end like this," Calhoun said.

"They never do," the deputy answered. He shook his head, then stepped aside so Calhoun could see two more men standing behind him, holding rifles of their own just in case he had any ideas about making a run for it. He wouldn't get far if he tried, but he didn't have it in him now. The pain was too bad knowing he had been sent to the gallows by the likes of Gladdy O'Connor.

The deputy walked over to Calhoun and stopped before him. "You can make this easy or hard. It's up to you."

Calhoun thrust his bloody hands forward, wrists together, surrendering to the deputy.

The task of physical capture was done in a matter of

seconds. Then the deputy walked Calhoun out of the cell. He started to shake once sunlight hit his eyes and he realized that he'd lost the ability to shade his vision. There was no way he was going to close his eyes. That would come soon enough for him. His mouth went dry, but he managed to say, "Would it help if I said I was sorry?"

The deputy behind him kept pushing, kept guiding him toward the gallows. "Probably a little late for that now, ain't it?"

"Well, you can tell 'em I asked."

They got to the stairs of the gallows sooner than Calhoun expected to. Calhoun made his way up and took his place before the rope. His mind screamed for him to run, but that was impossible. Instead, he said nothing, just stared out into the crowd. A man said some words from the Bible and asked him if he had anything to say for himself. He shook his head no.

"I'll see you all in hell," he said to no one, not willing to give up having the last word, but hoped Gladdy O'Connor was close enough to hear.

Vance Calhoun still believed he was going to get away with being Vance Calhoun and everything he'd done, all of the way up until his neck snapped and everything went black.


A pair of boots burst through the gallows, toes aimed straight to the ground. The single snap of a neck echoed on the wind like someone had broken a small glass bottle. Pigeons lit into the air and a delicate woman standing next to Trusty gasped loudly. In a quick last breath and the final blink of the eye, Vance Calhoun swung from the gallows, wet from the waist down, staring sideways in a state of shock like he never thought he was going to die.

This world was cold and harsh, awash in the black-and-white judgment of law and order once again. It was a rare occurrence for two hangings to happen so close together in Kosoma. The gallows from the first, when the Darby brothers had met their deserved fate, had yet to be disassembled before they were put into use again. Every citizen of the growing town hoped this would be the last spectacle for a while, that the judgment against senseless killings would be a deterrent to any man who thought he could get away with such a thing.

"Well, that will be that," Judge Bartlett Tripp said to Trusty. Judge Tripp was a head shorter than Trusty, a little soft in the belly, bald on top of his head, and dressed without concern about his appearance. His spindly gray beard still held crumbs from his morning toast.

"You'll be wanting to get going as soon as possible, then?" Trusty said.

"That would be fine. I'm ready to get back to the Dakota Territory. The air seems to be sweeter the farther north you go."

"I hope you're right."

"You've never been in my part of the world?"

"Can't say that I have."

"It's not so bad. You'll see."

Trusty shrugged and let silence settle between him and Judge Tripp. He was ready to be free of Kosoma and the sight of Vance Calhoun dangling at the end of the rope. The crowd seemed to agree, was ready to depart quicker than the last time Trusty had witnessed a hanging in Kosoma.

Three shiny black birds stood atop the pitch of the jail, staring down at the crowd looking for something shiny to steal. A few clouds pushed overhead on a wind growing in intensity out of the south. A baby started to cry in the distance. The piercing, uncomfortable sound drew Trusty's attention in a way it never had before. He turned away from Judge Tripp and scanned the crowd, his height giving him a slight advantage over shorter men and women. As soon as the baby cried again, Trusty locked eyes with a familiar man: Theodore Marberry, standing tall in his fine clothes. The man looked like he was dressed to go to a social instead of a hanging.

Trusty lost his breath for a second and tried to reason why Marberry was there. To see Vance Calhoun die, make sure that he was dead? It was as good a reason as any. But in truth, that didn't matter to Trusty. What mattered to him was the woman standing next to Marberry. Jessica's mother. An older version of the girl he had thought he had loved. The only girl he had ever loved. Now she was gone. But . . . had left something behind. A baby. A bundle that squirmed in the older woman's hands, face hidden, only a chubby little hand reaching out of the pink blanket.

Marberry grabbed Jessica's mother by the arm, nodded toward Trusty, then pulled her back into the crowd. They disappeared, leaving a brief indentation in between the people where they stood. The baby cried again, only this time the cry was distant and muffled. The sound of the crowd overtook the existence of the baby, leaving Trusty poised to give chase. His feet moved faster than his brain. He was ten feet into the crowd, pushing people aside, looking desperately for Marberry and the baby, before he stopped. He looked back to see Judge Tripp staring at him curiously, wondering what was going on.

Trusty shook his head, then searched again for a sign of the baby. There was no sight of her, no sound of her. Her. A revelation. A daughter? He wasn't sure. He would never be sure until he saw her, held her, and was able to see himself in her face. But that would have to wait for another day. Marberry was gone. Vanished like an angry ghost of the past. And so was the baby. Silent. The promise of new life and hope smothered, but not snuffed out. Not now. Trusty had got a glimpse of what Calhoun had told him existed. The baby was real. And he knew that no matter where he went, he would always look for her, wonder about her, pine for her. Just like he had Jessica.

He turned, walked back to the judge and said, "Come on, let's get your things. I want to get through Lost Mountain Pass before night falls."

"Are you all right, Trusty?" the judge said.

Trusty smiled and nodded. "You know, I think I might be, Judge. Thanks for asking. Now come on, let's get goin'. I want to make sure and get you home safe and sound."

Trusty looked over his shoulder one last time, hoping to see Marberry and the baby, but they were gone, swallowed up by the good people of Kosoma—who were just as happy to get on with their lives and their day now that all of the excitement was over with.

## Author's Note

There are several historical characters and events portrayed throughout this book, along with locations in the Indian Territory that existed in 1888 and continue to exist. Please note that some timelines, locations, and characters have been altered in service to the story. While it is always my intention to be as historically accurate as possible when I write a novel, one of the joys of writing and reading fiction is delving into a reality that might be a little different from what really exists. Any research mistakes are my own.

# Acknowledgments

It's been my experience that no book finds its way to the bookshelf without the help of a special group of dedicated people. Special thanks goes to my agent, Cherry Weiner, who championed this book for a long time. Thanks also goes to my editor, Gary Goldstein, Western editor extraordinaire, for taking a chance on Trusty (and me).

I am in constant awe of the men and women who serve in the United States Marshal service on a daily basis—past and present. I hope this book reflects the hard and decent work they do and have done throughout the history of the organization. Finally, no book leaves my desk without it first passing through my wife's, Rose's, hands. She has been a great source of strength, support, and encouragement for most of my life. This book most likely wouldn't exist without her presence and honest critiques. Our journey continues . . .

Thank you all.

Keep reading for a special early preview of

# THE BROKEN BOW,

the next book in the Trusty Dawson,
Deputy U.S. Marshal series
by acclaimed author Larry D. Sweazy!

**A Trusty Dawson, Deputy U.S. Marshal Novel**

# Chapter 1

Trusty Dawson cinched the saddle as tight as he could without causing his durable strawberry roan gelding that he called Horse to object. He wanted to be ready to ride after seeing Marshal Delaney in his office. He'd had enough of the rickety and windblown capital city. Too many people to be concerned with, even this far north. Any happiness in this new place would be found alone on the trail.

Once he was finished with the chore of preparing Horse, Trusty remained inches from his ride, his head down with the rim of his faded blue Cavalry Stetson resting on the saddle. He was listening to the two men in the next stall talk among themselves. The pair had got his attention and made him want to know more about them. Caution and suspicion came easy to him these days.

At first glance, the men seemed harmless enough, sewing machine salesmen making their way across the prairie, plying the marvel of the Singer Manufacturing Company to women in need of more time that the modern invention afforded them. It was the taller man of the two especially bothered Trusty. There was a darkness about the man's choice of dirty gray clothes and his sidearms—a Colt .45 on each hip—that seemed out of place for a salesman. This man's hardened eyes suggested that he was more of a hired gunslinger than a man who hocked wares for a living; they were as black as the steel and cast-iron sewing machines that sat in crates loaded on a wagon outside the livery. The shorter of the two men was tending to a lone horse, a swayback black draft mare with white stockings above her hooves that Trusty supposed was set to lead them on their sales route.

"We've hit a vein of luck with this weather, Miles, but I fear it's not going to hold. I think we should head south instead of west." Miles was the one that Trusty was concerned about, dark and unamused by the shorter man's expression of fear. Names always helped—if they could be relied on to be true. The man speaking was short and thin in a fit way, not a hungry, sickly way. He was outfitted in natty clothes fresh off of a tailor's needle, a crisp blue shirt, clean white collar, and a brown tweed vest. He wore a thick suede overcoat with a rabbit fur collar, clean of any lint or dirt and open, not buttoned down for extreme temperatures. A struggling farmer would see the short man coming from a mile off and know he was a huckster of some kind; though at the moment, the sewing machines appeared to be a legitimate concern, not snake oil or other flights of fancy. A Singer could change the life of any woman who could afford and learn how to operate the mechanical contraption.

Miles shook his head, objected to the change in plans with a grunt, then said, "West is the route we agreed upon, Mister Carmichael, and that's the route we take. I got my reasons to go west and you've got your prospects along the way. I say we go now like was planned."

Carmichael held fast, planted his feet firmly on the straw-strewn floor, acting as if he were the one in charge. "Do you know where you are?"

Trusty peered over the saddle as he began to fuss with his bedroll—a thick buffalo blanket—tightening it down again, giving himself a reason to stay inside the stall and listen. Horse snorted and kicked his rear leg hard enough to toss a bit of straw into the air. The roan had a restless streak in him that Trusty recognized and appreciated, but he wasn't going to be called off the two men by the beast. Both of the salesmen knew he was there but weren't paying any attention to him that he could tell.

Carmichael and Miles stood opposite each other, both of them looking like mules refusing to budge. The short man made the first move. "It was my friends and colleagues, Holland Freeman and Earl Lancaster, who set out on a fine winter day much like this one that brung us here in the first place. They journeyed away from Bismarck enjoying a rare, warm January day with coats unbuttoned, immune to any icy touch, or so they thought, as they made their calls on one soddie to the next. Them and a whole lot of other folk who'd lived on this land for the ages thought they'd been allowed to breathe safely from the wrath of winter who should have knowed better. A whoosh of wind straight down from the north with the force of a monster, bringing with it a blizzard that no one was prepared for or had seen the like of ever before. Them two fellas, as fine a Singer salesmen as was ever seen in this territory, plum froze to death, just like more than two hundred other people, a lot of them children, lost in the blizzard, seekin' their way home with nary a coat or scarf around their necks. Just because the sky is clear right now don't mean it can't change on the turn of a bird's wing. This is the Dakota Territory. You can't trust what you see with your own eyes. I ain't ready to freeze to death, Miles, and I doubt you are either. South is a safer bet for livin' another day. I am certain of it."

Miles stiffened, looked down on Carmichael since he towered over him a good five inches, and shook his head again. "Don't matter if we go south or west. A wind like what you say shows up, ain't nobody gonna outrun it. We go west, you hear?" It was then that Miles tore his attention away from Carmichael and made eye contact with Trusty. "You got a problem, stranger?" His voice was hard, and his jaw set forward as he took in the man he saw, assured now that he was being listened to.

"Not at all," Trusty said. "Just finishin' up with my horse and I'll be on my way. Your friend there is right though. From what I've seen around here it's best not to trust the sky overhead. I heard tell of that Children's Blizzard that befell so many families back in January. Winter up this way seems to have an appetite for fools and the unattended."

"You callin' me a fool?"

"I'm not callin' you anything. Just makin' a statement is all."

"If I want to know what you think, I'll ask you."

Trusty forced a smile, patted Horse, and walked to the front of the stall the two men stood in and stopped, blocking any exit from it. Like Miles, he was outfitted to ward off trouble if it came his way. One holster was armed with a Colt .45 with carved ivory grips and a six-inch barrel. His belt was fully complemented with cartridges, and a Bowie knife hung opposite the pistol. A single gun was enough for him. If it wasn't, then his Winchester '73 was waiting in the scabbard on Horse's right side. "Suit yourself, friend, but I'd heed your partner's warning. Blizzards are as common here as rattlesnakes in Texas."

Miles judged Trusty head to toe like he was an opponent of some kind. He let his gaze stop on the badge on Trusty's chest. "Never been to Texas so I wouldn't know. Like I said, you need to mind your own business, Marshal. Ain't nothing that concerns you here. We're honest, hardworkin' men, lookin' for our next sale is all."

"If you say so."

"I do."

"Now, now, Miles," Carmichael said, butting in, "it ain't prudent to be rude to a Deputy U.S. Marshal. He didn't mean no disrespect, Marshal, we're just starting out as a team. We've got a lot to learn about each other's ways."

Miles sneered at Carmichael, and for a second Trusty thought the tall man was going to smack the short man in the mouth, but that didn't happen. Miles unclenched his fist and smiled, offering the first bit of charisma since the conversation began.

"You gentlemen have a fine day, and be careful out there," Trusty said, holding Miles's stare before he set one boot in front of the other and headed for the open door of the livery. "I hope you have good luck on your trip." He didn't wait for a response, just kept on walking until he was outside the wind-blasted gray barn, glad to be free of the tension, smell of horse shit, and to have the warmth of the winter sun beating down on his face. It was then, just beyond the door, that Trusty glanced over his shoulder and caught sight of Miles's gaze following him outside. Trusty nodded, then headed toward Delaney's office, allowing his hand to dangle as close to his Colt as it needed to be—just in case the call for the pistol came from a man Trusty was sure had come to collect the generous bounty that sat upon his head. It was better to be prepared and wrong than to be dead.

Marshal Michael Delaney remained sitting behind his simple oak desk when Trusty walked into the office. Delaney wore a perfectly trimmed horseshoe mustache, white as Dakota snow and thick as a drift, the size of a thumb. He wore gold-rimmed spectacles and was hunched over a stack of papers, mumbling to himself as he ran his long, narrow finger down a ledger. "I've been expecting you, Dawson. Sit down." Delaney didn't look up, didn't dare losing his place among the numbers. The order was firm enough launched as it was by his deep, gravelly voice.

Trusty did what he was told and took a seat in a solid chair that fronted the desk. A curtainless window stood behind Marshal Delaney with bright, golden light penetrating the office, making the room more hospitable than it would any other time of the day; the color tones were usually marked by cold, gray uninspired shadows. This wasn't Trusty's first visit to the marshal's office, and it wouldn't be the last, but there was an institutional smell to the place and a sense of confinement that didn't appeal to any of his senses. He was always quick to leave after any necessary marshal business had been conducted.

"I'm assuming you've already cashed out?" Delaney said, looking up as he settled back into his red leather chair.

"Yes, sir. I plan on stopping at the bank on my way out of town."

"In a hurry to leave Bismarck?"

"No more than normal. I had enough of city life as a boy."

"Saint Louis if I recall."

"That'd be correct, sir. My father still owns a blacksmith shop there."

"Explains your build and demeanor a bit, doesn't it?"

Trusty didn't show the flinch on the outside that he felt on the inside. He'd given up the hammer and all of the work that came along with forging iron in exchange for something useful a long time ago. The early days of his life, however, muscles to some extent, broad shoulders, and workingman hands, gave away the experience and forced occupation of his boyhood. He tried not to think too much about the past, those days when fire and smoke seemed to be his only kin. His father was a cold and distant man with a taste for whiskey, especially after Trusty's mother had died and left the two of them to survive each other's presence.

"I suppose so," Trusty said with a glance to the toes of his boots.

"You get back to Saint Louis often? I'm partial to the city, myself. It's always buzzing with excitement. People coming and going every day."

"I try to avoid going home if I can. Especially now."

"There's still no word on Marberry's location, if you were wondering. He's disappeared."

"I've been given to understand that Marberry isn't my problem or my assignment."

"You understand correctly." Delaney drew in a deep breath and leaned forward. "It makes no difference why he has offered a bounty for your life; the fact is he has, and we will find him and hold him to account while you continue on with your duties here. I will ask you again, do you want to ride with another marshal to help look over your shoulder?"

"I ride alone."

"I figured that's what you would say. Have it your way, then. I have a warrant I want you to collect on, Dawson. I think you're the right man for the job. It will be your sole focus until the paper is served."

"Just one warrant, sir?"

"There'll be plenty of mileage to compensate you for the lack of multiple assignments."

"It's not that, sir. I'm not concerned about the money."

"What then?"

"Coming back to town so soon after I leave."

"This won't be an easy card to pocket. You'll head south, then back north again if what I've been told proves true. I think you'll have a challenge with this one. The ride will be long. You won't be returning to Bismarck anytime soon."

"Okay, that suits me. What do you have?"

"A Yanktonai Sioux called Charlie Littlefoot. Tried and accused of raping a white woman in Fort Yates, a captain's wife who is now with child. Littlefoot escaped the jail and is thought to be heading north into Canada. On the run, dangerous and smart. Just the kind of challenge you like. First thing I need you to do is head to Fort Yates and make sure the story is straight. Then if everything adds up, you'll need to track down Littlefoot."

A grin flashed across Trusty's face. He liked the sound of a long tracking journey. "Canada's a little out of our jurisdiction, isn't it?"

"I've paved the way for you to meet up with a Mountie from Wascana, Henri Bisset, if it comes to that. That is if you have to cross the border. Bisset is a good man. You'll like him. We've had some dealings in our time."

Trusty settled back in the chair and began to have second thoughts about the assignment. He tried to think of a way to get out of the orders. Canada in December was the last place he wanted to be. "Why me, Marshal? You have deputies who have more experience with the Yanktonai and that part of the country than I do. I don't have any knowledge at all of that corner of the world, especially Canada if I end up there."

"You'll be a fresh set of eyes. Besides that, I'm hoping nobody knows who you are that far north—including Charlie Littlefoot. He's faced trouble before and knows most of my badges by their first names."

"What kind of trouble?"

"Whiskey arrests. The usual. Nothing violent or mixed with white folk from the fort, which is why I want you to poke around before you try to pick up his trail. Something about this smells off to me."

What Delaney said made sense to Trusty, but it still felt like more punishment for his unresolved troubles than a tried-and-true strategy. Sooner or later, he was going to have to find a way to travel to St. Louis to confront Theodore Marberry, the man who had put a price on his head and the grandfather of Trusty's infant daughter—if the assumption of her lineage was true—and put an end to the bounty once and for all. For now, he'd been warned off—forbidden by superiors—from taking care of things himself, his way. Once he confronted Marberry himself, it would be the only way he would ever know for sure if the baby born to Jessica Marberry, dead in childbirth, had been sired by him. But such an act would demand that he disobey orders or give up the badge. Neither of those things were something he wanted to do. Being a Deputy U.S. Marshal was the only life he knew, the only life he wanted.

In good weather the ride south to Fort Yates was a two-day journey. Luckily, the temperate day had held without turning into an unexpected blizzard like the natty Singer salesman in the livery had worried about. Not that it wasn't cold beyond Bismarck, out in the open, as Trusty was. But the ride could have been a lot worse. Less than an inch of snow sat atop the ground, and the wind was mild, a soft push out of the southwest instead of a constant, angry rage out of the north. With the right gear and layers of coats, Trusty had been comfortable as he rode. Glad to be free of Bismarck and all of its confinements, though he was wary as a mouse ducking a hawk's shadow every time he approached any kind of traffic on the trail.

Starting late as he did and considering the shortened length of the days in December, Trusty didn't get as far as he hoped he would. Darkness forced him off the trail a few miles outside of a thick spot in the trail called Cannonball, which was nothing more than a trading post on the Standing Rock Reservation.

Luck had accompanied him so far on the trip, offering a thin grove of cottonwoods that reached up a slight ravine to protect his campsite from the wind. To make things even easier, he had spied a jackrabbit before the light faded away into the fullness of night, and a quick, accurate shot had allowed for a dinner of roasted meat instead of jerky and beans.

Trusty slept close to a pile of orange coals, dressed in his riding clothes and coats, hunkered down under a buffalo blanket. The night was clear with thousands of silver stars pulsing overhead. It wasn't long before Trusty fell asleep, though with one ear open for the sound of trouble. The downfall of riding alone was the fear of sleeping too deep, but there had been no sign of riders on the trail for hours, so it had been easy enough to relax, which as it turned out was a mistake.

The snap of a twig and a snort and rustle from Horse roused Trusty from his slumber straight to his feet, his hand reaching for the ivory grips of his Colt as he stood, half-awake, half-unsure if he was dreaming a nightmare, or truly standing before a short man with a scattergun aimed straight at his belly. Trusty's finger was on the trigger out of habit and preparedness.

"Well, well," Carmichael, the shorter of the two sewing machine salesmen said, smiling with the glint of the moon bouncing off his teeth. "We meet again, Trusty Dawson. Only now I know who you are and what you're worth. A thousand silvers can change a man's life. Especially a man like me who has to travel hundreds of miles in hopes of making a sale, riding with idiots, and freezing my ass for pennies instead of dollars."

There was no sign of his partner, Miles. Carmichael didn't demand that Trusty drop his gun or raise his hands in surrender. He didn't say anything else. The huckster just smiled wider and pulled the trigger of the scattergun. But he was too late. Trusty pulled his trigger first. The two explosions of gunfire joined together, rumbling across the frozen prairie like the thunder of a coming storm.

**Look for THE BROKEN BOW in Winter 2022!**